SUMMER DESIRE

Hearing his approach, Katelyn halted her brushing in mid-stroke. She turned to look at him, uncertain how he would react to finding her still up. "I . . . I washed my hair earlier, and I was brushing it dry."

"So I see."

"I'll move, so you can sit by the fire," she said, noticing his hair was also wet. She pulled her nightdress from beneath her legs and rose onto her knees.

Brit inhaled sharply. The fire behind Katelyn perfectly outlined her curves through the thin gown. He watched her gather her hair at her nape, then deftly separate the blond tresses into three sections. "No," he said, startling her. "Leave it down."

Keeping her gaze riveted on his, Katelyn let her hair slip from her fingers, then shook her head to release the beginnings of a braid. As her hair swayed from side to side, then settled in waves down her back and over one shoulder, she watched the heat build in his eyes.

"Come here," he said in a soft growl.

She did not hesitate, but stepped into his embrace. Brit wrapped his arms around her, lowering his face to nuzzle her neck and inhale the sweet scent of her hair. "I need you," he whispered against her ear.

"And I need you," she whispered, as Brit swept her up into his arms and carried her the few feet to the bed . . .

SUMMER WIND

ARLENE HOLLIDAY

ZEBRA BOOKS
KENSINGTON PUBLISHING CORP.

ZEBRA BOOKS are published by

Kensington Publishing Corp.
850 Third Avenue
New York, NY 10022

Copyright © 1995 by Arlene S. Hodapp

Zebra and the Z logo Reg. U.S. Pat. & TM Off. The Lovegram logo is a trademark of Kensington Publishing Corp.

First Printing: July, 1995

Printed in the United States of America

*Dedicated to the very special woman who
continues to teach me about kindness,
strength of spirit, and devotion to family.
To you Mom, with all my love.*

One

"Would you look at that! See how *la señorita* twitches *sus caderillas*," Armando said in a loud whisper. "She is something, eh?"

"*Sí*," Juan, youngest of the three men, replied, then added with a grin, "*y los pechos magníficos. Eh, compadres?*"

The third man merely grunted noncommittally to his companions' remarks about the woman's hips and breasts, but she had his full attention. Keeping his posture outwardly relaxed, he studied her shapely form and pale blond hair. As she moved down the boardwalk on the opposite side of Sacramento's K Street, he tried to summon the hatred that ate at him constantly. Instead, a sudden, intense coil of desire gripped his insides. How could he react so strongly to a woman he'd only just seen? The question made him shift uncomfortably in the chair he occupied in front of a miner's supply store.

His jaw clenching with sudden anger, he snorted with disgust at his unexpected reaction to the woman he'd been waiting to see. The woman he'd been surprised to learn owned the *Sacramento Argus,* the newspaper whose editorials he'd been reading for six months. At first, he'd found the scathing articles amusing. But the increasingly acrimonious writings no longer amused him, prompting his decision to see for himself the owner of a paper which printed such rubbish. He hadn't planned on that person's being a woman. There were few women in California, fewer still who owned a business. But it didn't matter; she was just another *gringa* bitch who didn't deserve the time of day.

Yet, he was helpless to keep his gaze from taking in every nuance of the woman. The way the dark green fabric of her dress stretched across her full bosom, hugged her small waist, and outlined her shapely hips sent another lick of unwanted desire dancing up his spine. He shifted in his chair again, silently cursing his body's traitorous reaction. Forcing his mind back to the reason he'd been sitting in front of the supply store for over an hour, he watched the woman stop in front of the newspaper office, pull a key from her handbag, and stick it into the lock. The corners of his mouth lifted in a satisfied smile.

"At last," he murmured.

"Hello, Katelyn," an older woman called from the doorway next to the *Argus,* her voice carrying to where the three men sat across the street.

The blonde's head turned at the greeting, a smile lighting her face. She replied with a nod and a wave, then pushed the door open, and stepped inside.

Katelyn. He liked the sound of it. He longed to savor the way it would roll off his tongue, but stifled the urge. Even after she'd disappeared behind the newspaper's door, her image stayed with him. She hadn't appeared to be particularly beautiful, at least not from his vantage point. Her plain features and pale hair were a direct contrast to the sultry, dark-haired beauties he was accustomed to. Yet there had been a palpable sensuality about her that touched something deep inside. A stirring in his soul he hadn't felt in a very long time.

With a grunt of annoyance, he came out of his chair in an easy, lithe motion, his right hand unconsciously seeking the reassurance of the Colt Navy pistol strapped to his hip.

"What is it, *jefe?*" Armando said, starting to rise.

"*Nada.*" Motioning for his companion to remain seated,

he stepped off the boardwalk and started across the street. "Stay here. I will be right back."

Armando flashed Juan an anxious look. He already thought their boss *loco* for coming to Sacramento in broad daylight. Yet, *el jefe* apparently thought his reasons worth the risk.

At the sound of the door opening, Katelyn laid down the rag she'd been using to clean print type and called over her shoulder, "I'll be right with you."

As she brushed a wisp of hair off her forehead, her nose twitched with distaste. She'd never gotten used to the smell of turpentine, so necessary in the printing business. Putting a smile on her lips, she turned to greet her customer. A tall man lounged negligently against the front counter. Straight, jet black hair brushed his wide shoulders. He wore a white, ruffled-front shirt and a leather vest. A black silk bandana, rolled and wrapped around his neck several times, was knotted at his throat.

"Good afternoon, sir." She stared up at him, trying to see his face. Only a square chin with a small cleft was visible beneath the shadow of his wide-brimmed hat. "How can I help you?" she prompted when he remained silent.

Deeply engrossed in the newspaper lying on the counter, the man ignored her questions. Pointing to an article with a long finger, the dusky color of his skin a sharp contrast to the cuff of his shirt, he said, "It seems someone who writes for your newspaper has taken a particularly strong dislike of the bandit people are calling *El Buitre.*"

Katelyn's brow wrinkled at his soft, cultured voice. "No one likes *El Buitre.*" Her pronunciation of the Spanish word for vulture sounded so much different than his. He was obviously bilingual. "Is that why you came here, to discuss my articles?"

His head snapped up at her words, the tilt of his hat still

hiding his features. *"Your* articles?" he asked in a silky whisper.

"Yes. I not only own the *Sacramento Argus,* but I'm its editor as well." Her spine stiffened in preparation for taking up the all-too-familiar argument about a woman alone in the wilds of California gold country, and worse, trying to run a business. Swallowing the sudden rush of anger, she continued, "I wrote the editorials about *El Buitre."* She nodded to the newspaper spread on the counter between them. "Including that one."

His gaze dropped back to the article beneath his hand. He silently reread the last paragraph. *How can we allow this vile bandit to continue his reprehensible acts of violence against our citizens? When are we going to rise up for what's right and stop this animal? I say the time has long since passed!*

The hair on the back of his neck prickled with the urge to grab the blond *gringa* and shake some sense into her. He wasn't vile or violent. And he wasn't an animal. But she'd never believe that. Clamping down on his temper, the initials at the end of the editorial caught his attention. KAF. He traced the letters with a fingertip. *Ah, Katelyn with a* K. Aloud he said, "If you are the editor, these must be your initials. I heard someone outside call you Katelyn, which explains the *K,* and the *A* stands for . . ."

"Ann." For the first time, she experienced a moment of apprehension. In a town where at least ninety percent of the population was male, a single woman couldn't be too careful. Yet, for a reason she didn't understand, she felt no real fear of this man. "Listen, what's this about? I'm afraid I have other things to do. So if you'd just state your business . . ."

"Katelyn Ann Ferguson," he said under his breath, her name as sweet and tantalizing on his tongue as he'd imagined. "Why do you hate *El Buitre?* Your editorials sound like you have a personal vendetta against him."

Katelyn pressed her lips into a firm line. Her cheeks

burning with a flush, she said, "That's none of your business, Mr. Whatever-your-name-is. Unless you have some newspaper business, I'd appreciate it if you'd take your leave."

Straightening to his full height, he tipped his head back and looked down his straight, patrician nose at her. Pulling a coin from his vest pocket, he slapped it on the counter. "I just came to buy a paper. It was a pleasure meeting you, Miss—it is Miss, is it not?"

She nodded curtly, certain her response caused his severe mouth to curve into a brief smile. The startling flash of white teeth against his dark face caused her heart to do a strange flip-flop.

"Adiós, Miss Ferguson." He touched two fingers to his hat brim. *"Hasta luego."*

Lips pursed, brow furrowed, Katelyn watched the man tuck the paper under one arm, then turn and stride from the newspaper office. Long after he departed, she stood staring out the front window, her mind filled with visions of a soft-spoken, dark-skinned man. She didn't know his name, nor had he touched her, yet the few minutes he'd spent in her office made her feel as if they had shared an intimate encounter.

Shrugging off the strange sensations hanging over her, she turned from the window, crossed the room to her desk, and sat down. She opened the paper's ledger, flipped to the cash account page, then frowned at the meager balance. The paper was barely holding its own, requiring all of her energy to keep it afloat. Glancing toward the window, her frown deepened. She had to give her full attention to saving the *Argus,* not mooning over a stranger . . . no matter how he made her feel.

"Are we leaving town now, *jefe?"* Juan asked when his boss returned from the newspaper office. Looking up at the man he admired, Juan hoped some day he would be as powerfully built. At eighteen, he was nearly as tall as the other man, but he still had a long way to go before he matched the strength of *el jefe*. His grandfather kept telling him he must be patient, but Juan chafed at the wait.

El jefe turned to look at the youth. Juan's narrow face was taut with tension, his dark eyes filled with hope. "No, not yet." At his words, Juan swallowed hard, but said nothing.

"*Por favor, jefe,* we must leave this place," Armando said, removing his hat and running a hand through his heavily graying hair. "It is not safe here."

El jefe shifted his gaze to the older man. Seeing the apprehension on Armando's round face and how his friend tugged on his long, sweeping moustache, he said, "You worry too much, *amigo mio.*" Idly slapping the newspaper he'd bought against one thigh, his gaze strayed to the building he'd just left. "No one knows what I look like. Of all the *gringo* artists' pictures of me, not one has it right. Would you agree, Armando?"

"*Sí, jefe,* that is true." Pulling on his moustache again, Armando glanced up, then down the street. "But we are *Californios,*" he said in a fierce whisper. "That is reason enough to suspect us. Being here *es muy peligroso.*"

After a long silence, their leader pulled his gaze from the newspaper office. "We will not be here much longer, so it is not that dangerous. I have decided there is something else I want to do. But I cannot do it until tonight. Can you wait that long, Armando?"

Armando took a deep breath. "*Sí, jefe,* but the sooner the better."

Katelyn opened the door to the small apartment behind the newspaper office and stepped inside. It was after ten and she was exhausted. She'd spent the entire evening at the city council meeting, trying to talk some sense into those fools about doing something about *El Buitre*. She had tried to convince the councilmen they couldn't keep sitting on their hands, hoping the bandit would simply disappear. They just listened to her impassioned speech, then replied as they always had: Yes, something must be done. But what that something was no one wanted to suggest. Anything, Katelyn thought, closing the door behind her, would be an improvement over the lethargic posture they had maintained for the six months since she'd taken over the newspaper.

Lighting the oil lamp on the parlor table, she started to turn around when she felt a presence behind her. Before she could move, a hand suddenly clamped over her mouth. Another hand jerked her wrists behind her back, and held them captive in a fierce grip.

"I have been waiting a very long time for you to return, Miss Ferguson," a man said next to her ear.

A scream welled up in her throat, but was stifled by the gloved hand pressing more firmly against her lips. She tried to twist free of his grasp, but he increased the pressure on her wrists. The next words from the soft voice halted any attempt to try again.

"I suggest you do not try it, Miss Ferguson. I do not want to hurt you. But if you make even the smallest of sounds, I will not hesitate."

Somehow her brain managed to push aside her fear long enough to analyze the man's voice. It was the voice that had haunted her all afternoon. The man who'd come into her office and asked about the author of the editorials on *El Buitre*. Remembering the strength she'd seen in his hands and the enormous width of his shoulders, she went limp against him. She could never win a physical battle against such a powerfully built man.

"Muy bien," he said at her compliance, then added, "Now, I am going to drop my hand. When I do, you are going to gather up some of your clothes, enough for a few

days, then we are going to take a little trip. You will make no sound. Do you understand me, Miss Ferguson?"

Her spine stiffened once more at his commands, but she managed to nod her agreement.

Slowly, he removed his hand from her mouth. He released her wrists, but kept his hand pressed to the small of her back. Before she could think of some way to avoid his instructions, she was propelled toward the door to her bedroom.

"What's the meaning of this?" she whispered fiercely. "How did you get in here? And what do you mean I need clothes for several days? I'm not going anywhere with you."

He chuckled at her rush of questions. "I see you are a true newspaperwoman. Your questions will be answered in good time, Miss Ferguson. Until then, *silencio*. Now, do as I say and pack a bag." When she didn't move, he raised his voice a fraction to add, *"¡Pronto!"*

Stumped on how to thwart him, and yet strangely not afraid for her safety, Katelyn moved stiffly to her chest of drawers and began pulling out underclothes, stockings, and a nightdress. Dumping them in a pile on the bed, she turned to where the rest of her clothes hung on pegs on the bedroom wall. She arbitrarily selected a handful of dresses, then tossed them onto the bed.

As she stuffed everything into a carpetbag, her mind worked furiously to comprehend what was happening. She'd only met this man that afternoon, so she couldn't imagine what he wanted with her. Holding her for ransom didn't seem likely, when there was no one who would pay to have her returned. But maybe this dangerous man didn't know that.

Abruptly, she stopped her packing and turned to face him. "If it's money you want, I don't have much, but . . . but I could get more."

He chuckled dryly. "I do not want your money, *gringa*. Now, hurry up."

Releasing an exasperated breath, she turned back to the bed. On top of her wadded-up clothing, she placed her journal and hairbrush.

As she glanced around for anything else she might need, he pulled her woolen shawl from its peg on the wall. Shoving it toward her, he said, "You had better take this."

"Why? It's the middle of July, so—"

"Just do it, *gringa,* and do not argue."

"Okay, fine," she snapped, jerking the shawl from his hand, then stuffing it into her carpetbag.

Before she could pick up the bag, he reached around her and snatched it off the bed. His other hand clasping her by the elbow, he nearly pulled her back into the parlor. "Is there someone you should notify about your absence?"

"I— Yes, I should tell Jacob Fletcher. He works for me, and he'll worry if I don't show up at the office in the morning. I'll just go tell him right now." When she tried to pull from his grasp, his fingers tightened.

"Hold it. You are not going anywhere. You will write the man a note." Releasing her, he ordered her to fetch pen and paper, then stood behind her at the small desk. "I can read, Miss Ferguson," he whispered softly, running one hand along the side of her neck. "So make it convincing, and do not try to tip him off."

Resisting the urge to shiver in reaction to his touch, Katelyn exhaled a frustrated breath. Unable to think of a way to get out of this mess, she complied and wrote a quick note to her close friend and employee, saying she'd been called away on urgent business and didn't know how long she'd be gone. After asking him to tell Grace about her unexpected departure, she closed by telling him to take care of the newspaper until her return.

When she laid down the pen, the man behind her grunted, then picked up the envelope. "Who is Grace?"

"She's a friend of mine. I was supposed to have supper

with her tomorrow night. I knew she'd worry, if I didn't show up. So that's why I asked Jake to talk to her."

He merely grunted again. "Tell me where this Jacob Fletcher lives, so I can have your note delivered," he said, pulling her from the desk chair and giving her a none too gentle shove toward the door.

Swallowing a retort about his high-handedness, Katelyn said, "He has a room in a lodging house on the corner of Seventh and M."

He responded with another grunt. Opening the door, he pushed her across the threshold, then followed her out into the night.

When they reached an alley several blocks from the newspaper office, two men on horseback, leading a third horse, moved out of the protective darkness into the street.

"This is the *something* you wanted to do, *jefe?*" Armando asked in Spanish.

"*Sí*, Armando," he replied in the same language. "I am ready to leave now."

"Does *la señorita* speak Spanish?" Juan asked.

"I do not know for sure. Just to be safe, watch what you say."

"We must leave now, *jefe*," Armando said.

Katelyn swung her gaze back and forth between the men, wishing she could understand their conversation. Although Spanish was commonly heard in Sacramento, she'd been too busy for the year and a half she'd lived there to pick up more than a word or two. Now she could kick herself for not taking the time to learn the language.

She was startled out of her thoughts by the voice of the tall man next to her. "I trust you will forgive me, Miss Ferguson. I seem to be without an extra horse. I hope it does not inconvenience you overly much, but you will have to ride double with me."

Tipping her head back, she tried to see his face. Although he'd tendered an elegant apology for the state of their traveling arrangements, she couldn't shake the feeling his words were couched in sarcasm. The feeble light the half-moon provided made it impossible to distinguish his features or gauge his mood. "Fine," she finally answered.

The word had barely left her mouth when she felt him move away from her. A burst of hope surged through her. *It's now or never.* She took a step back, then another. When he didn't seem to notice, she sucked in a deep breath, hiked up her skirts, and bolted down the street.

Two

Katelyn heard the snarl of an angry voice behind her, then the pounding of booted feet. Her lungs burning, she tried to run faster, but her full skirts impeded her progress. She'd gone only a short distance when a hand gripped her shoulder, spun her around, and pulled her flush against a hard chest.

"You cannot get away from me, *querida*," he whispered, surprised at how easily the endearment slipped off his tongue. "And besides," he said with a soft chuckle, "since your home is in the other direction, perhaps you are only playing games."

She wanted to scream at the unfairness of her aborted escape, at how she was badly winded, her heart pounding wildly; and he wasn't even breathing hard. Instead she clung to his heavily muscled arms, struggling to keep herself from sliding to the ground.

Before she could catch her breath enough to voice a protest, she found herself lifted into his arms and carried back to the other men. In spite of his burden, he mounted his horse with ease and settled her across his thighs in front of him. Such proximity momentarily snatched away what little air was left in her lungs.

She inhaled a deep, ragged breath, hoping to steady her nerves. His scent filled her lungs, nearly making her swoon. Not at all what she expected, he smelled faintly of leather, wood smoke, and horses. But mostly, he smelled of spice—

sandalwood, she thought—and his potent musky, male scent. The combination was extremely heady.

After the man holding Katelyn gave her note to the smallest of the other men, then gave him what she assumed were his instructions in Spanish, they started out of town. At the first corner, they split up. The man with her note went one way, the others turned in the opposite direction.

Keeping the horses at a walk and sticking to the shadows, the two men moved single file through Sacramento's streets. At the edge of town, Katelyn felt the man behind her jab his heels to his mount's sides, then the muscles of the horse bunch beneath her, before the animal lunged forward at a run.

A few miles into their journey, they pulled up and waited. In just a few minutes the third man appeared out of the darkness. After a brief conversation in Spanish, the three men and Katelyn continued their journey.

They traveled for several hours, then stopped along a rocky riverbank to water their horses. Katelyn was allowed to relieve herself in whatever cover she could find, but her captor stood not more than ten feet away. She was thankful for the darkness, certain her cheeks were fiery red with embarrassment. Much too soon, he remounted his horse, hauled her back up onto his lap, and continued their journey.

After a few more hours of riding, the darkness and the lulling rhythm of the horses' hooves racing over the gently rolling hills made Katelyn's eyes grow very heavy. Still, she fought sleep, determined to watch for something in the passing scenery that she could use as a landmark, if she had the chance to escape. Keeping watch proved useless in the deep shadows of night. Even the half-moon didn't provide enough light to see anything other than the eerie silhouette of a tree, or an occasional glimpse of moonlight sparkling on water when there was a break in the hills.

Unfortunately, the only thing she could be sure of was the road they traveled closely followed a river. But what road and which river? There were several roads leading into Sacramento, and more than one river in and around the town.

Being unfamiliar with the California countryside was a definite disadvantage. Not that such a shortcoming mattered much; her sense of direction was nonexistent. Her father had always teased her about not being able to find her way out of a gunny sack without having detailed instructions.

Although filled with growing despair, she finally could not keep her eyes open a moment longer. Giving in to her exhaustion, she slumped against the hard-muscled chest behind her. She pressed her cheek against the ruffles of his shirtfront and instantly fell asleep.

When she felt herself being pulled from the horse, she awoke with a start. "What—"

"Hush, *querida,* it is almost dawn, so we are stopping to get some rest. In just a moment you can lie down."

She allowed him to assist her to the blanket one of the other men had spread for her, then curled up on her side. When another blanket settled over her, she whispered her thanks, then feigned sleep. Looking through partially closed eyes, she watched the three men move around the small campsite.

After unsaddling the horses, each man gave his own mount a quick rubdown, then tied hobbles on their front legs. The men spread blankets for themselves near her feet, then sat quietly talking. Katelyn strained to hear their conversation, but caught only snatches of softly spoken Spanish. Though she wanted to remain awake to see if she could learn anything about what the men planned, sleep plucked at her. Exhaling a weary sigh, she gave in and slept.

When she awoke the next time, the sun was high, the sky a clear, brilliant blue. She rose up on one elbow and looked around. Seeing the sleeping forms of three men just a few feet away, she frowned. So she hadn't dreamed she'd been abducted by a mysterious stranger and his cohorts.

Under the brightness of daylight, she studied the area where they'd camped. They were in a small copse of oak trees on a hill overlooking the rocky banks of a river. The horses stood placidly on the opposite side of the trees.

Yawning, Katelyn considered getting up to look around, but she was just too tired. She rolled over, pulled the blanket over her face, then went back to sleep.

Jake Fletcher stared at the note left for him at the lodging house where he lived. Why in the world would Katelyn send a note, when she could have just left it in the *Argus* office?

More puzzling was why she had left town so abruptly. Tucking the note into his pocket, he headed down M Street, then cut north on Third. It wasn't like Katelyn to do something as impulsive as taking off. But then the girl had been working especially hard since her father died.

She'd been such a brave little gal, stepping in to take over the paper like she did. But bravery didn't pay the bills. He reckoned the *Argus* had to be going through real hard times, especially since most of Cyrus's advertising customers had refused to trust a woman at the helm of a newspaper, and had withdrawn their business. That was enough to send even the bravest of souls scurrying from town. No, to Jake's way of thinking, Katelyn wasn't on a business trip. She probably just wanted to get away from the pressures for a while, and was too embarrassed to say so.

When Jake turned the corner onto K Street, and the *Argus* office came into sight, his heart rate picked up. Next to the newspaper was the laundry owned by the Widow Grace Barnes.

He slowed his strides, hoping to catch a glimpse of the lovely Mrs. Barnes as he passed the front window of her building.

Recalling Katelyn's note, he stopped. *Durn you, Katie,*

for asking me to do this. He pulled the note from his pocket, swallowed hard, and approached the Barnes Laundry.

He pushed open the door, then stepped inside. He waited at the counter for a few minutes and was just about ready to leave, when a woman came through the curtains leading to the back room.

Jake felt the heat of a flush creep up his face. He silently cursed his nervous reaction to seeing the woman he'd admired ever since his first sight of her, when he had started working for Cyrus Ferguson in the fall of '51.

Though he'd never said more than an occasional hello to Grace Barnes, he'd made a point of learning all he could about the lovely widow. Originally from Ohio, she came to the Sacramento area with her husband back in '50. After the man's death that same year, she moved into town and opened her laundry in the building next to the *Argus.* He would guess her to be a few years younger than himself, perhaps forty-five, since Cyrus once told him she had two grown sons living back East.

Watching her approach, Jake took in everything about the woman who was never far from his thoughts. She was just a little thing, not much more than five feet tall, with a full, ripe figure, light brown hair worn in a coronet of braids atop her head, and the brownest eyes he'd ever seen.

"Why, Mr. Fletcher, what a surprise!"

Her voice startled him from his ruminations. "Mrs. Barnes," he replied, turning the envelope containing Katelyn's note over and over in his hands.

When he said no more, she said, "What's that you're holding, Mr. Fletcher?"

Realizing that he was acting like a schoolboy, he cleared his throat and said, "It's a note from Katelyn. She says she was called away on business, and she wanted me to tell you."

Grace's eyebrows lifted slightly. "Really? She left Sacramento?" At his nod, she added, "Does her note say where she was heading?"

"No, she didn't say. Here, you read it and see what you think."

Grace accepted the envelope, pulled out the single sheet of paper, then studied Katelyn's note.

While she was preoccupied, Jake drew in a slow deep breath, hoping to fill his lungs with her scent. She smelled of soap and just a hint of flowers—violets, he thought. His head reeled with the heady combination, his palms suddenly damp.

Much to his embarrassment, he always changed whenever he was around Grace. He was a grown man, almost fifty years old for cripes sake! But for some reason, being near Grace made him feel like a tongue-tied boy. Rather than face her possible ridicule, he'd never tried to pursue the widow, but kept their relationship formal whenever they chanced to meet.

Now being so close to the woman he longed for, he wasn't sure what he should say, how he should— Once again, her voice jerked him from his daydreams.

"What do you think this means, Mr. Fletcher? Do you really think she left on business?"

Needing a few moments to gather his thoughts, he exhaled slowly, then lifted his gaze to her face. But seeing the sprinkling of freckles on her nose and cheeks, her wide-eyed stare, he felt the familiar uneasiness start to settle over him. Determined not to act like a complete idiot, Jake pushed his discomfort aside and managed to find his voice. "I'm not sure what to believe. She never mentioned anything about a business trip yesterday, so it doesn't seem likely something could come up so quickly."

"Yes, it is a puzzle," she said, handing the note back to him.

His fingers brushed hers, sending his pulse into a gallop. Not able to look at her, he summoned all his strength and said, "Maybe we should get together and discuss this. What do you think, Mrs. Barnes?" He raised his head enough to peek at her face. Her bright smile came as a pleasant surprise.

"Don't you think it's about time we started calling each other by our Christian names? After all, we've known each other for nearly two years."

When he nodded, she said, "And I think getting together would be a good idea. How about supper tonight? I'm a great cook."

He smiled. "I'd like that, Grace." In spite of another rush of heat to his face, he didn't look away. "Is seven okay?"

"Perfect. See you then, Jake."

"Gringa, it is time to get up."

"Go away," Katelyn murmured, then gasped when her shoulder was given a none too gentle shove. Opening her eyes a crack, she saw a pair of boots next to her. She didn't have to guess who stood beside her, or that he'd used a boot-clad foot to prod her awake. "What do you want?"

"I said it is time to get up. Hurry and take care of your personal needs, so we may leave here."

She glanced at the sky. It was now a deep pink, shot with the last of the sun's golden rays. Had she really slept the entire day? Apparently she had, since the sun would be setting in a few hours. Shifting her gaze to the tall man who had issued the order, she looked up at him through narrowed eyes. Feet widespread, arms crossed over his broad chest, he stared down at her from beneath his hat brim. Wishing he'd remove his hat so she could see his face, she bit back a retort, then shoved the blanket aside.

"Would you mind helping me up?" She raised one hand toward him.

After a moment, he uncrossed his arms and reached down to grasp her hand. With one quick jerk, he pulled her to her feet.

"I didn't mean pull my arm out of its socket," she said, giving him a fuming look. Rubbing her shoulder, she added, "I'm not a—"

"I would not waste time talking, if I were you," he said, cutting off her complaint. "We are leaving in five minutes. So I suggest you take care of your personal needs immediately, or you will have to wait until the next time we stop."

"Fine," she said, shaking out her rumpled skirt, then marching deeper into the stand of trees.

When she returned, she mechanically ate the food he handed her, barely tasting it, but knowing she had to keep up her strength if she was to survive whatever lay ahead.

Again, she rode sitting across the hard-muscled thighs of her captor. Each time they stopped to rest and water the horses, she was allowed to stretch her legs, though ordered to stay close by. After their second stop, they turned away from the river, heading into the foothills of a mountain range. Katelyn thought the distant peaks resembled the Sierra Nevada, which she and her father had crossed on their trip to California. Her spirits lifted at the possibility, then immediately sagged. Even if she were correct, the Sierras were a very large mountain range, and since she had no idea which area they were in, the information was useless.

Still hoping something in the passing terrain would prove helpful later, she continued to watch for some distinguishing landmark. The chaparral-covered hillsides and deep canyons all looked alike in the deepening dusk. As they wound their way higher into the mountains, oak and pine trees mixed with the chaparral. Still she saw nothing unique enough to remember, if she were to see it again. From her perspective, they could be going in circles, and she'd never be the wiser.

After riding for several hours in full darkness, she grew drowsy from boredom and once again drifted to sleep against the hard chest behind her.

* * *

The lack of the horse moving beneath her woke Katelyn with a start. She opened her eyes a crack, then squeezed them closed. The late afternoon sun pierced down at her with a blinding fierceness.

The man holding her shifted in the saddle, rolling her head to the side with his movement. She groaned in protest, bringing a deep chuckle from his chest. *"Un momento,* Miss Ferguson, then you can go back to sleep."

She heard the rustle of cloth, then felt something soft brush her face. The fabric was pulled across her closed eyes and tied securely behind her head. When she lifted one hand to the silk blindfold, a soft voice stopped her. "No, *querida,* you must leave the bandana over your eyes. If you try to take it off, I will have to tie your hands as well."

"Why?" she managed to croak through her tight throat.

"We approach my camp. No one except my men has ever been here, and I cannot risk having someone from the outside know its location."

Katelyn wanted to tell him he had nothing to fear. But there was no point in telling her captor she could never find her way home, let alone back to his camp. He'd never believe her. Sighing with resignation, she dropped her hand and let her head fall back against the warmth of his chest.

"Bueno," he whispered softly, brushing a stray lock of hair off her face. He glanced up to see Juan and Armando staring at him incredulously. He pulled his hand away from the blond hair as though he'd been burned, his jaw clenching with anger. *Fool! How can I treat this* gringa *bitch with kindness?*

The next time Katelyn woke, the blindfold was still in place, and the man behind her was preparing to dismount. With one arm wrapped around her shoulders, the other under her knees, he lifted her off his thighs. Then, just as easily as he'd mounted the horse with her in his arms, he swung out of the saddle.

As he removed his hand from beneath her knees, she

slowly slid down his body, until her feet touched the ground.
When he dropped his other hand, her wobbly legs started
to buckle. Cursing softly, he grabbed her waist, preventing
her from falling. After she'd gained her balance, he moved
his hands to the back of her head. His fingers worked at
loosening the knotted silk, then the blindfold was whisked
from her face.

She blinked at the sudden brightness, trying to clear the
spots before her eyes. As she became accustomed to the
light, her gaze settled on the man standing beside her. His
hat hanging down his back by a leather thong, his face was
revealed to her for the first time. She sucked in a surprised
breath. Never had she seen a more handsome man. But
more than his high prominent cheekbones, long narrow
nose, and square clefted chin, her attention was captured
and held by his eyes. Dark as pitch, they glowed with an
intense inner fire—a fire she couldn't help thinking was
directed at her.

Suddenly some of his words came back to her, filling
her with apprehension. His camp. His men. Dear Lord, what
kind of man had abducted her? From the scowl on his face
and the anger burning in his eyes, she judged him to be an
extremely dangerous one. She swallowed her fear, determined not to show even the tiniest bit of cowardice.

"I think it is time I introduced myself," he said in that
warm, silky voice she was beginning to know well. After
bowing in a gesture of gallantry, he said, "I am Roberto
Cordoba, Miss Ferguson. Since you have devoted so much
space in your newspaper to me, I thought perhaps we should
meet in person."

Her brow furrowing, Katelyn replied, "Roberto Cordoba?" Deep in thought, she repeated the name several
times under her breath. Then, shaking her head, she said,
"The name doesn't sound familiar. Are you sure I've printed
something about you?"

He chuckled. "Yes, indeed. You have printed many articles about me. In fact, I have recently learned you were the author of all of them." His voice turned hard as he added, "You have called me every vile name imaginable with that poison pen of yours."

Something niggled at the back of her mind, yet the unlikely possibility didn't bear consideration. There were numerous gangs of bandits in this part of California; he must be the leader of one of them. Then another recollection came back, making her eyes widen with shock. When he visited the newspaper office, he'd been fascinated with her editorials about— Her eyes widened even more. *Oh, my God, was it really possible? Could he be—*

His voice interrupted her thoughts. "Ah, I see you are beginning to unravel the mystery of my identity." He flashed a chilling smile. "Yes, just as you suspect, Miss Ferguson, you know me by another name. One your fellow *gringos* gave me."

He lifted her chin with his fingers, forcing her to meet his gaze. When he was sure he had her undivided attention, he dropped his hand from her face. Watching her closely, he whispered, "They call me *El Buitre.*"

Three

"El . . . El Buitre?" Katelyn repeated softly. As the name sank into her befuddled brain, she shook her head with disbelief. *This can't be happening.* Trying to hide the quaking of her insides, she lifted her chin and met his gaze with a cool stare. "I don't believe you."

His mouth curved into another smile, this one also lacking amusement. "Believe it, Miss Ferguson."

Swallowing hard, she took a step back. *No, it can't be.* He wasn't *El Buitre;* that wasn't possible. She knew what The Vulture looked like; she'd envisioned meeting him a hundred times, although always in a courtroom or jail cell. Ever since her father's death, she'd dreamed of the day *El Buitre* was brought to justice—the day she'd personally witness his demise, the day he'd die at the end of a hangman's noose. The bandit in her imagination looked like his namesake—ugly as sin, with small beady eyes, a great hooked nose, and jagged teeth protruding over his bottom lip—nothing like the study in pure masculinity staring down at her. His face was finely sculpted, all sharp angles and plains, with whisker-roughened cheeks, and those piercing black eyes. Never had she met a man who was so blatantly male.

Meeting his penetrating stare, she saw again the anger lurking in the depths of his eyes. Though his anger alternately intrigued and frightened her, it didn't keep her from feeling the tug of his potent virility, drawing her closer with an invisible pull she was helpless to fight. When she finally broke eye contact, she was strangely breathless.

"I . . . you . . . Why did you bring me here?" she finally managed to say.

"I have already told you, Miss Ferguson. Since you have revealed your fascination with *El Buitre,* I decided you should be given the opportunity to meet him in person. What better way to learn about someone than on his own territory. Would you agree?" Not giving her an opportunity to answer, he continued, "While you are here, I intend to show you the error of your ways."

"That's ridiculous," Katelyn retorted, pleased her voice revealed none of her inner quaking. "I know what you are, what you've done." She planted her hands on her hips and glared up at him. "Nothing you say or do will change my mind."

He stared at her long and hard, silently enjoying the apprehension he saw flit across her face. For a tense moment he took in her disheveled appearance, the horribly rumpled and stained green dress, hair in a wild tangle, and smudges of purple beneath her eyes. Finally, he said, "I accept your challenge, Miss Ferguson." With that he turned to Armando, who had been standing quietly behind them. In Spanish he said, "See that she is given something to eat. Then take her to my cabin; she is exhausted."

Armando gave his boss a startled glance. "Your cabin, *jefe?*"

Turning toward his horse, *El Buitre* lifted the left stirrup and loosened the saddle's girth. He didn't spare Armando a look when he replied, "You heard me."

Recognizing the futility of arguing, Armando stepped over to Katelyn. *"Señorita,* you must come with me."

"With you? But where are you taking me?"

"You are hungry, *si?* And tired?" When Katelyn didn't respond, but stared at him blankly, Armando grasped her by the arm and turned her toward the center of the camp.

"Come, Armando will see you are fed and given a place to sleep."

Stunned by the events of the last day and a half, Katelyn allowed the older man to lead her to where another man, white-haired and weather-wrinkled, tended the campfire.

The old man turned at their approach, heavy white eyebrows lifting slightly above deep-set black eyes. "Who has he brought here?" the man asked in Spanish.

"She owns the newspaper *el jefe* has been reading."

"He reads many newspapers. So why did he choose this one to bring here?"

"She also wrote the editorials *el jefe* has found so entertaining."

The old man stared at the woman for a few seconds, then nodded. "Well, introduce us, Armando."

Switching to English, Armando dropped his hand from Katelyn's arm and gestured toward the other man. "This is our cook, Lutero, *Señorita* Ferguson. Lutero, this is Katelyn Ferguson. She will be our guest for a while."

"Guest? More like prisoner," Katelyn groused under her breath, then extended her hand. She blinked when Lutero lifted her hand to his mouth and brushed his lips across her knuckles. *At least one of these barbarians has some manners.* Her mouth curving into the brightest smile she could muster, she said, "Pleased to meet you, Lutero."

"My pleasure, *Señorita* Ferguson. Please sit down, and I will find you something to eat."

Perched on the piece of log he indicated, Katelyn realized she was famished. Her stomach rumbled loudly at the thought of food, bringing a chuckle from Lutero.

Although the food on the plate he handed her looked like nothing she'd ever had, she was too hungry to protest. Picking up her fork, she dug into her first real meal in almost two days. Beneath a thick sauce was some sort of flat pancake, filled with chunks of meat. The smell of onions and spices wafted upward, making her stomach growl again. She stuck a forkful into her mouth, chewed, and swallowed, her eyes closing with delight.

Just as quickly, her eyes popped open again, the pleasure replaced by shock and accompanied by a sudden spurt of tears. Her lips and tongue on fire, she croaked, "Water." She grasped the cup Lutero handed her and gulped down its contents in one breath. Staring at her plate, she whispered, "What is this?"

Lutero smiled. "It is an *enchilada;* a *tortilla* filled with dried beef, onions, and chili peppers. It is good, *sí?"*

Poking the *enchilada* carefully with her fork, Katelyn had to admit the flavor was very good, even if the inside of her mouth still burned like fire.

Refilling her cup with water, Lutero said, "You will get used to the spices. Now, try another bite. *Señor* Brit will be very unhappy if you do not eat."

"Señor Brit?"

"Sí, nuestro jefe," he said, waving one hand toward a man across the camp, the man she knew as *El Buitre.* Realizing she didn't understand Spanish, he translated. "Yes, our boss."

"Brit? But I thought his name is Roberto?"

"Sí, it is." Seeing the confusion on her face, he added, "I will say no more. You must ask your questions of him. Now, eat," he ordered softly.

Promising herself to get some answers, Katelyn obeyed. She was surprised to find the spicy food more and more appealing with each bite. By the time Lutero took her empty plate, she was pleasantly full and barely able to keep her eyes open.

Armando reappeared at her side, then helped her to her feet. One hand on her elbow, he escorted her across the campsite to a small cabin built in a stand of oak trees on the opposite side of the wide canyon floor.

The interior of the cabin was clean, the only furniture a chair pulled up in front of the fireplace at the opposite end of the single room. A bed had been built against the wall in one corner. A pile of blankets formed a mattress atop the wooden platform. On the floor next to the bed sat her carpetbag.

Armando's voice pulled Katelyn from her contemplation of how she could get away. "You are to sleep here, *Señorita* Ferguson." As if reading her mind, he added, "I will be standing guard outside."

Embarrassed her thoughts could be read so clearly, Katelyn's cheeks burned as she moved toward the bed. Too exhausted to think rationally, she decided she'd get a good night's sleep in a real bed, then try to figure out what to do about her situation.

"Thank you, Armando. You needn't worry that I'll try to escape tonight. I could never find my way out of these mountains in the dark." Unfortunately, she also knew she could never find her way in the brightness of daylight either. Sighing with frustration, she sat on the bed and opened her carpetbag.

She wasn't even aware Armando had left until she heard the door close softly behind her. Sighing again, she picked up her journal. Despite her need for rest, she didn't want to give in to sleep until she'd put some of her thoughts down on paper.

After changing into her nightdress, she brushed her hair, then deftly braided it into one long plait. Picking up her journal, she sat back down on the bed to write.

I met El Buitre *yesterday, or was it the day before? I've lost track of time. He came into the newspaper office, then later abducted me from my home. He is undoubtedly the most handsome man I have ever seen, yet he is also just as dangerous as I have reported him to be. There seems to be some sort of raw fury driving him. I see anger burning in his dark eyes and wonder at its cause. He is holding me prisoner at his camp somewhere in the mountains. To what end I do not know.*

She wanted to write more, but her complete exhaustion changed her mind. Carefully placing her journal back in her carpetbag, she stretched out on the pallet of blankets. The bed was surprisingly comfortable, and in seconds she was sound asleep.

Something woke Katelyn from a sound sleep. Glancing up at the cabin's only window, the deep purplish black of the middle of the night met her gaze. She felt a slight movement next to her and froze. As her eyes grew more accustomed to the darkness, she took care to keep her body relaxed. The movement came again, this time accompanied by the soft breathing of someone or something. Stifling the scream clawing at her throat, she forced herself to roll over.

There was someone lying next to her. Just as she drew in a deep breath to vent her protest, her nose detected a familiar scent. It was him! Not some wild animal or depraved criminal, the man beside her was Roberto Cordoba, Brit, *El Buitre.* The last of his names caused her breath to hang suspended somewhere between her lungs and her lips. Hadn't she described the bandit in exactly those terms— wild animal and depraved criminal? And even though she agreed that yes, he'd done all of the things she'd reported, for a reason she didn't understand, she strangely felt no fear having him so close.

She lay awake for a few minutes, trying to analyze why she wasn't scared out of her wits by the bandit. She found no answers. As her eyes drifted closed, she inhaled deeply. Her lungs filled again with the soothing scent of musk, sandalwood, and leather. Shivering suddenly, she scooted closer to the man lying with his back to her. Though she didn't touch him, the warmth of his body seeped into her chilled flesh and eased her back to sleep.

When Katelyn woke soon after daybreak, she was alone in the cabin. If it weren't for the indentation on the blankets next to her, she would have thought she'd dreamed that someone shared the bed with her. She reached out and tentatively touched where he'd slept. Realizing what she was doing, she jerked her hand away with a groan of disgust. With a sudden craving for fresh air, she jumped out of bed. The cabin smelled like sandalwood and leather, and she had to get away from the potent reminder.

"He's nothing but a damned robber and a murderer," she grumbled while pulling off her nightdress, then tugging on clean drawers and chemise and a dress of lavender lawn. "And he says he brought me here to meet the real *El Buitre*. Hah!" she ranted while tying her shoes. "I already know all I need to know about The Vulture, and I—"

She straightened abruptly, her lips pursed thoughtfully. Maybe this was a blessing in disguise, a chance for her to learn something new. Wouldn't that make a splendid headline for an extra edition: "Newspaper owner gets private interview with *El Buitre*." She liked the sound of that.

Katelyn's buoyed spirits fled, replaced by the sting of tears. That was exactly what her father had been trying for—an exclusive interview with the renowned bandit. Then Cyrus Ferguson's unexpected death ended his dream. She swallowed hard. "Oh, Papa, why'd you have to be so bullheaded?" she whispered.

When she had composed herself, Katelyn tried to smooth some of the wrinkles from the full skirt of her dress, then left the cabin. She nearly tripped over someone lying in front of the door. So she had been guarded!

Throwing off his blanket, Armando scrambled to his feet.

After allowing her a few minutes to tend to her personal needs, he escorted her back to Lutero for breakfast.

While she ate a bowl of corn porridge and drank a cup of delightfully sweet hot chocolate Lutero called *champurrado,* Katelyn made a decision. She'd use her time in the camp—however long her captor deemed to keep her there—to her advantage. She'd talk to the other men; they were bound to tell her something useful sooner or later. And she'd talk to The Vulture himself. He said he wanted her to see how she'd been mistaken about *El Buitre,* so he shouldn't object to answering a few questions.

Then, when she got back to Sacramento, she'd have material for two, perhaps more articles that were sure to increase sales. If she could sell more papers, maybe she could keep the *Argus* from going under for a while longer.

Her course of action decided, Katelyn still wasn't prepared for her reaction to seeing the man filling her thoughts stride across the campsite. He had bathed, shaved, and changed into clean clothes. If he was handsome before, the black trousers, black shirt open at the throat, and red bandana made him even more breathtaking. As he drew nearer, her heart threatened to pop right out of her chest. Schooling her features not to betray her inner trembling, she met his dark gaze with a glare of her own.

"Good morning, Miss Ferguson." He nodded curtly, then added, "I trust you slept well last night." While the words sounded friendly enough, there was no mistaking the brusque tone of his voice.

"Yes, I slept fine."

"You did not get cold?" His lips curved upward slightly, the usual anger in his eyes momentarily replaced by secret humor.

Her face burning, Katelyn refused to drop her gaze or take the bait he dangled in front of her. "No," she said emphatically.

In a voice meant for only her ears, he said, "Hmm, that

is strange. I was sure I felt your lovely little body pressing against mine during the night."

Lifting her chin, she gave him a scathing look. "You must have been mistaken."

Accepting a cup of hot chocolate from Lutero, *El Buitre* tilted his head in mock concession and murmured, "Perhaps." He lifted the cup to his lips, never taking his gaze from her face. Testing the temperature of his drink with the tip of his tongue, he saw the widening of her eyes and felt an instant response in his groin. With a muffled curse, he shoved the cup back to Lutero and stalked away.

"Wait," Katelyn called, running after him. "I wanted to talk to you."

He stopped short, his shoulders lifting with a deep inhalation of breath. He turned to look at her, the anger back in his eyes, hot and dangerous.

But this time another emotion shone there as well, an emotion Katelyn thought she must have imagined. As she stared at him, she could tell he struggled to compose himself.

A muscle jumping in his cheek, he finally managed to say, "Just what did you want to talk about, Miss Ferguson?"

Katelyn swallowed the sudden apprehension his harsh voice caused, and said, "You . . . you said you wanted me to get to know the real Vulture. So, I . . . um . . . was just going to ask you some questions."

After a long silence, he waved to Armando, who came puffing across the campsite. "Armando will give you a tour of our camp. I have things to do this morning."

"But—"

"You heard me, Miss Ferguson. I will talk with you later." With that he turned on his heel and headed for the trees surrounding his cabin.

"Well!" Katelyn said, balling her hands into fists. "If he isn't the rudest, most obstinate man I have ever met."

"He is not really like that, *señorita*," Armando said in a soft voice. "He was not so rude before—"

Intrigued, her aggravation instantly forgotten, Katelyn turned to look at Armando. "Before what?"

Clearing his throat, he shrugged. "I am sorry, *señorita,* I have said too much already. I can say no more."

Accepting his hand on her elbow, Katelyn allowed him to escort her around the campsite. Now that she was completely rested, she carefully studied her surroundings.

They were in a steep-sided canyon, deep in the mountains. A fast running stream ran across the rocky canyon floor, providing sufficient water for the men and horses. Abundant oak and a few pine trees shaded the main area of the camp; hazelnut and black cottonwood trees hugged the banks of the curving stream.

Behind the campsite, deeper into the canyon, were several corrals. The smallest corral held a single cow, while a half-dozen horses stood quietly in the larger enclosure. In spite of not wanting to find anything favorable about *El Buitre,* Katelyn had to admit building the horse corral past the campsite was a good idea. Intruders would not be able to make off with the horses without alerting the entire camp. Something about that discovery made her frown.

Armando's voice jarred her from her thoughts. He was introducing her to the others. As she smiled and returned the greetings of each of the half-dozen men, her mind kept straying to their leader. She wondered where he'd gone and what he was doing.

Brit knew exactly where Katelyn was, and how she spent every minute since he'd left her in such a huff. He headed up a steep incline to his private hideaway on a wide plateau partway up the canyon's side. He'd specifically selected the spot because it was level enough for a small corral, and because the plateau's higher elevation allowed him an unhindered view of the entire camp on the canyon floor.

Normally, he didn't spend his time secretly watching the

goings-on of his men; they were competent and did as they were told. But today he couldn't keep his gaze from constantly straying to the campsite. Every few minutes, he searched for the pale blond head among the dark ones of his men.

Picturing Katelyn's face in his mind, Brit was at a loss as to why he found her so attractive. His first impression of her had been correct—she wasn't a beautiful woman. Though her light hair and clear blue eyes were lovely, there was nothing extraordinary about her too-pointed chin, her too-full mouth, or any of her other plain features. Yet, in spite of her lack of classic beauty, there was an erotic essence about her, a rare sensuality he found strongly appealing.

Finally admitting he couldn't concentrate on what he'd intended to do, he settled down to watch Katelyn's every move.

His obsession—with a woman he wanted no part of—filled his gut with an all too familiar helpless anger, this time directed more at himself than at its true source—those responsible for the life he led. Squinting his eyes, he watched Armando escort their guest around the campsite. He couldn't help wondering if he'd made a mistake in bringing Katelyn Ann Ferguson to his hideout.

No! The intensity of his reaction surprised him. It had been necessary to bring Miss Ferguson to his camp. He wanted her to meet the real *El Buitre,* then perhaps she'd stop venting her spleen about him in her newspaper. Remembering his reason for abducting her from Sacramento, Brit sighed wearily. She had asked to talk to him—exactly what he wanted—yet he'd boorishly rebuffed her request.

"Damn," he murmured softly, rubbing a hand wearily over his eyes. He hadn't slept much last night, not with the soft body of Katelyn Ferguson snuggled next to him, making little kitten noises in her sleep. He sighed again, realizing it was inevitable he speak to her and answer her questions. He just hoped he could keep his hands off the *gringa* bitch. For a reason he hadn't figured out, he wanted more from Katelyn than just setting her straight about *El Buitre*. That thought made his anger flare even hotter.

He turned from the view of his camp below, and the woman who played havoc with his determination to seek retribution for the way his people were treated. He stalked over to the small corral and the pale golden horse he called Solazo standing inside. The mare lifted her head at his approach, nostrils flaring at his familiar scent.

"Easy, my pretty one," Brit crooned softly in Spanish, his anger fleeing at the sight of the skittish horse. He slipped through the rails of the corral and moved closer. "I will not hurt you. You should know that by now."

As he ran his hand down the mare's neck, it wasn't the golden coat of the horse he saw beneath his fingers, but the silken strands of Katelyn Ferguson's hair. When he realized where his thoughts had wandered, he jerked his hand away so quickly, the mare tossed her head in fright.

A burning rage sprang to life again in his chest. How was he going to get through his interview with the woman, when he couldn't keep her out of his thoughts for five minutes? Drawing on his thirst for vengeance, he managed to put aside all thoughts except one. He'd speak with her in the morning, then in a day or two, he'd see she was returned to Sacramento.

Four

Katelyn sat next to Armando near the camp's main fire; one of the two camp dogs, a large, brown hound named Paco, was curled up next to her. Though it was mid-July, the mountain evenings were much cooler than in Sacramento. She pulled her shawl closer around her shoulders, glad *El Buitre* had insisted she bring it with her.

The rest of the men sat in groups of two or three, near the fire but not close enough for her to overhear their conversations. It didn't really matter, they spoke entirely in Spanish.

Absently running her hand through the rough coat of the hound, she searched the surrounding area. The darkness made it impossible to see beyond the fire's glow. *El Buitre* hadn't returned to camp. She couldn't keep the fear his absence spawned from intruding into her thoughts. If something happened to him, or he chose not to return, what would happen to her? Would the others decide to return her to Sacramento, or would they think she wasn't worth the bother? Maybe they would keep her at the camp and pass her around. Maybe they would kill her. She shivered violently, pulling the shawl even tighter around her shoulders.

Forcing her panic to recede, she rose from the blanket Armando had spread on the ground for her. "I think I'll go to bed now, if that's all right."

Armando jumped to his feet. *"Sí,* I will escort you."

"That isn't necessary. I can find my way."

"It is my job to look after you, *señorita,* so do not argue."

Katelyn merely nodded, knowing it was useless to protest further.

After Armando bid her good night and before she curled up on the mattress of blankets to sleep, she wrote another entry in her journal.

I tried to speak to The Vulture today. He refused, that same, strange anger swirling in his dark eyes. But I noticed something else in those mesmerizing eyes— something I would classify as very close to desire. Yet, I must be mistaken. Such a handsome man would never want a plain-as-mud woman like me. I do know his gaze seems to penetrate to the center of my being, making me quiver all over in a way I've never experienced. He is the most exciting and at the same time most frightening man I have ever met. After our aborted conversation, he stormed from camp in a fit of temper, and to my knowledge he has not yet returned. While his absence means I do not have to withstand his angry glare or listen to more of his cutting words, I still cannot entirely halt a chilling fear from gnawing at my vitals. I pray I do not have to find out what will happen to me if he does not return.

After everyone else had retired, Brit headed for his cabin. Just inside the doorway, he halted, his gaze snared by the vision on his bed.

Katelyn lay curled on her side, one hand tucked beneath her chin, her lips slightly open. The glow of the fire danced over her sleeping features, making her hair shimmer like liquid gold. When his gaze lowered to the prim and proper nightdress, buttoned up to her chin, a faint smile eased the harsh line of his mouth. In his mind, he pictured her without the white gown, sleek and curvaceous.

The trace of a smile fled instantly, replaced by a scowl. Although he longed to slam the door of the cabin, just as he'd slammed the door on the path his thoughts had taken, he eased it shut and moved quietly across the room. Unbuckling his gun belt, he laid it carefully on the floor next to the bed, then pulled off his boots.

He lowered himself down next to Katelyn, wishing he could strip off his clothes as he usually did. But he didn't dare. Actually, he didn't trust himself. If he were to try sleeping beside her in the raw, he wasn't sure he could resist pulling her into his arms, or kissing her sweet mouth—or worse.

He tossed and turned fitfully before sleep finally overtook him. Even then his dreams were filled with a blond-haired woman who made his blood boil and his heart sing.

He awoke in a foul temper, gathered up three of his men, and rode out of camp.

When Katelyn saw nothing of *El Buitre* by noon, she decided she'd ask Armando about his uncooperative leader. At least she knew her fears from the previous night regarding her immediate future if the Vulture didn't return were unfounded. Sometime during the night, she'd awoken to find him sleeping beside her. Yet for some reason, he continued to avoid her during the day. No matter, she vowed, there were other ways to find out what she wanted to know.

After she finished the noon meal, Katelyn waited until the rest of the men had wandered away to their various chores before she said, "Armando, where did he go?"

"Who are you talking about, *señorita?*"

"Don't play innocent with me, Armando. You know I'm talking about your boss, the one you call *el jefe.*"

"Ah, him." Armando chuckled. "He went on a . . . mission."

"A mission? What kind of a miss—" Her eyes widened. "Oh, you mean as *El Buitre?*"

"*Sí*, that is who *el jefe* is, *señorita.*"

"He went to rob someone. Is that what you're trying to say?" Katelyn said, her eyes widened even more.

Armando shrugged. "Perhaps. I did not speak to him before he left, so I cannot tell you any more."

After mulling over his words, she finally said, "Can I ask you something else?"

Armando hesitated before replying. "You can ask, *señorita*, but I cannot promise I will answer."

Swallowing her disappointment that he was either naturally cautious or had been warned to watch what he said, Katelyn flashed him a bright smile. "Do not worry, *amigo mío*, I will not ask you anything that will anger *el jefe.*"

Armando smiled in return. "Your Spanish, she is improving, *sí?*"

Katelyn giggled. "Well, *she* isn't as good as I would like. That's what I wanted to ask you. Will you help me with my Spanish?"

Armando stroked one side of his moustache. "I must ask *el jefe*. If he agrees, then I teach you."

Realizing she had no other alternative, Katelyn nodded, then changed the subject. "Speaking of your boss, why does Lutero call him Brit? That doesn't sound like a Spanish name."

"No, it is not. Don Ricardo, the father of *el jefe*, is from England, and he named his son Roberto Brit. From the time *el jefe* was a little boy, those closest to him, all except his *madre*, call him Brit."

"So he's half English. Interesting," Katelyn said in a low voice, finding the puzzle of the man more and more intriguing. "How long have you had a camp here?"

After a long silence, Armando finally said, "For a very long time."

"But don't you miss your home and your family?"

"*Sí,* I miss them very much."

"Won't he let you visit them? Surely he understands how a man misses his family."

Armando's back stiffened slightly. "Of course, *el jefe* understands. But we have work to do here. When our work is done, then we will see our families."

"Where's home for you, Armando?"

"Far to the south, on a *rancho* in the broad valley, *señorita.*"

"What brought you to this part of California?"

"The same thing that brought many others. My people also wanted to become rich by taking gold from the earth." He stared off into the distance, his expression harsh. "And we were very good at mining—better than most Yankees. Then things changed."

"Changed? How?"

Armando turned his gaze on Katelyn. "How long have you been in California, *señorita?*"

"My father and I arrived about a year and a half ago, in October of '51."

"Ah, then you were too late."

"Too late for what?"

"It does not matter now." Rising from where he sat on the ground next to her, Armando held out his hand. "Come, I will show you more of the camp."

As she placed her hand in his, Katelyn studied his face. The set of his jaw told her he would say no more.

Late in the afternoon two days later, Brit returned to camp amid a flurry of yipping dogs, rearing horses, and shouts of greeting. Katelyn watched him from across the camp, wishing the jubilant smile on his face were directed at her.

Holding up what looked like several leather pouches with his left hand, he threw back his head and laughed. She watched Armando hurry over to greet the men, sorry she was too far away to hear their conversation.

"Your mission was successful, *jefe?*" Armando said, grabbing the reins of Brit's horse to still the gray's nervous prancing.

"*Sí*, very successful. We will eat well for a while. And there will still be plenty to send home to your families, eh, *compadres?*" he replied, glancing at the men who returned with him.

The others nodded and laughed, then swung down from their horses. Brit tossed the pouches to Armando, threw his right leg over the saddle horn, and slid to the ground in one lithe motion. Slapping the trail dust from his trousers, he walked with Armando to the campfire.

When his gaze landed on Katelyn, his smile faded. For a moment he had put the *gringa* from his mind, one of the few times in his two-day absence his thoughts hadn't been filled with her. Accepting a plate of food from Lutero, he circled the fire and sat down near Katelyn.

"So, are you enjoying your stay at my camp, *gringa?*" he said between bites of his meal.

Katelyn clenched her hands in her lap, determined not to lose her temper. "If you call living in primitive conditions, eating food I've never heard of, and sharing the camp with a group of Spanish-speaking bandits enjoyable, then I guess the answer is yes."

In spite of her less then glowing description of his camp, Brit would have laughed had he not caught the flare of blue fire in her eyes. His blood warmed. Her show of temper made her even more appealing. "If you are angry because I left you here while I attended to business, I am sorry you feel that way, but it could not be helped."

"Business! You call robbing and assaulting innocent victims, business?"

"Robbing *is* the business of *El Buitre.*" His voice was a low snarl. There was no use pointing out he had never assaulted anyone. In her current frame of mind, she wouldn't listen anyway. "Have you forgotten that so quickly?"

"No, I haven't forgotten. But apparently you've forgotten why you brought me here." She glared at him, waiting for his response.

A muscle jumping in his cheek, one hand tightening on his plate, he continued eating.

After a moment of silence, she said, "Let me remind you what you told me. You said—"

"I know what I said, Miss Ferguson," he said, setting his plate aside. "I will tell you what I want you to know about *El Buitre.*" When she opened her mouth to speak, he held up one hand. "But not today. I have just returned from a long ride, and I am in no mood for talking or answering your questions."

Late the next morning Katelyn sat beneath a large oak tree, watching the man she now thought of as Brit work with a palomino mare in a small corral on the other side of the plateau. Armando, her constant companion, stood nearby. After eating breakfast, she'd asked if they could take a walk, and he'd agreed. She was anxious to see more of the canyon, secretly hoping to find a possible escape route. That they ended up on the wide strip of land hugging the canyon wall behind Brit's cabin had been part of her plan from the beginning, a plan Armando had thankfully not been aware of.

"What a beautiful horse," she said in a low voice.

"Sí, she is very beautiful. *El jefe* captured her himself. He lets no one else near her."

"Captured her? Do you catch wild horses?"

"Sí. There are many *mesteños* in the valley stretching between the Sierra Nevada and the smaller mountains to

the west. *El jefe* has a good eye for fine horses. He looks over the herds we capture, then selects the best for his—"

Katelyn looked over at Armando. "The best for his what?"

"It is not important."

Resolved to wait a little longer before she got answers to her growing list of questions, she shifted her gaze back to the corral. Watching Brit and the palomino, she was struck again by the sharp contrast between the patient, gentle man handling the horse, and the man she'd painted as a vicious, savage animal in her editorials.

Was it possible her father had been right? Perhaps there was another side to *El Buitre,* a side no one knew. Perhaps there was a story to tell behind the man who'd chosen the life of a bandit. Was *El Buitre* truly what her father suspected, a good man turned bad?

Thinking of her father brought a lump to Katelyn's throat. She'd tried so hard to discourage Cyrus Ferguson from continuing his search for *El Buitre.* But it was her father's dream to interview the bandit and learn the real reason for the life the man led.

Even after Cyrus's health began to deteriorate, Katelyn couldn't convince him to stop making his forays into the surrounding countryside. Sometimes his trips kept him away from Sacramento for several days. Each time he swung onto his horse and headed out of town, Katelyn's fear grew. Then one day, her fears became reality. Cyrus returned slumped over in his saddle, clutching his chest.

He lingered through the night, then finally slipped away—his dream of an exclusive interview with *El Buitre* dying with him.

Though Katelyn hadn't loved the newspaper business as much as Cyrus Ferguson had and never planned to run a paper on her own, his passing changed the future she'd envisioned since losing her mother. Katelyn had thought to spend her life caring for her father, keeping their home, and perhaps working a few hours a week as a reporter for his paper.

At first Cyrus had objected to her decision, but she finally convinced him she was content. As the only family she had, her father came first in her life. There was never any thought given to looking for a husband. She remembered the housekeeper Cyrus hired after his wife's death telling her time and again, men want more from a woman than physical beauty. Katelyn knew the woman had only been trying to boost her self-esteem. But her mirror didn't lie, and she'd never tried to sugarcoat the truth. She *was* plain. In spite of the housekeeper's claims to the contrary, Katelyn refused to entertain any fanciful notions of finding a man willing to marry her—especially after the heartbreaking relationship with the one and only boy who had come calling.

Happy with the choice she'd made, her contentment abruptly came to an end with her father's death. His passing created a steely resolve to carry on the family tradition, to keep the *Argus* going. But running the newspaper was a constant struggle, the profits continuing to decline. Still, she remained determined to keep the paper from having to close its doors—at least until she'd extracted revenge.

Placing the blame for her father's death on the man Cyrus had become obsessed with, Katelyn had decided to use the newspaper as a means of retaliation. By writing editorials about *El Buitre,* she intended to stir up enough outrage among the local citizenry to launch a successful campaign to put an end to the bandit forever.

She also attended all town meetings. Though the Sacramento councilmen shilly-shallied over a decision, other townsfolk were beginning to put pressure on the local government to take some sort of action. After six months of her efforts, Katelyn's planned revenge had finally started making some headway.

Then, the very man she'd devoted all her time and energy

to putting out of business, had abducted her from her home. The man in the horse corral on the other side of the plateau.

Seeing Brit's dark hands run over the horse's coat in slow, gentle strokes, Katelyn shivered, feeling as though his fingers had glided over her skin. She pressed her lips together, her hands balled into fists in her lap. She forced thoughts of her unwanted reaction to the back of her mind, calling up her father's last words.

Cyrus had roused enough to grasp her hands and plead in a surprisingly strong voice. "Katie, lass, don't hate me for looking for him. I know you thought I was chasing after nothing more than a foolish dream. But if you had spent as much time as I have studying the man, you'd agree. I'm certain he is not what he appears to be."

Tears streaming down her face, Katelyn choked back a sob to say, "Oh, Papa, I don't hate you. Everyone has a dream they have to follow. I love you."

The anxiety left his face at her words. He even gave her a weak smile. Then he fell back on the pillow, his eyes drifting closed. He never reopened them.

She'd meant what she told her father. She didn't hate him; before his death she'd never hated anyone. Yet, as she watched her father's coffin being lowered into the ground, she knew how people could come to hate—that was exactly what she felt toward the man responsible for putting Cyrus in his grave.

Remembering her final conversation with her father and the day she discovered her need for revenge, a lump formed in Katelyn's throat. She swallowed, determined to hide both the threatening tears and her pain.

Unable to bear watching Brit any longer, Katelyn rose and brushed the grass and leaves from her skirt. "Can we go back to camp now, Armando?"

His brows pulling together, Armando searched her face. "We only just got here, *señorita*. Are you sure you want to return so soon?"

"Sí. I'm sure you have other duties besides being my nursemaid."

Armando straightened his spine, puffing out his chest. "It is my job to take care of the *mesteños* after we capture them. We have no horses now, so I do whatever *el jefe* say."

Katelyn didn't reply, but turned and headed back down the steep path to the campsite. Armando followed a few feet behind.

Brit had been aware of Katelyn's presence from the moment she stepped onto the opposite end of the plateau. Against his will, he had developed a sixth sense regarding the woman in his camp. He meant what he'd told her the day before, he did intend to talk to her. He should tell her the things he wanted her to know and be done with it, so he could send her back to Sacramento.

But each time he looked at her, the words wouldn't come. Instead he fought a constant battle with an intense desire to taste her lips, to run his hands over her body. Never had he known such a need for a woman, not even with Mirabella.

Thinking of the fragile Mirabella with the enormous black eyes, golden skin, and waist-length ebony hair, Brit's desire for Katelyn cooled, leaving a bitter taste in his mouth. His gut twisting with rage, he vowed to get on with his plans and not be affected by Katelyn Ferguson.

Ross Carter picked up his pace on Sacramento's K Street. Nearly a week had passed since Jacob Fletcher had shown him Katelyn's ridiculous note, and he was still no closer to learning where she went or why. No one saw her leave town: none of the agents at either the Forrest Stage Line or the steamship office had sold her a ticket. So where the hell had she gone, and how? He wasn't buying her "called away on urgent business" line, but so far he'd turned up nothing to prove otherwise.

Thinking again of the note she'd left Jake, Ross clenched his teeth in irritation. *Why the hell did she tell Jake to notify Grace Barnes, and not bother to mention me? That woman can be so infuriating. Thinking she could run a newspaper was bad enough, but now she has to pull a stupid stunt like this.*

Entering the *Argus* office, Ross nodded at Jake, moved past the counter, and stopped in front of Katelyn's desk. "Any word from Miss Ferguson?" he said as casually as he could, flipping through the stack of mail on the desk.

"No, sir, not a peep. You don't think something's happened to her, do you?" Frowning, Jake searched Ross's profile for some sort of reaction. The owner of the *Sacramento Tribune,* one of the competitors of the *Argus,* was just past thirty, of average height and weight, with light brown hair, dark blue eyes, and a full, neatly trimmed beard. Jake could detect no undue worry in Ross's expression.

Turning to meet the gaze of the newspaper's printer's devil, Ross noticed the furrows on the older man's forehead were deeper than usual, concern for his boss reflected in his hazel eyes. Ross moved next to the shorter man, laying a hand on his heavily muscled shoulders.

"No, I don't think something's happened to her, Jake. I just thought she might have sent word when she'd return. After all, leaving you to run the newspaper alone for who knows how long is a mighty big imposition."

Jake shrugged off Ross's hand and brought himself up to his full height. Shoving a lock of his graying hair off his forehead, he said, "I was working in a newspaper office long before you were more than a gleam in your daddy's eye, and I don't mind taking care of the *Argus* 'til Miss Katelyn gets back."

"Take it easy, Jake, I know you can do the work. I'm just upset Katelyn took off the way she did. If she got wind of a story, I can't imagine why she didn't tell me. You know we collaborate our efforts whenever we can."

Jake stared at him through narrowed eyes. He knew Katelyn shared news material with Ross out of professional courtesy, but he didn't want to point out how little she received in return from the *Tribune* owner. Clearing his throat, he said, "Aye, I know you did."

"I just find her leaving so abruptly most . . . er . . . distressing," Ross replied, turning from the other man's gaze to conceal what his face might reveal. "Especially since we're engaged."

"Engaged?" Jake's brows pulled together. "Miss Katelyn ain't said yes to your proposal, and you damn well know it."

"Well, she would have," Ross snapped, then added in a softer voice, "I know she would have agreed to marry me, but she left town before she gave me her answer."

Jake cocked his head to one side, eyeing Ross suspiciously. He had the distinct impression Katelyn wasn't in love with Ross Carter, and would not accept the man's proposal in spite of what Ross thought. Taking a deep breath, he exhaled slowly. He knew some folks tied the knot regardless of whether they loved each other. Though he never figured Katelyn to be one to enter into a loveless marriage, he wouldn't put it past Ross. To Jake's way of thinking, Carter had a reason completely separate from love for wanting the marriage—the *Argus*. Jake had never mentioned his suspicions to Katelyn, but seeing the way Ross's gaze moved greedily around the office, he wished he had.

Moving to the printing press, Ross picked up a copy of the edition Jake had just run. On the second page, in the space reserved for the newspaper's editor, was an editorial entitled, *Desperado Must be Stopped*.

"Did you write this week's editorial?"

"No," Jake responded. "Miss Katelyn wrote it the day before she left."

Ross nodded absently, silently reading Katelyn's work.

News has reached us that The Vulture has struck again, adding another foul and daring crime to his list of atrocities. This time another innocent traveler was relieved of his hard-earned coin near Angel's Camp, then beaten senseless by the villainous Vulture. The actions of this despicable bandit are beyond human endurance. This scourge on mankind is well named. He is indeed a Vulture, picking his victims clean at every turn and making a mockery of our law enforcement. I say again, citizens of Sacramento, The Vulture must be stopped. How long will we allow travelers in this part of our fair state to feel insecure, their very lives at risk? We must do something now!

Laying the sheet of newsprint aside, Ross smiled. "She does have an acrimonious way with words, when it comes to *El Buitre.*"

"She has her reasons," Jake said softly.

"What? Oh, yes, I know she blames him for her father's death. Cyrus was certain there was a good man beneath his life of crime. Hell, Cyrus must have been as mad as an old coot. The Vulture is just another damned greaser, as far as I'm concerned. I'm not so sure Katelyn is right to blame him for Cyrus's death. But I have to admit, her stinging editorials should help bring the bandit to the punishment he deserves."

Jake merely grunted. While it was true *El Buitre* was a bandit, robbing at will, Jake had also read all of Cyrus Ferguson's notes on the man called The Vulture. Cyrus may well have been right in his assessment of the man who led a life of crime, but Jake wouldn't tell Ross Carter that. No use stirring up trouble with a man who lumped all Mexicans, *Californios,* and other Latins together, and labeled them with the horrible epithet *greaser.*

Jake turned back to the press. He had a paper to get out. "I'll let you know if I hear anything from Miss Katelyn."

Ross stared at the older man's back for a few seconds, then said, "Please do." After glancing around the office one last time, he turned to leave. "I'll stop by again tomorrow, to see if you need any help."

Frowning, Jake shrugged. "Suit yourself."

Five

Three days later, Brit returned to his cabin late in the afternoon to find Katelyn rummaging through her carpetbag. Leaning against the doorjamb, he watched her in silence, tracing the lush curve of full bosom beneath the tight bodice of her gray dress with an intense gaze. Forgotten was the vow he had made several days earlier, his body responded with shocking speed.

Sensing his presence, Katelyn's hands stilled. She lifted her head to look toward the door. "What are you staring at?"

One dark brow lifted at her snippish tone. "Ah, you are certainly in quite a snit. What is the problem, *querida?* You cannot find your favorite set of hair combs?"

Lifting her chin, she flashed him an annoyed look, then said, "Very funny. I thought I brought a bar of soap, but I can't find it."

He moved away from the door frame, sauntering across the room with his usual easy grace. Sitting down next to her on the mattress of blankets, he said, "Why are you looking for soap?"

"You seem to have forgotten an important part of being my host. You haven't provided bathing facilities."

His dark brows shot up. "Bathing facilities? You want to take a bath?"

Her back stiffened. "Yes, I want to take a bath. Is that so hard to believe? Or don't bands of thieves bathe?"

When he didn't respond, she glared at him. "I want to

take a bath, because I smell like the east end of a horse going west."

He stared at her for several seconds, then burst into laughter. Seeing the fire spark in her eyes, he couldn't resist testing her temper. Pretending to sniff the air, he said, "I agree, you do."

Katelyn's mouth dropped open. "Well, of all the rude, obnoxious— How dare you say I smell like a horse!"

"Do not get yourself all upset. I was only agreeing with you to be polite. You were the one who said you smell like a horse, and I—" Her swinging fist cut his rebuttal short. When the punch missed its target and glanced harmlessly off his shoulder, Brit burst into laughter again.

He let her release her pent-up anger, easily deflecting her fists from causing him any real injury. *"Sí, cardillo mío,* take your frustration out on me."

After a few more wild punches, Katelyn dropped her arms to her sides. Her anger and strength gone, she slumped her shoulders in defeat. As she tried to catch her breath, she realized she'd never heard Brit laugh before, and suspected it was a rare occurrence.

She stole a glance at him through her lowered lashes. His sparkling eyes and smiling lips softened his normally fierce demeanor and emphasized his good looks. She felt a sharp tug of need from deep inside. Ignoring the sensation, she lifted her head and said, "What did you call me?"

Giving in to his urge to touch her, Brit ran one hand through the silk of her hair. "I called you my golden thistle. You are just like the *cardillo*—all prickly on the outside and the color of precious gold."

He dropped his hand from her hair, a frown replacing his smile. No woman in his culture would dare lift a hand against a man. Yet he found Katelyn's boldness only added to her growing appeal.

"Who is the man called *El Buitre?"* she whispered. "Tell me about him, Brit." It was the first time she'd said the name aloud. The unsettling feeling of having an intimate knowledge of the man sitting next to her returned, warming her cheeks and igniting a throbbing heat low in her belly.

Her question erased the last dregs of amusement from his eyes. Once again anger swirled in their black depths. His *El Buitre* expression slipping back into place, he glared at her.

"You would not understand, *gringa.*" Rising from the bed, he stalked to the door. He stopped in the open doorway. "I will instruct Armando to bring soap and towels, then take you to a place where you can bathe."

With that he was gone.

Katelyn sighed with pleasure. Though the mountain stream was much colder than she would have preferred, the chance to bathe and wash her hair felt too good to find fault with the minor inconvenience of the water temperature. After dipping her head under a final time to rinse the last of the soap from her hair, she rose and headed for the stream's bank. She shivered. She'd dawdled too long; the sun was slipping behind the ridge of the canyon. Already the air had turned much cooler. Wrapping one length of toweling around her head, she quickly dried herself with another, then pulled on clean underclothes and a two-piece dress of sapphire muslin.

When she was dressed, she approached where Armando stood with his back to the stream.

As they walked back to camp, Armando said, "You feel better now, *señorita?*"

"*Sí,* I feel much cleaner. But I'm starved. I wonder what Lutero made for supper."

Armando chuckled. "*Puchero,* I think."

"Stew! I love Lutero's stew." She ran her tongue over her lips. "Come on, Armando, let's hurry. I still have to brush my hair dry."

Chuckling again, he quickened his pace to keep up with the spirited Katelyn.

After stuffing herself on Lutero's *tortillas* and tasty beef stew, Katelyn set her plate down with a sigh. "I haven't eaten this much since the last time my mother made—"

"Made what?" Brit said, approaching the fire and crouching down on his haunches across from her.

"Chicken and dumplings. Mother was a good cook, but her chicken and dumplings was my favorite. She promised to show me how to make her recipe, but she . . . she died before she had the chance."

"When was that, *querida?*"

"The summer I turned ten. After Mama died, I didn't try cooking again until after I finished school. Though Papa never complained, I never got very good. For the past several months, my friend Grace has been trying to teach me, but I'm afraid I'm a poor student."

"That is not true, *señorita,*" Armando said. "Your biscuits from last night, they were *muy delicioso.* Is that not so, *jefe?*"

Scowling, Brit shot Armando an annoyed look. After a moment, he said, "Yes, they were delicious." Accepting a plate from Lutero, he rose and walked away from the fire. Pushing Brit's curt words from her mind, Katelyn summoned a smile for the man beside her. "Grace would be pleased to hear I've learned something. *Gracias,* Armando. You are very kind to say so."

Staring thoughtfully at the back of his boss, he replied, *"De nada."*

Several hours later, Katelyn bid Armando good night, then entered the cabin, expecting to have it to herself. She was surprised to find Brit sitting in the chair by the fireplace, an opened book in his lap. He glanced up when she stepped into the room.

Meeting his dark gaze, she said, "I'm sorry. I didn't mean to disturb you. Would you like me to come back later?"

He couldn't get his throat to work so he could speak. His power of speech as well as his gaze were hopelessly trapped by her glorious hair. Used to seeing the pale golden tresses pulled atop her head and secured in a tight knot, or in a single thick braid while she slept, he found the soft tangle of long, wavy hair mesmerizing.

He realized her hair must have been down when he stopped at the campfire to get his meal, but apparently the shadows had concealed the fact. It was probably just as well, otherwise he might have sat there staring like a callow youth.

When she started to turn to leave, he snapped out of his momentary lapse. "No." His voice was a near shout, making her jump. "No," he said more gently. "You do not have to go. I was just reading. Go to bed, if you want."

She moved toward the fire. "Actually, I'm not very sleepy. Do you mind if I sit by the fire for awhile?"

He started to rise. "Here, take the chair."

"No, that's all right. I don't mind sitting on the floor."

Wanting to tell her that no gentleman ever let a lady sit on the floor while he took the only chair, Brit clamped his mouth shut and sat back down. "Fine."

After a few moments of silence while she settled on the floor in front of the fireplace, she glanced over at the book he held. "What are you reading?"

Unable to concentrate with Katelyn so close, her unbound hair just inches from his itching fingers, he closed the book and held it out to her.

She gingerly took the slim volume from his fingers. Bending so she could read the book's title in the firelight, she started. "The sonnets of Shakespeare?"

He smiled grimly. "Shocked, Miss Ferguson? I am sure

you are thinking a depraved criminal such as *El Buitre* would never be capable of reading something as complex as Shakespeare."

"That's not what I was thinking. It just seems strange for anyone in California to be reading Shakespeare. I mean, I read his work in school, but that was back East." She gave the book back to him, surprised at how he ran his large hands over the leather cover almost reverently. "When did you start reading his writings?"

"When I was at Oxford."

"Oxford?" Eyes wide, her voice was little more than a squeak. "In England?"

Brit moved his gaze from the book to her face. The reflection of the fire's flames danced wildly in her loose hair, sending a bolt of desire to his groin. He shifted in the chair to ease the ache. "Yes, in England."

"Armando said your father is British. Is that why you went to Oxford?"

"Both my older brother and I were sent to England for our education. Antonio did not like school very much, so he left after only one year at the university. I stayed and completed my studies."

"Then you came back to California?"

"No. First, I toured Spain and the rest of the Continent for a year, then I returned to California."

"Where does your family live?"

"Many days south of here. My parents live on the *Rancho del Sol Poniente*. My brother and his wife and my youngest sister live there as well. My other sister is married and lives with her husband's family less than a day's journey south of our parents."

"What does *Rancho del Sol Poniente* mean?"

He smiled at her pronunciation. "It means Ranch of the Setting Sun."

"Hmm, I like that. Where did the name come from?"

"My grandfather said the name was chosen by the first

Cordobas to live there. When the sun sets, a reddish gold is cast across the entire *rancho,* making the land appear to be part of the sunset."

"Sounds like a beautiful place. Is that where you send the horses you capture, to the *Rancho del Sol Poniente?"*

His eyes narrowed. "How do you know we capture horses?"

"Armando told me."

"Armando talks too much."

"Do not be angry with him. He was only trying to satisfy my curiosity by answering some of my questions."

His voice turned cold when he said, "And you never lack for questions, do you, *gringa?"*

Sensing the newfound peace between them was about to end, she said, "That's part of my job as a newspaper owner, to ask questions."

He opened the book of sonnets and idly flipped through the pages. "Apparently you do not always listen to your own advice."

"What do you mean?"

"You should have asked questions before you started writing your editorials."

"If you have something you want to tell me, Brit, why don't you just say it."

He closed the book with a resounding snap, then rose from the chair. "Not tonight. I am tired. Get ready for bed, I will be back in a few minutes." After carefully tucking the book into his saddlebags, he left the cabin.

Wondering what had brought about the abrupt change in his mood, Katelyn got to her feet, changed into her night-dress, then braided her hair.

Though still awake when he returned, for a reason she didn't completely understand, she pretended to be asleep. There were too many new pieces of information swimming around in her head, and she needed time to sort them all out.

Facing the wall, she listened to the sounds of him moving around the cabin: the crackle of sparks shooting up the chimney as he banked the fire, the soft thud of his boots as they hit the floor, the swish of leather against his trousers as he removed his gun belt. When he sat down on the bed, then stretched out next to her, she forced herself to remain relaxed.

In a few minutes, she recognized the soft cadence of his breathing and knew he slept. Wishing she could get up and sit by the fire, she settled for rolling over so she could look at the man next to her.

She studied his relaxed face, longing to brush a lock of black hair from his brow, to test the roughness of the dark stubble on his cheeks, to touch her mouth to his slightly parted lips. Shocked by her train of thought, she squeezed her eyes closed. Forcing herself to concentrate on the next entry she'd make in her journal, she drifted to sleep composing what she'd write.

I asked Armando questions about Brit today. Though he was very evasive, he did give me a few answers. It was from Brit that I learned the most interesting pieces of information. He captures wild horses; his father is British; he has a brother and two sisters; his parents live on a ranch south of here called the Ranch of the Setting Sun; and most surprising, he was educated at Oxford and reads Shakespeare. I wonder if I will ever learn all there is to know about this complex man. It shocks me to realize I hope so.

The following morning, Katelyn awoke to learn the man she found so interesting had once again ridden out of camp with three of his men. With the subject of her curiosity away, she had no alternative but to bide her time until his return.

She spent the remainder of the forenoon washing her dirty clothes in the stream. The work was boring, the water so cold her fingers were soon numb. As she twisted the water from each piece of clothing, then spread it over the bushes along the banks of the stream to dry, her thoughts turned to home.

Had Jake delivered her message to Grace? She hoped her friends weren't worrying too much about her abrupt disappearance. She missed Jake and Grace so much. Her leaving town was so unfair to both of them. But then, perhaps they were consoling each other. Katelyn smiled.

Maybe there would be one positive outcome to her abduction by The Vulture. She had always been sure Jake and Grace were made for each other, though the subtle hints she dropped had done no good. Maybe her absence would finally bring them together.

Her thoughts shifted to the *Argus.* Was Jake having any problems running the paper? She hoped Harold Danbury hadn't found out she'd left town. If he had, he was sure to raise a ruckus, maybe even pull the advertising for his clothing store. After her father's death, she had devoted a lot of time and effort into keeping the paper's advertising customers. Trying to convince the half-dozen men had been a real trial. They didn't believe Katelyn, a mere woman, was capable of running a newspaper. Most had refused to stay with the *Argus,* but Mr. Danbury had finally given in to her pleas and agreed to remain a paying customer. At the time, keeping his account had been a real boon, but now there was a very real possibility her efforts had gone for naught. The paper was on the brink of folding as it was, and she didn't need the coffers to drop any lower.

Whispering a quick prayer that Jake would be able to soothe Mr. Danbury enough to keep his business, she tossed the last of her clothes over a bush. As she straightened from her task, she wiped her hands on the length of toweling tied around her waist as an apron. *Now what do I do?*

By the middle of the afternoon, having nothing to keep her busy began to grate on her nerves. Used to working long hours at the *Argus* office, the inactivity proved to be a trial. Although Armando and Lutero treated her well, neither would answer personal questions about their boss or say anything about the gang's non-horse-capturing activities.

Armando did like to talk about the wild horses he helped capture, but that subject soon grew old for Katelyn. When she asked if she could go for a ride, she was told *El Buitre* had forbidden it.

"Am I allowed to do anything? Or is everything forbidden?" she'd snapped in a fit of temper.

"I am sorry, *señorita,* but I am only following orders. If I could, I would take you for a ride, but *el jefe* said I was not to allow you on a horse."

Katelyn sighed, her pique forgotten. "I know, Armando. It isn't your fault. When will he be back?"

"He is always gone two days, never more."

"Two days. What am I going to do for two days?" she whispered.

On the evening of the third day since his departure, Brit finally rode into camp. The arrival was less jovial than the first one Katelyn had witnessed, and she wondered at the reason. She remained by the campfire, and though his conversation with Armando carried to her, she could not understand their quietly spoken Spanish.

"You were gone longer than usual, *jefe*. There was trouble?"

"No, everything went well. I wanted to see what is being written about *El Buitre,* so I took an extra day to pick up the newspapers Jorge had for me."

Armando nodded, relieved his boss's delay was not because of trouble. "How is Jorge?"

Leading his horse to the corral, Brit replied, "He is well. Glad to see me, as always. He is a good friend."

"Sí," Armando replied, walking beside him. "It is good he found work with the stage line." Jorge had once worked for Brit's father, but decided to try mining with Brit, Armando, and the others when they first came north. When the trouble with the Yankees began, Jorge moved to Stockton.

"Yes, he has been a great help to me. I was disappointed when he declined my offer to stay with us and help with the horses. But I understand his wanting a permanent home. Working for the stage line has proven to be a true blessing. Without Jorge's help, I could not have kept up with the news of *El Buitre*. He is a *very* good friend."

Even though Brit had not wanted one of his friends to run the risk of coming under the scrutiny of the law for aiding an outlaw, Jorge was adamant about helping. And since Brit wanted to keep abreast of what was known about his activities as The Vulture, he had accepted Jorge's offer. They decided he could best serve Brit by collecting newspapers from the area on his runs for the stage line. Jorge hid the papers at his home, until Brit or one of his men could get to Stockton.

Thinking of the invaluable service Jorge provided reminded Brit it was through his friend's efforts that he'd first read the editorials in the *Sacramento Argus*. He pressed his lips together in annoyance.

Seeing the harsh set to his boss's jaw, Armando said, "There was something interesting in the newspapers Jorge had for you?"

Brit pulled the bundle of papers from one of his saddlebags. "Nothing any more interesting than usual." Handing Armando all but one of the newspapers, he turned toward the center of camp. "Put those in my cabin."

As Katelyn watched Brit approach, her pulse increased. Seeing the determined look on his face, she frowned. *What's set him off this time? He looks mad enough to chew a saddle in half.*

He stopped in front of her, then hunkered down on his haunches. "How is it," he said in a deceptively soft voice, "that you are here at my camp, yet your newspaper still prints an editorial which could only have been written by you?"

Her frown deepened. "What are you talking about?"

He tossed the newspaper onto her lap. She glanced down to see the paper's masthead was that of the *Argus*. The date at the top was the edition she'd been working on when he'd snatched her from her home.

Lifting her chin, she sent him a chilling glare. "I'm at your camp because you brought me here against my will. And the editorial is in my newspaper because I wrote it the day you kidnapped me. I left it on my desk, so obviously Jake found it and put it in this week's edition."

Brit straightened, returning her glare. "Once again, your editorials do not speak the truth. You make up facts to fit your own cockeyed opinion of the bandit you *gringos* call *El Buitre*. You are only interested in selling newspapers with your made-up stories, instead of printing the truth."

"That's not true," she said, trying valiantly to remain calm.

"And I say it is the truth. The man near Angel's Camp was not beaten, yet you reported he was. With such shoddy reporting, it is a wonder you report any news correctly."

Katelyn jumped to her feet. "Well, if you don't want to see more editorials like this one," she yelled, waving the newspaper in front of his face, "then do what you said you would do."

"And what is that?" he yelled back.

"Let me get to know the real *El Buitre*. That's the reason you brought me here, isn't it?"

He didn't respond, but stared at her for several seconds. Finally, he turned around and started walking away.

"Well, isn't it?" she shouted at his retreating back. When he never broke stride, she stomped her foot in frustration.

Brit stood at Solazo's corral, staring into the deepening shadows. The heated words he'd just exchanged with the exasperating Katelyn Ferguson kept running through his head.

He should have known better than to try to win an argument with his golden thistle, especially when most of his brain had been thinking about how much he wanted her.

Closing his eyes, he could still see her in full dudgeon, her beautiful blue eyes sparkling with inner fire, those magnificent breasts rising and falling with each agitated breath. His body reacted instantly to the picture.

When he had his desire under control, he opened his eyes and sighed. Katelyn was right. He had told her he wanted her to get to know the real *El Buitre*. But since taking her from Sacramento, he'd done little to see his plan carried out. Turning back towards camp, he decided he would do something to change that.

Six

The next morning, Brit approached where Katelyn sat by the campfire. "I am going up to the high corral to work with Solazo. Would you like to go with me?"

She looked up from the hounds, Paco and Pepe, sprawled at her feet to meet his gaze. His eyes revealed no clue as to why he had offered the invitation. "Who is Solazo?"

"The golden mare I have been training." Seeing the uncertainty on her face, he said, "I thought we could talk while I work with Solazo."

Giving the rough coat of each of the hounds one last pat, she got to her feet. "Okay, let's go."

Brit shortened his strides to accommodate Katelyn's, keeping his hands tucked in his trouser pockets. The soft curls of hair at her nape beckoned his fingers, but he refused to give in to the temptation.

While walking up the steep path to the hidden corral, she said, "What does your horse's name mean?"

"Solazo means scorching sun. Her coat shines like the brightest of suns, so I thought it an appropriate name."

Katelyn nodded, wondering again at Brit's behavior. After their argument the night before, she figured he wouldn't come within ten feet of her. Now he walked next to her, carrying on an easy conversation as if they were old friends. Had their heated exchange brought about the abrupt reversal? Frowning, she found such an explanation hard to believe.

When they reached the corral, Brit motioned for her to

remain on the outside of the crude fence, while he slipped inside and approached Solazo. Catching the scent of someone other then her master, the mare stomped a front hoof and flattened her ears in annoyance.

"Take it easy, my pretty one," Brit said in Spanish. "You need not be afraid. The *gringa* will not hurt you." Immediately the mare settled down, nickering softly, ears swiveling forward to catch his gently spoken words.

Katelyn pulled her brows together, wondering what he said to the horse. She watched his dark hands stroke across the golden withers, and the mare's skin ripple in response to his touch. Katelyn had to force herself not to shiver in reaction. Feeling Brit's stare, she lifted her gaze from his long fingers to his face.

Something hot and potent passed between them, a brief searing exchange that made her heart pound hard against her ribs. A pulsing warmth settled between her thighs. Unable to stand a moment more of the tension hanging in the air, she looked away.

Brit forced himself to concentrate on Solazo. His body throbbed with need, his blood running hot with a desire to have a woman he should hate, just like he hated all other *gringos*. Once again he found his hatred wavering where Katelyn Ferguson was concerned.

After a few minutes of silence while he recomposed himself, he said, "When did you come to California?"

Uncomfortable with her reaction to him, she was careful to keep her gaze averted when she said, "My father and I came by wagon train late in '51."

He pulled a brightly colored saddle blanket from where it was draped over the corral fence, then carefully laid it on Solazo's back. With slow measured movements, he rubbed the blanket forward over her withers, then back to her hindquarters. He repeated the motion several times, then ran the blanket down each leg. "Where did you live before that?"

"Chicago. I was born there, as were both my parents. What are you doing with the blanket?"

"Getting her used to the feel of it." He pulled the blanket from the mare and tossed it over the fence. "Why did you leave Chicago?"

"It was Papa's idea. After Mama died, my father spent more and more time at the newspaper office. He lost interest in everything else. Anyway, when word of the gold strike reached Chicago, he became fascinated with the stories about California. He read everything he could, and got so swept up with the excitement he decided he had to come out here and see it for himself. So he sold our house, most of the furniture, and everything at the newspaper except his new printing press. Then we left Chicago and went to St. Joseph, Missouri, where we joined a wagon train."

Slipping a hackamore over the mare's head, Brit said, "Have you always worked in your father's newspaper office?"

"Yes, Papa taught me to set type almost as soon as I learned to read. And later I learned how to run a press. I loved going to his office; I went there with him every day, when I wasn't in school. He said I would be his star reporter some day." A faint smile lifted the corners of her mouth. "Anyway, when Mama died, Papa hired a housekeeper to look after the house and me. As I got older, my schoolwork kept me too busy to help him very much." She draped her arms over the top rail of the fence, then dropped her chin onto her crossed forearms. "After I finished school, I insisted Papa let the housekeeper go, so I could take over her duties. He thought I shouldn't be cooped up in the house all day and asked me to work full time at the paper. With Mama gone, I insisted the running of our house and taking care of him were more important. Once in a while, he asked me to write an article on some social event. I really enjoyed doing those articles, and I'd hoped to do more writing after we moved here. Even so, I don't love the newspaper business the way Papa did. I never wanted to work full time for him, and I certainly never considered running the paper myself." She sighed. "But he gave me no choice."

"What happened to him?"

Her gaze met his, then skittered away. "He died while working on a story. It was his heart."

"So, if you never wanted to run a newspaper, why did you take over the *Sacramento Argus?*"

"I owe it to Papa. He worked so hard, and I'm determined to make sure—" She cleared her throat, appalled at what she'd almost revealed. "To make sure the *Argus* is successful. And besides, since I had no other way to support myself, at least I knew something about running a newspaper."

Brit glanced up from Solazo, his eyes narrowed. "And why are you so determined to see *El Buitre* punished?"

She lifted her head, chin tilted at a defiant angle. "Because he deserves to be punished for what he's done."

"And just what has he done that is so terrible?"

"He's a common thief and a murderer."

His hand tightened on the rope lead of the hackamore, a muscle in his jaw twitched. *"El Buitre* has never killed anyone."

"Never killed—" Her voice rose sharply. "What about last year, when your band terrorized a group of men north of Marysville, killing three? Or the Chinese man near San Andreas, who was stabbed to death when he refused to give up his money? Or what about the deputy sheriff of Santa Clara County? He was found murdered; a murder *you* committed."

"I have never been to Marysville. I have no quarrel with the Chinese, only with Yankees. And as for the deputy, he was killed by a band of Mexicans."

"Mexicans? What's that supposed to mean? You and your men are all Mexicans."

"No, *gringa,* we are not." He drew himself up to his full height. Thumping his chest, he said, "We are *Californios.*

We were born in California. My mother's ancestors were among the first *gachupíns* to settle here. *Gachupíns* are from Spain, not Mexico."

After a moment to think about his statement, she said, "Well, even if I believed you—which I don't—there have been other men murdered by The Vulture."

Pressing his lips together in a severe line, he glared at her. When he spoke, his voice was cold and menacing. "I told you, *El Buitre* has never killed anyone."

Her chin came up a notch higher. "That's not true." No longer caring what she revealed, she added, "He killed my father."

"You just said it was your father's heart that killed him."

"Yes, his heart was weak, but he would still be alive if he hadn't been so bent on—" She swallowed the sudden lump in her throat. "If he hadn't been so bent on getting an interview with the bandit. The Vulture is responsible for Papa's death, as surely as if he had killed Papa with his own hand."

"How can you say that?" His voice was a low growl. "If his heart was weak, many things could have brought on his death."

Refusing to agree, she pushed away from the corral fence. "I thought we came up here to talk about you."

Brit led the mare around the corral, coaxing her to follow him. When she obeyed his commands, he praised her in soft Spanish. To Katelyn, he said, "Okay, *gringa,* ask your questions."

Unsure where to begin, she finally decided to find out if what Armando told her was true. "Why do some of your men call you Brit?"

He glanced over his shoulder at her, then shrugged and returned his gaze to the mare. "It is part of my name. Roberto Brit Livingston. I was called Brit as a child, and many still use the name."

"Livingston? You told me your name was Roberto Cordoba, when you first brought me here."

"As you have also learned, my father is British, hence Livingston. I use the name Cordoba when it suits me. My full name is Roberto Brit Livingston y Cordoba."

"Armando also said your father's first name is Ricardo."

"He was born Richard Anthony Livingston. After he decided to stay in California, he changed his name to Ricardo Antonio."

So, Armando had told the truth. "How did your father end up in California?"

Katelyn thought he wasn't going to answer, then finally he said, "My father left England to make his fortune. Like me, he is a second son, and thus would not inherit his family's wealth. He visited many places, and he liked several of them enough to settle there. But it was here in California that he lost his heart."

"Your mother?"

"Yes. They met at a *fiesta*. He said he fell in love with Margarita Cordoba at first sight. My grandparents objected to his pursuit of their youngest daughter, because he was British and not of the Catholic faith. He changed his name and embraced our religion to win the approval of the Cordobas. My parents were married a few months—" He clamped his mouth shut, silently chastising himself for rattling on like an old woman. "That is enough about my father, what do you want to know about me?"

Surprised by his answer and his abrupt change in mood, her thoughts swirled aimlessly for a moment. At last she said, "What are you going to do with Solazo?"

"After I have finished training her, she will be taken to my *rancho*."

"Your ranch? You have a ranch?"

One side of his mouth lifted at the disbelief he heard in her voice. "Not exactly. I have purchased the land, but it will not be a true *rancho* for a long time."

"Where is this land?"

"Near the *Rancho del Sol Poniente*. There is good water on my land, and it will make a fine place to raise horses. Solazo will be my prize mare. From her I will get the finest foals in California. I already have a stallion waiting for her. He comes from one of the oldest and best bloodlines in Spain."

He stopped his slow circling of the corral and reached out to run his hand down the mare's sleek neck, smoothing her snow-white mane. "You will like the mate I have chosen for you, my pretty one," he said to the horse. "His coat is the color of midnight, as black as yours is golden. He is intelligent, strong, and proud. You will like joining with him, for he will be eager and virile."

Katelyn struggled to breathe. His words sounded as though he had been talking intimately about the two of them, not Solazo and her unknown stallion. The throbbing between her thighs returned, intensifying until her knees became weak and threatened to fold under her. She grasped the fence to keep from falling.

Brit turned back to Katelyn, a banked fire glowing hot in his eyes. She had never felt so totally flustered. She cleared her throat, shifting her gaze to a stand of pine trees across the plateau. She had to think about something else, anything but the man inside the corral and her physical response to him. How could her body respond so strongly to this man, a man she professed to despise?

Near dusk, Paco and Pepe lifted their heads, ears perked forward, noses testing the wind. Giving a yip of joy, the pair of hounds left their usual spot next to Katelyn and raced to the edge of camp. Their tails wagging wildly, they took up a position at the head of the trail leading out of the canyon.

In a few minutes, Katelyn heard what the dogs' keen

hearing had detected. A group of about a dozen men on horseback rode into the clearing. Remaining near the fire, she watched as the newcomers swung out of their saddles and were greeted by the men in the camp. After everyone said their hellos, Brit approached the group. She couldn't hear their conversation, but after speaking to one of the newly arrived men, Brit clapped him on the back, turned, and walked with him toward the fire.

Katelyn watched the two approach, studying the man next to Brit through partially lowered lashes. He was only slightly shorter than Brit, but built as powerfully. A flat-brimmed, felt hat with silver braid around the crown hid his face. He wore a leather vest, similar to Brit's, and dark trousers tucked into his boots. As the two drew closer, she dropped her gaze to the fire.

After giving Lutero a hug, the new man started to sit down. Glancing across the campfire and seeing a woman, he jerked upright. In Spanish, he said to Brit, "It is good to be back, *jefe*. Especially when you have brought us a *gringa* to enjoy, eh?"

The man's laugh and his bold smile made Katelyn's skin prickle with apprehension. The only word she caught in his rapid Spanish was *gringa*, but the way he looked at her, she probably was better off not understanding the rest.

Forcing himself to smile, Brit replied in Spanish, "She is not here to pleasure anyone, Tomás. I brought her here to learn about the real *El Buitre*."

"I do not understand."

"She is the one who wrote the newspaper editorials about me in the *Sacramento Argus*."

Tomás looked sharply at the blond woman. "She is the one who called you a 'bloodthirsty villain who has no qualms, no mercy, no conscience'?"

"Yes, she is the one."

Tomás threw back his head and laughed. "That must have been quite a shock, eh? To find out the newspaper editorials were written by a *gringa*. I must meet this woman." Pushing his hat off his head so that it dangled down his back by its leather thong, he said, "Introduce us."

Brit gave him a fuming look, but complied. Turning to meet Katelyn's confused gaze, he said, "Katelyn, this is Tomás Sanchez. We grew up together, and now he works for me. Tomás, this is Katelyn Ferguson."

Tomás circled the fire, then reached down to take her hand. Bowing, he placed his lips on the back of her knuckles, then whispered in only slightly accented English, "*Señorita* Ferguson, it is my pleasure to make your acquaintance."

Her brows drawn together, she replied, "Thank you." Annoyed when he didn't release her hand, she pulled her fingers free of his grasp. "What is your part in The Vulture's band, and where have you been?"

Blinking with surprise, Tomás flashed Brit a grin before saying in Spanish. "Is she always so full of questions? I can think of many ways to keep her quiet, if you need some suggestions."

Brit's answering smile vanished, his back stiffening. "Yes, she always has countless questions. And I told you, she is not here for anything other than to learn about *El Buitre.*" He didn't add that he, too, knew ways to keep Katelyn quiet, but he could never make such an admission to one of his men, not even to his closest friend. "You may answer her questions, if you like."

Tomás gave him a startled look. "She knows what we do?"

"She knows we capture horses and send them to my parents' *rancho*. She does not yet know the truth about the rest of our activities, so be careful what you say."

Turning back to Katelyn, Tomás said in English, "I am leader of a group of men who take the *mesteños* to another camp a few days from here, where they are allowed to rest before making the rest of their journey. Normally, the men at our southern camp take the *mesteños* to the *Rancho del Sol Poniente,* and my men and I return here. But on occasion, when *nuestro jefe* asks me, we make the entire trip. We have just returned from such a mission. Does that satisfactorily answer your questions, *señorita?"*

Katelyn studied Tomás for a moment. His hair was as black as Brit's, though his eyes were a soft gray. He wore a neatly trimmed moustache, and his square jaw bore the stubble of several days' growth of dark beard. Lowering her gaze to his hips, she frowned. His gun belt sported an ivory-handled revolver on the right side, a deadly-looking knife on the left. Remembering what these men were, she snapped, "Yes, for now."

Tomás gave another bark of laughter at her prim tone. Switching back to Spanish, he said to Brit, "She is a prickly one, eh? I bet she could cut a man to ribbons with only her tongue as a weapon."

Brit grunted a reply. He could think of better uses for her tongue. Forcing his mind away from such a tantalizing thought, he said, "Get yourself something to eat, then I want to hear the news of my family."

Accepting a heaping plate of food from Lutero, Tomás followed Brit to the far side of the camp. After allowing his friend a few minutes to eat, Brit said, "You had no trouble?"

"No, everything went well. We made good time."

"What about my family, everyone is well?"

"Sí, Don Ricardo and Doña Margarita said to tell you they have not seen you in many months; they miss you and wish you would return."

"That is what they always say. I have told them time and again, that I must have enough horses to start my own *rancho* before I can leave here for good. They forget Antonio will one day inherit the *Rancho del Sol Poniente.* Since I am the second son, I have to start my own from nothing."

"They know that, Brit." Away from the others, Tomás reverted to calling his friend by name. "Capturing horses is not why they fear for your safety. It is your actions as *El Buitre* that frightens them."

"Why do they not understand I have work I must do?"

"I think they do understand. Revenge is a very powerful motivator. But they worry about you just the same. They fear your revenge will end up costing you your life."

"Mirabella's death has to be avenged regardless of the cost. Besides, I am always careful."

"You were not careful when you brought the *gringa* here."

Brit shot his friend a peeved look. "I took precautions. We traveled at night as much as we could, and when we got close to the mountains, we doubled back several times. And as an added measure, I blindfolded her before we got close to the camp. She does not know where we are."

Sensing the anger lurking just beneath Brit's calm demeanor, Tomás merely shrugged.

After a minute of silence, Brit said, "What of my sisters? They are well?"

"*Sí, Señorita* Rosita is as beautiful as ever, but she has not lost her sharp tongue or fiery temper." Tomás smiled. "She reminds me of your *gringa.*" Placing a hand over his heart, he said, "Ah, such hot-blooded women are hard to find."

Ignoring his friend's theatrical attempt at humor, Brit said, "So, you are still interested in my baby sister?"

Tomás's amusement fled; his back stiffened. "You object to my interest in Rosita?"

Brit grinned at the challenge in Tomás's voice. "No, I have no objection. But what of Rosita, does she welcome your attention?"

"*Sí,* why would she not? I would make a fine husband, eh?"

Chuckling, Brit replied, "You are very sure of yourself, Tomás. I hope you will not be disappointed if Rosita does not share your opinion."

"I will make sure she does," Tomás said in a determined voice, then fell silent.

After a moment, Brit said, "What news do you have of Natalia?"

"She sends her love, as does Rosita. *Señora* Natalia also gave me a message for you. She said you must return before All Saints' Day."

"All Saints' Day? What does she mean?"

"Natalia and Vicente want you to be the *padrino* of their child."

"Padrino? Child?"

"Sí, Natalia will give birth to her first child in October. She is planning to have the baptism on the first Sunday after All Saints' Day, and she has chosen you to be the child's godfather."

Brit sat back, stunned. It was hard for him to think of his nineteen-year-old sister as a married woman, much less as a mother. "I must send her my congratulations. You will take a message to Father John?"

"Sí. I will leave first thing in the morning."

"Good. I want to go after another herd of horses, but I will wait until you return. That will give your men a few more days of rest."

"And a few more days for you to get to know the *gringa,* eh?"

Brit bristled at Tomás's teasing. "I did not bring Katelyn here so I could get to know her. She is here to get to know me."

"I do not think you can do one without doing the other."

"I did not ask you what you think."

Tomás held up one hand. "I was only making a joke. What is wrong with you? You have never been this touchy before."

Brit shrugged, unable to put into words what was wrong with him even if he'd wanted to. "I just want to finish here and go home."

After studying his long-time friend for a moment, Tomás replied, *"Sí,* I want that, too, *amigo mío.* I want that, too."

After bidding Tomás good night some time later, Brit remained by the fire. That night he was reluctant to make the short walk across the camp.

Katelyn had retired several hours earlier. And although he knew she'd likely already be asleep, he couldn't make himself move. He kept thinking about his reaction to her at the corral that afternoon. A woman had never affected him this way, and he was at a loss on how to deal with his lust-crazed reaction whenever she was near. Closing his eyes, he wondered what he was going to do with her.

He still hadn't told her everything he wanted her to know about *El Buitre.* Yet he didn't know if he could control himself if he had to continue being around her. For a moment, he considered giving in to his lust and taking her. But his training as a gentleman cooled the idea. In his culture, a single woman's virtue was protected at all costs. Unmarried women were revered, not used then tossed aside.

Perhaps he should have one of his men return Katelyn to Sacramento. Yes, that would be the wise thing to do—get her away from his camp, away from him. But could he do it?

Seven

The morning following the return of Tomás and his men, Brit gave his friend the message to deliver to Father John in San Andreas, then went to Solazo's corral. He still hadn't made a decision about Katelyn, and he had to put some distance between himself and the tempting *gringa* so he could think rationally about her.

When he finally made his way back down to the floor of the canyon, dusk had descended over the campsite. He had spent the entire day away from Katelyn, yet an answer continued to elude him.

Coming around the corner of his cabin, Brit abruptly halted. He heard voices coming from the direction of the campfire, voices hushed but urgent. Forgetting about changing his dusty clothes, he headed toward the center of camp.

Just beyond the circle of light cast by the fire, Brit stopped to listen to the man speaking.

"Think about what I said, *compadres*. You will do better with me as your leader. I am not afraid to take the purse of a Yankee, then shoot him through his black heart. The man who leads you now is a coward, because he will—"

"You have said enough, Marco," Brit said, stepping closer.

Straightening from where he was crouched by the fire, Marco Chavez turned to face his former leader. "Ah, *el jefe magnífico* returns at last."

Brit's eyes narrowed at Marco's mocking tone. "I told

you, you were not welcome in this camp unless you changed your ways. From what I just heard, you are no different."

"*Sí,* that is what you told me, but I decided I did not want to stay away." Moving around the fire, he added, "So, what are you going to do about it? The same thing you do to the Yankees you rob—turn your back and run like a coward?"

"Marco, we have had this discussion before. You and I will never agree. One day your thirst for violence could very well cost you more than you are willing to give."

Marco's lips twisted into an evil smile. "Perhaps you would like to put my thirst for violence to a test, eh?" With one swift move, he pulled his knife from the leather sheath on his hip. "Shall we fight to see who leads these men, or are you the coward I know you are?"

Armando saw the flash of Brit's knife blade as he pulled it from his boot, and silently signaled the others to move back. Grabbing Katelyn's arm, he hauled her away from where she sat near the campfire.

"Who is that man and what are they saying, Armando?" she whispered. "Their Spanish was too fast for me to understand."

"Marco used to be one of us," he replied. "A few months ago, he and *el jefe* had a disagreement, and Marco left."

"Why did he come back?"

"He is trying to talk some of us into going with him."

Keeping her gaze on the two men as they slowly circled each other, knives gripped tightly in their hands, Katelyn swallowed hard. "Shouldn't someone stop this before one of them gets hurt?"

"No, *señorita,* this must be settled once and for all. Marco has been spoiling for a fight for a very long time. He will just keep coming back if *el jefe* does not end it now."

Her gaze snapped to his face. "End it? Brit won't kill him, will he?"

Armando shrugged. "I do not know. Perhaps it will be necessary in order to save his own life."

She turned her gaze back to Brit, a terrible pain wrenching her heart. What would she do if he were badly hurt, or worse, killed? She couldn't even think about the latter possibility. For surely, if something happened to Brit, her existence at the camp would change. Recalling the way Marco had looked at her, his gaze probing through the darkness from across the campfire, she knew it wouldn't be for the better. She shuddered violently.

Fisting her hands in the fabric of her skirt, she watched the two men square off.

"Make your move, Marco," Brit said in a low growl. "You have wanted a fight for a long time. Now I will oblige you."

Marco felt a momentary chill at the gleam in Brit's eyes and the hard edge of his voice. But he refused to back down. He would not be labeled a coward. In one easy movement, he lunged forward, his knife aimed at his opponent's belly.

Brit jumped back, chopping at Marco's wrist with his left hand, deflecting the blade heading for his middle. Immediately Brit went on the attack. With quick, light-footed movements, he stepped forward, then retreated, his knife slashing with each advance. Each time, the tip of his razor-sharp blade connected. Three places on Marco's shirt bore rips. Blood oozed from each cut.

Marco glanced at his tattered shirt, then back to Brit. His lips curled into a snarl, he said, "If you can draw my blood, why can you not spill the blood of the Yankees you say you hate?"

"You know why I do not spill their blood."

"*Sí,* you told me. But I do not agree with your reasons."

"Apparently, we will never agree. I do not want to fight you, Marco. Drop your knife and leave, and I will forget about this."

Marco laughed, an evil, almost demented sound. "You have proven you can draw first blood, but can you finish what you have started?"

Brit heaved a weary sigh. "If this is the only way to make sure you stay away from my camp, get on with it." He curled the fingers of his left hand and wiggled them at Marco. "Come on, Marco. You think you are a better man than I, the man who should lead these men. Now you must prove it, Marco. Prove *you* are the better man. What are you waiting for? Come on, show them how good you are."

His goading had the desired effect. Marco growled with rage, then lunged toward him again. Only that time Marco's knife hit its target. Brit sucked in a hissing breath, surprised by his opponent's sudden display of agility. Ignoring the sting of the cut on his upper arm, he crouched and circled to his left.

He flashed Marco a grin, a baring of his teeth which bore no semblance of amusement. "You have scored once, but now you must win the fight."

"I am very good with a knife. Perhaps you forgot who taught me."

"No, I did not forget. But there are things I did not teach you. A good teacher never shows the student everything he knows." Brit grinned again. "Watch and learn, student." He leaped toward Marco. Using one foot, he swept Marco's legs out from under him. Marco hit the ground with a grunt.

Before Brit had time to savor his success, Marco was back on his feet and coming at him. Amid grunts, strained muscles, and knives swishing through the air, they exchanged a series of vicious slashes. Most missed, but enough hit their mark to be effective. Soon both Marco's and his own shirt were soaked with blood.

Katelyn bit her lip to keep from crying out each time Marco's knife touched Brit's flesh. For each wound he suffered, she flinched, feeling the bite of the blade as if her own skin had been cut. As much as she wanted to look away, she found she couldn't tear her gaze from Brit. Wiping the tears from her cheeks, she watched him continue the fight.

His strength slowly slipping away, Brit knew he had to make his final move, or his exhaustion could easily spell disaster. Maneuvering so he was just out of Marco's reach, he feigned a movement to the right. When Marco responded and moved to defend himself, he shifted to the left. Catching his opponent off guard, Brit grabbed Marco's right wrist and twisted it behind his back, forcing the man to drop to his knees. Brit knelt next to him, maintaining the pressure on Marco's wrist.

With a groan of both agony and frustration, Marco's hand went numb. Though he tried to keep his fingers closed, they opened on their own. The knife slipped from his grasp, landing in the dirt with a soft thump.

Keeping the pressure on Marco's wrist with his left hand, Brit raised his right hand and held the blade of his knife against Marco's throat. "You see, Marco, you have not yet learned to best your teacher." He pressed the blade deeper. Marco swallowed hard, the knife scraping his skin from the movement.

"I could end this permanently right now. You know that, do you not, Marco?" At the man's slight nod, he said, "Good. At least we agree on something. But I will not take your life. Enough blood has already been needlessly spilled. Still, I think you need a reminder of this day to carry with you forever."

Seeing the fear leap into Marco's eyes, Brit's lips curved into a sinister smile. With one swift movement, he drew the blade across Marco's neck, leaving a line of blood in its wake.

"Now you carry the scar from my knife, so you will remember this day forever. But you must also remember these words. Do not return to my camp again, Marco. If you are stupid enough to do so, I promise I will not spare your life a second time. Do you understand me?" Releasing Marco's arm, Brit rose, then stepped back.

Holding a bandana to his neck with his left hand, Marco looked up to meet Brit's gaze, hatred burning in his eyes. "*Sí*, I understand you. But soon I, too, will be *el jefe* of my own band of men, and then I will become even more famous than *El Buitre.*"

"You may form your own band, and you may even become its chief. But I am warning you, recruit the men foolish enough to follow you from somewhere besides my camp." Wiping his knife on his tattered shirtsleeve, he stared at Marco's mutinous face.

"Armando," Brit called over his shoulder. "See that Marco is put on his horse and leaves our camp. Have one of our men follow him to make sure he does not double back."

Armando left Katelyn and rushed forward. "*Sí, jefe.* I will take care of it immediately."

Brit stood stoically in the middle of camp, while Marco was helped to his feet and onto his horse. Brit's expression never changed, not even when Marco turned in the saddle, shook a fist at him, then spat in his direction. Only after the man disappeared down the path with Juan following close behind did Brit move.

Katelyn watched him carefully as he turned toward the campfire. The light from the fire fell on his face, revealing the tension of pain etched on his features. She quickly moved to his side. "Let me help you," she said in a low voice.

He stared at her for a moment, then surprisingly gave her a nod. He allowed her to drape his right arm across her shoulders and made no protest when she wrapped her left arm around his waist. She walked slowly toward his cabin, trying to support part of his much greater weight. By the time they reached the cabin door, she was breathless from the exertion.

"Sit on the bed, while I get some water to clean your cuts."

Sinking onto the mattress of blankets with a sigh, he lifted his head to look at her. "I can take care of myself." He reached for the top button of his shirt, unable to stop a flinch as one of the cuts on his arms pulled with the movement.

"Don't be silly. You're exhausted, and you've lost a lot of blood. Just sit right there. I'll be right back."

Brit stared at the open door of his cabin and smiled. His golden thistle's offer to tend him came as a surprise. And not an unwelcome one, he realized while waiting for her to return.

A few minutes later, Katelyn entered the cabin with a pan of water and some pieces of cloth. Her eyes widened at the sight meeting her gaze. Brit had somehow managed to remove his shirt and now lay stretched out on the bed. Across his chest and upper arms were numerous cuts where Marco's blade had sliced into his flesh. Some looked only superficial, no longer bleeding, while several appeared to be deeper and still bled steadily.

Kneeling next to the bed, she set the pan on the floor and dipped a cloth into the warm water. "I told you to wait for me," she admonished softly.

Brit's eyes snapped open at her voice. "I only wanted to help you, *querida,*" he answered, giving her a weak smile.

"Stubborn man," she murmured, wringing out the cloth and applying it to the worst of his cuts. He sucked in a sharp breath. "I'm sorry, Brit. I don't want to hurt you, but I have to clean your wounds."

Closing his eyes, he said, "Do what you must."

With slow, careful movements, she cleaned the dried blood from each cut. While tending him, her thoughts drifted to the side of this man she had just witnessed first-hand—the calculating, brutal side. Though she had previously thought of *El Buitre* as a harsh, viciously cruel man with absolutely no compunction about killing another in cold blood, the man who had abducted her had thus far shown no signs of such characteristics. The man she was getting to know—the man she found so attractive—had a kind, gentle heart. And though he had shown flashes of temper and was sometimes harsh and demanding, he was still nothing like her preconceived opinion of him.

Surprisingly, she realized that she was not frightened to be alone with Brit, even after seeing the savage side of this complex man. Forcing herself to concentrate on her task, she tried not to think of the powerful muscles beneath her hands, or how touching him made her feel. She did not succeed. The raw, masculine strength of him ignited the familiar fire low in her belly. It took all the willpower she could summon to still the trembling in her hands, to keep her breathing at a normal cadence.

She pressed her lips together in annoyance. How could she react so strongly to a man she was determined to see punished? She had to try harder to ignore the way he affected her.

When she finished bathing him, she reached for the bottle of mescal. Lutero told her to use the liquor to disinfect Brit's cuts and help them heal. Wetting another cloth from the bottle, she said, "This will probably hurt like the devil, but I have no choice." She touched the cloth to one of the smaller cuts. Brit flinched, but remained quiet. Moving to a deeper cut, his inhaled breath hissed through his clenched teeth.

"Do it quickly," he murmured in a thick voice.

Working as fast as she could, she bathed each cut a second time using the mescal, then sat back on her heels. One of the cuts on his chest and another on his upper arm persisted in bleeding, and would have to be wrapped.

"Brit," she said, touching his shoulder. "Brit, wake up. I need your help."

Slowly his eyes opened, the pain in their dark depths completely cooling her wickedly wonderful reaction to him. "How can I help you, *cardillo mio?*"

She took a deep breath, forcing herself not to shiver at

the deep, intimate tone of his voice. "I have to bandage some of your cuts, but you will have to sit up."

He lifted his upper body off the bed, biting back the urge to groan aloud. Obediently, he lifted his arms when she told him to do so, inhaling her earthy, female scent when she leaned close. His body reacted instantly to her nearness. How he could want a woman when his body hurt in a dozen places completely astounded him.

After wrapping the cuts with the strips of cloth Lutero gave her, Katelyn secured them in place by tying the ends into tight knots. "I'm afraid that's the best I can do."

"You did fine, *querida*. Now give me the bottle of mescal. I have another, more important use for it."

Her brow furrowed, she handed him the bottle. When his fingers brushed hers, another jolt of need rushed through her.

As he started to lift the bottle to his lips, she said, "But you don't drink." At his raised eyebrows, she added, "The others imbibe occasionally, but I have never seen you take even one drink of spirits."

"That is true. I seldom have more than a glass of wine. But tonight . . ." He tried to smile, but it was more of a grimace. "Tonight, I need something stronger." He tipped the bottle to his mouth and took a long drink. The potent clear liquor burned his throat, then warmed his stomach before having a blessedly dulling effect on his pain. He took another draught before setting the bottle on the floor.

"Does it help?" she asked, her eyes wide with curiosity and something he didn't dare identify.

"*Sí*, it helps." He shifted on the bed, wondering what would help his painful arousal.

The next few minutes passed in silence while Katelyn started a fire, discarded the pieces of cloth and what was left of Brit's shirt, then dumped the basin of water outside. From beneath partially lowered lashes, he watched her every move, frequently taking another sip of mescal and silently cursing himself for finding her so attractive.

"Are you comfortable?" she asked, after returning the basin to Lutero and fetching a cup of *champurrado* for herself.

He nodded, unable to speak around the lump in his throat. The concern on her face was nearly more than he could bear.

Uncertain what to do, Katelyn looked around the Spartan cabin, her gaze finally landing on his saddlebags. "Would you like me to read to you?"

He swallowed. "I would like that."

After retrieving the book of sonnets, she set her cup aside, pulled the chair closer to the fire, and sat down. "Is there something you'd like to hear?"

He shook his head, unable to take his eyes off the way the firelight behind her cast a golden halo around her blond hair.

"Okay, I'll pick something. Let's see," she murmured, flipping through the book. Making her selection, she drew her feet up under her and began to read.

> *When, in disgrace with fortune and men's eyes,*
> *I all alone beweep my outcast state,*
> *And trouble deaf heaven with my bootless cries,*
> *And look upon myself, and curse my fate . . .*

Brit's lips twisted into a bittersweet smile. *She would select the sonnet which parallels my life as an outcast. I do not think I can bear to hear the rest, the part where thinking of the woman he loves lightens his mood.* Pulling himself out of his thoughts, he cleared his throat and said, "I have changed my mind, I do not want to hear Shakespeare tonight."

Startled by his gruff voice, Katelyn closed the book. "Fine. Do you want to talk?"

Another smile curved his lips, this one of amusement. "Why, so you can ask more questions?"

"I won't ask you questions, if you don't want me to."

After taking another draught from the bottle of mescal, he said, "Go ahead and ask, *querida.*"

"Tell me about Marco."

Brit exhaled heavily, then said, "He used to be one of my men, then we had a disagreement and I sent him away."

"What did you disagree about?"

"Marco is young and foolish, and unfortunately, he has a lust for blood." At her confused look, he said, "Marco wanted to be a bandit by his own set of rules: steal everything valuable, then leave no witnesses. I do not believe killing is necessary. Taking the purse of those we stop on the road is sufficient."

After a long silence, Katelyn said, "Tell me how you came to be *El Buitre.*"

He scooted closer to the wall, wincing with the effort, then patted the bed beside him. "Come sit next to me, and I will tell you."

Katelyn hurried to do his bidding, anxious to hear his story. Once she was settled, he began speaking in a low voice.

"After I returned from England, I had nothing to keep me busy. I helped on my parents' *rancho,* but I was not really needed. I wanted to be a *ranchero* and own a place of my own, but I did not have the money to buy the land. So, some friends of mine and I came to the gold fields late in '49. We mined for placer gold at Calaveritas, just south of San Andreas. For six months we did very well, making enough so we could send a large percentage of the gold home. But the Yankees did not like us taking what they thought of as *their* gold."

"What happened?"

"The Yankees wanted all competition out of their way. They said no one other than citizens of the United States could dig for gold. We tried to tell them the terms of the Treaty of Guadalupe Hidalgo gave the people born in Alta California the same rights as other citizens, but they would not listen. They insisted we were trespassers, and tried to chase us from the mines.

"The Yankees believed chasing off all those who spoke Spanish—the ones they called greasers—completely justified. Since Mexico lost the war, Mexicans were considered part of a conquered race and could be ordered to do whatever the *gringos* wanted." He made a sound of disgust. "What they wanted was to run out all those they labeled foreigners. We had to leave the best mining areas or face being attacked or killed." He paused to take another drink. "We were willing to defend our claims and might have stayed, but the Foreigner Miner's Tax changed everything."

"The Foreigner Miner's Tax?"

"Each foreigner was ordered to pay twenty dollars a month for a mining permit. We argued that we could not afford such a sum. We were already paying inflated prices for food and supplies, and another twenty dollars would have taken most of our profits. We offered to pay three, or even five dollars a month, but again the Yankees would not listen."

"So, is that why you became The Vulture?"

"No. My friends and I stayed near Calaveritas for a few months, working an inferior claim and waiting to see if conditions would change." He drew a deep breath. "Then in September, my fiancée arrived."

Katelyn started. "Your fiancée?"

"Our marriage was arranged by our parents when we were just children. We were to marry when Mirabella reached the age of seventeen. After the *fiesta* to celebrate her birthday, she wanted to set a date for our wedding, but I would not let her. I did not have a home where we could live, and I refused to stay with my parents. I told her then, as I told her many other times, I would not take her as my wife until I had my own *rancho,* my own house. I nearly had enough money saved when Mirabella grew impatient at the wait and decided to visit our camp." He lifted his gaze to stare at the cabin's roof, his features taut. A muscle jumped in his jaw.

After a moment, Katelyn reached out and touched his forearm. "Brit?"

Starting at her touch, he was jarred back to the present. After clearing his throat, he said, "By a miracle, she traveled without incident through the areas where there was growing violence. She arrived safely with her escorts: her *dueña* and two of her father's men. Three nights later, our camp was attacked by at least a dozen drunken *gringos.* Since some of my friends had given up mining and returned home, there were only six of us, counting the men who came with Mirabella, to defend ourselves and the women. We fought as hard and as long as we could, but eventually we were overpowered. When we came to, Mirabella and her *dueña* were missing."

"Did . . . did you find them?"

"Yes. The *gringos* left them a few miles from our camp, right where they had all used them."

Katelyn gasped. "Oh, my God. Were they—?"

"Mirabella's *dueña* was dead; her throat had been slit. I found Mirabella a few feet away, alive. Her nightdress had been torn from her, her fingernails broken and bloody from trying to fight them off, her face and body were covered with bruises." Brit took a deep, shuddering breath. "But it was the look in her eyes I will never forget—the look of shame and defeat."

"Surely, she didn't think you would blame her for what happened."

When he turned to meet her gaze, Katelyn's eyes widened at the raw fury she saw on his face. "You do not understand, *gringa.* In my society, women value their purity above all else. If a woman's purity is taken from her by someone other than her husband on her wedding night, she considers herself no longer worthy of marriage."

"But—"

"After Mirabella had been used by the *gringos*," he said, ignoring Katelyn's attempt to interrupt him, "she no longer considered herself worthy of me. She said she was contaminated, and would not let me touch her. She lost the will to live, refusing to eat. Nothing I said could change her mind." He paused to take another deep breath. "She died several weeks later. I knew she would want to be laid to rest on her family's land, so I took her home.

"Mirabella was so young and innocent, and I let her become another victim of *gringo* greed. For months, I prayed for God to take me as well. I did not deserve to live. Finally, I realized my prayers went unanswered because I had been given a new purpose in life. I was to return to this part of California, not as Roberto Brit Livingston y Cordoba, a miner filled with dreams, but as a *bandido* filled with hate."

"Oh, Brit, I'm so sorry. I had no—"

"I do not want your pity, *gringa*. I only told you this to explain why I became the bandit your people named *El Buitre*."

"You wanted revenge for your fiancée's death."

"*Sí*, but I also want the Yankees to pay for what they have done to all *Californios*. By taking away our right to mine gold, the greedy Yankees have brought poverty and hunger to many of my people. As *El Buitre*, I take money and sometimes cattle from those I hold responsible to help my people survive."

Katelyn didn't respond; she couldn't. The shocking story he'd just told her stunned her to silence. She wasn't sure she believed him—perhaps his grief and rage had embellished the facts. She had to admit though, his obvious pain seemed genuine enough.

Neither of them spoke for a long time, for which Katelyn was extremely grateful. By the time she rose to prepare for bed, Brit was sound asleep, the mescal apparently doing more than numbing his pain.

After lying on the pallet of blankets for a few minutes, sleep continued to elude Katelyn. Glancing at Brit's profile, his words replayed in her head. She shivered, then pulled the blanket up under her chin. How would Brit react when he found out she, a woman he knew had never been married, wasn't as pure as his Mirabella?

Although he'd made no move toward her, Katelyn had a bone-deep premonition her relationship with Brit would become intimate. Surprisingly, before tonight she hadn't feared such an eventuality. But now that she'd heard how his culture looked upon virtuous women, she experienced a very real fear.

Would the desire she saw smoldering in his eyes change to hate? The possibility sent another shiver up her body, a shiver leaving a knot of cold fright in her belly.

Eight

Brit slept soundly for several hours, then began tossing fitfully, mumbling in Spanish. Concerned he could not get the rest he needed with her lying beside him, Katelyn got out of bed. After checking his forehead for fever, she wrapped her shawl around her shoulders, pulled the chair closer to the bed, and sat down. Worried he would take a turn for the worse, she knew she'd never be able to get back to sleep, so she didn't try. Instead, she was prepared to keep watch over him throughout the night.

Occasionally he roused enough to ask for water, but more often he wanted mescal. She did not refuse him, hoping the liquor would lull him into a deep healing sleep. Near dawn he ceased his restless thrashing; at last he slept peacefully. After checking him for fever, Katelyn quickly dressed and left the cabin. She would talk to Lutero while she ate a hurried breakfast.

"He has a fever, *señorita?*"

"No," she said between mouthfuls of porridge. "He's warm, but I don't think it's a fever. Not yet anyway."

Lutero nodded. "Bathe him with cool water to keep his temperature down. He is young and strong, so he should be able to fight off a fever if it comes."

"What about the mescal? Should I continue giving it to him?"

"*Sí,* he may have the mescal for a little longer, then only water." He flashed a smile. "We do not want him to wake up with a hangover. He may wake up like a wounded bear as it is."

Katelyn returned his smile. "I'm sure you're right." Handing her bowl and cup to Lutero, she got to her feet. "I'd better get back."

"Let me know if you need anything. I will have Juan check on you later."

Katelyn returned to the cabin and Brit's bedside. He was still asleep. Deciding to rest while he was quiet, she curled up in the chair. A few minutes later, she fell into a light sleep.

It seemed as though she'd just closed her eyes when Brit's voice jolted her awake. Getting out of the chair, she dropped onto her knees next to the bed. Eyes closed, his face pinched with pain, he was talking in his sleep.

"They cannot make us pay such a fee. We have every right to mine here. We must fight the tax." Though he spoke in English, his words were slightly slurred, forcing Katelyn to listen closely to catch his ramblings.

"No, you cannot want to die." His voice rose to a near shout. "You cannot leave me, Mirabella. We are to be married."

Hearing the hurt in his voice when he said his fiancée's name, a stab of pain ripped through Katelyn's chest. The story he'd told her the night before was obviously haunting his dreams. Laying a hand on his arm, she gave him a gentle shake. "Brit, wake up."

He groaned, then shuddered.

"Brit. You're dreaming." She gave him another shake. "Open your eyes and look at me."

Very slowly his eyelids lifted. He looked around, his eyes clouded with pain. Blinking several times, his gaze cleared, then finally settled on Katelyn's face. "Ah, *cardillo mío,* you are still with me."

Katelyn smiled. "Yes, your golden thistle is still here. Do you want anything?"

His brow furrowed. "Yes, I need to . . ."

"What? What do you need? Tell me, and I will help you."

"No, I do not think you can help me this time, *querida*." He flashed a weak smile. "I need to relieve myself."

"Oh," Katelyn murmured, feeling her cheeks warm with a blush. "I'll get Armando." Pulling her skirts out from under her knees, she got to her feet, then hurried to the door.

When she stepped back inside, she said, "Armando is on his way."

"*Gracias.*"

"*De nada,*" she replied, unable to meet his gaze.

When Brit returned from his trip outside, his face was ashen, his breathing labored. Sinking onto the bed with a moan, he said, "The mescal, *querida, pronto.*"

She handed him the bottle, watching anxiously as he took a long draught. The liquor did its work quickly, sending him into another deep sleep. Taking the bottle of mescal from his limp fingers, she reached down to touch his face. His skin was dry and hot. A soft gasp escaped her lips.

After calling to Armando to fetch a basin of water, she spent the rest of the morning bathing Brit's face, arms, and chest. When he was still resting quietly at noon, she stopped her ministrations long enough to get something to eat and to stretch her legs. Filling a canteen with fresh water, she headed back to the cabin.

Though his skin was warm to the touch, she was certain he wasn't as hot as he'd been earlier. Ringing out a cloth, she laid it across his forehead. Her gaze moved over his face, past his prominent cheekbones and straight nose to his square chin and the small cleft she found so fascinating. Giving in to temptation, she pressed the pad of her right forefinger into the indentation. A perfect fit. She smiled.

Brit sighed in his sleep, startling her and erasing her

smile. Her heart pounding in her ears, she jerked her hand from his face, but couldn't make herself withdraw completely. She held her hand just above his chest. Closing her eyes, she tried to talk herself out of what she was about to do. She let her breath out slowly, then opened her eyes. Though she knew it wasn't right, she couldn't stop herself from lowering her hand to the center of his muscular chest.

Her fingers clenched spasmodically, then threaded through the silky black hair above the white bandage. She bit her lip to stifle a groan of pleasure. The muscles beneath her hand were firm and well-defined. She moved to his upper arm, curling her fingers around his bicep. They barely went halfway around his arm. She traced the prominent vein in his arm from shoulder to wrist with one finger, marveling at the smooth texture of his skin, the raw strength beneath her fingertips. She was about to continue her explorations, intent on running her hand across the hard expanse of belly above his trousers, when the cabin door opened.

Katelyn inhaled sharply, pulling her hand away from its intended target. She glanced toward the door, unable to stop the heat of a blush from creeping up her cheeks. "Lutero," she said, her voice breathless and high-pitched.

If the old man thought anything amiss, thankfully he said nothing, but moved to stand at the end of the bed.

"He is better?"

"Yes, I used cool water like you said, and I think I stopped the fever from getting worse." She kept her gaze on Brit, unable to look at Lutero for fear he'd see the shame reflected on her face.

"Bueno." He remained silent for a moment, studying the stiffness of Katelyn's shoulders and back. At last he shrugged, and said, "I must get back. *Señor* Brit is in good hands." Turning to leave, he added, "I will have Juan let you know when the evening meal is ready, *señorita.*"

* * *

As darkness fell on the mountain campsite, Katelyn made her way from the cabin to the campfire. Brit had suffered another bad spell in the middle of the afternoon, but had finally settled down into another deep sleep. Having eaten only a small meal at noon, Katelyn was famished. Though Juan had offered to bring her something several hours earlier, she had refused, wanting to make sure Brit was out of danger before she left his side.

"Ah, *señorita,* I am glad to see you," Lutero said. "I was just about to send my grandson up to the cabin with a plate of food."

"Sí," Juan said with a smile. *"Mi abuelo* told me I must stay at the cabin until you cleaned your plate. He is worried about you, *señorita."*

Lutero cleared his throat, then said, "You must eat or you will fall ill. Then who will care for *Señor* Brit?"

Katelyn gave the men a weak smile. "I'm fine, Lutero. Just tired and hungry." Accepting a plate from the cook, she sat down beside Juan.

As she ate, she watched Lutero mix something in a clay bowl. "What are you making?"

"Bread."

"Really? But how can you bake bread?"

Lutero chuckled. "I will bake the bread in the *horno."* He nodded toward a pile of rocks.

Juan leaned closer to Katelyn, and said, "It is an oven, *señorita.* Grandfather built it when he first came here. He dug a hole in the ground, lined it with rocks, then piled more rocks on top."

"So how can you bake anything inside a pile of rocks?"

"It is hollow in the center," Lutero replied, shaping the bread dough into loaves on a long wooden paddle. "I built a fire inside, and when the rocks are very hot, I will remove the ashes and put the bread in to bake." He flashed her a smile. "It is easy, *sí?*"

Katelyn returned his smile. "For you maybe. But I doubt it would be easy for me. I wish I'd known about the oven when I made biscuits the other night."

"There was no fire in the *horno* that night. But it did not matter, everyone liked your biscuits. Did they not say so?"

"Yes, but the oven would have been easier."

Chuckling, Lutero picked up the wooden paddle and moved to the oven.

While she finished eating, she watched him get the oven ready, then slip the bread inside to bake. When he had the rocks back in place, she said, "Lutero, can I ask you something?"

"*Sí.*"

"Why do you lead such a hard life? Surely you would rather live inside a comfortable house, instead of here in the open."

"I live the life I want, *Señorita* Katelyn. I love the outside, the open skies, the mountains. Besides, I want to be near my only grandson." He glanced over at Juan, who smiled sheepishly.

"You may love the outdoors, but don't you get tired of sleeping on the hard ground?"

"My lumbago bothers me sometimes, like it is today. But otherwise, I do not mind making my bed on the ground, or sleeping beneath the stars. Someday, when *Señor* Brit says it is time to go back to his parents' *rancho,* I will once again live in a house. Until then, I am content in the mountains."

"But isn't the winter hard on your lumbago?"

"*Sí,* it would be, if we stayed in this canyon when the snow comes. But *Señor* Brit will move our camp to a warmer place to the south before then. We will spend the winter in another mountain canyon, where it does not get so cold."

Katelyn thought about that for a moment, then turned to Juan. "What about you, aren't you anxious to go home?"

"Sometimes. But I, too, like being in the open air. And as long as *el jefe* says we are to remain here, I will stay."

"But, what about being a member of a band of thieves? You certainly realize what could happen to you if you're caught, don't you?"

"*Sí,* I am aware of what could happen. That does not matter. We all willingly follow *el jefe.*"

"Were you with him when his fiancée was killed?"

"No, I was at my parents' *rancho.* After Mirabella was buried and *el jefe* decided to come back here, I asked to go with him. He said I was too young. But Mirabella was my cousin, and I wanted badly to help avenge her death. He told me I had to wait until I was seventeen before I could join him. I did not like the idea of waiting, but I agreed. Grandfather and I have been here almost two years."

Katelyn swung her gaze back to Lutero. "Mirabella was your granddaughter?"

"*Sí,* she was the child of my oldest daughter. My youngest son is Juan's father."

"So, you came north not only to be with Juan, but also to help avenge your granddaughter's death?"

"I do not believe in seeking revenge, *señorita. Dios* is the only one who can extract vengeance. But I will not try to stop *Señor* Brit, or my grandson, or any of the others from the mission they have given themselves. They believe in their cause too strongly to listen to one old man."

He reached over and patted her hand. "Since you have never thirsted for revenge, *señorita,* you cannot understand their need to accomplish it at any cost. But you must believe me when I say, revenge is an all-consuming, driving force which cannot always be controlled."

Katelyn merely nodded. How could she tell Lutero she did indeed know what the thirst for revenge did to a person? She couldn't tell him the man who had been engaged to his granddaughter was the same man she had sworn vengeance against—the man she feared she was beginning to care about a great deal.

Brit came awake slowly, the fuzziness in his brain clearing enough for him to remember his fight with Marco. He could remember sending the man away, coming back to his cabin, Katelyn tending his wounds, and a bottle of Lutero's mescal. After that, everything was a blur.

Though his head hurt from the mescal and the worst of his wounds still pained him, he felt surprisingly good, his spirits unaccountably high. More memories flooded back: a soft female voice, the cool touch of a woman's hand on his brow. He smiled. Katelyn had taken good care of him.

Then he recalled telling her about Mirabella, and his smile changed to a scowl. Was that the reason behind his good mood? Had recounting his fiancée's tragic death lifted, at least briefly, the enormous weight he carried on his shoulders?

His scowl deepened. That wasn't possible. He'd sworn on Mirabella's grave to let nothing or no one distract him from carrying out the oath he'd made. He would never forget his sworn promise to avenge her senseless death, or to make the hated *gringos* pay for their heartless treatment of his people.

Katelyn stirred next to him, jerking his thoughts back to the present. His teeth clenched, he turned his head to look at the woman next to him. Her eyelids fluttered up, revealing eyes that looked even bluer than usual. As her sleepy gaze focused on his face, her lips curved upward. Desire, intense and as hot as the sun-baked desert between his parents' *rancho* and the border of Mexico gripped him.

Though he knew he should get out of bed and away from the temptation Katelyn presented, Brit found he could not move. He wanted desperately to taste her mouth, to bury his throbbing flesh inside her warmth. The need was so overwhelming he could think of nothing else. Making a sound deep in his throat, a half-moan, half-growl, he rose onto one forearm, then slowly lowered his head.

When his lips grazed hers, Katelyn's breath caught in her throat. The emotion surging through her from their first intimate touch made her head reel. Looping one arm around his neck, she pulled herself closer, groaning when her breasts pressed against the hard muscles of his chest. The tip of his tongue teased her closed lips, urging them to open. She complied, gasping when his tongue slipped into her mouth. Never having known the sensations his exploring tongue caused, she was equally shocked and excited by his actions.

Just as Brit started to push Katelyn flat on her back and cover her with his painfully aroused body, another pain ripped through him. His wounds throbbing their objection, his senses returned. He stiffened, then pulled his mouth from hers. *"No más!"*

Though Katelyn wasn't certain she knew what he'd said, there was no mistaking the anger in his voice. She carefully removed her arm from his shoulder and sank back onto the bed. "Brit, I'm—"

"Do not say anything, *gringa,*" he said, cutting off her words. He rolled onto his back, trying to cool the white-hot need still coursing through his veins. "It is my fault." He swung his legs off the bed and started to get to his feet. He bit back a groan.

"Here, let me help you," Katelyn said, scurrying off the bed. "You've been sleeping for nearly a day and a half, and you're bound to be weak. Give me your hand, and I'll help you up." She reached for him.

"No!" he shouted. After taking a deep breath, he said

more softly, "Do not touch me, *querida,* I must do this by myself."

Katelyn backed away, biting her bottom lip to keep from telling him he was too stubborn for his own good. She watched him straighten, saw the pain he fought to control reflected on his face.

Brit swayed from side to side, remaining on his feet through sheer dint of will until his bout of dizziness passed. Moving slowly, he managed to pull a clean shirt from his saddlebags.

As he struggled to get dressed, Katelyn turned away, unable to bear watching the flex of his arm muscles without remembering the feel of his skin.

She kept her back to him until she heard the door open and close. Sighing, she pressed a hand to her breast, where her heart still beat in the wild rhythm caused by the kiss they'd shared.

As she dressed, she wondered why he'd stopped. Then she remembered what he told her the night before. Mirabella.

After speaking with Armando, then eating a small breakfast, Brit decided to visit Solazo, though he would do nothing requiring more than a minimum of physical exertion. The walk to the corral loosened his stiff muscles, the worst of his pain subsiding. But as much as he hated to admit it, Katelyn was right, he was weak. He would have to work on regaining his strength as soon as possible, but also taking care not to tear open his healing wounds.

For the time being, he settled for grooming Solazo, talking to the mare in soft Spanish, while he made plans for his next horse-capturing venture. He hoped Tomás would return soon, so they could leave the hidden canyon and head down into the lower foothills.

In spite of his injuries, Brit was anxious to get away from camp—away from the temptation Katelyn presented. Once he was racing after a herd of *mesteños,* the wind blowing against his face, his mind would no longer be filled with thoughts of his captive. After the kiss they'd shared that morning, he was determined to rid himself of the tantalizing memory. If he didn't, he could easily become ensnared by the powerful allure of his golden thistle.

He finished brushing Solazo's coat and glanced up at the sky. The sun was not yet straight overhead. How would he pass the rest of the day? He closed his eyes for a moment, praying Tomás had no trouble making the trip to the church in San Andreas.

When Brit first changed from law-abiding citizen to *bandido,* he had been concerned about being able to stay in contact with his family. As a wanted criminal, he had to be careful about putting in an appearance in any of the nearby towns for fear of being arrested. Though the description of him being circulated in the area was not completely accurate, Brit rarely took the chance.

Father John had been receptive to acting as courier for the man he knew only as Roberto Cordoba, an occasional worshipper at his church after the priest's arrival in the spring of '51. Since Brit's first request soon after he became the bandit later named *El Buitre,* Father John had followed through on his promise to see that Brit's messages to his family arrived safely.

For the good father's assistance and the risk he ran in helping, albeit unknowingly, a bandit, Brit made sure a portion of each purse he stole was given anonymously to the Catholic church in San Andreas.

Two days later, Katelyn watched Brit saddle his horse in preparation for leaving. When Brit came to his cabin the night before, he had been in a particularly jovial mood. He announced that Tomás had returned, and he and his men would be leaving in the morning to go after another herd of wild horses. When she asked how long he'd be gone, he said it depended on how far they had to travel in their search. If they were lucky enough to find a herd in a nearby canyon, they would be gone only a few days. But if their search took them to the meadows in the lower foothills of the mountains, they could be gone a week or more.

Brit checked the saddle's girth one last time, then secured the bags of food Lutero had packed behind the cantle.

"You should not leave *la señorita* behind, *Señor* Brit," Lutero said in a quiet voice. "You should send her home. Have you not done what you set out to do?"

Brit could not make himself meet the old cook's gaze. *"Sí."*

"Then you must do the right thing and return her to her home. What is stopping you?"

Brit glanced over his shoulder to look at the topic of their discussion. Katelyn stood off to one side, arms crossed at her waist. Finally, he said, "I do not know. You are right, but I . . ." He cleared his throat. "I can do nothing until I return."

Lutero eyed him for a few moments, then, nodding his white head, turned and went back to the campfire.

Pushing Lutero's words aside, Brit walked over to Katelyn. "Do not be frightened to stay here, *querida*. You will not be alone," he said in a low voice.

"I know," she replied, looking up to meet his gaze. He had told her Lutero and several other men would be staying behind to take care of the camp.

He longed to kiss her again, but held himself in check. He could not let his men see him lose control where this *gringa* was concerned. Still, he couldn't stop himself from reaching up to run his knuckles down one cheek. "I will see you soon, *cardillo mío.*"

Katelyn's eyes widened at his touch, gooseflesh popping out on her arms. *"Vaya con Díos,"* she whispered.

Brit started at her words, then smiled. "Your Spanish is

becoming very good." He dropped his hand, gave her a small bow, and returned to his horse.

Katelyn watched him swing easily into the saddle, signal for the rest of the men to follow him, then kick his horse into a trot. She stared down the trail, not moving until long after the last of the horses disappeared from view. With a deep sigh, she headed back to the campfire.

She sat down next to Lutero and smiled when Paco stretched out beside her, laying his head in her lap.

Rubbing her hand over the dog's muzzle, she said, "Lutero, Juan said the two of you have been in this part of California for two years. Is that correct?"

Lutero looked up, his brow furrowed. *"Sí,* it will soon be two years."

"Did you ever try mining for gold?"

He nodded. "When *Señor* Brit first come north to look for gold, I came, too. But the work was very hard, so I quit after a few months and went home. The mine fields are no place for an old man. I came north a second time with Juan, but only to cook."

"The night of his fight with Marco, Brit drank a lot of the mescal you gave me. He told me about his fiancée and why he became The Vulture."

"Sí, I knew he must have."

"I know her death must have hurt you deeply. But was her death also very hard on Brit?"

"Sí, he grieved for a very long time. He spent many hours of each day on his knees in his family's chapel. His parents worried they would lose him as well."

"He must have loved Mirabella very much."

"Love?" The creases on Lutero's forehead deepened. "I do not know the answer to that, *señorita.* The parents of *Señor* Brit and *Señorita* Mirabella's *madre y padre,* my daughter and her husband, agreed to their engagement when he was only six or seven, and she but a baby. *Señor* Brit grew up knowing Mirabella would be his wife one day, and

I know he was very fond of her. But as to whether it was love . . ." He shrugged. "As I said, I do not know the answer. But I have always thought he has not yet found the woman of his heart."

"But surely, he wouldn't have been so grief-stricken unless he was in love with her."

Lutero thought about her statement for a moment, then said, "I think his grief came mostly from guilt. He blamed himself for Mirabella's death."

A long silence passed between them while Lutero cut up vegetables for another *puchero,* and Katelyn continued petting the hound. Finally, in a low voice she said, "Was she beautiful?"

Lutero smiled. *"Sí, muy bella.* Her skin was the color of cream, her lips like a ripe strawberry. I think all of my grandchildren are beautiful, but everyone said Mirabella was the most beautiful woman they ever saw in all of California."

Katelyn released the breath she'd been holding. She should have known Brit's fiancée would be nothing less than extremely beautiful. Still, knowing for sure hurt more than she wanted to admit. There was no way a plain-faced woman like herself could compete with a real beauty—alive or dead.

Her hand stilled on Paco's head. Where had that thought come from? She wasn't trying to catch Brit. Was she?

Pushing the hound off her lap, she jumped to her feet. "I think I'll go for a walk."

"Do not go too far, *señorita.* There are many dangers in these mountains. It is not safe for a woman alone." Lutero watched Katelyn hurry across the campsite, wondering about the sudden change in her mood. Both *Señor* Brit and *la señorita* were acting strange.

Perhaps there was more to their relationship than either was aware. In spite of the strong attraction he sensed they felt for each other, could two people from such opposite cultures find happiness? Could Brit lay his hatred of Yankees aside?

Wishing he knew the answers, Lutero sighed and went back to his pot of stew.

Nine

Marco Chavez sat staring into the fire in brooding silence, his thoughts filled with anger. Lifting one hand, he touched the bandage on his neck. As he probed the healing cut with his fingertips, he felt only minor discomfort from the four-day-old wound. Though still weak from the loss of blood, he would be strong enough to ride in a few more days. Marco couldn't wait.

"You are feeling better?" one of his men asked from across the campfire.

"Sí. We will be leaving this place very soon."

"Where are we going?"

"We need money. So we will find someone who will give us their gold." Marco had spent nearly every waking hour since he had been escorted from *El Buitre's* camp in disgrace planning his revenge. He would begin by robbing as many people as he could, making sure his victims believed they had been robbed by the famous bandit. Then, when he tired of that game, he would move on to his next step.

Since he knew *El Buitre,* surely the information he had about the bandit would be of value to someone. Perhaps he should tell someone the bandit's true identity. But what good would that do? Knowing *El Buitre's* real name wouldn't lead the authorities to Brit. There was a better way to accomplish that. And Marco knew exactly how he would start.

Stretching out on his bedroll, he closed his eyes. Just as

he did every night, he relived his last visit to *El Buitre*'s camp in his mind before he allowed himself to sleep. By reliving that night and feeling the humiliation, the burning anger, Marco kept his thirst for revenge primed.

Once again, he wondered about the woman in Brit's camp. Who was she, and what was she doing there? As far as Marco knew, Brit had never allowed a woman in his camp. He wished he could have gotten a better look at her. Such information might be just as valuable as what he knew about Brit and his camp.

The day seemed to drag on forever for Katelyn. Without Brit, time crawled. She hadn't realized how accustomed she had become to his presence in camp, spending time in his company, watching him from across the canyon, or at least knowing he was nearby. Grateful when darkness finally fell, she excused herself and headed for Brit's cabin.

She hadn't written in her journal for several days, so she pulled the book from her carpetbag and sat down in front of the fireplace. For several seconds, she stared into the fire one of the men had lit, then opened her journal and began writing.

I witnessed a knife fight between Brit and a former member of his band named Marco. I have never felt such terror for someone else's safety. Much to my relief, Brit won the fight, though he suffered numerous cuts. After he sent the other man on his way, I tended his wounds. Later, Brit told me why he became the bandit called El Buitre. *He is seeking vengeance for the death of his fiancée, and retribution for the way he and other* Californios *were treated in the mine fields. After hearing his story, I am no longer certain what to believe. If what he told me is true, he should have sought justice by letting the law handle it, not by becoming a vigilante. One cannot take the law into his own hands!*

Katelyn paused. Should she write the rest? Deciding to be honest, she turned the page and began writing again.

Brit contracted a fever while recovering from his wounds and talked in his sleep. The pain in his voice when he spoke to his now-dead fiancée was almost more than I could bear. When his fever broke, I could have cried with relief. The next morning he awoke lucid, but weak. Before I realized his intention, he kissed me. I know I should have stopped him, but truth to tell, I wanted him to kiss me. I think I have wanted him to do so since the first time I saw him. His lips were so gentle, so soft at first, then so demanding and fierce. His kiss set my entire insides afire. Dare I say it? Yes, I want him to kiss me again. I have thought of little else. But I cannot allow it. If he were to kiss me again, I cannot be sure I could resist any further advances. And it is a schoolgirl's dream to think he will ever want me, not when the memory of his beautiful fiancée still burns so brightly. I've made up my mind, I must leave here. He and most of his men have left to capture more wild horses. There are only three men in camp, the fewest Brit has ever left during one of his absences. This will be my best chance—perhaps my only chance to escape. I don't know if I can find my way out of these mountains, for as Papa so frequently pointed out, my sense of direction is sadly lacking. But I cannot stay here any longer, for if I do—well, I will just say it is imperative that I leave.

Closing her journal, Katelyn rose and readied herself for bed. After selecting the clothes she would wear in the

morning and stuffing the remainder of her belongings into
her carpetbag, she stretched out on the bed. Even though
she knew she must leave, her heart was heavy. She had
come to like the men in Brit's band, and in particular Brit
himself. She refused to entertain the idea that she might
feel more than *liking* for him. She couldn't love Brit, for
to do so would break not only her vow to see the man
responsible for her father's death brought to justice, but
also her heart.

Jake shoved the plate away from him and sat back in his
chair with a sigh. "Grace, that's the best apple pie I've ever
had."

She looked at him over the rim of her coffee cup. "That's
what you said about tonight's roast, and the chicken last
night."

"Well, it's true. Your cooking is the best there is."

She smiled, then took a sip of coffee. "Thank you." Setting the cup on the kitchen table, her brow furrowed. "I'm
so worried about Katelyn, Jake. She's been on my mind a
lot lately."

Jake reached across the small table and placed his hand
over hers. "I know. I think about her a lot, too."

"It's been almost three weeks since she left town, and
neither one of us has heard anything. Do you think we
should send someone to look for her?"

Giving her hand a squeeze, he said, "I'd like to look
for Katie myself. But I don't have the faintest idea where
to start. We don't know which direction she took, or even
how she left town." Releasing her hand, he pushed his
chair away from the table. "Come on, I'll help you with
the dishes."

"Don't be silly, Jake. I can do them later."

"Are you sure? I'd be happy to help you."

Grace chuckled. "Yes, I'm sure. Come on, let's go sit in the parlor."

After they were settled on the settee, Jake said, "Ross Carter stopped by the *Argus* again today. He keeps trying to take over, but I just ignore him. He thinks I can't run the paper on my own. He's even started going through the mail."

"You don't think he's involved with Katelyn's disappearance, do you?"

"No. The day I showed him her note, he was fit to be tied that she hadn't mentioned his name." Jake laughed. "There's no way he could've faked his reaction. I think he's just as stumped on her leaving as we are." He sobered to add, "I sure don't like how he keeps eyeing Cyrus's printing press. I never told Katie, but I think he only asked her to marry him so he could get his hands on both the press and the *Argus.*"

"Jake, what a terrible thing to say!"

"Maybe so, but it's how I feel. She never kept company with any man, though plenty asked, until Cyrus said he approved of Ross Carter. But Cyrus was too caught up in his work to see how Carter looked more lovingly at the printing press than at Katie."

"Well, if that's true, shouldn't you tell Katelyn when she gets back?"

"I don't want her to think I'm sticking my nose where it doesn't belong. Besides, I don't think she'll marry Carter."

"Why do you think that? Has she said something?"

Jake scratched his head. "No, she hasn't said anything. I guess it's the way she looks at him, like she's looking right through him. She don't love him. I'd bet my last nickel on that."

Grace scooted closer and placed her hand on his forearm. "Not all folks feel the way we do."

Jake's eyes widened; his heart pounded in his ears. "What are you saying, Grace?"

"I'm saying, the last few weeks, seeing you every day, have been the happiest I can remember, and—" She took a deep breath. "And I think I'm falling in love with you, Jacob Fletcher. And, unless I miss my guess, I think you're falling in love with me, too." She squeezed his arm. "Am I wrong?"

"No," he said in a strangled voice. "You ain't wrong. Except, I'm not *falling* in love with you, Grace. I already love you. I have from the moment I first laid eyes on you." He chuckled. "I can't believe I just told you that. Guess it's 'cuz I feel so comfortable around you." Giving her a sheepish grin, he added, "I can even talk to you now without stumbling over my words, or acting like a gun-shy idiot. And to think you're—" He grasped her hands. "Grace, are you absolutely certain you could love an old printer's devil like me?"

"Positively. Now would you please stop carrying on and kiss me?"

Releasing her hands, Jake moaned deep in his throat, then lowered his face to hers. With infinite gentleness, he captured her lips with his. "Oh, Gracie, Gracie," he whispered against her mouth. "I love you."

When he finally lifted his head, both he and Grace were breathing hard, her face as flushed with desire as his. Though the look in her eyes told him she wouldn't protest if he tried to do more than kiss her, Jake forced himself to grasp her arms and ease them from around his neck. He wasn't about to risk losing what he'd so recently found.

"I have to be going, Grace."

She blinked, her eyes slowly focusing on his face. Giving a soft, little gasp, she dropped her gaze to where she twisted her hands in her lap.

Putting his fingers under her chin, he tilted her face up until she met his gaze. "Don't be embarrassed by our passion, Gracie. It's a fine and wonderful thing, and I'd like to take it even further. But it's late, and I have to be getting home." He pressed a brief kiss on her lips. "I want our first time to be special. Do you understand what I'm saying?"

Two bright splotches of color staining her cheeks, she didn't look away, but held his gaze. She finally nodded.

"Good, now walk me to the door, before I change my mind and have you right here on the settee."

Grace laughed, easing the sexual tension hanging over them. "You're something, you know that, Jake Fletcher? You're really something."

Just before daybreak, Katelyn rose from the bed in Brit's cabin where she'd barely slept. After changing into a dress of golden brown pique, she twisted her hair into a knot atop her head and pinned it in place. She picked up her carpet-bag, then opened the cabin door.

Lutero was busy at the campfire as usual; the other two men were still lying in their bedrolls. Deciding the time was right, Katelyn looked around the cabin one last time, then slipped outside, closing the door softly behind her.

Taking care to move slowly, she made her way to the corral. From the four horses left in camp, she selected a sorrel mare as her means of escape. Slipping a bridle on the horse proved relatively simple, but the saddle wasn't so easy. She'd never actually saddled a horse, though she'd watched her father and the men at Brit's camp do it many times.

After considerable straining and silent groaning, she managed to get the saddle onto the mare's back and the cinch tightened. As she tried to catch her breath, she looped the handles of her carpetbag over the saddle horn. One of the other horses nickered softly. Katelyn looked over at the animals and frowned. *What am I going to do with the other horses? I can't leave them here.*

A few minutes later, she opened the corral gate, then swung into the saddle, the lead ropes she'd attached to the hackamores of the other horses clutched in one hand. Realizing she couldn't take the trail heading out of the canyon because she'd have to pass Lutero and the other men, she experienced a moment of panic. Could she find her way out of the mountains if she had to leave the canyon by another route?

Forcing herself to remain calm, she decided her poor sense of direction made her chances about the same either way. She swung the mare around and urged her toward a stand of oak trees at the rear of the clearing.

A hundred yards beyond the edge of camp, Katelyn halted, holding her breath and cocking her head to listen to the sounds around her. The only things she heard were the horses' impatient stomping on the leaf-covered ground, the distant chatter of a squirrel and the heavy pounding of her heart in her ears. Satisfied her escape had not yet been discovered, she touched her heels to the mare's sides.

It was only a matter of time before her absence became apparent, so she intended to get as far as she could before that happened. Though she had the extra horses with her, she wouldn't feel safe until she put as much distance between herself and Brit's camp as possible.

Not wanting to be out in the open where she could easily be spotted, Katelyn kept to the trees. Unfortunately, trying to move through the trees and skirt heavy thickets of chaparral while leading three horses, proved to be a difficult task. Every time she tried to pick up the pace, one of the horses invariably chose that moment to balk. She finally gave up and settled for a slow walk.

Every few minutes, she looked over her shoulder, expecting to see approaching horses bearing down on her, a very angry Brit riding his big gray in the lead. She couldn't explain why seeing only an empty trail came as a disappointment.

* * *

Lutero heard the pounding of boots on the hard-packed ground and looked up from the pot of corn porridge bubbling over the campfire. His grandson, Juan, and Lorenzo Sanchez, Tomás's younger brother, raced toward him.

"Abuelo, la señorita, she is gone," Juan said, sliding to a stop next to his grandfather.

Lutero's eyes narrowed. "What do you mean?"

"Señorita Katelyn, she has taken the horses and escaped! Lorenzo and I went to feed the horses, but the corral was empty. I thought they must have run off, until I went to *Señor* Brit's cabin. It, too, was empty. Everything belonging to *la señorita* is gone."

"I thought it was your job to watch her, Juan?"

"Sí, Abuelo. But I heard nothing from her cabin when I checked earlier, so I thought she was still asleep. She has never given us reason to think she would try to escape, so I thought . . ." He bowed his head, unable to meet his grandfather's piercing gaze.

"Which way did she go?"

"To the east," Lorenzo said. "She headed deeper into the canyon. We tracked the horses to the edge of the clearing."

Lutero rubbed a hand across his eyes, then pinched the bridge of his nose. *"Madre de Díos."*

"What are we going to do?" Juan asked. "We cannot go after her without horses."

Heaving a sigh, Lutero turned back to the campfire. "There is nothing we can do. When *Señor* Brit returns, you will tell him what happened, then do as he tells you."

Juan gave Lorenzo an anxious look, then sat down by the fire, memories of their boss's knife fight with Marco still vivid in his mind. *"El jefe* will not be too upset, will he, *Abuelo?* I mean, he took her from Sacramento as part of his revenge on the *gringos.* So what should it matter that she has escaped?"

"I do not know, Grandson. *Sí,* it is true he brought her here as part of his revenge. But you know as well as I, these mountains are very dangerous."

"But she is just a *gringa!*"

"Perhaps. Still, I do not think *Señor* Brit would want her hurt or killed."

Juan swallowed hard, meeting Lorenzo's gaze and seeing his own fear reflected in his friend's eyes.

"I suggest both of you pray to the Heavenly Father," Lutero said. "Pray that *Señor* Brit will not want to make you pay too dearly for your negligence."

"*Sí, Abuelo,* we will," Juan replied.

Katelyn looked at the late afternoon shadows, then back at the mare standing a few feet away. She frowned at the way the horse kept its weight off the right foreleg.

Just her luck. Not more than several hours had passed since she'd decided it was safe to turn the rest of the horses loose. They had slowed her down long enough. She'd swatted the horses on their rumps and sent them off at a gallop, thankful to finally be able to make better time. Shortly after she watched the three horses disappear through the trees and continued her journey, the mare developed a limp.

Not wanting to risk permanent injury to the horse, Katelyn had pulled up to contemplate her alternatives. She realized she really had only one choice. Though she didn't like the prospect of going back to Brit's camp, there was no way she could make it out of the mountains—let alone all the way to Sacramento—on foot.

Shoulders slumped with defeat, Katelyn grabbed the reins and started walking. The mare followed docilely behind her. At least the long summer days were in her favor. Small consolation when she had no idea where she was or how far she'd traveled. If she made good time, she should make it back to the campsite before dark. She prayed that was true.

An hour later, she stopped. Nothing looked familiar. But then, all the rocks, pine trees, and shrubs looked alike to her, so perhaps she had passed through this area and not realized it. Again she started walking, picking up her pace in the deepening dusk.

The next time she stopped, almost total darkness pressed down on the mountains, the setting sun providing only meager light. Determined to press on, she continued walking.

The terrain changed abruptly, the slightly rolling ground giving way to a sharp decline. Katelyn inched forward, then a little farther. Thinking she could navigate the hill with no problem, she took a tentative step, then another. On the next step, her foot made contact with smooth rock, then immediately slid forward. Yelping with surprise, she struggled to keep her balance, but she continued to slide. She took a couple more quick steps, but it was no use. Her feet went out from under her, and she sat down hard.

When she tried to stand, she stepped on her skirt and fell sideways. Before she could scramble to her feet, the momentum of her fall sent her rolling down the steep embankment. Forced to let go of the mare's reins, she tried without success to grasp something to slow her descent. Brush and weeds slapping at her face and arms, sticks and stones poking into her back, she was vaguely aware of the mare's struggles to maneuver down the hill. Katelyn prayed they'd both survive.

When she rolled up against a tree stump, her unconventional descent of the hill abruptly ended. The sudden contact with the tree knocked the wind out of her. Lungs on fire, she lay still for several seconds, forcing herself to draw one painful breath after another. When she could breathe without pain and felt reasonably sure nothing was broken, she slowly got to her feet.

Her dress was covered with a coating of powdery, red

dirt, her now-loose hair a mass of snarls, her arms and hands crisscrossed with scratches and scrapes, but thankfully she had sustained no serious injuries.

She glanced around, exhaling a relieved breath when she spotted the mare standing a few feet away, apparently no worse for wear.

Pushing her hair back off of her face, she checked her surroundings. She was in a narrow, steep-sided canyon. Katelyn studied the surrounding scenery with a frown. She knew she'd never been *here* before. Closing her eyes, she drew a shuddering breath. *Looks like you've done it again. You're lost!*

Katelyn hadn't thought about the first time she'd gotten lost in many years. But as she acknowledged the fact that her poor sense of direction had gotten her lost again, the memory came flooding back.

She had just turned seven, and insisted she was old enough to walk a few blocks by herself to visit a friend. Though she had no problem getting to her friend's house, returning from her visit was a different matter. Somehow she managed to turn the wrong way. Before realizing her error, she was blocks from home, wandering in an unfamiliar neighborhood.

Spotting a group of boys she recognized from school playing marbles in a vacant lot, she approached them. Her plea of being lost and needing directions was met with hoots of laughter. When one of the boys told her babies shouldn't leave the nursery by themselves, she turned and ran as fast as she could. Their taunts and laughter ringing in her ears, she was too frightened and too embarrassed to ask anyone else for help. Tired and hungry, she cowered in a doorway and prayed her parents would find her soon.

When Katelyn hadn't returned by the time her father came home from the newspaper office, her mother was in a state of panic. Cyrus immediately set out to look for her.

An hour later, he found her huddled on the stoop of a vacant building, frozen with fright.

After that terrifying experience, it was years before she would go anywhere alone.

Now she was not only alone, but lost in the mountains with darkness fast approaching. Though no longer an easily frightened seven-year-old, at twenty-two the paralyzing fear she'd first experienced so long ago filled her once more. The mare nickered, pulling Katelyn from her somber thoughts.

"What is it?" Glancing around, she said, "I don't see anything."

Katelyn hesitantly moved forward a few feet, then smiled. "Water!" The canteen she'd taken from Brit's cabin was nearly empty. She rushed to the small stream cutting across the canyon floor and dropped to her knees. After both she and the mare quenched their thirsts, Katelyn used a piece of her torn skirt to bathe her face and arms.

Looking around her again, she tried to sound cheerful when she said, "Guess this is as good a place as any to make camp." While she didn't relish the idea of spending the night alone in the wild, she had no alternative. To continue walking was out of the question. She didn't want to risk another fall in the dark, and besides, she was too tired to go on. The combination of not much sleep the night before, the hours of walking, and the blisters on her feet, had taken its toll. She was completely exhausted.

After unsaddling the mare and removing the bridle, Katelyn soaked her burning feet in the stream, then sank gratefully onto the bed she'd made for herself—the saddle blanket covered by one of her dresses. In spite of the strange noises, Katelyn pulled her shawl tighter around her shoulders, then fell into an instant, deep sleep.

Something awakened Katelyn, but she wasn't sure what. She opened her eyes a crack. It was still dark, though the sky had begun to change from a purple-black to soft gray. Then she heard it again. A loud shrieklike cry came from atop the ridge of the canyon. Her shoulders convulsed with a shudder. Squeezing her eyes closed, she prayed she never had to meet whatever bird, animal or— She shuddered again at the thought of what other kind of creature could have made such an unnerving sound. Opening her eyes, she looked around, then rolled over to check on the mare.

With a gasp she rose up onto one elbow, her eyes wide. She searched the surrounding area again. No, she hadn't been mistaken. The horse was gone. She dropped back onto her makeshift bed with a little sob. Though keeping the horse with her had been more for the companionship, rather than harboring a hope the mare would lead her back to Brit's camp, Katelyn was sorry the animal had taken off during the night. Now she was truly alone.

Swallowing the bitter taste of fear, she drew a deep breath, then sat up. She'd better make use of every hour of daylight she could.

After drinking from the stream, changing into a dress of solferino pink muslin, and pulling on her shoes over two pairs of stockings—in spite of her protesting feet—Katelyn started walking. She had no idea which direction she should take, but for the time being, she decided to follow the winding canyon. At least it was relatively flat and had a water supply. She scolded herself for not thinking to pack food. What she would be willing to give for one of Lutero's *tortillas!* Her stomach rumbled at the thought, but she ignored it. *How could I be so stupid? I take off in the mountains, with not one iota of a clue on how to get home, and don't even bring a smidgen of food!*

But then, her lack of forethought should have come as no surprise. Ever since she'd met Brit, her thinking had been clouded—constantly wavering between her intense attraction to the man and wanting to club him over the head for the hateful things he said to her.

Pushing thoughts of food from her mind, she tightened her grip on her carpetbag and kept walking.

Ten

Two days. Had only two days passed since Brit left his camp, only two days since he'd seen Katelyn? It seemed much longer.

Thankfully, he and his men had found a small herd of wild horses late in the afternoon of their first day of searching. The mustangs were grazing on the sparse, yellowed grass in a canyon north of Brit's camp. He and his men had chosen a spot at the mouth of the shallow, U-shaped canyon to spend the night. Their position would block the horses' escape, should they try to slip away under the cover of darkness.

That morning, the men had mounted up and divided into two groups. After surrounding the herd, they drove the horses out of the canyon, then turned them south.

Though the horses numbered only several dozen, Brit was satisfied they were in good health and would not suffer from the long trip to his parents' *rancho*. The herd's lead mare was an especially fine-looking animal, a bay with a white star on her forehead, and would be an excellent addition to his own growing stable of breeding stock.

On the ride back to his camp, Brit found he could not keep his mind from drifting to Katelyn. He could still taste the incredible sweetness of her mouth, feel the silky, softness of her cheek. He imagined her on the bed he had shared with her for so many nights, the single golden braid laying on her chest, rising and falling with each breath. He longed to push the braid aside and bare her breasts, to touch her with his fingers, then with his tongue and lips.

His body reacted instantly to the picture he'd created in his imagination. He shifted in the saddle, trying to ease the tightness in his groin. But to no avail. Though he tried to concentrate on keeping the herd of horses bunched together and moving at a steady pace, his mind refused to cooperate. Once again his thoughts continued to dwell on the woman back at his camp in the hidden canyon.

Pressing his lips together in a firm line, he jerked his horse's reins to the left, then touched his heels to the gray's sides. The animal instantly bolted forward.

When Brit drew even with Tomás, he slowed his horse to a walk. "I am going back ahead of you," he said. "You are in charge."

Tomás started at Brit's words. Never had his friend taken off while herding wild horses—he had always worked as hard and as long as the rest of his men. Narrowing his eyes, Tomás said, "Is something wrong? Are your wounds bothering you? You have always helped escort the horses we have captured back to our camp."

"No. Nothing is wrong, and I feel fine." Seeing the questions in Tomás's eyes, Brit was unable to hold his gaze. He didn't like having to explain his actions, especially when the explanation was his weakness for a *gringa*. Angry at himself for not being able to overcome such a weakness, his voice turned harsh. "You do not doubt your ability to get these horses to our camp without me, do you?"

Surprised by Brit's sarcasm, Tomás stiffened in the saddle. "No, I can handle the horses as well as you," he replied, then added with a sneer, *"jefe."*

Brit wished he could take back his words, but perhaps it was better to leave his friend this way. As long as Tomás was angry, he would ask no more questions. "You will have no problem with this small herd. Just keep them moving, and you should arrive at our canyon by nightfall."

Not waiting for Tomás to reply, Brit pulled his horse away from the herd, then kicked the gray into a trot.

Tomás watched Brit disappear ahead of the herd, his mouth pulled into a frown. What was on the mind of his friend? When the answer came to him, he threw back his head and roared with laughter. A yellow-haired *gringa* with a sharp tongue. *Oh, my friend, you are getting yourself into deep trouble. You cannot continue to hate all* gringos, *when you are falling for one of their women.*

Several hours later, Brit arrived at his camp, his gaze immediately searching the area for the blond-haired woman he could not keep from his thoughts. After dismounting and turning his horse over to Lorenzo, Brit strode to the campfire.

Lutero rose to greet him. "I did not expect you so soon, *Señor* Brit. Why have you returned without the others? Is something wrong?"

His jaw clenched at being asked again about his motives. "No. Everything is fine." His gaze continued to scour the campsite. "I decided to come ahead of the rest, so I left Tomás in charge of bringing in the herd of horses we captured."

Seeing Brit glance around the area, Lutero took a deep breath, then said, *"Señor* Brit, I must tell—"

Before he could finish, Brit said, "Where is she?"

Juan jumped up from where he'd been sitting by the fire and stepped in front of Lutero. *"Jefe,* it is my fault. I take full responsibility, and will accept whatever punishment you say I deserve."

Brit's eyebrows pulled together in a scowl. "What are you talking about, Juan? What is your fault?"

Juan forced himself to meet his boss's fierce gaze, then said, *"La señorita* is gone. She took all of our horses and left yesterday morning."

Brit's scowl deepened. "If that is true, then how is it all of the horses are now in the corral?"

Swallowing hard, Juan said, "Three horses came back last night. She must have let them go when she thought she was far enough away that we would not be able to follow her."

"And the fourth horse?"

Juan's Adam's apple bobbed several times. In a strangled voice, he said, "That horse, the sorrel mare, returned this morning. She is favoring her right foreleg."

Brit drew in a sharp breath. If the horse Katelyn rode had returned injured, did that mean she had also suffered some mishap? The possibility filled him with a gut-wrenching fear. Though he was angry she had escaped, at the moment he was more concerned for her safety.

Pointing toward the fire, he said, "Lutero, get me a plate of food. And, Juan, saddle one of the other horses. I will look for her as soon as I have something to eat."

After a hastily eaten meal, Brit swung into the saddle. Turning to the three men who stood watching him, he said, "Do you know which direction she took?"

"The tracks led to the east, deeper into the canyon," Juan replied. "And that is the direction the horses came from when they returned."

Brit nodded, then said, "I will not be back until I have found her." Jabbing his heels to the horse, he leaned over the animal's neck as it raced across the clearing, then agilely moved through the oak trees.

Katelyn tripped over a fallen tree and went down hard on her hands and knees. Sitting down with a half-sob, she willed herself not to cry. Crying wouldn't solve anything, and it certainly wouldn't get her out of the maze of the mountain wilderness.

She looked down at her hands. They were filthy, and

covered with more scrapes than she could count, the result of trying to pass through a thicket of chaparral with long thorns. An encounter that had left several scratches on her right cheek as well. She ran her palms over her skirt to wipe off the worst of the dirt, but with little success. The pink muslin was in the same sorry state as her hands.

Her shoes and the hem of her dress were covered with a black, oily residue from a fernlike plant growing in a thick carpet beneath the pine forest. Only after she'd walked through a dense patch of the foot-high plants did she realize their sticky leaves were responsible for the coat of oily film on her shoes and clothes. When she discovered the oil gave off a horrible resinous odor and was nearly impossible to remove, she took care to avoid areas where the plants were plentiful.

Taking a deep breath, she grabbed the handles of her carpetbag, then slowly got to her feet. She had to keep moving. Though she'd been walking all day, and had yet to stumble on Brit's camp, she knew she had to continue. She was bound to find the camp, or a road to lead her out of the mountains. At least, she prayed that was true.

She started walking again, struggling to contain her growing fear. Having no food and only the water in the canteen she carried, her future didn't look very promising at the moment. But she couldn't let panic overtake her. Glancing up at the sky, she nearly lost her precarious self-control. Darkness was fast approaching, which meant— She shivered at the terrifying thought of having to spend another night in the mountains.

Forcing herself to push on, she decided she'd better use what little daylight was left to find a place to sleep.

Brit halted his horse. He'd been looking for hours, and with each passing minute his fear for Katelyn grew. Sometime during his search, he'd made a startling realization—he truly cared for Katelyn. It wasn't just concern for her safety, but a much deeper, more substantial feeling, a feeling he couldn't remember ever having experienced. Even his feelings for Mirabella—and he had truly cared for his fiancée—didn't compare to what he now felt for Katelyn.

He shook his head to clear such thoughts. He couldn't allow himself to feel anything but hatred for the *gringa*. Blowing out an exasperated breath, he nudged his horse forward.

Checking the trail in front of him, he wondered why Katelyn continued to head north. Once she left the canyon where his camp was located, she should have circled around and headed west. Instead, she had changed to a northerly direction. Perhaps she thought she could better elude him, if she took an unexpected route out of the mountains. Whatever her reasons, he only had an hour of daylight left, and he wanted to put it to good use.

If he didn't find Katelyn soon, he would be forced to end his search for the night and find a place to camp. He meant what he had told Lutero and the others. He would not return until he found her.

Just as darkness was ready to throw its cloak over the mountains, Brit spotted a place next to a fallen tree where the ground had been disturbed. Dismounting, he examined the area carefully. Leaves and pine needles had been shoved aside, exposing a small patch of damp, reddish-colored earth. Brit bent closer, then smiled. There was a distinct impression of a hand in the dirt. He knew in his heart the impression was that of Katelyn's hand.

Closing his eyes for a moment, he lifted his face to the sky and whispered a brief prayer of thanks. At least he knew she was alive.

Standing, he circled the fallen tree, searching for a sign to indicate which direction she had taken. Finding places where the ends of tree branches were bent or broken and the undergrowth trampled, he swung back onto his horse.

It seemed like hours before he finally found what he'd been praying for. Huddled against the trunk of a yellow pine, Katelyn sat like a statue. Knees drawn up under her chin, arms wrapped around her legs, she held her carpetbag clutched against her ankles. Head resting atop her knees, her face was turned away from him.

Brit slipped off his horse, looped the reins around the branches of a manzanita, then moved toward her.

"Katelyn," he called softly.

Her head came up with a snap. She turned to look at him, eyes wide, mouth opened and ready to scream. The absolute terror on her face caused an intense pain in his chest.

"It is all right, Katelyn. I have found you, *cardillo mío*. You will be fine," he said, keeping his voice gentle.

He moved closer, stopping a few feet from her. When she did not respond, or appear to recognize him, his own fear grew. "Katelyn?"

He held his breath, his gaze never leaving her face. Her carpetbag clutched in one hand, she struggled to her feet. As he reached for her, she took a step back, slowly shaking her head. "No, don't touch me."

"Do not be afraid. It is over now." In one quick motion, he closed the distance between them and wrapped her in his arms. She tried to pull away, wiggling and twisting against him.

"Leave me alone. Get your hands off me."

"Katelyn, you are safe now. There is no need to fight me. I will not hurt you." When she continued to struggle, he held her at arm's length, then said, "Look at me, *querida*. I am Brit. I mean you no harm."

She ceased her efforts to free herself. Her breathing a labored wheeze, she lifted her face to stare up at him.

As recognition dawned, he watched her panic recede. Her eyes lost their glazed appearance, the tenseness of her body relaxed. He released his hold, then dropped his arms to his sides. "Are you—" His words were interrupted by her carpetbag coming at him.

Dodging her wild swing, he snatched the bag from her hands. "What are you doing?"

"You scared the wits out of me," she said. "How dare you frighten me like that?"

Biting the inside of his lip at the sudden display of temper on the heels of her previous terror, he swept his gaze from the tangled mass of blond hair to the badly stained hem of her dress. "Are you hurt? I found a place not far from here where you fell."

She shook her head. "I have some cuts and scrapes. I made the mistake of trying to tangle with an uncooperative chaparral and its thorns." She flashed a smile, then turned serious. "I am truly glad you found me. If you hadn't, I would have wandered through these mountains until—" His fingers pressed to her lips cut off her words.

"Do not speak of it, *querida*. I did find you, that is the only thing that matters."

At her nod, he said, "Come, we have a long ride back to camp." He took her hand and turned toward his horse. When her knees started to give way, he grasped her arms to steady her.

"I hate feeling so weak," she said.

He smiled. "You have had quite an ordeal. There is no shame in feeling weak." Seeing the uncertainty on her face, he couldn't resist pressing a brief kiss on her lips.

When he lifted his head, he met her luminous gaze and smiled again. "We must get back, so I can see to your cuts." Before she could reply, he put one hand around her shoulders, the other beneath her knees, and lifted her into his arms.

He was nearly to his horse, when she said, "My carpetbag!"

"I will get it. Can you stand?" When she nodded, he dropped the hand beneath her knees and let her feet slide to the ground. He kept his other hand around her waist until she could stand without his assistance, then turned to walk away.

"Wait!"

He swung back to her. "What is it?"

"I'm afraid I lost one of your horses. The mare I rode—"

Again he cut off her words with his fingers. "The mare is not lost. She returned to camp, limping but otherwise fine."

"Really? She isn't seriously hurt?"

"No. Juan said it is only a stone bruise." He started to turn away, when he saw a look of distress cross her face. "Is there something else?"

"I had to leave the saddle after the mare left me. It was too heavy for me to carry."

"Do not worry about it, *querida*. I will have one of my men get it. Do you know where you left it?"

"In a small canyon, umm . . . that way." She pointed behind them. "Or was it that way?" She pointed in the opposite direction. "I'm not sure where the canyon is."

"Well, it cannot be too far away. I will tell my men where I found you, then they will be able to find the canyon."

When she said no more, he retrieved her carpetbag. He tied it behind the cantle of his saddle, then swung onto the horse. Reaching down to Katelyn, he pulled her up in front of him.

Trying to hold herself away from him, she murmured, "I don't think you're going to want me too close to you."

"Why not?"

She made a face, then said, "There's something all over my dress and my shoes. I couldn't wash it off, and it smells terrible."

He chuckled. "I noticed." Hearing her small gasp, he said, "Do not be embarrassed, the smell is fading. Everyone who has been in these mountains has smelled like that at least once. Did you walk beneath trees where a plant resembling a fern covered the ground?" She nodded. "The Indians call the plant kit-kit-dizze, but as you have learned, it is also called mountain misery. You now know, like the rest of us, to avoid the plant."

Wrapping one arm around her and pulling her close, he picked up the reins with his other hand. "Ready?" he whispered.

At her nod, he directed the horse forward at a slow walk.

They had traveled for only a few minutes when Katelyn's head fell back against Brit's chest. Sighing, she cuddled closer, pressing her nose and cheek to the base of his throat. The slow, easy cadence of her breathing told him she had fallen asleep.

The feel of her full breasts beneath his arm, her soft bottom sitting across his thighs, the gentle whispering of her breath on his neck, quickly stoked Brit's desire into a raging inferno. Never had he wanted a woman as much as he wanted Katelyn. She was a fever in his blood, a fever that could only be cooled in one way. He closed his eyes, fighting his lust for the woman nestled so trustingly in his arms.

The teachings of his culture, that a woman's virtue is both precious and sacred, were hard to ignore. Even so, he was ready to risk whatever punishment might be doled out for such a breach in conduct. He had always prided himself in following the rules he'd been taught. This time he had fought the battle and lost.

Accepting the bitter taste of defeat was made easier by another revelation. Making Katelyn his would not only satisfy his physical hunger, but it would have another more important ramification—putting a stop to her newspaper editorials. Surely she would not continue writing about a man with whom she had become intimately involved.

Then another thought occurred to Brit. Taking Katelyn's virginity would be the perfect revenge for Mirabella. Like the Bible said, an eye for an eye. Only in this case, the verse would be modified to one maidenhead for another.

Though he intended to carry out the decision he'd just made to use Katelyn as a pawn in his thirst for vengeance, his conscience objected vehemently. Squashing such misgivings, he turned his thoughts to the pleasure awaiting him, the pleasure of sinking into Katelyn's sweet body and claiming her as his.

The hour was well past midnight by the time Brit arrived back at his camp. He pulled the horse to a halt by the campfire, roused the sleeping Katelyn, lifted her into his arms, and dismounted.

Lutero stirred in his bedroll next to the fire. Sitting up, he looked up at Katelyn's torn clothes and scratched face. "Did you hurt her?" he asked in Spanish.

"No!" Brit glared at the older man, hurt and angry that Lutero would think such a thing. He tried not to think about what the cook's reaction would be to the decision he'd made just hours earlier. "She has only a few small cuts from a fall. She said she is not hurt seriously. I will examine her later to see if she spoke the truth." Feeling Katelyn stir in his arms, he switched to English. "Get her something to eat. I will see to the horse, then come back for her."

Brit lowered Katelyn to the ground, then led the horse to the corral.

Lutero threw off his blanket and got to his feet. *"Un momento, señorita,* and I will get you a plate of *puchero.* I kept it warm for when *Señor* Brit brought you back. I knew you would be hungry."

Katelyn thanked him, then dug into the tasty stew.

Brit returned just as she finished. "You can go back to bed now, Lutero." Turning to Katelyn, he held his hand out to her. "Come, I will take you to my cabin."

Her heart thrumming wildly, she looked up at him, then

laid her hand in his. She resisted the urge to shiver at both the feel of his palm and the husky tone of his voice.

Inside his cabin, Brit motioned for Katelyn to sit on the bed. After pouring water into a basin, he removed his hat, gun belt, and vest, then moved to the bed. Kneeling in front of her, he pulled off her shoes and stockings, then lifted his hands to the placket of her dress. She shrank back from his touch, eyes wide, lips slightly parted.

"I will not hurt you, *querida*. I only want to make sure you have no serious injuries."

She nodded, holding still while he unbuttoned her dress, then slipped the pink muslin off her shoulders and arms. While he gently washed her many cuts and scrapes, she watched his face. His dark eyebrows drawn together in concentration, a muscle jerked in his jaw. She longed to run her fingers over the severe line of his lips, to press a fingertip into the cleft in his chin once again. She could do neither, since he held her hands firmly in his.

"Your poor hands. And your cheek," he murmured, raising his head to look at the long scratches on the right side of her face. "You should not have gone into the mountains alone."

"I know," she replied, refusing to meet his gaze.

"You should have stayed here and waited for me to return."

"*You* think I should have waited here. But I didn't, did I? For all I knew, I could have died of old age before you returned."

He glared at her. "So, you are not sorry you tried to escape?"

"Yes, I'm sorry," she snapped. "Sorry I wasn't successful."

Her blatant spark of defiance should have fired his smoldering temper. Strangely, it not only cooled his irritation, but also ignited another emotion.

"I am not sorry you did not succeed, *cardillo mío*," he said, lifting her hands and placing a kiss on each palm.

Raising her face, she met his gaze. The heat of his mouth flowing from her hands to her breasts, then lower to her belly, she sucked in a ragged breath.

The look in his eyes told Katelyn what was about to happen, something she had intuitively known would take place from the moment they met. Some time over the past weeks, she had accepted the fact that she and Brit were destined to become lovers.

Seeing the desire throbbing in his body reflected on her face, Brit quickly pulled off her dress, then reached for the hem of her chemise.

Before she realized his intent, he pulled the garment up and over her head in one swift movement. She gasped, crossing her arms over her breasts. No one had ever seen her naked, not even— She halted that line of thinking. She forced herself to remember that the man with her was Brit—handsome, wonderfully masculine Brit.

Grasping her hands, he pulled them away. "No, let me look at you," he ordered softly. Her full breasts rose and fell with each breath, their dark coral tips tightening into hard buds under his watchful gaze. He longed to cover them with his lips, to draw them into his mouth, to suckle them and lave them with his tongue. But he held himself in check. There would be time enough for that later.

As he reached for the ribbon at the waist of her drawers, she stiffened, but made no move to stop him. When he gave the ribbon a tug, freeing the bow, she closed her eyes, certain her cheeks had turned scarlet.

"Raise up, *querida*."

She complied, then felt the soft rasp of her drawers being pulled down over her hips and thighs. Then she sat before him, completely naked. Her cheeks warmed even more.

He gently cupped her shoulders with his hands and pushed her down onto the bed until she lay flat on her back.

He dropped his hands and sat back on his heels. Taking a deep breath, his gaze moved slowly over her body with its cream-colored skin, high, full breasts, and narrow waist above flaring hips. When he lowered his gaze to the dark blond hair at the base of her concave stomach, he nearly lost control. Gritting his teeth, he forced himself to move his gaze beyond the temptation hidden between her silky thighs. Long, well-shaped legs and small, thigh-arched feet completed his perusal.

She was even more beautiful than in his imagination. He closed his eyes for a moment, willing his breathing to return to normal. He reached out to touch her. To his amazement, his hand quivered slightly.

As Brit ran his fingers across the scratches on her cheek, down the length of her neck, then over her collarbone, he whispered something in Spanish.

Her eyes still closed, Katelyn's brow furrowed. Surely she'd heard wrong. No one had ever called her beautiful. Though she had accepted her looks as nothing grander than pleasingly plain long ago, she was almost certain Brit had said *bella*. Was it possible this handsome man saw beauty in her, where others had not? The idea seemed inconceivable.

Feeling the coolness of something wet on her skin, Katelyn's eyes popped open. Brit was bathing her! Her gaze riveted to his face, she didn't move as he rubbed a cloth over her body. A fire blazed hot and dangerous in his eyes, burning her wherever his gaze touched. Then he followed with the cloth, the cool water soothing the heat.

Katelyn could not think of anything more erotic than having the man she loved bathe her. It was like nothing she had ever— She blinked. Love! Did she love Brit?

The answer was immediate. Yes, she loved him. She wasn't sure how it happened, but it was true. Though he professed to hate her as he hated all other *gringos,* and she had promised herself to see him punished for his part in her father's death, she had somehow fallen in love with him.

Otherwise, she would never consider allowing what was about to happen. And she desperately wanted him to make love to her. There might never be another chance for her to experience the joy of making love with the man she would want, under different circumstances, to spend the rest of her life with.

She started when she realized he had finished bathing her. Looking up, she met his intense gaze.

"Soon, you will be mine, *querida,*" he whispered. "All mine."

Eleven

Katelyn nodded, never taking her gaze from his. Brit stared at her long and hard, then abruptly got to his feet.

He pulled off his boots, then reached for his shirt. As he fumbled with the buttons, he silently cursed his shaking hands. He had never been this eager for a woman, not even before his first time many years ago, when he and his brother had been initiated into manhood by a Mexican widow old enough to be their mother.

Brit remembered sitting nervously in the woman's parlor after Antonio had been ushered into her bedroom. But the anticipation he'd experienced while waiting for his turn was nothing compared to the eagerness he felt for his golden thistle.

In that instant, he hated himself for not being able to control his desire for a *gringa,* for wanting to make love with her. He clenched his teeth. It would *not* be making love, he reminded himself. It would simply be a brief coupling to accomplish his goal. Somehow the rationalization only increased his anger, though he could not pinpoint exactly why.

He had decided taking Katelyn's maidenhead fit perfectly into his plans for revenge. However, he hadn't expected the decision would make him want her so much. He tried to slow his fingers' hurried fumblings, with little success.

For modesty's sake, Katelyn knew she should look away, or at least close her eyes while Brit hastily removed his clothes. But she found she could not make herself do so. She watched with growing fascination as he ripped off his shirt, revealing his heavily muscled chest still swathed in the bandages she had put on him several days before. Visually checking each place she had wrapped his knife wounds, she sighed with relief when she found no fresh bloodstains on the white cloth.

Her gaze dropped lower, tracing the narrowing, dark line of hair from his chest to where it disappeared beneath the waistband of his trousers. As if drawn by her gaze, his dark hands moved to the place of her perusal. With agile fingers, he worked the buttons free, then slowly pushed the dark cloth down over his hips.

As he shoved the fabric lower, Katelyn held her breath. The skin beneath his trousers was not as dark as his upper body, though still several shades darker than her own. Her fingers twitched with the need to touch him, to again test the texture of his dusky-colored skin. When the source of the dark hair she found so fascinating was revealed, her eyes widened, her pent-up breath escaping in a soft rush.

Cheeks burning, she lifted her gaze. The look on his face was so fierce, his features could have been made of stone. His clenched jaw and hooded eyes gave her no insight as to what he was thinking.

"You like what you see, *querida?*"

She started at the anger in his voice. Though she wished she could throw an equally sarcastic remark back at him, her mind went blank. When he tipped his head to one side in anticipation of her answer, she swallowed hard, then nodded.

His face softened somewhat at her response, a slight smile curving his lips. "I like what I see as well," he said, tossing his clothes aside. He put one knee on the bed, then lowered himself down beside her.

Unable to resist his nearness, Katelyn lifted one hand to touch his chest. Her fingers skimmed over the hair-covered muscles, reacquainting herself with their contours and sending a tingling throughout her body.

"Ah, you are eager," Brit whispered, grasping her hand and pulling it lower.

Shivering at his words, she realized she was eager, more eager than she could have imagined. "I . . . Yes, I do want to—" Her words came to a halt as he wrapped her fingers around his engorged shaft. Reacting instinctively to the velvet feel of him, her hand closed tighter.

His hips bucked forward at the ecstasy of her touch, a low groan rumbled in his chest. Squeezing his eyes closed, he threw back his head and gritted his teeth. He had not been with a woman in a very long time and was extremely close to losing control.

He pulled her hand from his throbbing flesh, then took several deep breaths to cool the fire raging in his blood. For the moment, the reason for her lying naked in his bed was forgotten. All he could think of was the pleasure awaiting them.

"We will take it slowly, *querida*. I do not want to hurt you."

Katelyn blinked with surprise. Hurt her? What was he— She closed her eyes, holding in a sob of panic. *Oh, God, I'd forgotten. He thinks I'm a virgin. How will he react when he finds out I'm not?* For a moment, she considered jumping up off the bed, so she wouldn't have to learn the answer to that question. But then Brit's fingers settled over one breast, gently rolling the nipple between his fingertips. Her misgivings instantly melted away. No matter what he did when he discovered the truth, no matter how fierce his reaction, she would have this one memory to keep forever.

Opening her eyes, she stared up into his face. Though still harsh, his features were now taut with concentration. When his gaze lifted from her breasts, moving up her neck and across her cheek, she could feel the raw heat of the desire burning in his eyes. When their gazes met and locked,

Katelyn bit her lip to prevent her feelings from tumbling out. He would not take kindly to such a confession. After all, he hated all Yankees, including her.

Wise enough to realize his desire for a *gringa* was tearing him apart, she knew she could not speak of her love now, perhaps never. Rather then saying the words, she would show him in the only way she could. Putting her arms around his shoulders, she pulled him down until their mouths were only inches apart.

"Kiss me, Brit," she whispered. "Kiss me and make everything but the two of us disappear."

He blinked, then smiled at her boldness. *"Sí cardillo mío.* I will take us to a world where only you and I exist."

Closing the distance between them, he touched his lips to the scratches on her cheek, then moved to her mouth. What started out as a gentle kiss soon escalated into a more savage blending of their lips. He suckled her lower lip, then nibbled on the soft flesh with his teeth. He explored the interior of her mouth with his tongue, until she lay panting and writhing in his arms.

He finally broke the kiss and lifted his head. His own breathing labored, he watched her eyelids flutter upward. Her eyes were dilated with desire, their color darkened to a deep blue. He placed a kiss on her chin, then moved lower to take one coral nipple into his mouth.

Katelyn moaned, her hips coming up off the bed. Brit smiled around the hardened flesh he held between his lips. Her response and obvious eagerness stoked his already blazing desire to even hotter heights.

Determined to make her first time an enjoyable one, he moved his hand from the soft underside of her breast to trail across her sleek belly. His fingers delved into the silky blond triangle of hair. She moaned again, her hips jerking in reaction to his touch. When he opened the soft folds and found the bud of flesh already swollen and damp, his moan joined hers.

Working the hardened bud with his fingers, he continued alternately licking and suckling her nipples. Her breathing a rasping pant, she rolled her head from side to side. "Brit," she groaned. "Please. I can't stand— Please!"

The urgency in her voice nearly broke his grip on the iron fist he used to control his own desire. His fingers stopped their insistent movement. Releasing her nipple, he lifted his head and stared at the wet coral tip for several seconds, then moved his gaze to her face. Her parted lips beckoned him, and he heeded their welcome. Capturing her mouth with his, he shifted positions, pushing her legs apart and settling on his knees between her opened thighs.

Breaking the kiss, he sat back on his heels. He took the time to savor one more look at the kiss-swollen lips, the heaving breasts wet from his mouth, the pink nubbin of flesh peeking from the dark blond hair between her thighs. As he bent over her, he pushed her legs farther apart and leaned closer. When his manhood grazed the soft skin of her inner thigh, a low, keening groan escaped his throat.

Now that the moment Brit had been waiting for was upon him, his desire cooled enough for him to recall why he had decided he must have Katelyn. Grasping his engorged shaft, he guided himself to her and pushed forward until he had barely entered her warmth.

"You will soon know *El Buitre* in the most intimate of ways," he murmured, grasping her bottom and lifting her off the bed. The movement pushed him deeper. He bit back another groan.

Katelyn flinched, but made no move to stop him. Unable to stand the strange look in his black eyes, she let her eyelids drift closed.

"No! Look at me," he commanded, bringing her eyes open with a start. "I want you to look at me when I take your—" He clamped his mouth shut, unable to finish what he'd wanted to tell her. His control was quickly slipping away, requiring every bit of his concentration. The muscles of his chest and arms bunched, then relaxed.

Unable to speak, he was determined to end this quest for revenge quickly. With one mighty thrust of his hips, he pushed forward until he was completely sheathed inside her. He heard her sudden indrawn breath, then only the loud pounding of his heart in his ears. Though vaguely aware she had not cried out in pain, his mind was focused solely on the incredible feel of her slick, tight passage.

In a slow, steady rhythm, he rocked forward, then back. He buried himself as deeply as possible, then withdrew until only the tip of his manhood remained within her body. He wanted this to last forever, but feared he could not go on much longer, not with the way her inner muscles milked his throbbing arousal with each stroke.

Katelyn locked her arms around his neck, then pulled his head down to hers. When his mouth was just above hers, she rose up to press her lips against his. She kissed him as he'd kissed her, licking and biting, then slipping her tongue into his mouth. His groan told her she had learned the lesson well.

Her heels digging into the mattress of blankets, she lifted her hips to meet each of his downward thrusts. Pressure began to build where their bodies were joined. Warmth radiated outward from that place, rushing through her with lightning speed. She whimpered, knowing she needed to find relief from such delicious torment, but unsure how to reach that elusive end.

Sensing her distress, Brit tore his mouth from hers. His breathing ragged, he braced his weight above her on one forearm and shifted his position so he could lower one hand to between her thighs. When his fingers touched her swollen bud, she gasped, her hips bucking against his hand in reaction.

Holding onto his control with all the strength he had left, he was determined she would not be denied her pleasure.

He didn't take the time to analyze why the pleasure of a *gringa* was important to him, he only knew it was.

Using both his fingers and hips, he began moving again. He carefully watched Katelyn's face, picking up his rhythm when he sensed her release was near. He didn't have long to wait. With a high-pitched scream, her body tensed, then convulsed with tremor after powerful tremor.

At the first contraction of her inner muscles, Brit held back as long as he could, then gave himself over to what his body craved. After several quick thrusts, he pushed as far into her as he could, then held perfectly still. Keeping his lips clamped shut so he wouldn't shout out loud, he allowed himself to seek relief. His release began, a wild throbbing against Katelyn's womb. Her continuing contractions brought forth a groan he could not stop.

Arching her back, she pushed against him one last time, then collapsed on the bed. A few seconds later, he fell atop her, his face pressed to her neck.

Though his breathing came in harsh pants, he managed to whisper, "You are mine now. You are mine."

Through the haze of her incredible climax, Katelyn heard Brit's words and wished they were true. But she knew he had been aware he had not taken a virgin to his bed. She had felt his body tense at the exact moment he realized he had not broken through the barrier he had expected. And she knew it was only a matter of time before he, too, remembered.

Closing her eyes, she drew a deep breath, then exhaled slowly. If only things could be different. But for now, she was determined to be content with just being with Brit. For now she would enjoy what pleasure she could in being with him and not think about the future. Because she knew all too well, for them, there was no future.

After Brit's breathing and heart rate returned to normal, he rolled off of Katelyn without saying a word. He was appalled at what had just happened. He had actually enjoyed taking her! No, he had not only enjoyed the most spectacular coupling he had ever experienced, he had taken the time to make sure she, too, reached her peak of pleasure.

Pinching the bridge of his nose, he stifled a groan. How had he let it happen? How could he actually find so much enjoyment in the taking of a *gringa*'s virginity?

He jerked his hand from his face. Lips pressed into a thin line, he sat up, then swung his feet to the floor. Looking down at himself, he saw no blood on his manhood. So, it was true. *Miss* Katelyn Ferguson had not been a virgin.

He clenched his hands into fists on his thighs; a muscle ticked in his cheek. Just as quickly as his temper flared, a new thought immediately cooled his ire. Though not happy about being thwarted in his attempt to avenge Mirabella in the same way she had been used, there was a positive side to this latest turn of events. At least he could have the woman lying in his bed whenever he wanted.

And based on how his body was beginning to respond even after the unbelievable climax he'd just experienced, he would have her often. The fever in his blood for her should have abated after their initial joining. Yet, even now, just minutes after his first taste of her passion, his desire continued to run hot and rampant through his veins.

Snorting with self-derision, he rose from the bed and stalked across the cabin.

Katelyn watched Brit's movements, her bottom lip caught between her teeth. She wished she knew what he was thinking. Would there be even more hatred in his eyes when he looked at her? As if responding to her thoughts, he turned toward the bed. She immediately sought his gaze with hers. Her brow furrowed. She could detect no hatred, or even anger in his dark eyes. What she saw looked more like desire. She lowered her gaze, then gasped.

Using the cloth he'd used on her cuts, he was washing himself, his manhood swelling more with each stroke of his hand. Her gaze darted back to his face, where she found him staring at her, a faint smile twisting his lips.

When he finished with the cloth, he hunkered down to rinse it in the basin. Then he stood up and crossed the room to the bed, the cloth once again in his hand.

Raising up on one elbow, she said, "What are you going to do?"

He made a sound, somewhere between a laugh and a snort, then replied, "I am going to bathe my seed from your thighs, then I am going to enjoy your body again. After all, since you were not a virgin, I do not have to be concerned that you are too sore." His eyebrows arched. "Do I, *Miss* Ferguson?"

Katelyn could say nothing; there was nothing she could say. He would never believe she was already sore, that it had been four years since the one and only time she had been with a man. From the look on his face and his aroused state, he would not listen even if she tried to explain. With a sigh, she dropped back onto the bed.

At the first touch of the cool cloth on her leg, her body jerked in reaction. Murmuring for her to lie still, he wiped the sticky wetness from her inner thighs. She complied, her cheeks burning with embarrassment as he moved to cleanse her most intimate place. Keeping her gaze on the roof of the cabin, she tried not to be affected by his touch. Her efforts did little good. In spite of not wanting to respond to him, her breathing became erratic, her body tingling with renewed desire. Soon she squirmed restlessly beneath his hands.

When he tossed the cloth aside and stretched out on the bed beside her, she welcomed him with open arms and eager lips. Katelyn knew she would likely be condemned to hell for what she was doing, but she couldn't help herself. Brit sparked a fire in her veins which only he could put out. But not before fanning the flames even hotter and taking her to incredible heights of rapture she had only dreamed of attaining.

He rolled atop her and slipped inside her spread thighs in one swift movement. Pulling her legs up around his waist, he sank even farther into her welcoming depths, wrenching a moan from deep inside his chest. He repeatedly thrust, then nearly withdrew in a gentle, easy rhythm, letting the tension build slowly.

Keeping their bodies joined, he suddenly rolled to his left, until they lay face to face on their sides. He continued thrusting into her, picking up the pace and brushing her mouth in brief kisses.

"Tell me when you are close to your finish, *querida*," he whispered against her mouth. "I want to feel you convulse around me before I spill myself inside you." At her nod, he pressed another kiss on her parted lips, then moved his mouth to her neck and the wild throbbing of her pulse below her ear.

His fingers again working their magic on her sensitive flesh, she felt the pressure build, the heat increase until an explosion was imminent. Her hips bucked against him, faster and faster.

"Now. Now, Brit," she managed to croak before she lost the ability to speak, her body throbbing and quivering with the strength of her release.

He stopped the movement of his hips and leaned back to watch her climax overtake her. He saw her neck arch backward, felt her fingers grip his arm, her inner muscles tug at his manhood. With a growl, he began thrusting again. Harder and faster. Then before he could stop it, he was spilling himself deep inside her and shouting his pleasure at the top of his lungs.

A few minutes later, he summoned what strength he had left to ease away from Katelyn, then roll onto his back. He closed his eyes, cursing himself silently for letting his plans go awry once more. He had planned to take her for only his own enjoyment. He had never allowed himself to lose control while in the arms of a woman. Much to his shame, he had not only shouted like a madman, he'd also been compelled again to make sure their joining left her totally fulfilled.

A sharp rap on the cabin door jarred Brit from his thoughts.

"Jefe? Is everything all right?" Juan said in an anxious whisper through the closed door.

"Sí, Juan. Everything is fine." Avoiding Katelyn's gaze, he added, "I just . . . I just removed my bandages and tore open one of my cuts."

"Should I bring you another bottle of Grandfather's mescal?"

"No. It is nothing. Go back to bed," Brit replied.

After Juan's footsteps faded, Brit wondered if he should have agreed to the mescal. Perhaps the potent liquor would ease his hurt—not the hurt caused by his cuts, which had lessened to little more than an occasional dull ache, but the hurt caused by the unfamiliar pain deep in his chest.

He never thought the hatred he'd harbored for so long would waver. Before he'd met Katelyn, it had always burned hot and strong—a constant reminder of his purpose in life. Now the hate he wanted so desperately to keep alive was inexplicably undergoing a change. And even worse, he seemed unable to stop the transformation into an emotion on the opposite end of the spectrum, an emotion he did not want in his life.

If he allowed himself to love Katelyn, he would never satisfy his need for vengeance. But he wasn't sure there was anything he could do to keep his heart uninvolved.

Katelyn stirred, rolling away from him to face the wall. In seconds, he heard the slow, even cadence of her sleep. Ignoring the urge to snuggle behind her, to press his body against the length of hers, he willed himself to get the rest he needed.

Tomorrow, he'd figure out how to stop the progression of his feelings for Katelyn, but not tonight. Tonight, the pain of her not being a virgin was too fresh, his emotions too raw, his exhaustion too complete.

Twelve

Ross Carter opened his jackknife, then slipped the blade under the envelope's flap. He had started opening the *Argus'* mail a week after Katelyn's disappearance, thinking he might learn something about her whereabouts. The responsibility of running two newspapers was wearing thin, and in spite of Jake's obvious objection, Ross continued to read every piece of mail the *Argus* received.

Folding the knife and slipping it back into his trouser pocket, Ross pulled a single sheet of paper from the envelope and unfolded it. One hand lightly stroking his beard, he read the scrawled message addressed to the Editor of the *Argus.*

Since you believe El Buitre *should be stopped, I have information you will find most interesting. If you are willing to pay for what I know, meet me at midnight on Friday behind the Orleans Hotel.*

A wide smile replaced Ross's frown of concentration. Well, perhaps he hadn't learned anything about Katelyn, but he had stumbled onto this one stroke of luck. Even if Katelyn had been in town, he knew she couldn't afford to pay whoever sent the note, so he would go in her stead. It was about time his *Tribune* had a chance to be the first to print a new story about *El Buitre.*

He tucked the letter into his jacket pocket, wished Jake good day, then left the *Argus* office and headed up K Street.

Whistling a carefree tune, Ross decided the day had turned out better than he'd thought—a whole lot better.

Over the first few days following Brit's discovery regarding Katelyn's lack of innocence, he worked himself harder than usual—checking the new herd of horses for sickness or signs of lameness, helping with their feeding, working with Solazo, continually pushing himself to the very limits of his endurance—all so he wouldn't think about Katelyn.

His efforts proved successful for only short periods of time. No matter what he did or where he looked, everything served as a reminder of her. The sun glinting off Solazo's coat reminded him of Katelyn's glorious hair, the clear blue of the cloudless sky was a perfect match for her lovely eyes, the warm summer wind rippling across his skin felt like her gentle touch.

Each time thoughts of Katelyn intruded into his mind, he worked all the harder to keep them at bay. He wanted to be so exhausted, so physically spent, that his desire would not stir when he finally sought his bed. But even on the nights he purposely worked until well past dark, then stayed away from his cabin until he was certain she had fallen asleep, his plans went for naught.

Though he tried to be quiet when he entered the cabin, she always stirred as soon as he stretched out next to her. Then she would roll toward him and snuggle close. At the first touch of her soft skin against his body, his desire roared to life, his exhaustion forgotten. On each night following their first joining, Brit had made love to Katelyn, sometimes at a leisurely pace, sometimes in a feverish rush. And on each night after he had slaked his lust, he promised himself he would not touch her again.

Making his way from the stream to his cabin, Brit recalled the previous night and frowned. Again, he had broken his own promise. Last night he had been in a near panic to consummate their lovemaking. He snorted with disgust. So much for his theory that his desire for Katelyn would wane after having her a few times. He wanted her more now than he had when they first met.

Being honest with himself, he knew what he felt for Katelyn wasn't just physical lust. He needed to see Katelyn, to be near her, to talk to her—all things he had denied himself since he had claimed her as his four nights earlier.

He opened the cabin door and stepped inside, then carefully eased the door shut. When he turned to face the room, his eyes widened. Katelyn sat before the fire brushing her hair. As the blond strands shifted through her fingers, they caught the fire's glow, sending shards of golden light around the room.

His heart leaping at the picture she made, Brit took a step toward her, then another. Forgotten once again was his resolve not to touch this woman.

Hearing his approach, Katelyn halted her brushing in mid-stroke. She turned to look at him, uncertain how he would react to find her still up. "I . . . I washed my hair earlier, and I was brushing it dry."

"So I see."

Noticing his hair was also wet, she said, "I'll move so you can sit by the fire." She pulled her nightdress from beneath her legs and rose onto her knees.

Brit inhaled sharply. The fire behind Katelyn perfectly outlined her curves through the thin gown. Desire, torrid and throbbing, ignited instantly.

Cursing himself under his breath for not being able to control his lust, he moved closer. When he stood in front of her, he reached down to cup her chin with his hand. In Spanish, he whispered, "I have tried very hard to fight it. But my efforts have done little good. I fear you have stolen my heart, perhaps even my soul."

Katelyn furrowed her brow. Recognizing only a few of his softly spoken words, she wondered at the meaning of the rest and at the hoarseness of his voice. When he dropped his hand from her chin and held his palm out to her, she hesitated only a moment before placing her fingers atop his.

He helped her to her feet, then immediately pulled her into his arms. With her pressed full-length against him, he had the sensation of feeling whole again. Pushing such thoughts aside, he set her away from him, then quickly stripped off his clothes. When he turned back to her, she had removed her nightdress. Another surge of desire stormed through him.

Through glazed eyes, he watched Katelyn gather her hair at her nape, then deftly separate the blond tresses into three sections. "No," he said, startling her. "Leave it down."

Keeping her gaze riveted on his, she let her hair slip from her fingers, then shook her head to release the beginnings of a braid. As her hair swayed from side to side, then settled in waves down her back and over one shoulder, she watched the heat build in his eyes.

"Come here," he said in a soft growl.

She did not hesitate, but stepped back into his embrace.

He wrapped his arms around her, lowering his face to nuzzle her neck and inhaling the sweet scent of her hair. His arousal throbbed against her belly; his heart pounded in his temples. "I need you," he whispered against her ear.

His statement brought a lump to her throat. If only he needed her for more than the release of his desire! But there was no point in wishing for what could not be. Willing to accept whatever he gave her, she swallowed, then said, "And I need you."

He swept her up into his arms and carried her the few feet to the bed. Laying her on the blankets, he remained standing for a moment, staring down at her and trying to cool the fever in his blood. Just as a wildfire raging out of control was impossible to stop, he was unable to halt the blaze burning inside him. Dropping his chin onto his chest, he closed his eyes.

Through partially lowered lashes, Katelyn watched the way he clenched his jaw, the muscles of his throat moved as he swallowed. From the intense look on his face, it was almost as if he were in pain, struggling to win some inner battle. After he took a deep breath, he opened his eyes, then lowered himself onto the bed. As soon as he touched her, she forgot about the strange expression she'd seen on his face. With Brit's hands and mouth working their magic, she could think of nothing save the pleasure he brought her.

After caressing and kissing Katelyn to her orgasm, Brit finally slipped into her still-pulsing center. Sighing at the unbelievable feel of her tight passage surrounding him, he began thrusting in a frantic rhythm. Unable to delay his almost immediate release, he gave himself over to the nearly heart-stopping climax. His body shuddering with the intensity of his release, he threw back his head and thrust one last time. As Katelyn continued moving beneath him, he had to bite his lip to hold in a shout of triumph.

A few minutes later, Katelyn lay nestled against Brit's chest. His fingers lightly stroked her arm. Only the crackle of the fire broke the silence in the cabin.

"Who was he?" he said, shattering the peaceful quiet.

Katelyn stiffened, her breath caught in her throat. There was no need for her to ask who Brit meant. She had known the question would come eventually. Sitting up, she scooted to one end of the bed. She pushed her hair away from her face, refusing to look at him. "I—" Her voice cracked. Clearing her throat, she said, "I need my brush."

"I will get it," he said, swinging his feet to the floor. Returning with her brush, he sat down on the opposite end of the bed. Silently, he watched her work the brush through her snarled hair.

After a few moments, she began speaking in a low voice. "His name was Mason. Mason Webster. He and his family lived down the street from me in Chicago. His youngest sister was a friend of mine; that's how I met him. After I finished school, he started calling on me. I was flattered by his attention, and we became secretly engaged that summer. A few months later, he told me he had to go out of town on a business trip. He said he couldn't bear for us to be apart, and he wanted a memory of our last night together to carry with him."

When Katelyn fell silent, Brit said, "He wanted you to lie with him?"

She nodded, unable to meet his gaze. "Mason swore he loved me, and he promised we would announce our engagement and get married as soon as he returned from his trip. I . . . I believed him, so I . . ."

"You gave yourself to him," he said in a harsh whisper.

At her nod, he added, "Why did you not marry him when he returned?"

"I would have married him. But as the months passed, I knew he wasn't coming back. Then, two years later, I learned he'd married the heiress of a Boston shipping magnate not long after he left Chicago." Her voice turned bitter. "That's why he insisted we keep our engagement a secret; he never intended to marry me. He just wanted to use me, and I fell for his entire selfish scheme. I gave myself to him for nothing."

She finally worked up her courage to look at Brit. The fierceness of his features made her wish she hadn't. Eyebrows drawn together, nostrils flared, mouth a harsh slash, he stared at her with those penetrating black eyes.

Unable to bear the disgust she saw on his face, her hackles rose. "How dare you judge me! Have you never done something you later regretted?"

"I was not judging you."

"Oh, no? Then why are you looking at me like I'm the lowliest of vermin, or a bug you'd crush beneath your heel without a second thought?" When he didn't respond, she lifted her chin and glared at him. "Maybe you think my contamination has tainted you. Or maybe you can't stand the thought of having another man's leavings. Is that what you think?"

Shocked by her words, Brit's head snapped back as if he'd been struck. How could she think him so shallow? His momentary hurt quickly gave way to white hot anger. "That is not what I think. When a man takes a *puta* to his bed, he knows there was one before him, probably many, just like there will be more after him."

Katelyn clenched her teeth, her fury growing. "Are you calling me a liar?"

Lifting his shoulders in a shrug, he said nothing.

"I'll have you know, Mason was the only man I was with before you." Eyes blazing, she said, "One man hardly qualifies me as a whore."

He still didn't speak, but rose from the bed and pulled on his clothes. Without giving her another glance, he stalked to the door and left the cabin.

Katelyn stared at the door in stunned silence. *Damn him. He wanted the truth, then he won't believe it and calls me a whore.* Heaving a weary sigh, she finished brushing her hair, then braided it into one plait. She curled up on the bed, one hand tucked beneath her chin, the other twirling the tuft of hair at the end of her braid.

The soft light of dawn had just begun filtering into the cabin when Katelyn finally fell asleep. For the first time, Brit did not return to sleep beside her.

Brit was jolted out of the sleep he'd fallen into only minutes before by someone kicking his feet. Rolling over to direct a glare at whoever had roused him, he met Tomás's amused gaze.

"Ah, *jefe,* I did not know it was you. What brings you

to sleep by the campfire? Perhaps it was a lovers' quarrel, eh, *amigo mío?*"

"Enough, Tomás," he growled, his lack of sleep and the hard ground making him irritable. "You do not know what you are talking about." Getting to his feet, Brit stretched to ease the stiffness of his muscles.

Staring at his friend for a few seconds, Tomás finally said, "You cannot fight what is meant to be."

Brit looked at him sharply. "What nonsense are you spouting?"

Tomás started to say something, then changed his mind. Shrugging, he finally replied, *"Nada.* Come, let us get something to eat. We have work to do, *sí?"*

Brit followed Tomás to where Lutero was serving breakfast to the rest of the men. He accepted a cup of hot chocolate and a bowl of porridge from the old cook, then moved off by himself.

His thoughts dwelling on the conversation he'd had with Katelyn the night before, the porridge stuck in his throat. He kept seeing the look on her face after she told him about the man who had taken her innocence. Obviously, she'd lashed out at him because she thought his anger was directed at her.

Finally, giving up on trying to eat, Brit set the bowl of porridge aside and settled for drinking the *champurrado.* He closed his eyes, wishing he hadn't spewed such angry words at Katelyn. Opening his eyes, he glanced over at his cabin. He longed to go to her, to tell her he wasn't angry with her, but with the man who stole her virginity with false promises. But he did not move.

Having no experience with such matters, he didn't know how to tell her how he felt. And besides, his pride was still bruised from her scathing words. Just then the door of his cabin opened, and Katelyn stepped outside.

His gaze immediately sought her face, but the distance separating them concealed her expression. When she turned to look in his direction, he jerked his gaze away. Getting to his feet, he hurried to leave his cup and bowl with Lutero before she arrived at the cook fire. As he strode toward the corral, he heard Lutero tell her good morning. Though he strained to hear her reply, he could not catch her words, leaving him with an inexplicably empty feeling.

Ross checked his pocket for the pistol he carried when he went out at night, then eased from the shadows behind the Orleans Hotel on Second Street. He could hear the soft lapping of the river two blocks away, the creaking of the boats pulling against their moorings, the laughter of men enjoying a night of gambling and whiskey at one of the local gaming houses.

He stopped, prepared to wait ten minutes, no more. He had only waited for a minute or two, when a voice came from his left.

"You are the editor of the *Argus, señor?*"

Ross turned slowly. He could make out the silhouette of a man, but was unable to see his face. "No, the editor of the *Argus* is out of town, and therefore unable to make this meeting. But even if that weren't the case, the *Argus* is in no position to pay its sources. That's why I came instead. My name is Ross Carter. I'm the owner and editor of the *Sacramento Tribune.*"

After a moment's hesitation, the man said, "You will pay for information about the man you Yankees call *El Buitre?*"

"If the information is of use to me, then yes, I will pay."

"Tell me, *señor,* what is your feeling about *El Buitre?*"

"The man is a menace to society, a reprehensible blight on the people of California who must be stopped."

The mysterious man chuckled. "So, you share the *Argus* editor's views on the famous *bandido?*"

"Yes, we agree on the subject." Ross rubbed his hands

together in anticipation. "Now, what's this interesting information you have?"

"I can tell you about the hideout of *El Buitre*. Would that be of use to you, *señor?*"

Ross smiled in the darkness. "Most assuredly." He started walking toward the man. "Yes, most assuredly."

Marco stepped back. "Take it easy, *señor.* I have not decided if we can work together. Other than what you have told me, I know nothing about you."

"What are you talking about? You were willing to make a deal with the editor of the *Argus,* a person you have obviously never met, yet you hesitate to work with me because you don't know anything about me?"

"A man cannot be too careful, *Señor* Carter."

Trying to calm his irritation, Ross took a cheroot from his inside coat pocket. After lighting the cigar, he exhaled a puff of smoke, then said, "How is it you selected the *Argus* to be the recipient of the information you claim to have?"

"I have heard the words the editor of the *Argus* wrote about *El Buitre,* and I know how angry they made him."

"You know The Vulture personally?"

"*Sí,* I know him."

Tamping down his growing excitement, Ross said, "So if I'd told you I was the editor of the *Argus,* would you have handed over the information you're selling?"

Marco laughed softly. "No, *señor,* I am not that stupid. Just as I am going to do now, I would have made sure the person who met me here was who he claimed to be."

When the man said no more, but started backing away, Ross said, "Wait! When can we meet again?"

"If I am satisfied with what I find out, I will let you know."

The man silently disappeared, leaving Ross alone to ponder the possibilities of where their relationship might lead.

* * *

By the evening of the fifth day after Katelyn's heated exchange with Brit, her anger had long since cooled. But his continued avoidance of her, told her that he was still angry. Picking up her journal, she sat down in front of the fireplace in his cabin and began writing.

Brit still hasn't spoken to me since the night I told him about Mason. He avoids me at every turn. His brooding silence has become harder and harder to accept, until the strain between us is now unbearable. I'd like to apologize for the terrible things I said to him, but I'm unable to read the expression on his face whenever his gaze happens to meet mine. Without knowing his mood, I am hesitant to approach him. As strange as it seems, I truly understand his anger. His culture is even more strict about their women going to the marriage bed untouched than the most puritanical of beliefs. Still, I thought perhaps he, too, felt what we shared was special, and eventually he would overlook my past. I was obviously very wrong. He will never forgive my fall from grace. The realization is all the more painful, because I know there will never be anyone to take his place in my heart. Though I am resigned to spend the rest of my life as a spinster, at least I can take comfort in the fact that I will not leave this earth without having experienced a few nights of bliss in Brit's arms.

Blinking back tears, Katelyn reread her entry, then closed the journal. She sat for a very long time, unmoving and staring into the fireplace, too weary to go to bed. Writing in her journal was the only thing that kept her going. By putting her thoughts and feelings down on paper, she was able to get through the days. But then the endless nights followed.

If only she could get some rest. Without Brit beside her,

she tossed and turned each night, getting only a few hours of sleep. Each morning she got up feeling more exhausted than when she retired.

She finally summoned her strength and rose to get ready for bed. As she undressed, her thoughts turned to Sacramento and the *Argus*. If there was any chance she could sneak away undetected, she would take it, even if it meant facing the risk of getting lost again. Donning her nightdress, she knew she could never get away without being seen, not with all of Brit's men in camp at the same time. And after her first attempt at escaping, she was certain he had taken measures to see she wasn't allowed a second chance.

She sighed and lay down on the bed, resolved to endure another long, fitful night.

Katelyn spent the next morning as she'd done the previous several, sitting against the smooth trunk of a black cottonwood near the stream and writing in her journal. Intent on her entry, the sudden crunch of boots on the ground behind her made her jump.

When she started to turn toward the sound, her journal was snatched out of her hands. Gasping with surprise, she struggled to her feet and swung around to find Brit standing a few feet away. Legs widespread, one hand clutching her journal, he glowered down at her through narrowed eyes.

"What are you writing, *gringa?* Tales of our exploits in the pleasures of the flesh? Did you mention the birthmark I have on my right hip? Or perhaps you wrote of how virile I am?"

Katelyn's mouth fell open. Snapping it shut, she reached for her journal. "Don't be so egotistical. Why would I want to write about any of those things?"

Until that moment, she'd forgotten about her decision to

use her time at his camp to gather information for the *Argus*. Somewhere over the past weeks, her plans had taken an unexpected detour. Though there were bits and pieces of useful material in her journal, most of her writings were of a more personal nature—things she certainly didn't want him to read.

She lunged toward him, fingers stretching for the book he held in one hand. "Give me my journal."

He stepped back, keeping the book just out of her grasp. "I think not." He pressed his lips together, his anger increasing after finding her writing in her journal once again.

In spite of her denial, he wasn't so sure she hadn't written about their intimate relationship. Though it occurred to him that she couldn't write about their intimacy without revealing her own wanton behavior, he dismissed the idea. After all, she'd been no innocent, so her reputation was not at stake.

Over the past several days, he'd spent a lot of time thinking about Katelyn's motives for becoming his lover. And each time he'd come to the same conclusion. She wanted him caught and punished so much she had been willing to go to whatever lengths were necessary to see it accomplished—even subjecting herself to an intimate involvement.

Remembering the way she had responded to his kisses, his touch, his body moving above hers, he clenched his teeth in impotent fury. Was it possible she had faked such wanton passion?

Though he tried to clamp down on his anger, it continued to climb. While a large part of his fury was directed at Katelyn, for willingly becoming his lover on the pretext of gathering information for use in her editorials, another part was directed inward. His plans had failed again. Not only had his idea of beginning an intimate relationship with Katelyn not kept her from continuing her writings, he discovered an even more startling result. He was falling in love with her.

How had it happened? When had his lust for this infuriating *gringa* begun changing to love? Katelyn's voice pulled him from thoughts of the paradox of his life.

"I said, I'd like my journal back."

"And I said, no." Grabbing her arm, he swung her around to face the camp. "Come on. It is time for you to go home."

Katelyn pulled free of Brit's grip and stopped. "What did you say?"

Squeezing his eyes shut for a second, he exhaled heavily, then lifted his gaze to meet hers. "It is time I took you home. I will saddle our horses, while you pack your things."

"What about my journal?"

"You cannot have it. I am keeping the book."

"Why? It's just my personal journal."

"Ah, *gringa,* that is where you are wrong. It is more than a journal. If I keep the book, you will not have your notes when you write more editorials for your newspaper. Now, get moving. We have a long ride ahead of us."

"But—"

"Do not argue. We are leaving as soon I have readied the horses. Do you understand?"

Katelyn nodded, stunned by his sudden decision. Now that he'd agreed to take her home, she wasn't so sure she wanted to return. Once he deposited her back in Sacramento, there was a very real possibility she would never see him again. That prospect was far, far worse than his avoidance of her at his camp.

Brit turned from saddling two horses to find Tomás waiting nearby.

"It is time for the *gringa* to return home?" Tomás said in Spanish.

"Sí, we are leaving in a few minutes."

"You are going to put her on a stage?"

"No, I am taking her back to Sacramento."

Tomás's eyebrows pulled together. "Sacramento? But it is not yet noon. You could put her on a stage only a few miles from—" The harsh set to Brit's jaw ended his statement. He cleared his throat, then said, "The herd is ready to travel. Should I wait for your return before I take the horses to our southern camp?"

"No, leave whenever you are ready. I am not sure how long I will be gone."

Brit shook Tomás's hand, then turned to Katelyn. He took her carpetbag, then waited until Tomás was out of earshot before he said, "Before we leave, I want you to promise me something. I do not care what tales you tell about me in your newspaper, but I want your promise you will reveal nothing about this camp."

Katelyn met his dark gaze, her cheeks warming with anger. Momentarily stunned by his words, she could not speak.

Interpreting her flush and hesitation as signs of guilt, his voice turned harsh. "You should care about the men who have become your friends. Think of them when you pick up your poison pen. Think of how their lives will be put in danger, if you write about our camp." He paused to let his words sink in, then added, "I want your promise, *gringa.*"

Though she knew there was no way she could reveal the location of *El Buitre's* camp—other than being somewhere in the mountains—she wouldn't give him the satisfaction of confessing she didn't possess a sense of direction. Besides, in his current mood, he wouldn't believe her anyway.

After a moment, she said, "All right, I promise."

He stared at her for several seconds, noting the defiant tilt of her chin, the blue fire in her gaze. He closed his eyes briefly, willing his body not to react to her nearness. When he had gained the upper hand on his desire, he motioned for Katelyn to mount up, then moved to his own horse.

As they left camp, Brit prayed he wasn't making a mistake, prayed her word was good.

Thirteen

As Brit led the way through the unusual formation of rocks which hid the entrance to the canyon, then down the winding trail into the lower foothills, he belatedly realized he should have waited until nightfall to start their journey. Once again his ability to think rationally had been hampered by Katelyn. Nothing was as it had been before she entered his life.

He glanced over his shoulder to make sure she was still following him. When she caught him looking at her, she straightened her back, tilting her chin at a defiant angle. Her full breasts strained against the bodice of her dress.

Brit turned back to the trail in front of him, his mind filled with visions of her bare breasts, the nipples hardened peaks. He bit back a groan. Cursing the fact Sacramento was too far from his camp to make in a single day's ride, he wished he hadn't acted so rashly. Perhaps he should have had one of his men take her back. As soon as the thought formed, he discounted the idea. He never would have allowed anyone other than himself to be her escort, or spend the night on the trail with her.

The trip out of the mountains seemed to take forever. When the horses finally left the foothills, he urged them to a faster pace, pushing them as hard as he dared over the gently rolling terrain.

As the sun sank into a purplish-red bank of clouds, Brit

started looking for a place to camp. He finally settled for a relatively flat, tree-dotted area along the riverbank.

Dismounting, he tied his horse's reins to the branches of a valley oak, then turned to Katelyn. "We will camp here for the night."

She stared at him for a moment, her heart giving a little leap in her chest. Finally, she swung off her horse.

After he made a small fire and spread out their blankets, he unsaddled the horses, then led them down to the river to drink. When he returned, Katelyn had a pan of biscuits sitting over the fire and was sorting through the bag of food Lutero had packed.

They ate their meal of biscuits and dried beef in silence, Brit's gaze constantly on her face. He smiled at her refusal to look at him. *Stubborn woman. I named her well; she is in truth a golden thistle.*

"I'll wash the dishes," she said, jumping up when he set his plate aside. Gathering the plates and biscuit pan, she nearly ran down the bank to the river, slipping and sliding on the rocks. When she returned a few minutes later, she found Brit lounging against one of the saddles, rolling a long blade of grass between his thumb and forefinger.

He watched her repack his saddlebags, then take a seat on her blanket on the opposite side of the campfire. Arms wrapped around her drawn-up legs, she stared into what was left of the fire.

Though Brit wanted to feel nothing when he looked at her, his body refused to cooperate. Desire pounded in his veins, making every nerve ending throb with longing. Determined not to act on his need, he tried to shift his thoughts to something else. Then he remembered there would be no more nights with Katelyn. Tomorrow he would leave her in Sacramento.

Tossing the blade of grass aside, he got to his feet. He removed his hat, then reached for his vest. When he started unbuttoning his shirt, he heard Katelyn gasp. He looked over at her and smiled.

Recognizing the gleam in his eyes, she wet her lips and said, "Stay away from me."

His smile broadened. "I do not think you mean that." He pulled his shirt from his trousers, then shrugged the fabric off his shoulders.

"Yes . . . yes, I do."

He threw his shirt aside, then took a step towards her.

"I mean it, Brit. Stay away from me." She scrambled to her feet. "Tomorrow you're taking me home and we'll—" She swallowed the sudden lump in her throat. "We'll never see each other again, so let's just end it here."

"Yes, I am taking you home tomorrow. Can you think of a better reason for us to experience another taste of the passion we create so well?"

She shook her head and took a step back.

"You want me, I know you do." She shook her head again. "Do not deny it, *querida*. Now, come here." He held out one hand. "Come here, and let us stir our passion to new heights."

Katelyn halted her retreat, unable to resist the fire in his dark eyes, or the soft timbre of his voice. She stared at his hand for a few moments, her love for him making her waver on her decision.

She released a long, shuddering sigh. Though she knew she'd hate herself later for giving in, she reached out and placed her hand in his.

He wrapped his fingers around hers, then pulled her into his arms. He dropped his chin on top of her head and drew a deep breath. In Spanish, he said, "I wish our lives were not so much at odds, my beloved. Perhaps then I would not have to tell you good-bye tomorrow. And though I know I should not touch you tonight, I cannot stop myself. Forgive me, if my need only makes our parting more painful."

He kissed her hair, then grasped her shoulders and held

her away from him. Unable to resist her trembling lips, he bent his head and pressed a brief kiss on her mouth. In English, he whispered, "Do you still say you do not want me?"

Never taking her gaze from his, she shook her head. She lifted one hand and placed it on his chest. Running her fingers through the dark, silky hair, she said, "I want you." Shifting her gaze to the bulging muscles beneath her hand, she added in a soft murmur, "Tonight and always."

Her light touch sent a wildfire through Brit's veins, wrenching a moan from deep in his throat. With trembling fingers, he reached for the row of buttons running down the front on her dress bodice. In just a few moments, he managed to get both Katelyn and himself out of their clothes.

He held her at arm's length, running his gaze from her head down to her toes, then back again. Dropping to his knees, he pressed his cheek to her belly. "You are so beautiful," he whispered against her satiny skin.

One hand threading through the dark hair on his head, she said, "You don't have to say that, Brit. I've already agreed to this, so it isn't necessary to ply me with pretty words to gain my consent."

He pulled away from her, then got to his feet. "I was not using pretty words to try to seduce you. I meant what I said. You are beautiful."

She gave him a small smile. "Then you must be losing your eyesight. I know I'm as plain as—"

"Stop it!" He grabbed her shoulders and gave her a little shake. "I want you to listen to me, Katelyn Ann Ferguson. Perhaps you do not have a classic beauty, but to me you are beautiful just the same. Your hair, your eyes, your mouth . . ." He smiled. "Even your stubborn chin—all make you uniquely beautiful. A beauty no other woman could ever match."

Blinking back the sting of tears, Katelyn reached up to

push a lock of hair off his forehead, then whispered, "Thank you."

Brit grabbed her hand and placed a kiss on her palm. "There is no need to thank me, *querida.*" Moving to her blanket, he sat down, then pulled her down next to him.

Deliberately taking his time, he made slow, leisurely love to her. He touched and kissed wherever he could reach, concentrating on the places he knew were particularly sensitive.

The night was nearly gone before he allowed her to slip into the depths of slumber. More of the night elapsed while Brit remained awake, watching Katelyn sleep, tucking more memories away in his mind. At last he, too, yielded to his exhaustion and slept.

Marco opened the door to the *Argus* and stepped into the office. An older man stood on the other side of the counter, deep in conversation with a man whose back was to the door.

Jake looked up as the door closed. Nodding, he said, "Be right with you." Shifting his attention back to the man across the counter from him, he said, "Look, there's nothing I can do for you today, Mr. Roberts. You know Cyrus always paid his bills on time, but after the fire last year, things have been real tough. The *Argus* isn't the only business behind in its payments. If you'll just be patient, I know things will improve."

"They'd better, Jake. Or I'll have to take other measures to get the money this newspaper owes me." With that the man turned from the counter, opened the door, and slammed it shut behind him.

Jake took a deep breath, exhaled slowly, then turned to the other man standing quietly to one side. "What can I do for you?"

Marco shifted his gaze from his perusal of the rest of

the newspaper office to the man on the other side of the counter. "I would like to speak to the editor."

Jake pushed a hand through his hair. "You're not the only one," he muttered in a low voice. Then louder, he said, "I'm afraid that isn't possible. The editor is out of town. Is there something I can help you with?"

"*Gracías, señor,* but it is not important." Turning to leave, Marco touched his fingertips to the brim of his hat, then opened the door and stepped into the street.

The sun was high when Brit awoke. Angry at himself for sleeping longer than he intended, he vented his frustration on Katelyn when she stirred. "Get up and get dressed."

Rubbing her eyes, she sat up. "What?"

"I said, get up and get dressed," he said in a harsh voice, pointedly keeping his gaze from her naked breasts. "We are leaving as soon as I can saddle the horses."

Confused on how he could change so abruptly from last night's tender, considerate lover to such a contrary, ornery brute by the light of day, Katelyn shot him a peeved look, then rose and reached for her clothes.

Once they were back on the trail to Sacramento, Brit was filled with conflicting emotions. Though eager to deposit Katelyn back at her home, he felt an equally strong urge to turn around and spirit her away.

Forcing such thoughts from his head, he concentrated on his reasons for taking Katelyn from her home in the first place—the anger and hatred that had consumed him since Mirabella's senseless death.

Mirabella. He tried to conjure up her image. Her beautiful face was less distinct in his mind now; memories of her were no longer as sharp.

He had been a fool to abduct Katelyn, to think having her get to know the real *El Buitre* would make a difference.

What had he been thinking when he made the decision? Perhaps even then she had already bewitched him.

He clenched his teeth with suppressed fury. This was all Katelyn's fault. It was Katelyn's fault he could no longer picture his fiancée's face, Katelyn's fault he was being pulled in two directions at the same time, Katelyn's fault he wanted her so much he could think of little else.

During the rest of their journey, he allowed his anger to fester inside, hoping it would kill his remorse over leaving Katelyn in Sacramento. When the building housing the *Argus* came into view on the darkened streets of town, he looked at it passively, refusing to show any outward reaction.

He directed his horse down the alley to the back of the newspaper office, and pulled up in front of the door to her apartment. He dismounted, then assisted Katelyn from her horse. Before releasing her, he said, "Do not forget your promise, *gringa.*"

Katelyn lifted her face. The hard set of his jaw and the harsh line of his mouth snuffed out the hope that he'd show some sign of regret at leaving her. She shrugged off his hands. In a stiff voice, she replied, "I won't."

Brit stood in front of her for several seconds, trying to decide if he could believe her. At last, he stepped aside. As she moved past him, he whispered, *"Adiós, cardillo mío."*

An enormous lump in her throat, she managed a choked *adiós,* before hurrying into her apartment and closing the door behind her.

Brit stared at the door for a very long time, then finally turned toward the horses. Picking up the reins of the horse Katelyn had rode, he swung back into his saddle. After one last glance at Katelyn's home, he turned his horse toward the street, then touched his heels to the gray's sides.

Katelyn watched Brit's departure from the window of her darkened parlor. Biting her lip, she held in a sob until he was out of sight, then ran to her bedroom. Throwing herself across her bed, she let the tears come. With deep, heart-rending sobs, she cried for the loss of the man she loved, cried for the man who hated her, yet who would always have her heart. She cried until there were no more tears.

Weak and exhausted, at last she rose, washed her face, and changed into a nightdress. Pulling back the coverlet on her bed, she crawled between the sheets and almost immediately fell into a deep sleep.

Not far from Sacramento, Brit made camp. He wanted to put more distance between himself and the woman he'd just left, but the horses were spent. He'd put them through a lot over the last two days, and he couldn't risk pushing them any further.

Stretched out on his bedroll, he stared up at the stars, unable to keep his thoughts from straying to Katelyn. Grunting with disgust, he rolled over and closed his eyes. Still, a vision of blond hair and blue eyes persisted in taunting and tormenting him. Again he felt the pull of desperately wanting and needing to go to Katelyn, and the equally powerful pull of getting as far away from her as he could.

As sleep slowly crept over him, the last line of one of Shakespeare's sonnets filtered into his mind. "My grief lies onward and my joy behind."

A sharp pain clutched his heart. Was that how it was to be for him?

The following morning, Katelyn awoke soon after dawn. She looked around, seeking confirmation that she really was back in her bedroom. With a deep sigh, she threw back the covers and sat up. Her carpetbag sat on the floor by the door; the dress she'd worn the day before lay in a tangled mass at the foot of the bed.

Feeling the sting of tears, she took a deep breath, willing

herself not to cry. Her eyes hurt, and her throat was raw from the tears she'd shed the night before.

After bathing and pressing a cool cloth to her puffy eyes, Katelyn dressed and fixed her hair. Though a last look in her mirror told her she looked far from her best, she left her apartment and headed for the *Argus* office.

Stepping into the office, Katelyn abruptly halted. Ross Carter sat at her desk, going through the newspaper's files.

"What are you doing here?" she said, unable to keep the irritation out of her voice.

Startled, Ross looked up. His eyebrows pulled down into a scowl, then immediately lifted. "Katelyn! It's about time."

Katelyn closed the front door, walked around the counter, and crossed the office to stand next to her desk. "I asked what you're doing here, Ross."

"I was just helping Jake in your absence." He rose from the chair and bent to give her a kiss.

She turned her head at the last moment so that Ross's lips barely grazed her cheek. His brows beetled again, his mouth turning down in annoyance. "Just where have you been, anyway?"

"I was . . ." Katelyn swung away from him, uncomfortable under his intense scrutiny. "I was away on business."

"What kind of business?"

She took a deep breath and exhaled slowly. "I don't think that's any of your concern."

"None of my concern," he nearly shouted. "Everything a man's betrothed does is his concern."

Katelyn turned back to face him, her eyes narrowed. "Betrothed? We aren't betrothed."

"Only because you never gave me an answer. You promised to think about it." He approached her and grasped her hands between his. "Katelyn, is that why you—"

Pulling her hands free, she took a step back, then another. "Where's Jake this morning?"

"He went next door to see Grace. He should be back soon."

"Grace? Jake went to see Grace?"

"Yes, he's been seeing her a lot lately. Now listen to me, Katelyn, are you going to tell me where you've been? You're acting . . . well, different."

Her smile at the surprising news that Jake and Grace were keeping company faded. "I don't see why you need to know, Ross. Suffice it to say, it doesn't concern you. Now, I don't want to discuss it anymore."

Sitting down at her desk, she frowned. The envelopes of all the newspaper's mail had been opened. Picking up several envelopes, she waved them in his direction. "Did you open all of these?"

"Yes, I did." Seeing her frown deepen, he added, "Now, don't get all huffy. I thought one of them might give Jake and me some information about your whereabouts. You were gone for weeks, and no one heard a thing from you. I'll have you know, Jake and Grace were very worried. And me, too, of course." He lowered his voice to add, "Especially me, Katelyn."

She glanced up at Ross. "Well, you all worried for nothing. As you can see, I'm back, safe and sound. So let's get on with our lives, shall we? Now, if you'll excuse me, I have a newspaper to run."

His brow furrowed, he replied, "Okay, fine. I have my own business to take care of. The *Tribune* has suffered with me having to look after both newspapers."

"Jake is more than capable of running the *Argus,* and you know it. There was no need for you to take time away from your own paper to come here."

"Don't get so riled. I was only trying to help the woman I hope to marry." When she didn't respond, he said, "Can I take you to supper?"

"I suppose. But it will have to be late," she replied, rifling through the mail piled on her desk. "I have a lot of work to catch up on."

Ross's back stiffened at her indifferent attitude, but he held his tongue. Determined to eventually find out where Katelyn had spent the past few weeks, he placed a kiss on the top of her head, then left the *Argus* office.

Walking back to the *Tribune* office, Ross's thoughts shifted from the exasperating woman he'd just left to the meeting he was to attend later that night with his mysterious informant.

Perhaps this time he would actually get some information from the man. He snorted, hawked, and spat into the street. *Damned greaser! Won't tell me anything until he's sure I can be trusted to print whatever it is he wants to sell.*

Other than having a Spanish accent and being of average height and weight, Ross knew nothing about the man. He hated the disadvantage that put him at, but since he'd met the man at midnight, his hat pulled low over his face, Ross didn't have a clue to the stranger's identity. *He'd better have some damn good stuff after the delay.*

On their first meeting over a week ago, the man had been on the verge of selling Ross information about *El Buitre,* when he abruptly decided to wait, claiming he wouldn't do business with just anyone. *Fool! The man acts like he's conducting a legitimate business deal. And he's nothing but a greaser snitch.*

Left with no other choice, Ross had been forced to wait until the man contacted him. He was beginning to wonder if he'd ever hear from the Mexican again, when a message had finally arrived at the *Tribune*'s office the day before. Unfortunately, the note set their meeting for that night at midnight, something Ross had forgotten when he'd asked Katelyn to supper.

Entering the office of the *Tribune,* Ross decided he could still pull it off. He'd take Katelyn to a late supper, then get her home in plenty of time to make the midnight meeting.

She was as cold as a January wind blowing across the Sierras, so there was no reason for him to dawdle in her parlor.

He'd always hoped she would eventually thaw for him, but so far he'd seen no signs of a warming trend. Perhaps he'd misjudged her. Perhaps his belief that a fire simmered beneath her cool reserve had only been wishful thinking.

His shoulders rippled with a shudder. He hated the thought of being married to a woman capable of giving him frostbite. But there was one compensation—a married man could still find a warm bed and a willing female in Sacramento. A parlorhouse down by the river had a new French beauty he particularly liked.

Ross smiled. Everything would work out perfectly. He could continue enjoying the talented Colette whenever he wanted, and he'd have the *Argus* and its assets—especially the impressive and valuable Washington Printing Press. There was just one matter yet to be resolved. Katelyn still hadn't agreed to marry him.

Taking off his jacket and draping it over the back of his chair, Ross chuckled. *All in good time. After all, I'm the only man in town she has ever kept company with; she turned down flat the others who'd asked. Yes, sir, all in good time.*

Fourteen

Marco watched Ross Carter pace back and forth behind the Orleans Hotel, yet he did not move from the deep shadows. He had to be certain this *gringo* newspaper owner could be trusted, that the man would come alone when summoned for a meeting. Marco also reveled in the power keeping Carter on the end of a string like a marionette gave him. He could jerk the man to his whims whenever he chose.

As he continued watching, Marco saw Carter take a cheroot from his inside coat pocket, then strike a match. The light from the flame momentarily revealed the newspaper man's face. *Ah, so he is not happy about the delay. That is good. I do not want him looking confident, like he has someone watching his back.*

After a few more minutes of pacing and smoking his cigar, Ross finally tossed the cheroot to the ground, crushed it with his boot heel, and strode away. Once he was out of sight, Marco stepped from his hiding place. "Going to visit your French *puta?*" he whispered. Chuckling, he hurried to see where Carter was headed.

Marco had been checking on both the owner of the *Argus* and Ross Carter. So far the man had told the truth. The *Argus* owner was indeed out of town, and Carter was the owner and editor of the *Sacramento Tribune,* whose editorials indicated he had no use for the bandit *El Buitre.* But Carter was also very full of himself, a cocky *gringo* with a penchant for a young whore at a local parlorhouse, a *Mademoiselle* Colette Dubois.

In spite of Marco's opinion of Ross Carter, he was nearly satisfied that they could do business. But he would wait a few more days, before letting the man know his decision. He was enjoying adding to the man's agitation.

"Did you get a fat purse this time, *jefe?*" Armando watched Brit count the money from *El Buitre*'s return to the life as a bandit.

Brit shrugged. "Enough." When Armando looked at him expectantly, he added, "We will not starve, if that is what you want to know."

Wondering at his leader's strange words regarding a successful mission, Armando said, "That is good, eh?" When Brit did not respond, his concern grew. "Is something wrong, *jefe?*"

"Nada." He couldn't very well tell Armando the money he had stolen from two Yankees on the Auburn Coloma Road made him sick. He couldn't tell Armando how his life as a *bandido* no longer held the appeal it once had. He couldn't tell him how relieving the unsuspecting Yankees of their wallets and pouches of gold dust had given him none of his usual satisfaction, but instead had left him feeling nothing but disgust.

Brit abruptly rose, handed the spoils to Armando, then turned toward his cabin. "I am going to bed."

"Buenas noches, sleep well," Armando called.

Brit nodded, but did not reply. Sleeping well was something he hadn't done since returning from Sacramento. Everything he did, every place he went at the camp, held something that reminded him of Katelyn. But nights in his cabin were the worst. The single room held too many memories—memories constantly swirling in his head and allowing him very little sleep.

Entering the cabin, his gaze went immediately to Katelyn's journal, just as it did every time he came through the door. For a reason he didn't completely understand, he refused to pack the book away. It was always in plain view. In spite of his inability to stash the journal somewhere out of sight, so far he'd managed to curb his curiosity about what was written inside.

That night his control slipped. Picking up the leatherbound book, he took a seat in the chair and opened the journal's cover.

Katelyn had neatly penned her name on the first page. Brit slowly ran a finger over each letter, saying her name in a soft whisper. He swallowed hard, then flipped the pages to her first entry. After shifting to a more comfortable position in the chair, he started reading.

May 1, 1851 Our train of wagons finally left St. Joseph today. Got a late start because we had to wait for the spring grass, otherwise there would have been no forage for the oxen as we cross the plains. Though I feel both excitement and apprehension about leaving civilization behind, I'm glad the wait is over, and we are finally embarking on this trip.

We've been on the trail thirty days now. I don't think Papa realized the hardships of this undertaking. We have to haul water from creeks, cook over an open fire, and sleep on the ground because Papa's printing press takes up most of the room inside the wagon. Nothing in our daily routine is like what we left behind. For the past week, the favorite topic of discussion has been Indians. The others take great delight in recounting hair-raising stories of the savages and their bloody deeds. I shudder at the thought of such atrocities befalling our wagons.

June 22 Cholera has struck the folks of our train of wagons. We lost three of our number this morning, and more are taken with the sickness every hour. It is a horrible disease, claiming adults and children at will. So far Papa and I have had no signs of illness. I pray to God we remain healthy.

A pain clutched at Brit's heart. Though Katelyn had survived the threat of cholera, he felt the immense fear she must have experienced. Taking a deep breath to ease the tightness in his chest, he continued reading.

Had to stop and bury more victims of cholera today. A husband, wife, and their baby were laid to rest in the same shallow grave, in the middle of this endless prairie. I shall never forget the sadness of that burial, how the family will have no headstone to mark their passing, how any remaining relatives back East may never know of their loss.

Arrived at Fort Laramie today. We are told we have completed only one third the distance to our destination of Sacramento. We will stay here for a few days to replace our supplies, let our teams of oxen rest, and see to any necessary repairs to our wagons and harnesses. It will seem good not to feel the constant sway of the wagon beneath me.

Four months have now passed since we left St. Joseph, and I am so weary of the life we must live. Papa appears to be holding up well, and is in surprisingly good spirits. I know this life is very hard on him, but he never complains. Though the scenery we are passing is magnificent, I would give anything to be at our journey's end.

Brit wanted to continue reading, but he made himself close the journal. He would read more from the book on other nights, for his eyes had grown heavy. He yawned. Perhaps the sense of feeling closer to Katelyn from reading her entries had relaxed him enough to allow him to sleep.

He rose from the chair, removed his clothes, then stretched out on the bed. Katelyn's journal clutched in his hand, he fell into the first sound sleep he'd had since returning her to Sacramento.

The next morning, Brit's mood was considerably lighter. Fully rested, he ate breakfast, then headed for Solazo's corral.

"How are you my pretty one?" he said to the mare. "Are you ready to allow me to sit on your back again?"

The horse tossed her head, her white mane fluttering in the light breeze. Brit chuckled. "Ah, I see you are anxious to begin. Perhaps we will even go for a short ride today."

Solazo nickered, butting her head into Brit's chest. As he ran a hand over her golden coat, his thoughts wandered. Pressing his forehead to the mare's neck, he struggled to curb memories of another head of golden hair. His voice was thick when he said, "Let us get to work. You will soon be ready to go to your new home."

The lesson with Solazo went very well, her acceptance of the saddle and Brit on her back going better than he'd anticipated. For the first time since he'd captured the palomino mare, Brit took her outside the corral. Though she was eager to run, she flawlessly obeyed his command to hold her ground, her hide rippling with anticipation.

When he finally signalled her to move forward, her hooves moved lightly across the ground. He directed the horse down the narrow path to the canyon floor, then gave her the signal she'd been waiting for. Running like the wind, Solazo carried her rider along the edge of the stream with ease. As they neared the rear of the canyon, Brit pulled back on the reins. The mare slid to a halt, sides heaving, golden coat damp with sweat.

"You have done well, my pretty one," he said, leaning forward to pat her neck. "How I will hate to see you leave. But I will try to visit you soon."

Reining the mare back in the opposite direction, Brit kept Solazo at a slow walk to allow her to cool down. As they made their way back to the corral on the plateau, his words about visiting the horse after he had her moved south continued to fill his thoughts. Perhaps he could pay a visit to someone else as well.

His heart picked up its rhythm at the idea.

He kicked Solazo into a canter, anxious to get back to camp. As soon as Tomás returned—which, unfortunately, could be a week or more—he would have his friend take the mare to his father's *rancho*. Then, once Tomás started his journey, Brit would see to paying the visit he'd just decided to make.

That night, he read again from Katelyn's journal.

We have traveled almost two thousand miles, and yet the most dreaded part of the journey—a forty-mile trek across the desert to the Carson River—now looms before us. We will rest our teams during the day, then fill our canteens and start the crossing during the cooler hours of the night.

Crossing the desert was every bit as bad as we'd heard. The sand was very deep, making the already exhausted oxen strain even harder in their yokes to pull our wagons. Ours is especially heavy because of the printing press. We are grateful our team has shown great stamina, and that we didn't have to leave Papa's pride and joy, his new Washington Printing Press, behind on the desert. All along the route we saw bedding, cooking utensils, and other personal belongings people had tossed out to lighten the weight of their wagons. Such a shame, hauling their treasures all this way from their homes back East, then being forced to leave them beside the trail so close to their destination.

We have just survived the ordeal of the desert, and now we have yet another intimidating challenge to face. We must somehow cross the Sierra Nevada Mountains. I worry about Papa. He has felt so good this far into our trip, but last night he had a bad spell. Though he seems better today, I am still worried. He needs to be where he doesn't have to work so hard, where he can get plenty of rest. Will this journey ever end?

October 30, 1851 We have arrived in Sacramento at last. Papa is overjoyed to be so close to the place where gold was discovered, a place he has dreamed about visiting ever since word reached Chicago of James Marshall's finding gold at the sawmill of John Sutter. Papa's health is much improved, perhaps because he is so happy with the town where we will be living. I wonder if I will be happy here.

Closing the journal, Brit bowed his head and whispered a brief prayer. Many did not survive the grueling overland trip, and he felt the need to offer his thanks for her safe arrival in Sacramento. Lifting his head, he pulled his mouth into a frown. Why should he give thanks to God for sparing a *gringa?*

As much as it pained him to admit it, he knew the answer—he loved her.

Perhaps he wouldn't make the trip to Sacramento after all. He would be wise to stay away from the woman who had captured his heart. But as soon as the idea to cancel his plans formed, he shoved it aside. He would see Katelyn once more. Perhaps seeing her one more time would rout her from his blood, from his heart. To have fallen in love with a *gringa* was a slap in the face to his people.

He should hate *all* Yankees for what they did to the *Californios,* not be selective about the target for his hatred. But he was powerless to control his feelings for one blond-haired, blue-eyed woman. From the first time he'd laid eyes on Katelyn, his life had changed. He wondered if he would ever be able to change it back.

Grace Barnes entered the *Argus* office, then quietly shut the door behind her. When Jake looked up and saw her, a wide smile appeared on his face. She returned his smile, then pointed to Katelyn.

Glancing over to where Katelyn sat at her desk, Jake nodded his understanding, then said, "Katie, look who's here."

Katelyn turned from her work. "Grace! What a surprise. What are you doing here? Did you come to see Jake?" The sudden splash of color on Grace's cheeks made her smile. Looking over at Jake, she had to stifle a laugh. He, too, was flushed a dull red, and looked like a schoolboy with his head bowed, scraping the toe of one boot on the floor.

"Are you two going to supper?"

"Actually, Katelyn, I came to see if you'd like to have supper with me. I haven't seen much of you lately, and Jake tells me you've been working too hard."

Katelyn stared at Grace for a second, glanced over at Jake, then back to Grace. "Are you sure you wouldn't rather have supper with Jake?"

"I've fixed supper for Jake every night this week. It won't hurt him to eat somewhere else this once."

Seeing that her friend was serious, she said, "Well, if you're sure?"

"Absolutely. Now come on."

"Go ahead, Katie," Jake said, picking up a rag to wipe

the ink from his hands. "I'll finish cleaning the press, then lock up for you."

"Thanks, Jake. Just let me get my handbag, Grace."

Jake strode across the office to the front door. "Allow me, ladies," he said, opening the door with a little bow. When Grace passed him, he leaned close to her ear and whispered, "Bye, love."

Grace smiled her response, then stepped through the door.

Sitting on a stool in Grace's kitchen after helping with the supper dishes, Katelyn watched her friend roll out a pie crust.

"So, you've been cooking for Jake every night? That sounds serious."

Grace smiled. "If you hadn't gone out of town, Jake might never have worked up the courage to visit me, or to declare his feelings."

"I guess I should have left sooner," she said, returning her friend's smile.

"Do me a favor, Katelyn. If you ever decide to leave town again, promise me you'll give Jake or me some advance warning."

"I promise to tell you both." In a softer voice, she added, "But there's no chance of my disappearing that quickly again."

Grace was startled by the sadness she heard in Katelyn's voice, the pain she saw reflected on her face. "I know it's none of my business, and I'm not asking you to tell me anything. But if you ever want to talk, I'm a good listener."

She gave Grace a wan smile. "Thanks, but I'm not sure I can talk about it. Not yet anyway."

Grace nodded, then went back to rolling out the pie dough. After a few moments, she took a deep breath and said, "You were with a man, weren't you?"

Katelyn visibly flinched, her eyes widening. "Why . . . why would you say that?"

Looking up from her work, Grace gave her a gentle smile. "The expression on your face when you think no one is looking, the pain I see in your eyes. Things only a woman would notice."

Staring at her tightly clasped hands, Katelyn said, "Yes, I was with a man. But you must promise you won't tell anyone, not even Jake."

"Your secret's safe with me." Grace lifted the rolled-out dough with her rolling pin and positioned it on top of the fruit-filled bottom crust. "Do you love him?" she asked in a soft voice.

"Yes." Katelyn's reply was just as soft.

Using a knife to trim the extra dough hanging over the edge of the pie tin, Grace said, "What about him, does he return your feelings?"

"I wish I knew," she said with a sigh. "Sometimes I think he loves me, but then other times I'm sure he hates me."

"Hates you? Katelyn, why in the world would he hate you? You're one of the nicest people I know. Surely no one could hate you?"

"I can't tell you why, Grace. I wish I could, but I can't."

As Grace deftly crimped the edges of the pie crust together with her thumb and forefinger, she said, "I understand. Just remember, if you ever change your mind, I'll be here for you."

Brit's feelings about visiting Katelyn continued to vacillate over the next few days. He wanted desperately to see her, though he knew he should stay away. But the wild thrill of anticipation running through him when he heard the arrival of horses and saw Tomás striding toward him, told Brit the inner battle he'd waged was at an end.

"Tomás, it is good to see you."

"Sí, it is good to see you, too, *jefe."* His gaze swept the camp. "You left the *gringa* in Sacramento?"

"Sí."

"Bueno. I thought perhaps you would change your—" The flash of anger in Brit's eyes halted Tomás's words. He coughed, then said, "What do we do now?"

"You will take Solazo to my parents' *rancho."*

"I will take her to *El Rancho del Sol Poniente,* if that is what you want. But must I leave right away? I have just returned from our southern camp. That is a long journey, and I am very tired."

"You can rest for a few days before you go. Take two men with you. The others will go with me after another herd, when I return."

Tomás stared at Brit through narrowed eyes. "Return? Where are you going?"

Brit silently cursed the weakness he could not control. "I have some business to take care of. I am leaving at the break of dawn, and probably will not get back until after you leave. So, I will say good-bye now." Extending his hand, he said, *"Vaya con Díos."*

Tomás clasped Brit's hand and shook it firmly. *"Sí, vaya con Díos, amigo mío."*

Brit nodded to the other men, then made his way to his cabin. After packing his saddlebags for the trip, he planned to turn in early.

Several hours later, he was still sitting in front of the fireplace, Katelyn's journal opened across his lap.

He had read her entries about her new life in Sacramento, her efforts to make a home for Cyrus Ferguson, her concern about her father working too hard at the newspaper he'd purchased and renamed the *Argus,* and her fears for the man's health. He was about to close the book, when something in the next entry caught his eye and made him read on.

*Papa has gotten the idea into his head that the despi-
cable bandit,* El Buitre, *is not what everyone thinks,
that he has a story worth telling. Papa is obsessed
with being the one to write the man's side of the life
he leads. I think Papa is foolish to go traipsing across
the countryside looking for The Vulture, but he won't
listen to me. He insists on going out nearly every day,
hoping to find some clue to locating a desperado who'd
rather steal a man's wallet than talk to a newspaper
editor. I am so afraid Papa will have another of his
spells, but I can do nothing to stop him.*

The next few entries were more of Katelyn's concerns
for her father's deteriorating health, and how her pleas continued to fall on deaf ears. She reported the devastating fire
that swept through Sacramento in November of '52, turning
nearly the entire town to ash. Though their house was lost
to the blaze, by some miracle the *Argus* and several other
businesses survived the fire. With their home destroyed,
Katelyn and her father moved into the small set of rooms
formerly occupied by the newspaper's previous owner.
Though she tried to convince her father not to help with
the town's rebuilding, he paid her no heed. He helped those
less fortunate than himself, while continuing his efforts to
locate The Vulture.

Then came the entry where she reported what she had
feared most.

*Papa passed away yesterday. He had been out looking
for The Vulture again, when he was taken ill. Somehow
he managed to get back to town. I sent for a doctor
immediately, but he told me only the grace of God
would save my father. Papa lasted the night, then took
a turn for the worse. He roused only long enough to
plead with me not to hate him for trying to get the
exclusive story he had dreamed of for so long. When*

I promised him I could never hate him, he gave me a weak smile, then closed his eyes. At peace, he slipped away.

Her tearstains blurred some of the words on the page, and also in her next entry.

Papa was laid to rest today. I wish so much his final resting place could have been next to Mama, but it wasn't possible. I pray they are together in whatever existence there is after we leave this earth. As I watched the dirt being thrown over his coffin, I felt the anger burning and building inside me. It is The Vulture's fault my father was taken from me. If not for the horrible thief, I would have Papa with me still. I swear I will make it my first duty to see the bandit caught and punished. I will take over as editor of the newspaper Papa loved so much, and see justice carried out through the only means I have, the printed word. El Buitre, if it takes until my dying breath, I will see you hang!

Brit closed his eyes; a muscle jumped in his clenched jaw. The depth of Katelyn's hatred was now painfully clear. He swallowed, trying to ease the tightness in his throat. Opening his eyes, he took a deep breath, then exhaled slowly.

As hard as it was to believe, he actually sympathized with her. And more surprising, he even understood why she blamed him for her father's death, why she hated him so much. He would likely have felt the same way, had one of his parents died through a similar circumstance. Didn't he already feel a comparable hatred for the loss of another loved one, his fiancée, Mirabella?

Brit grunted, closing the journal with a snap. He knew what hatred did, how it ate at a man's insides slowly and inexorably, until he was turned into a bitter, cynical person who found no joy in life. He pushed himself out of his chair. Did he want that to happen to Katelyn?

While undressing, the answer came to him. He had to try to change the course of Katelyn's hatred, before it was too late. But what if her hatred was too deeply ingrained? What if he couldn't successfully defuse her hate? Stretching out on the bed, he tried not to think of those possibilities.

Thinking of how his hatred for Katelyn had wavered, then finally went through a complete transformation, he knew he had to try. Thoughts of visiting Katelyn filling his mind, he drifted to sleep.

Katelyn laid down her pen and cradled her head in her hands. She'd been working for hours on her first editorial since returning to town, and she still hadn't finished the article. What had come so easily for months was now a struggle. Lifting her head, she dropped her hands onto her desk and sat back in her chair. She heaved a weary sigh. She had to do this, no matter how difficult, no matter that she now loved the subject of what should be a disparaging editorial, like all her previous efforts.

She had to stop thinking about Brit as a kind and gentle man, as a tender and considerate lover, as the man she loved. She had to think of him as a vile, bloodthirsty villain, the way she had thought of him before he stole her from her home, before he stole her heart.

She reached for the pen, her lips pressed together in determination. What would Papa think of her, if he knew she couldn't keep her private emotions out of her writing? Recalling Cyrus Ferguson's words about the necessity of maintaining a separation between a reporter's subject matter and his personal feelings, Katelyn dipped the pen into the inkwell, then began writing.

When she laid the pen down a second time, the editorial

was finished. She reread the article, satisfied she had done her father proud. Though Cyrus would have approved, Katelyn's heart ached for Brit. Though he had kidnapped her, used her for his own pleasure, then dumped her back on her doorstep, she still loved the man she had gotten to know in his mountain hideaway. She always would.

Fifteen

Brit picketed his horse beneath a grove of valley oaks not far from the Sacramento River. Sticking to the heavy shadows of midnight, he made the half-mile walk to the rear of the *Argus* office. Though the town was deserted at such a late hour, he halted outside his destination, listening to the nighttime sounds. The bark of a dog echoed from a few blocks away. The music from a riverfront saloon drifted toward him on the faint wind. When he was satisfied his arrival had roused no one's suspicions, he moved up the steps and onto the small porch.

He grasped the doorknob and turned. The door wouldn't budge. In spite of the problem he faced—getting into the locked apartment—Brit was pleased Katelyn had locked her door.

Pulling his knife from his boot, he applied the blade to the keyhole. He turned the blade until he heard a soft click. He smiled. After slipping his knife back in its sheath, he carefully opened the door and stepped into the parlor.

He eyes accustomed to the dark, he moved immediately toward the room he knew to be Katelyn's. The door stood slightly ajar. Using his fingertips, he gently pushed the door inward. One of the hinges gave a low squawk, making Brit grimace. His gaze snapped to the woman on the bed. She didn't stir.

He moved across the small room and stood next to the bed. For a moment he was content to watch Katelyn sleep by the pale moonlight filtering through the room's small window. The incredible sense of emptiness plaguing him since he'd last seen her eased with each passing second. Being so close to the woman he loved, filling his gaze with her, hearing her soft breathing, gave him an indescribable sense of joy.

Slipping off his vest and gun belt, he lowered them to the floor, then pulled off his boots.

Katelyn sighed, then rolled onto her back. Brit straightened, smiling at the gown she wore. When would she learn to sleep without the restriction of a nightdress?

He placed one knee on the bed, then eased down beside her. Bracing his upper body on one forearm, he stretched out full length, then lifted one hand to her face. His fingertips had barely touched her cheek when she started, her eyes popping open.

She sucked in a deep breath, then opened her mouth to scream. A warm, silky voice halted her attempt to cry for help.

"It is all right, *querida*. I will not hurt you." He lowered his head, until his face was just above hers. "Did you miss me?" he whispered, flicking his tongue over her lips. "I missed you." His tongue made another foray across her mouth. "Are you going to give me a hello kiss?"

Before Katelyn could reply, Brit closed the distance between them and settled his mouth on hers. She groaned at the contact. Oh, how she'd missed the taste of him, the scent of him, the feel of him. Looping one arm around his neck, she pulled him even closer, pressing her breasts against his chest, her thighs against his groin.

He moaned, pushing his tongue between her parted lips, delving into the sweet depths of her mouth. Struggling for breath, he finally ended the kiss.

"What are you doing here?" she managed to ask, her own breathing labored.

"Ah, *querida,* do not tell me you have forgotten that you

are mine." He kissed her cheek, then her neck. "I always take care of what belongs to me." He opened the buttons at her throat and kissed the soft skin beneath. "Why do you insist in sleeping in such a demure gown? We both know you are not demure when I am between your lovely thighs. Is that not so?"

Katelyn stiffened, then immediately tried to scoot away from him. His voice stopped her efforts. "Do not go all prickly on me, *cardillo mío,* I meant no offense. I am pleased you like my kisses, my touch, my body joined with yours. A woman should enjoy the pleasures of the flesh as much as a man. Surely you would agree with such a premise."

Katelyn stared up at him through widened eyes. What was he doing here? Did he mean to kidnap her again? She finally found her voice and said, "What do you want?"

Brit did not look up, but continued working the buttons free on her gown. "I came to see how you are, and . . ." Her skin took on a silvery sheen from the moonlight. He leaned over to brush a kiss across a newly exposed nipple. When the rosy tip instantly puckered into a tight bud, he smiled. "And to taste your passion once again."

He lifted his head to look at her. "You want that as well. Your body tells me you do."

The stupor that had settled over her from his unexpected presence and drugging kisses vanished at his boldness. Pushing at his chest, she said, "No, I don't want you, you arrogant cad. How dare you make such an assumption! You break into my home, sneak into my bedroom, then try to assault me under the misconceived notion that *I* want you. I'll have you know, I—"

A finger pressed against her lips ended her tirade. "Hush, *querida.* There is no need to pretend outrage at my statement. We both know it is the truth. I want you, just as you want me. It is that simple." He removed his finger from her mouth. "Tell me you want me, Katelyn."

A shiver ran up her spine. She could not remember his

ever calling her by name. The effect was startling. Her anger fled. Her breathing quickening, she ached for his touch. A flame ignited in her belly, sending a sizzling heat throughout her body and settling between her thighs.

As much as she wanted to pretend otherwise, she was truly glad to see him, to know he was alive and well. And, yes, he was correct. She did want him. Unable to get the words through her tight throat, she finally nodded.

He chuckled, a low, husky sound sending her desire even higher. He pressed a brief kiss on her lips, then rose from the bed. The scratch of a match was followed by a flare of light as he lit the oil lamp on her bedside table. After blowing out the match and adjusting the lamp's wick, he reached for the buttons of his trousers.

He pulled and tugged at his clothes, grumbling under his breath when his fingers failed to work properly. Naked at last, he turned back to the bed. Katelyn hadn't moved. Eyes wide, lips parted, the placket of her nightdress opened to reveal her heaving bosom, she stared up at him. His already aroused flesh jerked in reaction to the enticing picture she made.

With a soft growl, he reached down to her, and with quick, efficient movements removed her gown. He tossed the garment aside, slipped into bed, and took her into his arms.

Whispering in Spanish, Brit made slow, delicious love to Katelyn. He knew exactly where and how to touch her, and she soon writhed in escalating passion. In only a few moments, his name escaped her throat in a strangled cry. She arched her back, digging her heels into the mattress. Hips moving to the rhythm of his fingers, her climax overtook her.

After the last of the tremors from her powerful release had racked her body, he laughed with satisfaction. "Only I can give you such pleasure," he murmured, rolling atop her and pulling her legs up around his waist. He entered her in one swift movement, gasping as her still-pulsing inner muscles gripped his manhood.

She smiled at the startled look on his face. "Now it's my turn to give *you* pleasure," she said, running her fingers through the hair on his chest. Lifting her hips, she took his engorged shaft even deeper. She started an easy rocking motion, one he quickly matched. Grabbing the backs of his thighs, she increased the rhythm, refusing to allow him to withdraw completely when he tried to pull away.

"No," she whispered. "You must stay inside me. You'll reach your finish like this." To emphasize her words, she lifted her hips even higher, forcing him deeper. Her second climax very near, she moved her hands from the back of his thighs, stroking and kneading his taut buttocks.

His sharply indrawn breath made her even bolder. Shifting enough to get one hand between their bodies, her fingers touched where they were joined. Their flesh was incredibly hot and slick with their mixed essence.

"Querida, do not—" His plea ended with a strangled groan. Each time he partially withdrew, her fingers rubbed his shaft, sending him closer to the edge.

"Yes, Brit, I will," she replied, her own voice raspy. Her hand continued its encouragement. "You are very near your release, aren't you?"

Brit couldn't reply, the buzzing in his ears was too loud, the incredible pleasure building too fast. Though he didn't want to end the sweet torment, his climax started before he could stop it. His hips bucking harder and harder, he pressed his face to Katelyn's neck.

Katelyn gave his forehead a fleeting kiss, then his nose and his cheek. Moving her lips next to her ear, she whispered, "I want you to yell for me, Brit. Shout your pleasure like you did when we were in your cabin. Shout so I will know I can pleasure you like no other woman."

Though taken aback by her request, he was too far into the throes of his release to make a comment. Spilling himself against Katelyn's womb, he lifted his head and yelled his pleasure as her own cries joined his.

A few minutes later, when Brit could breathe normally, he rolled to his side and said, "You have bewitched me. I have never behaved in such a way, and yet I cannot control myself with you."

"I'm not a witch, I'm the woman who—" Katelyn snapped her mouth shut, appalled she had almost revealed her love for him.

"You are the woman who . . . what?"

She swallowed, afraid to meet his gaze. "It isn't important." She ran a finger down the prominent vein in his arm. "Why did you really come here?"

He grasped her hand and squeezed her fingers. "I told you. I came to see how you are. Is everything all right, *querida?*"

"Yes, everything is fine. How is Armando? And what about Lutero's lumbago?"

"Lumbago?" He frowned. How did she know one of his men suffered from an ailment, when he did not? "Lutero has not complained of it."

"Good. I was worried about him."

Brit fought the immediate anger her words caused. "You should not worry about any of my men. I make sure they are well taken care of."

"I know that. I wasn't trying to imply you don't."

His anger cooling, he nodded.

"How is Solazo?"

"I have finished with her training, so I had Tomás take her to my parents' *rancho.*"

"Why not your ranch?"

"I have only land, no *casa,* no barns or corrals for the horses. It will not become a true *rancho,* until I can build a house and live there."

"What do you call your ranch?"

"I have not thought of an appropriate name, so I have not given it one."

After a few minutes of silence, Brit rose from the bed.

Pulling on his trousers, he said, "I must leave." He turned back to look at Katelyn. Her tousled hair and flushed cheeks made him smile. "You look very inviting, *querida*. I wish—" He abruptly looked away. His teeth clenched, he picked up his shirt.

"What do you wish?"

He fumbled with his shirt buttons, silently chastising his loose tongue. Once again he'd been a fool—a fool to come here, thinking he could change things. Instead of diverting her hatred as he'd planned, he felt the strong compulsion to feed it. He wanted to strike out and hurt her, just as he hurt inside.

Keeping his back to her so he wouldn't see her reaction, he said, "I wish I had time to sink between your thighs again. You have chosen the wrong profession, *gringa*. You would be rich if you were using that lovely body of yours to make a living."

He knew his words were cruel, but perhaps if he stoked her hatred enough, he could provoke her into saying or doing something to end his need for her, to kill his love.

Katelyn sucked in a surprised breath. Pulling the sheet up under her chin, she gave his back a fuming look. "How dare you speak to me that way." Her voice rose sharply. "I want you out of my house. Get out and never come back."

"Do not worry. I am leaving." He tucked his shirt into his trousers, then bent to pick up his gun belt and vest. When he straightened, he looked at Katelyn. As she bravely met his gaze, he could see the tears shining in her eyes, the quiver of her bottom lip.

Jerking his gaze away, he turned to leave. If he stayed a moment longer, he risked becoming more of a fool than he already was.

He stalked to the bedroom door. Unable to resist one last look at the woman he loved, he glanced over his shoulder, then quietly slipped from the room.

Katelyn stared at the empty doorway for a long time. She

flinched at the sound of the front door clicking shut. Brushing angrily at the tears on her cheeks, she sat up and reached over to turn out the lamp. She fell back on the bed, wide-awake, her heart breaking.

Why did she have to fall in love with such an exasperating, arrogant man? Even worse, she'd fallen in love with a wanted man, a man she had worked so long to see punished for his crimes. She drew a deep breath and let it out in a weary sigh. *What do I do now?*

Rolling over, she thought about the editorial she'd written earlier that evening. *I have to remember Brit is The Vulture. I have to remember my father is dead, because of this man! I cannot allow myself to forget that.*

Brit headed toward the mountains and the secret canyon holding his campsite, trying to keep his mind from replaying the scene with Katelyn. He never thought falling in love would change him, or make him act in such strange and contradictory ways. Yet his behavior in Katelyn's bedroom confirmed he had not only lost his heart, but apparently his mind as well. One minute he was a kind and gentle lover, the next a raving madman, spouting horrible words he did not mean.

Shaking his head to clear his disturbing ruminations, he urged his horse to a faster pace. He had to get his life back on the path he had set for himself. Unsure whether he had the strength to accomplish such a feat, he lifted his face to the heavens and prayed for guidance.

Several days later, Brit helped his men find and capture another herd of wild horses. But for a reason he didn't completely understand, he didn't allow *El Buitre* to continue his unlawful ways. He wondered how much time would pass before one of his men would comment on his change in behavior. Though he caught some of them giving him confused sidelong glances, no one said anything until one night a week after his return from Sacramento.

Though the first week of September continued to keep the daytime temperatures very high in the foothills where Brit and his men caught horses, the canyon containing his camp usually turned cool as soon as the sun slipped below the mountains. That night the air hadn't cooled much, leaving the evening pleasantly warm.

Brit sat near what was left of the campfire, watching the few remaining embers flicker and glow red-hot when the slight breeze stirred through the ashes.

"You are very quiet tonight, Brit," Tomás said in a low voice. "Something troubles you?"

Brit pulled his gaze from the campfire and turned to look at his friend. "No, everything is fine."

Tomás nodded, then said, "You have not asked any of us to go with *El Buitre* in search of prey. Is there something you have not told me?"

Brit shifted his gaze back to the dying fire. "There is nothing to tell. I have been thinking it may be time to stop playing *El Buitre*. Perhaps it is time to go home."

"You have avenged Mirabella's death to your satisfaction? You have taken enough gold and dollars from the Yankees to pay back what we have lost?"

Brit took a deep breath, then exhaled on a sigh. "I do not know, Tomás. I . . . I no longer know what I want."

Tomás mulled over Brit's words. After a moment of silence, he said, "It is the *gringa,* is it not? She is behind this confusion you feel." When his friend did not respond, he added, "Could it be you love her?"

Brit glanced over at Tomás, then stared into the deep shadows across the camp. "How could I love a *gringa?* How could I love my sworn enemy?" After a few seconds, he added in a soft voice, "I do not know how it happened, but, *sí,* Tomás, I love her. I have tried, but I do not think I can change how I feel."

"And that disturbs you?"

"Of course, it disturbs me," Brit nearly shouted, then lowered his voice to add, "How would my parents respond if they knew I loved a *gringa?*"

"You forget your *padre* was not always one of our people. He, too, was a *gringo* when he first came here. Then he fell in love with a *California*—your *madre*—and they have had a happy marriage for many years."

Brit's brows pulled together. "You are suggesting I marry Katelyn?"

Tomás rose from his place by the fire. Brushing off his trousers, he said, "I am suggesting nothing, *amigo mío.* What you do with your life and who you chose to marry are your decisions. I am only telling you, sometimes things are not as hopeless as they seem."

Brit watched Tomás until he disappeared in the night shadows. Looking back at the campfire, he contemplated his friend's words. While it was true his parents came from different cultures and had still found happiness, his own circumstance was very different.

Though Katelyn responded to him completely in bed, she didn't love him. She hated him and wanted to see him punished. And though he loved her more than he thought possible, he wasn't sure his own hatred of *gringos* would ever disappear entirely. There could be no happy outcome to that kind of relationship.

After a few more minutes of watching the last of the embers crumble to ash, Brit rose and headed for his cabin. Tomorrow would be another long day, and he was bone-tired.

Once he entered his cabin, Katelyn's journal beckoned as it always did. Unable to stop himself, he lit a candle, then picked up the book. Though he knew he was only bringing himself more pain, he opened the book and began reading.

I wonder if I will be able to keep the Argus going. I guess I never thought about how the running of a newspaper is an around-the-clock job. There's trying to sell advertising space, laying out the pages, writing the local news and the editorial, typesetting and printing, then distributing the newspapers. Thank goodness for Jake. He's the best printer's devil a newspaper could ask for. I don't know how I would have made it without him. He's so fast at the typecase, hand-spiking type faster than I ever could. But if finances don't improve, I may have to let him go. I don't know how I could possibly run the Argus alone, but I may be faced with that sorry state. Papa would be so disappointed in me. He never had trouble keeping the paper here, or the one in Chicago, afloat. Everything is so expensive in California, plus there's so much competition in Sacramento, and only so many people in the reading public. I wish I knew what Papa would do if he were alive.

Ross Carter came by again today. The man has been here eight of the last ten days. I don't know what's the matter with me—a moment of weakness, I suppose—but, I agreed to go to supper with him on Friday. He has been stopping by the office a lot since Papa's death, asking if there's anything he can do for me. He even asked if I wanted to sell the Argus. Though Ross has always been thoughtful and polite, I never thought seriously about accepting any of his invitations to dinner. When Papa was alive, he was always singing Ross's praises, the brotherhood of newspapermen, no doubt. So I guess going to supper with Ross will give me a chance to see if I agree with Papa's opinion of the man.

Brit skimmed over the next few pages of the journal, looking for more references to the man named Ross Carter. Katelyn wrote mainly about her continuing struggles to keep the newspaper going. Ross's name appeared occasionally in her entries, a brief mention of going out with him several more times, mostly to supper, and once to a play at one of Sacramento's theatres. She also mentioned, in at least a couple of places, how he repeated his offer to buy the newspaper. Then came an entry where Ross Carter was the main subject.

Ross and I went to supper last night. Afterward, we took a walk down by the river. It was such a lovely evening, the breeze off the water refreshing and cool. I was startled out of a quiet reverie, when Ross asked me to marry him. I cannot explain how shocked I was. I can only imagine he must have suffered some sort of brain fever, to propose to a plain little hen like me. When I told him he didn't know what he was talking about, he insisted he did, that he wanted me as his wife. I must admit, he did sound sincere. When he asked me for my answer, I told him I would have to think about it. He didn't seem very happy with my response, until I explained that marriage is a very big step, and we barely know each other. He reluctantly agreed to give me the time I need.

A stab of raw jealousy ripped through Brit, threatening to strangle him with its intensity. Trying to calm himself, he closed his eyes until he won the battle. When he had his emotions back under control, he exhaled slowly, then opened his eyes. As much as he didn't want to, he knew he could never sleep that night without finding out what Katelyn had decided.

His hands clenching the journal in a firm grip, he read the next few entries, his heart pounding in his ears. Katelyn told how Ross stopped by every day for a week. He always arrived with a hopeful look on his face, but each time he left disappointed. Finally, the man could wait no longer, and demanded she give him an answer. She insisted she needed more time to make up her mind, but would definitely give him her decision in a week.

Brit checked the date of the entry. She wrote it several days before he brought her to his camp. He heaved a sigh of relief. She hadn't had the opportunity to give Carter her answer.

His brows pulling together in a scowl, Brit closed the journal. What if her answer was to have been yes? If he hadn't spirited her away from Sacramento, would she now be Ross Carter's bride?

Brit's scowl deepened. He would not let her marry that *gringo,* Carter. Katelyn belonged to him.

Sixteen

A few days later, Katelyn awoke with a start. Someone was in her bedroom again. Rising up onto one elbow, she peered into the darkened room. "Brit, is that you?"

She heard the scratch of a match, and blinked against the flare of light as the wick of the oil lamp caught.

"Yes, it is Brit. I am pleased you were expecting me, *querida.*" As he moved closer to the bed, the light from the lamp fell across his chest.

Katelyn's eyes went wide at the expanse of hair-covered muscle revealed by his unbuttoned shirt. When he sat down on the edge of the bed, her gaze snapped to his face. "I *wasn't* expecting you," she said in a low voice. "Last time you were here, I told you not to come back."

He nodded. *"Sí,* that is true. But I think both our tempers have cooled by now, and we can forgive each other's heated words."

"You're sorry for what you said to me?"

He smiled at the dubious look on her face. "Yes, I am sorry. I was angry, and it was wrong of me to strike out at you that way." He picked up one of her hands and pressed a kiss on the backs of her knuckles. "Please say you forgive me, *querida.*" He turned her hand over and ran the tip of his tongue along the length of her palm.

She sucked in a surprised breath. She could actually feel the heat of his tongue between her tightly clenched thighs. She lifted her gaze to look into his eyes. Desire, hot and demanding, gleamed in their black depths. She repressed a shiver, then whispered, "I forgive you."

He smiled, really smiled, making her belly cramp with need. After pressing a kiss on her palm, he rose, stripped off his clothes, then stretched out beside her. "I have missed you, *cardillo mío*. I have missed your sweet mouth." He kissed her lips. "Your soft skin." He placed a kiss at the base of her throat. "I want to kiss and taste you everywhere," he murmured against her ear. "Would you like that, *querida?*"

Katelyn could barely speak. Her throat was clogged with love and need for the man running his tongue along her neck. She finally managed to whisper her response, bringing an immediate chuckle from Brit.

"Ah, I thought you would. First we must rid you of this ridiculous gown." Tossing the top sheet to the foot of the bed, he made short work of removing her offending nightdress. When she lay naked beside him, he nodded with satisfaction. "This is how you should always be when we are in bed. So that I may fill my eyes with all of you."

He moved his gaze from her head down to her toes, making her entire body flush at his bold perusal.

Reaching out with one hand, he settled his fingertips on her cheek. "So that I may touch all of you," he said. Slowly, he moved his fingers down her neck, over one breast, across her flat stomach, through the blond triangle of hair, then down one thigh, calf, and finally one foot. Moving his hand to the opposite foot, his fingers made the return trip back to her face.

"So that I may taste all of you," he said, lowering his head towards hers. He touched her slightly parted lips with his tongue, wrenching a groan from deep in her throat. He smiled again, then captured her mouth with his. She groaned again, lifting her head from the pillow. After a long, thorough kiss, he pulled away.

"Always so eager, just as I am," he murmured, shifting

to kiss one pert nipple. He pulled the coral bud into his mouth, suckling greedily and circling the tightened tip with his tongue. Reluctantly he released her nipple and moved lower. He kissed the indentation of her navel and gently bit her belly. She gasped.

Recognizing the sound as not one of pain but of pleasure, he smiled against her silky skin, then continued his downward journey. He pushed her legs apart, then planted a kiss on the inside of each thigh. She sighed, allowing her legs to fall open even more.

He spared a moment to glance up at her. Eyes tightly closed, breathing rapidly, her hands clutched the sheet at her sides. This time he grinned before returning to the pleasure awaiting them both.

Using his fingers, he parted the soft hair between her thighs, then touched the exposed nubbin of pink flesh with his tongue. Her hips came up off the bed, followed by a raspy moan.

When she made no move to stop him, he settled his mouth over the nubbin of flesh, tugging at it with his lips in a gentle, sucking motion. She grasped his shoulders, digging her nails into his skin, but he barely noticed. All he could think about was how unbelievably sweet she tasted, how incredibly wonderful it felt to love her this way.

Katelyn rolled her head from side to side on the pillow, unable to stand the intense building of heat between her thighs. Nothing Brit had ever done was like the sensations flooding her body at that moment. Never had she imagined anything could feel so wickedly wonderful, or so indescribably good.

Her hips bucking in a wild rhythm against his mouth, she cried his name, then gave herself over to her release. Wave after wave of tremors racked her, making her squirm and twist as the uncontrollable spasms continued. She arched her back one last time, lifting her hips as high as she could, then collapsed back on the bed with a long sigh.

For several minutes, Brit did not move. He kept his lips pressed to the hard bud until her tremors stopped. Then he filled his lungs with her intoxicating scent and eased his mouth from her. Rising up onto his knees, his gaze traveled from the parted thighs directly in front of him to her flushed face.

The totally wanton look about her made him smile. This incredible woman belonged to him—not that damn *gringo*, Ross Carter—and he would prove it.

Grasping Katelyn's legs, he lifted them and draped her knees over his shoulders. With a groan, he leaned forward and entered her in one swift thrust. For a moment he didn't move, willing himself to control the need thrumming through his body.

He drew a deep breath, then began a slow movement of his hips, forward, then back. With each stroke, he pushed a little deeper, until he was certain he brushed the mouth of Katelyn's womb with the tip of his manhood. Just the thought brought on his immediate release.

"No, not yet," he groaned aloud.

But there was no stopping what had begun. Pulling her knees from his shoulders, he pressed his body over hers, bracing himself on his forearms. The rhythm of his thrusts increased, his breathing grew more ragged. His head thrown back, he made one last mighty thrust, then held perfectly still.

Katelyn looked up at Brit. As he throbbed deep inside her, she saw how his nostrils flared, the cords on his neck stood out, the muscles of his jaw clenched. With a moan, he dropped his head forward and buried his face against her neck.

"You will not marry him, *querida,*" he said between deep breaths. "Promise me you will not marry him."

"What?" Katelyn tried to push him away so she could see his face. "What are you talking about?"

Brit gathered his strength and lifted his head to meet her

gaze. "I know about the marriage proposal you received." He pushed a strand of hair off her forehead with his fingers. "I want your promise that you will tell that man you cannot marry him."

"Ross?" She stiffened. "Are you talking about Ross?"

A muscle in his cheek ticked. "Yes, Ross Carter. I want your promise, *querida.*"

Katelyn stared at him for several long seconds. She knew he must have read her journal. There was no other way for him to have found out about Ross's proposal. Had Brit also read where she said she loved him? Was that why he wanted her promise not to marry Ross, because he knew it wasn't Ross she loved, but Roberto Brit Livingston y Cordoba who had captured her heart?

She searched his face for some sign of his feelings. His expression told her nothing. She'd already made up her mind to tell Ross she could not marry him. There was no way she would marry Ross, or any man, not after what she and Brit had shared. It wouldn't be fair, marrying one man when her heart belonged to another. But she still didn't like Brit demanding she do what he wanted.

"Ross and I have a professional relationship. As fellow newspaper owners we have a lot in common, exchanging information on newsworthy—"

"I do not care about any of that, *querida.* The man asked you to marry him. That does not sound like a professional relationship to me."

"Well it was." The narrowing of his eyes prompted her to add, "I never wanted to see Ross socially. Papa was the one who wanted us to keep company, urging me to accept if Ross proposed."

"You still have not given me the response I asked for."

Drawing a deep breath, she knew she couldn't lie to him. "I won't marry Ross." Seeing his eyebrows raise in anticipation, she added, "All right, I promise."

The tenseness seemed to leave his face at her words. A

smile replaced the harsh set of his lips. He lowered his mouth to hers. Just before he kissed her, in Spanish, he whispered, "You cannot marry another man, my beloved, for it is I who loves you."

Katelyn hoped her reaction to Brit's words wasn't obvious. Though she'd been working on her Spanish since coming back to Sacramento, she still didn't understand everything she heard. But she'd bet her last dollar, Brit had just told her he loved her. She longed to tell him she loved him, too, but she held the words inside.

Since there didn't appear to be any chance they could have a life together, not letting Brit know of her love seemed the wise choice for now . . . perhaps forever.

Hearing the crunch of boots on gravel, Ross pushed away from the rear wall of the Orleans Hotel, his gaze searching the shadows.

"You are here, *Señor* Carter?"

Ross stepped away from the hotel. "Yes, I'm here." He squinted at the man, wishing he could see his face. He hated dealing with this faceless, nameless stool pigeon, but he had no choice. "It's a damn good thing you showed up. It's been over three weeks since we were supposed to meet. I waited in this damned place for over an hour before giving up."

Knowing Carter exaggerated the time, Marco decided not to correct him. Instead, he said, "I am sorry, *señor,* but I was unavoidably detained. I was . . . let us say, sampling the charms of a lovely *mademoiselle,* a little French dove I believe you know very well." He chuckled at Carter's indrawn breath.

"You were with Colette?"

"*Sí,* I have been with her several times. She is very good with her mouth, is she not?"

Ross clenched his hands into fists at his sides. Though

he knew Colette sold her favors to other men, learning she had been with this greaser bastard nearly choked him with rage. Hanging onto his temper by a thread, he said, "Now see here, what's Colette got to do with the business we are going to do?"

"I had to make sure what you told me was correct, *Señor* Carter. I wanted to see what kind of man I might be working with, so I followed you around town. Since you spent so much time with the French *puta,* I wanted to find out what you found so appealing, and to see what she could tell me about you."

"You asked her questions about me?" At the man's nod, he said, "What did she tell you?"

Marco shrugged. "Not much, I am afraid. She said she has not known you very long, and could only tell me about what you do in her bedroom. She said you especially like her to take you into her mouth and—"

"Enough," Ross said in a fierce whisper. "What I do with Colette is none of your concern. Now, are we going to do business or not?"

The smile on Marco's face slowly faded. "Because what you told me was the truth, *sí,* we can do business."

Ross stroked his beard for a moment, wondering if he should continue with this deal. He was still furious about Colette, but finally he said, "Your information better be as good as you claim."

"I told you, I can tell you where *El Buitre* hides when he is not robbing Yankees. Are you still interested?"

"I'm interested, but I have to know if you're also selling what you know to other newspapers."

"I have contacted no one else."

Unsure whether to believe him, Ross said, "I'm also curious about something. Why are you doing this? Why are you willing to sell me information which could lead to the arrest of one of your fellow Mexicans?"

Marco stiffened, but didn't correct the man's assumption

regarding his heritage. Tracing the puckered scar on his neck with his fingertips, he said, "It is a matter of revenge, *señor,* of a personal nature."

"Personal nature? What'd The Vulture do, rob you, too?" Ross laughed, finding the idea of one greaser stealing from another vastly amusing.

"No, *El Buitre* did not steal money from me. But I intend to get even with him for what he did do. Now, if you want to hear about his hideout, I must see your gold."

Hiding his annoyance, Ross reached into his jacket pocket and pulled out a bag of gold dust. "Okay, here's your gold, now start talking."

Ross lit a lamp on his desk in the *Tribune* office, sat down, and pulled a piece of paper from a drawer. He wanted to write down his conversation with his secret informant before he forgot anything. The information about the hideout of The Vulture was very good. If he'd been told the truth, once he printed the details in his paper, the authorities should have no trouble finding the hidden campsite. The problem was, had he been told the truth on the location of the bandit's camp? And would the same information find its way into other newspapers?

Ross decided to delay putting the story in the *Tribune* for a week or two. He would wait to see if the same—or even conflicting—details about The Vulture's hideout appeared in other newspapers. He didn't like the idea of being played for a fool.

Having made the decision about the timing of his story, he contemplated what he would do with the rest of the information he'd learned. That a woman was seen at the camp of *El Buitre* hadn't come as a surprise. But his informer's description of a white woman with light hair and eyes had shocked Ross, spawning questions he didn't want to consider.

* * *

More than a week had passed since Brit's last visit, but Katelyn still thought about that night as if it had just taken place. She couldn't forget the first time Brit told her he loved her. Catching herself daydreaming again, she straightened her shoulders, silently lecturing herself to keep her mind on business.

You have a newspaper to get out, and you won't get it done if you keep mooning away the day. She glanced quickly in Jake's direction, to see if he'd noticed her lapse. Breathing a sigh of relief, she looked down at the editorial for this week's edition of the *Argus.*

She reread the article, trying to view it with a critical eye. Was it as scathing as her previous editorials? No, she didn't think so. Well, she didn't have time to write another one. Jake would need the article to set the type in a few more minutes, so what she'd written would have to do.

She squeezed her eyes closed, hoping to halt the threatening tears. She felt like a hypocrite, continuing to write editorials calling for the arrest of *El Buitre,* while consorting with the enemy. *Admit it, Katelyn, you're in love with a criminal.* Even admitting the truth didn't change how she felt. She loved Brit, and even though her position as newspaper editor required her to take a stand on the side of the law, she would always love him.

In spite of her mixed feelings, she knew she had to keep telling herself Brit made his living as a bandit, a bandit who would eventually be caught and punished. She also knew, though she would be condemned to eternal damnation for admitting it, if he came to her again, she would allow him back into her bed.

A few days later, Katelyn sat in the *Argus* office, staring at the opened newspaper in stunned silence. Unable to believe her eyes, she blinked several times, then reread the editorial in the latest edition of the *Tribune.*

*Word has reached this newspaper office by an anony-
mous source that the hideout of El Buitre is located
in a secret canyon deep in the foothills of the vast
regions of the Sierra Nevada Mountains. Though there
are reported to be many canyons in that range of
mountains, we are told the one in which The Vulture
makes his camp is east of Coloma, not far from the
southern fork of the American River. The entrance is
hidden by a rock formation resembling an upright
thumb and forefinger. Along with this welcome information regarding the bandit's camp, also comes some
disturbing news. It was reported to this journalist that
a woman was seen in the camp of The Vulture. Why
would a woman—a white woman—willingly be at the
hideout of a bandit? Has he committed yet another
crime against his fellow man? Has he kidnapped one
of our women for some dastardly purpose? With this
latest revelation, perhaps now our illustrious law enforcement will drop their claims that they do not know
where to look, and using the information we have fur-
nished, take up the hunt for the notorious bandit.*

"My God, where did Ross hear that?" Katelyn whispered.
Where had he gotten the idea a white woman was at The
Vulture's camp? Deciding he must be grasping at straws to
get the local citizenry riled up, she turned her attention to
Ross's claim regarding the location of Brit's camp. Unable
to imagine where he'd gotten the information, she wondered
whether it was accurate.

If only she had a better sense of direction, then perhaps
she'd know for sure. What Ross wrote in the editorial
sounded about right. She knew for a fact the camp was in
a canyon, deep in the foothills of the mountains. There was
some sort of rock formation at the entrance to the canyon,
but she couldn't remember what it looked like. And she
knew there was a river nearby, because she and Brit had

followed one for a long way on their trip back to Sacramento. As to the rest of Ross's information about the camp, she had no idea if what he'd written was accurate.

Aside from the fact that the *Tribune*'s editorial put Brit in danger, Katelyn was annoyed with Ross for not mentioning the information to her. In the past, they'd always shared any newsworthy stories one or the other had come across. Apparently, Ross wanted his paper to have an exclusive this time.

For the first time since she started her personal campaign to have *El Buitre* caught, she prayed the information about his camp and the possibility he held a white woman against her will would not incite the local government to take action. What would Brit think, or more importantly, what would he do, if he saw the article? A shiver racked her shoulders at the thought of his possible reaction.

Tucking the *Tribune* into a drawer of her desk, she stood up, then turned to Jake.

"I'm going out for a while."

Jake looked over at his employer, the young woman he loved like a daughter. Her face looked paler than usual, with dark shadows beneath her eyes. "Are you all right, Katie? You're looking a little peaked."

"I'm fine, Jake. I just need some air. I won't be gone long."

"Take your time. I'll take care of things here."

"I know you will," she said, giving him a smile before opening the front door and stepping outside.

"Katelyn!" Ross pushed his chair away from his desk and rose. "What a surprise. What are you doing here?"

Katelyn glanced at the other men in the *Tribune* office, then back at Ross. "I want to talk to you for a minute, Ross. Can we go for a walk?"

"Sure thing," he said, pulling his jacket off the back of

his chair. "Be back shortly, boys," he called over his shoulder.

Katelyn remained silent on their walk to the public square on Ninth Street.

"What is it you wanted to tell me?" Ross said. "Are you ready to give me an answer to my proposal?"

"No, that's not what I wanted to speak to you about. It's about the editorial in your paper. Where did you get the information about *El Buitre*'s camp?"

Ross frowned. There was something different about the way Katelyn said the bandit's name, a more Spanish pronunciation. For a reason he didn't completely understand, he didn't want to reveal his source to Katelyn. Ignoring her question, he said, "This could be the break we've been hoping for, the break leading to the man's capture. Don't you agree?"

"Ross, I asked you where you got your information."

Irritated with her persistence, he said, "I'll tell you, if you tell me where you were for over a month." Seeing her back stiffen, he couldn't help adding, "Why the particular interest in the man's hideout? Before you went away, you would have been thrilled to have learned such details."

When she didn't answer, he snapped, "What's the matter, Katelyn, isn't what I printed accurate?"

Stunned, Katelyn turned to meet his intense gaze. "How would I know?"

Deciding to be blunt and voice his suspicions, he said, "Were you at The Vulture's camp when you were supposedly out of town on important business?"

"How in the world would I get to the man's camp? I wouldn't have the slightest idea where to find his hideout. You heard Papa tell how I could get lost at the drop of a hat."

"Yes, well, perhaps the man found you and took you to his hideout!"

"Don't be ridiculous, Ross. Why would The Vulture want me?"

Stroking his beard, he stared at her thoughtfully for a moment, then whispered, "Why indeed?"

After a few minutes of uncomfortable silence, Ross cupped Katelyn's elbow with one palm and said, "Come on, I'll take you home."

As he escorted her to the *Argus* office, he thought about his conversation with his informant regarding a woman at The Vulture's camp. He scowled.

After the Mexican told him he'd seen a woman sitting by the campfire the last time he was at The Vulture's camp, Ross had asked what the woman looked liked. The man said he couldn't see her very well, because she sat in the shadows. But he was sure she had light eyes and hair. If he had to guess, he would say she was a *gringa*.

Remembering that shocking and enraging conversation, Ross clenched his jaw in frustration and glanced at the woman walking next to him. Now that he thought about it, Katelyn hadn't mentioned that part of his editorial.

Could it be she had lied to him, that she was the woman at the bandit's camp? He shook his head at the thought, unable to imagine a more preposterous possibility. Still, she continued to refuse to give him a satisfactory answer regarding her whereabouts during her month-long absence. He hated not knowing the truth.

But then, there were things she didn't know about him as well—like the lovely Colette. Though he'd been furious with Colette for taking his informant into her bed, he realized perhaps she could tell him about the man.

The Frenchwoman claimed she had been with him only three times, and each of those times, he insisted she douse the lamp in her room. She had never seen his face, but she did know he had a nasty-feeling scar on his neck. When Ross was satisfied she knew no more, he gave into her pleas to forgive her, but only after administering his own brand of punishment.

Shaking his head to clear such thoughts, he knew he could never risk having Katelyn find out about that little episode with Colette. For the time being, he wouldn't press Katelyn on the subject of where she'd been.

A week later, one of Brit's men returned to camp with another collection of newspapers from Jorge. Wanting to read them in private, Brit took the papers to his cabin.

He read the editorial in the *Argus* first. He smiled at Katelyn's words. Though her article painted him as a vile and dangerous criminal, he was pleased he hadn't broken the spirit of his golden thistle.

Still smiling, he laid her newspaper aside and picked up another from the stack. He opened the paper to the page containing the editorial and started reading. His smile faded.

Checking the masthead of the paper, an angry growl rumbled in his chest. *Damn her! I should have known I could not trust the word of a* gringa. He wadded the newspaper into a ball and tossed it across the room. Running a hand through his hair, he rose to pace the length of the cabin.

In spite of his fury, he had to tip his hat to her. Passing the information on to Ross Carter was a sly move, but one that had not slipped past him.

Now that he knew of her double cross, what would he do about it? He could not let this go unpunished.

Retrieving the wadded-up paper, he smoothed the page he wanted, tore out the editorial, and stuffed the piece of paper into his shirt pocket.

Seventeen

In the ten days since the publication of Ross's editorial, Katelyn's thoughts were never far from Brit. Though the local authorities had shown only minor interest in the information Ross had printed about Brit's camp, a few glory hunters headed for the Sierra Nevada, the *Tribune*'s editorial clutched in their hands.

Each time the men returned empty-handed, she breathed a sigh of relief. Her fear would ease until the next time someone was struck with the notion to try again and took off for the mountains.

"Where do you suppose Ross Carter got the idea some woman was at that bandit's camp?"

Grace's voice startled Katelyn, pulling her attention back to her cooking lesson. "I don't know," she murmured, stirring the batter for johnnycake.

"Funny none of the other newspapers around here printed the same story. Makes a body wonder who Ross's anonymous source could be, doesn't it?"

"Yes." Katelyn looked up at her friend. "It does make a person wonder." She'd thought a lot about that herself, and there was only one person she could think of who was privy to the information given to Ross. Marco Chavez. Just thinking about the man who'd fought with Brit made her shudder.

"Are you all right, Katelyn?"

Idly stirring the batter, Katelyn said, "Grace, I was the woman at *El Buitre*'s camp."

"What?" Grace dropped the cake pan she was greasing and turned to look at Katelyn. When her friend said no more, Grace whispered, "Do you want to talk about it?"

Katelyn lifted her gaze and saw only concern reflected in Grace's brown eyes. "He came to my home the night I wrote the note to Jake, and took me to his camp. He said he wanted me to get to know the real Vulture, that he wasn't the depraved criminal I made him out to be in the *Argus.*"

"He read your editorials?"

Katelyn smiled. "Yes. He's well educated, Grace. And he reads Shakespeare."

Grace's eyes widened. "Not at all what one would expect in a bandit."

"No, he's not."

"Did . . . did he treat you well? I mean, he didn't hurt you or anything, did he?"

"No, he didn't hurt me," she replied, unable to halt the rush of heat to her cheeks. Hoping her flush wouldn't be noticed, she said, "Grace, you have to promise not to tell anyone what I just told you." Seeing the strange look on the older woman's face, she said, "What is it?"

"You didn't tell Ross those things, did you?"

"No. I know some of what he wrote about the camp's location is correct. But even if my life depended on it, I still wouldn't be able to tell anyone how to find the camp. Besides, even if I'd wanted to tell Ross, I couldn't have told him anything about the camp without revealing how I came to have such knowledge. And I would never do that."

"You must love him a lot."

Katelyn frowned. "Ross? Heavens, no, I don't love him. I could never love a man as self-centered as Ross Carter."

"I wasn't talking about Ross. I meant you must love this Vulture fellow. Otherwise, you would have gone to the law as soon as you returned to town."

"Yes," she whispered. "I love him."

"So, what are you going to do?"

Sighing, Katelyn said, "What can I do? I can't go to the authorities, because I won't betray the man I love. And now that Ross's editorial has sparked new interest in hunting him down, I'm in constant fear for his safety, yet there is nothing I can do to stop it. If I reveal I was at The Vulture's camp for a month, then I might get arrested for withholding information."

"Yes, I see your problem." Recalling a conversation they'd had some weeks before, Grace said, "Does he really hate you?"

Katelyn glanced up, her face pinched and drawn. "I'm not sure. He says he hates me, yet he can be so gentle, so giving, when we—" Clearing her throat, she said, "Anyway, he's so filled with hostility and anger, that I think he must hate me."

After a few minutes while she watched Katelyn pour the johnnycake batter into a pan, then slip the pan into the oven, Grace said, "Love and hate are both very strong emotions. Though they would seem to be on opposite ends of the scale, I'm not so sure that's true."

"Are you saying love and hate are closely related?"

"In a manner of speaking. To love someone with all your heart comes from deep inside a person, and takes a great deal of effort. And I imagine hating someone would be the same."

"So, you're telling me, if love and hate come from the same place and take the same amount of effort, one can turn into the other?"

"All I'm telling you is that anything is possible."

Katelyn fell silent for a few moments, then said, "Even if he did come to love me, what good would it do? He's still a wanted man."

"I wish I had an answer for you, Katelyn. But I don't. The Lord works in mysterious ways, so we'll just have to pray for his help."

Katelyn nodded, not altogether certain even God could help this time.

After her conversation with Grace, Katelyn was unable to sleep that night. Having broken her silence and revealed where she'd spent her month-long absence, Katelyn wondered if she'd done the right thing. But Grace was a good friend, one of her closest, so Katelyn was worrying needlessly. Besides, she couldn't deny the enormous burden she'd been carrying now felt considerably lighter.

Her thoughts too much in a turmoil, she finally gave up trying to sleep and decided to read for a while. She'd just settled in the parlor rocking chair, when she heard the soft tread of boots outside the door.

Her heart pounding in her ears, she froze. Holding her breath, she heard the lock being forced open, then watched the door swing inward. As the person came into view, her breath rushed out in a relieved sigh. "Brit."

He turned in her direction, his face hidden by the brim of his hat. "I did not expect to find you up so late, *gringa*."

Katelyn's brow furrowed at the tone of his voice. Though he had often called her *gringa* when they first met, now he only used the word when he was angry. A moment of panic filling her, she knew why he had returned. Determined not to cower, she said, "Brit, I didn't—"

He pushed the hat back on his head, revealing the scowl on his face, the heat of fury in his eyes. "What did you not do?" He pulled something from his shirt pocket and held it out to her.

Seeing the piece of newsprint grasped in his hand, she didn't have to ask which newspaper he held. "I didn't break my promise to you."

He moved towards her, taking slow, measured steps. "Oh, and how is that? One of my men brings me a newspaper with an editorial telling where my hideout is located, saying a *gringa* was there, details only someone who had been at my camp would know, and you tell me you did not break your promise?"

"It's true, I swear it."

He stopped in front of her, a sound much like a growl rumbling in his chest. "Do you think I am a fool? I know you did not write the editorial yourself. But you broke your promise just the same." He gave a snort of laughter. "I have to give you credit, you tried to be clever. By giving the information to your *gringo* friend, you thought you were not breaking your word to me. I was such an idiot, believing your promise, thinking you could be trusted. I now know the truth, you have proven you are what I first thought you to be—nothing but a *gringa* bitch."

She flinched at the words he threw at her, but kept her gaze riveted to his face. "You were not wrong to trust me; I did keep my word. Think about it, Brit. Why would I give the information to my competition? The *Argus* is barely scraping by as it is. So, if I wanted to break my promise to you, doesn't it make sense that I'd try to capitalize on such a story by running it in my own newspaper?" She paused, waiting for her words to sink in. When he didn't look convinced, she added, "I didn't tell Ross anything, I swear on my father's grave."

He lifted a hand and grasped her chin. "Enough of your lies." His fingers tightened. "You will be sorry you did this, *gringa.* I will make you very sorry you crossed *El Buitre."*

He stared into her upturned face. Her eyes were wide and pleading, yet held no fear. Feeling his fury start to waver, he quickly sealed off the breach. "I despise you for what you have done not only to me, but to the rest of my men as well. I swear I will get even for your deceit."

Seeing the darkening of her eyes, her tongue peeking out to wet her lips, her breasts rise and fall with her quickened breathing, his desire sprang to life. He had just announced he planned to get even, and yet he continued to want her.

How could he extract revenge, if his body still craved hers? Releasing her chin, he smiled.

Katelyn watched his expression change, the bone-chilling twisting of his mouth. For the first time, a shiver of dread raced up her spine. What had brought about that sinister smile?

Grasping her shoulders, he held her at arm's length. "I have the solution on how I will avenge what you have done. You will have to withstand the touch, the kiss, the lovemaking of a man who hates you. Can you think of a more perfect revenge, *gringa?*" No longer did he care about trying to change her hatred. His only concern was feeding his own resurrected hate.

She slowly shook her head, not in answer to his question, but as a means to deter him. Finding her voice, she whispered, "Don't do this, Brit. You're so possessed with hate that you can't see what it's doing to you. It will destroy you."

Dropping his hands from her shoulders, he made a sound of disgust. "Who are you to give me advice on hate? The woman who hates the man she blames for her father's death, who wants—"

"I don't hate you," she shouted. Seeing his eyebrows arch, she lowered her voice to add, "All right, I did hate you, but I don't any more. Hating people doesn't solve anything."

"Are you saying you no longer want *El Buitre* caught and punished?"

"No, I didn't say that." She dropped her gaze, unable to look at him. "When people break the law, they usually have to pay for their crimes. I just meant, hate will eat you alive if you allow it to. And I . . . I don't want to see that happen to you."

He crossed his arms over his chest and looked down his nose at her. "Is that right? Well, thank you for the advice, but I have already decided on what I will do."

"I ask you again, Brit." Forcing herself to meet his gaze, she said, "Please, don't do this. Don't turn what we've shared into something ugly and vile. What we had was so wonderful, so right." She swallowed the lump in her throat, blinking back the sting of tears. "Don't spoil it by—" She bit her lip to keep a sob from escaping.

He wanted to tell her not to cry. He wanted to hold her close and rock her gently. But he did neither. Steeling himself not to be affected by the lone tear rolling down her cheek, he swept her up into his arms, blew out the lamp, then turned toward her bedroom.

He said nothing more about revenge, content to let his actions carry out his earlier words. But as soon as he pulled her nightdress over her head, his palms brushing her soft flesh, his plans to take her swiftly—with no preliminaries and without seeing to her pleasure—vanished. As soon as he captured her mouth with his, he could think of nothing but making their lovemaking last as long as possible.

As she moved beneath him, her breath warm against his neck, her hands clutching the backs of his thighs, he realized another of his plans had blown up in his face.

No matter how much he wanted to, he didn't hate Katelyn, he could never hate her. In spite of her betraying him, he still loved her. He would always love her. Though the urge to say the words clawed at his throat, he managed to keep his lips clamped shut.

Several hours later, he left Katelyn sleeping in her bed, slipped from her apartment, and retrieved his horse. As he headed out of Sacramento, he vowed he'd never return. Because if he did, Katelyn might find out his professed hatred didn't exist, that in fact he loved her more than life itself. If she were to learn the truth, he feared she would use such an admission against him. A risk he wasn't prepared to take.

* * *

As soon as Katelyn heard the front door of her apartment click shut, she opened her eyes. Rolling over onto her back, she straightened her legs, then winced. Every muscle in her body ached, having been pushed to the limit by Brit's almost frantic lovemaking.

She sighed. In spite of the angry words he spouted at her, his actions had been completely at odds with his accusations. He said he hated her and would get even, but it couldn't be hatred he felt toward her. Though she was no expert on matters of the heart, she knew instinctively no man could make love with such fierce intensity while still being so infinitely tender, if he hated the woman. Perhaps Grace had been right about hate and love being so close.

The problem was, Katelyn didn't know what it was Brit felt for her. Even if he loved her, there was no chance for them to be together. He was a wanted criminal, she the person calling for his capture.

Closing her eyes, she sighed again. Perhaps it would be better if he did hate her. Then maybe her love for him would die, unable to survive when faced with an obstacle as daunting as his true hatred.

More depressed than she'd ever been, Katelyn wondered what she was going to do. Being torn in two directions was beginning to take its toll.

Brit rode as if the devil himself were hot on his heels. He had to get as far from Sacramento and Katelyn as possible. Though he tried not to think about what he'd accused her of, his mind refused to cooperate. He kept hearing her say she hadn't broken her promise; she hadn't told Carter where his camp was located.

As much as it pained him to make the admission, she had sounded sincere, and her point about giving the story to a competitor made sense. But he knew differently. He knew she was a consummate liar. How else could she tell him she hadn't betrayed him, convincing him for a moment that she spoke the truth, yet all the while guilty of what he'd accused her?

He cursed himself for being a fool once more. There was a line in one of Shakespeare's sonnets which said it best, if he could remember it. Concentrating hard, the line finally came to him. "When my love swears that she is made of truth, I do believe her though I know she lies."

He snorted, then whispered to the night sky, "Exactly."

The front door of the *Argus* opened, and Ross Carter stepped inside. Carefully easing the door closed, he glanced over to where Katelyn sat at her desk.

Jake looked up from where he stood in front of the type case and frowned. When he turned to tell Katelyn they had a visitor, Ross held a hand up to stop him. Jake's frown deepened, but he remained silent as he returned to his work.

Ross came around the front counter and approached Katelyn's desk. When she didn't look up, he cleared his throat.

Katelyn lifted her head. Seeing Ross, her brows pulled together. When he just stood there staring at her, she said, "Did you want something, Ross?"

"You look tired, Katelyn," he replied, taking a step closer. Noting the shadows beneath her eyes, her pale cheeks, he scowled. "You're working too hard. Why don't you let me buy the *Argus?* Then you won't have to worry about ever having to work again."

Her back stiffened. "Is that why you came here, to extend another offer to buy my newspaper?"

"No, actually I came by to apologize for our last conversation." Lowering his voice, he said, "What I said to you last week was out of line, and I'm sorry."

She didn't reply for a few moments, the only sound in the room the rhythmic clicking of Jake's shoving each letter of type into his type-stick. As she studied Ross, his attention strayed. His gaze shifted to the other side of the room, sweeping appreciatively over the Washington Printing Press.

Katelyn pressed her lips together in annoyance. Was that why he wanted the *Argus?* Did he covet the press more than he wanted her as his wife?

"All right, Ross, I accept your apology."

His gaze snapped back to her face, a wide smile appearing in his dark beard. "Thank you, Katelyn." He moved closer. "Would you like to go somewhere this evening?" He placed one hand on her shoulder and squeezed. "We could—"

Her flinch halted his words, making him jerk his hand away. "What is it? Are you hurt?"

Katelyn turned her face, pretending interest in the pile of papers on her desk. "I'm fine. I just pulled a muscle when I . . . tried to . . . move a chest of drawers last night. It's nothing serious."

She absently rubbed her shoulder, hoping Ross would accept her story. If he pressed her further, she might throw caution to the wind and tell him what really happened. That she'd writhed in the throes of passion, twisting and turning, stretching and straining every muscle as Brit made love to her.

Ross's voice pulled her back to the present. "Are you sure you're all right? You're not yourself this morning. If fact, you haven't been yourself since—"

"I said I'm fine, and I am," she snapped, her voice sharper than she'd intended. She exhaled a weary breath, trying to calm her agitation. "Look, I'm sorry, but I'm tired. You're right, I have been working especially hard." She looked up at him, attempting a smile. "But we both know that's the life of a newspaper owner," she said, hoping to sound carefree. "All we do is work, work, work."

Ross nodded, stroking his beard and staring at her now-flushed face. He didn't like this *new* Katelyn. She was too independent, too quick to disagree. What happened to change her, and how could he change her back to the more biddable, agreeable woman he'd proposed to?

Thinking of his still-unanswered proposal, he dropped his hand to his side, his fingers curling into a fist. He opened his mouth, then snapped it shut. The flash of challenge in Katelyn's eyes kept him from bringing up the subject and pointing out her lack of response.

Careful to hide his growing annoyance, he shifted his gaze back to the printing press. "How's the press working, Jake?"

Jake turned, the partially filled type-stick held gently in his left hand. "She's doing just fine."

"You said she came from Cincinnati?"

"Aye. Cyrus said he ordered her from the Cincinnati Type-Foundry Company. Isn't that right, Katelyn?"

She jumped, Jake's voice pulling her out of more disturbing thoughts about Ross's fascination with her father's printing press. "Yes, it was delivered just before we left for Missouri. Papa might have delayed our trip, if the press hadn't arrived."

Ross gave the press one last look, then turned back to Katelyn. "Well, I guess I'd better be going," he said. He bent to place a quick kiss on her cheek, then turned and left the office.

Katelyn stared after him, wondering why she'd ever started seeing him. Her mouth drawn into a severe line, she realized she still hadn't told him she could not marry him. That was an oversight she would correct at the first opportunity. Drawing a deep breath, she turned back to her work.

Back at his mountain hideout, Brit refused to read more of Katelyn's journal. Instead he'd spent the evenings since his return reading from his book of sonnets. He had successfully kept thoughts of the woman he loved from his thoughts, though it was a constant, difficult task, until he came to one particular sonnet. One line made him sit up with a start.

"For thou art so possess'd with murderous hate . . ."

Katelyn's words came flooding back. It was almost as if she had quoted Shakespeare when she spoke about his hatred. Brit closed the book and shut his eyes, trying to ease the sudden ache in his chest.

She was right. Hate could destroy people. But what did love do to a person when nothing could ever come of it? The question haunting him, he rose from his chair and returned the book of sonnets to its place next to Katelyn's journal. He left the cabin to check on the guards he'd posted for the first time since he and his men set up camp in the canyon.

Satisfied the campsite was secure, Brit returned to his cabin and prepared for bed. He lay awake for a long time, his mind refusing to allow him to sleep. He relived every minute he'd spent with Katelyn, every time they'd made love. His body reacting to his thoughts, he bit back a groan and shifted restlessly on the mattress of blankets. Why had his life become so complicated?

Before he first arrived at the mine fields, all he'd wanted was to marry Mirabella, raise horses, and live his life in peace. Then the greedy Yankees changed the path he'd set for himself. Mirabella was dead, he loved a *gringa* he could not trust, and the possibility of ever moving to his *rancho* lessened with each passing day. Another wave of pain washed over him—pain for what he'd lost, pain for what could never be.

Two days after Ross's last visit, Katelyn stared up at Jake, her throat clogged with fear.

"What is it, Katie girl?"

"Did you say Ross has a map showing *El Buitre*'s hideout in the mountains?" she managed to croak.

"That's what I said. I heard tell his anonymous source drew the map for him. Now Ross is having copies made up so he can spread them around to other towns."

Katelyn sagged onto her chair, her heart pounding painfully. "Oh, my God," she murmured. "What will he think when he finds out?"

Jake cocked his head to one side, his graying eyebrows pulled together. "What are you talking about? What will who think?"

"Nobody." Seeing the concern on her friend's face, she reached up and grasped one of his gnarled hands. "Don't worry, Jake. Everything will be fine."

"Katie, are you in some kind of trouble? Are you in danger?"

She removed her hand from his, turning and folding her hands atop her desk. "No, I'm not in any trouble. And I'm not in danger." She squeezed her fingers tighter, turning her knuckles white. Under her breath, she added, "For now anyway."

Katelyn watched the group of men mount up, heard their laughter and jokes about the mission they were about to undertake. Ross's map had caused quite a stir among the citizens of Sacramento. Though some thought the map was a hoax, enough believed in its accuracy to call for volunteers to search for *El Buitre*'s hidden camp. The men would join groups from mining towns to the east and south, then head into the Sierra Nevada.

She should rejoice about the interest in finding The Vulture. She would have a few months ago. But she could find no joy in knowing the man she loved was about to be hunted like a wild animal. Now that what she'd worked so long to accomplish had finally come to pass, she was left with a bitter taste in her mouth, and even worse, a very large crack in her heart.

After getting over her shock at the existence of a map to Brit's camp, Katelyn had decided Marco had to be Ross's anonymous source. Apparently his defeat at Brit's hand had prompted him to seek revenge, and somehow Ross had ended up as the vehicle for that revenge.

Revenge. So much had happened to her in the past few months because of revenge. She had wanted to avenge her father's death, Brit had wanted to avenge his fiancée's death and the way his people had been treated, and now Marco wanted to avenge his loss to Brit.

Thinking about her father brought about a startling realization. She no longer sought revenge for his death. Blaming Brit had sprung from her grief, nothing more.

For months, she had known her father's heart was weak, that he could be struck down anywhere, anytime. His fatal attack happened to strike while he searched for *El Buitre,* giving Katelyn someone to blame. She now knew Cyrus would have wanted the end to come exactly that way— while doing what he loved. There never had been a reason for her to seek revenge.

But what about Brit? Had his thirst for revenge been quenched, or was he still riding the path of vengeance? And now there was Marco to consider. Would the man's desire for revenge lead to Brit's capture, or possibly his death?

As the search party turned their horses toward the edge of town, Katelyn whispered a prayer for Brit's safety.

Eighteen

A few nights later, Katelyn approached her apartment after a town council meeting. When she noticed the soft yellow glow of light shining through the parlor window, she stopped. She didn't remember leaving a lamp burning.

Hurrying to the door, she opened it slowly and stepped inside. Her back pressed against the closed door, she held her breath as she searched the room. The flame of the oil lamp next to her rocking chair danced with the puff of air from her entrance, the chair rocked gently. As her gaze moved to the door leading to her bedroom, Brit stepped through the doorway.

Sagging with relief against the door, her breath left her in a rush. She quickly locked the door, then checked to be sure the drawn curtains completely covered the window.

When she turned back to the room, Brit was sitting in the rocking chair, staring at her.

"I . . . I thought you weren't coming back."

He said nothing for a moment, then finally whispered, "I cannot stay away, *querida*. I have tried, but I cannot break the spell you have cast over me."

She moved closer. "I told you, I'm not a witch. I did not cast a spell over you."

"Then why can I not stay away from you?" he said, grabbing her wrist and pulling her down onto his lap.

"I don't know the answer to that," she murmured, unable to take her gaze off his mouth. "But I'm glad you're here."

Watching her tongue peek out to lick her lips, he moaned. *"Sí,* I am glad, too."

He wrapped his arms around her and pulled her close, his mouth settling on hers. He kissed her fiercely, then more gently, his tongue invading her mouth to taste her sweetness. When she reciprocated, he groaned. His breathing ragged, he pulled away.

"You make me crazy with need. I cannot stop wanting you." He moved his mouth down to her neck, nuzzling the soft skin behind her ear, licking the hollow at the base of her throat. "All I can think about is kissing you, tasting you, being inside you. My mind is filled with what I want to do to you. I want to make you quiver with a need as great as my own, to make you beg me to take you, to make you scream your pleasure. I want—"

"Shh," she said, placing her fingers on his mouth. *"¡No hablemos!"*

His eyes widened, then a low smile curved his lips. "All right, *querida,* we will not talk." Grasping her around the waist, he shifted her position until she straddled his thighs. "I am an impatient man. We will stay right here."

Blinking with surprise, Katelyn made no comment. The idea of making love with Brit in her rocking chair was highly appealing. Her fingers shaking with her burgeoning need, she reached for the buttons of his shirt.

When she'd managed to free the first three, she slipped her hands inside. His skin felt like hot silk beneath her exploring fingers. A moan rumbled in his chest, vibrating against her hands.

"Let me return the favor," he said, unbuttoning her dress. He shoved the opened bodice apart, then pushed her chemise down. Her heavy breasts filled his hands, their coral tips tightening under his scrutiny. Dropping his head, he took one nipple into his mouth. He worked the bud with his lips and tongue until it hardened into a tight rosette, then shifted to the other. When he lifted his head, her nipples glistened with the wetness of his mouth.

He moved his gaze upward. "Let your hair down," he said in a gruff, passion-laced voice.

She did as he bid, raising her arms to pull the pins from her hair. The motion lifted her breasts, bringing them closer to his face. He nuzzled each one, then ran his tongue over each peak. As she freed her long hair from the tight bun, he gathered her skirts in his hands, pulling them upward until they were bunched around her waist.

He lowered one hand to her drawers, pressing his palm against her belly, then moved even lower. Feeling the soft curls through the thin fabric, his manhood jerked in reaction. Groaning, his fingers shifted lower until he found the opening in her drawers.

As he touched her damp flesh, rubbing her gently, then slipping a finger inside, he watched her carefully. Back arched, head thrown back, her breath rasped through her parted lips. She pushed her hips forward. His finger sank deeper, making her gasp.

"Brit," she moaned over and over, her hands groping for the buttons of his trousers. When the last one popped free, she drew in a sharp breath. Her fingers closed tentatively around him. He was so hard, so warm. Gripping him tighter, she moved her hand up, then down.

"Sweet god in heaven," he groaned, his hips lifting off the chair in time to her hand's rhythm. When he could take no more of the sweet torture, he grasped her wrist to still her movements. "Enough. Or I will spill myself in your hot little fingers."

Moving his hands to her waist, he lifted her off his thighs, whispering instructions in her ear.

As he lowered her, Katelyn guided him to the place now throbbing with need. When she had taken him fully inside, her sigh joined his.

"Ah, *querida,* you feel like heaven."

She smiled in reply, but did not speak. Forming words was much too difficult with such heat building between her thighs.

He began slow and easy upward thrusts with his hips, setting the chair to rocking gently with his movements.

Bracing herself by grasping the back of the chair on either side of his neck, Katelyn soon found her own rhythm, using the rocker's backward and forward motion to push against Brit on each of his upward thrusts. Her pulse pounding in her ears, the incredible heat continued to build low in her belly, the pressure increasing where their bodies were joined.

His hands clamped around her waist so she wouldn't fall, Brit clenched his teeth against the overpowering need to find a quick release. He wanted this to last, to draw out the pleasure, but he feared he wouldn't be able to go on much longer. Hearing Katelyn's sudden gasp, feeling the tensing of her body, he realized it didn't matter.

Katelyn gave a high, keening cry, her fingers moving from the chair to dig into his shoulders, her body pushing against his faster and faster. He matched her movements, until his own climax began. Lifting his hands, he grasped either side of her face and captured her mouth with his to absorb the shout he couldn't hold in. He made one last thrust, pushing into her as far as he could, then held perfectly still.

Her hands flexed once on his shoulders, then relaxed. He pulled his mouth from hers, sagging against the back of the chair with a groan. She fell forward, collapsing on his chest, her head tucked against his neck.

When his strength returned, he wrapped his arms around her and pushed out of the chair. The muscles in his legs quivered, but held their combined weight.

He carried her to the bedroom and eased her onto the mattress.

Looking up at him through drowsy eyes, she scooted over and patted the bed next to her. "Stay with me tonight."

"It would not be a good idea."

"Please stay."

Her throaty plea and her disheveled appearance brought a smile to his lips. "You *are* a witch," he whispered, reaching to release the remaining buttons of his shirt.

After taking off the rest of his clothes, then helping Katelyn remove hers, he slipped into bed beside her. When she snuggled close, putting her head on his chest, a pang of longing swept over him. If only it could be like this, if only he could go to sleep each night with his golden thistle at his side.

But he knew it was an impossible dream.

Katelyn awoke slowly, the last dregs of sleep gradually dissipating. Keeping her eyes closed, she recalled the previous evening. Had they really been so hungry for each other that they actually made love in her rocking chair? She smiled. Brit was very inventive when— Brit?

She opened her eyes, wondering if she'd dreamed he spent the night in her bed. Turning her head and seeing his dark head on the pillow next to her, her heart swelled with love. She loved the dusky-skinned, infuriating, stubborn man so much. A tiny sigh escaped her lips. Yes, she loved Brit with her entire being. Yet, what future could there be for them?

Determined to put those thoughts from her mind, she scooted closer and placed a delicate kiss on his shoulder, then another. When he didn't move, she ran a lock of her hair over his skin.

Brit stirred, raising one hand to brush at something tickling his shoulder. His fingers found the culprit and tightened around it. A smile curved his lips. "Ah, *cardillo mío*," he murmured. He opened his eyes and turned to look at the woman lying next to him. "So, I did not dream we spent the night together."

She shook her head. "No, and you didn't dream about the other things we did, either," she said, flashing him an impish smile.

"Other things?" His eyebrows lifted, his dark eyes sparkling. "And what other things are you talking about, *querida?*"

"Don't tell me you don't remember?" When his eyes widened in an innocent look, she said, "Certainly you can't have forgotten what happened in the parlor? In my rocking chair? Or what happened later in this bed?"

"The rocking chair I remember. But later? I am afraid my memory has failed. You will just have to remind me what happened."

"Remind you?" Seeing the mischief in his eyes, she decided two could play at this game. "Of course, I'd be glad to. You carried me in here and slowly undressed me. Then after I helped you undress, you lay down on the bed and I . . ." She glanced around the room for something she could use to embellish her story.

She gave him a quick kiss before continuing. "I used your bandana to . . . to tie your hands to the headboard."

His eyes widened even more. "Really? And did I like such treatment?"

She shrugged. "Perhaps we should try it again, so you'll know the answer."

"Perhaps," he replied. "What did you do after you tied my hands?"

Shifting her position, she knelt on the bed next to him. "Well, I kissed you, and ran my fingers over you like this." She leaned over and pressed her mouth to his, her hands threading through the hair on his chest. Slightly breathless, she pulled away. "Then I kissed you here," she lowered her mouth to his neck. "Then here." She kissed his chest, licking one flat nipple until it stood up in a hard pebble. "And finally here," she murmured against him. She moved lower, her lips grazing the ridges of his stomach, the tip of her tongue darting into his navel.

Brit could barely breathe; his heart thundered in his ears. When her mouth moved even lower, actually brushing his throbbing arousal, his hips jerked upward of their own volition. Her hand closed around him and squeezed. Raising his head from the pillow, he looked down at her. Fascinated, he watched her lips move closer to the tip of his manhood, her tongue peek out to touch him. As his hips lifted again, straining to get closer to her warm mouth, a moan rumbled in his chest. He had never seen anything more erotic, experienced anything more stimulating.

Grasping her shoulders, he hauled her up so that she straddled his hips. "No more of your games, *querida*. I can take no more," he said in a grating whisper.

Katelyn looked down at him; his face was tense with desire. "Stay with me today," she said.

He shook his head, lifting one hand to brush a wisp of hair away from her face. "I cannot."

"Yes, you can. It's Sunday. I don't have to go anywhere," she replied. When he didn't answer, she reached behind her and gave his arousal a playful tweak. She smiled at his surprised expression. "We can spend the day in bed."

"Bruja," he said, returning her smile. Running his fingers through her hair, he murmured, "I love to feel your hair. It is as soft as the finest silk."

"Will you stay with me?"

"Sí, I will stay. Now, bring that beautiful body down here, so I can finish what you have begun."

A low, throaty laugh escaped her throat. "Oh, so you do remember?"

"As I told you, I remember the rocking chair. But as to the rest of your tale, we fell asleep as soon as we got into this bed, and you know it. Still, I enjoyed your reenactment of what you tried to convince me had taken place."

She shifted positions, stretching out next to him. Pushing her thighs apart, he rolled atop her and slipped into her warmth. He groaned at the unbelievable joy their joining gave him.

They quickly brought each other to the pinnacle of pleasure, their thrusts becoming increasingly urgent. As first one, then the other surged over the summit, he lowered his head and gave her a long, thorough kiss.

When the last ripple faded away, he rolled onto his back, pulling her close. "If you would like, next time we will try your fantasy of using my bandana."

Katelyn felt a hot rush of blood race up her cheeks. She turned to press her face to his neck. "Am I . . . I mean, is there . . ." She paused to clear her throat. "Is there something wrong with me for thinking and doing what I did?"

Brit gave her a fierce hug, then kissed the top of her head. "No, *querida,* do not ever think that. You have a healthy appetite for, shall we say, the pleasures of the flesh. There is nothing wrong with you." Only with our future, he added to himself.

After dozing for a few minutes, Katelyn rose and slipped on her robe. Deciding to let Brit sleep, she tiptoed from the room.

Half an hour later, she returned with coffee and hot biscuits. Setting the tray down on her bedside table, she sat down on the bed. "Brit. Wake up." She shook his arm.

He mumbled something, rolling towards her. His eyes opened a crack. "What is that smell?"

"Breakfast. I made coffee and biscuits."

"Coffee?"

"I have chocolate, but no milk, so I couldn't make *champurrado.* I hope coffee is all right. Come on, sit up. We'll be totally decadent and have breakfast in bed."

He smiled. Pushing himself into a sitting position, he scooted up to lean against the headboard. He accepted a cup of coffee from her and a plate of biscuits. When she started to get into bed, he said, "Wait a minute. You must remove the robe."

Her brows pulled together.

"If you want to be totally decadent, you must be as naked as I."

Giggling, she shed the robe and climbed in beside him. Brit ate three biscuits to Katelyn's one, then leaned over to lick the crumbs off her breasts.

"Umm, these are the best biscuits I have ever tasted," he said against one pert nipple.

Though she tried to sound outraged, she couldn't hide the amusement in her voice when she replied, "You are a rogue, Roberto Brit Livingston y Cordoba."

He lifted his head, then sank back against the headboard. "Is that so bad? Do you not like having a rogue in your bed?"

Dropping her gaze, she said, "You know I do."

He put his thumb and forefinger under her chin and forced her to look at him. "Do not be sad, *cardillo mío*. We should just enjoy our day together."

She nodded, swallowing the lump in her throat. Snuggling close to him, she said, "Tell me more about your ranch."

"There is not much to tell. I own twenty thousand acres. There are mountains on the western border, and I share the eastern border with my parents' *rancho*. There is plenty of water from a mountain stream, and enough grass to support many horses.

"But before I can think of raising horses, I must have a place to live. I will use adobe and stone from the nearby mountains to build my house on a site I have already selected. At the edge of the mountains, there is a small, tree-covered hill which overlooks a stream. It will be the perfect spot for my *casa*."

"Sounds wonderful," Katelyn said. "You should put a veranda on the side facing the stream. Wouldn't it be nice to spend evenings sitting on a veranda, listening to the wind in the trees and watching the water flow by?"

He closed his eyes, picturing the scene she'd described. *"Sí,* it would."

After a moment of silence, she said, "Do you think you'll ever get married?" When she felt him stiffen, she added, "Don't worry, I'm not talking about me. I know where I stand. I just . . . I just wondered if you'll have someone to share your ranch with."

He grunted. "I doubt I will ever find another woman I want to marry."

Ignoring the pain his words caused, she whispered, "Don't you want children?"

Not liking the direction of their conversation, Brit didn't reply. He seldom thought about his future. Considering the life he'd chosen, his future could be very short. He might never get to live on his ranch, or marry, or have children.

For a moment, he allowed himself to imagine everything working out. The hope he kept locked inside opened a crack. Perhaps one day he would be able to have a normal life with a family. Recalling the recent renewed interest in finding his secret camp, he refused to entertain thoughts of his life becoming normal. He shoved his hopes back inside and resealed the crack.

He would likely die early and single. In a low voice, he said, "Die single, and thine image dies with thee."

"Shakespeare?"

"Yes, from one of his sonnets. He is urging a friend to marry and have children."

"Oh." Sensing this wasn't something he wanted to discuss, she dropped the subject.

They spent the rest of the morning, all afternoon, and into the evening, alternately making love and talking. Brit was surprised at Katelyn's knowledge of Shakespeare's work, and thoroughly enjoyed their lengthy discussions on what the man was trying to say. Brit realized he and Katelyn not only suited each other intimately, but they were also a perfect match intellectually. Unfortunately, the realization pained him as much as it pleased him.

"Tell me something about you," he prompted, hoping to shake his sudden melancholy.

"What would you like to know?"

He shrugged. "Anything."

"Well, let's see. I like working in a flower garden, though I was never able to plant one here. And I like dogs."

He chuckled. "Yes, I know of your love of dogs. Paco and Pepe still mourn your leaving. They walk around with their great heads hanging down, their sad eyes constantly searching for you."

She gave him a weak smile. "I miss them, too. I also miss Lutero and Armando. They became my friends while I was there."

A little later, he looked out the bedroom window, then said, "It will be dark soon. I should be leaving. I have a long ride back to my camp."

Katelyn's head snapped up. "Camp! Oh, my god! I almost forgot." She grabbed his wrist. "Brit, a map showing the location of your camp has been circulated in the area."

He scowled at her. "What are you talking about?"

"Ross has a map. He says his informer gave it to him, and it's supposed to show the location of your hideout. He sent copies of the map to neighboring towns. Brit, you have to believe me. You have to move your men out of the canyon before one of the search parties finds it."

"Search parties have been sent?"

"Yes, some men from Sacramento were planning to join volunteers from other towns, then use the map to find you."

After a moment, he said, "Why are you telling me this?"

Selecting her words carefully, she said, "I'm telling you

because I care for your men, and also because I care a great deal for you."

He snorted at her declaration. "And you expect me to believe that? What I believe is that your conscience is bothering you. Or could it be you do not want to lose your lover? Does it pain you to think the man who makes you scream with pleasure may be taken from your bed forever?"

Katelyn lifted her chin and glared at him. "I think you have it backwards. You're the one who does most of the shouting while we're in bed." The flush of color appearing on his high cheekbones pleased her.

"Only because a *puta* like you knows how to twist a man inside out and make him behave like a wild beast."

She sagged against the headboard. "Why do you say such hateful things to me?"

He rose from the bed, keeping his back to her. "You know the answer to that. I told you last time I was here, but I will tell you again." He swung around to look at her. "I hate you, *gringa*."

In a soft voice, she said, "I don't believe you. I don't think you hate me."

"I also told you I would make you withstand the touch, the kiss and the lovemaking of a man who hated you. I think you will agree, I did a very good job of that last night and today."

Stung by his words, Katelyn said, "Are you saying everything you did to me was because you hate me?"

Crossing his arms across his chest, he gave her a curt nod.

"Well, I still don't believe you. No man could do the things you did to me, with me, purely out of hatred."

When Brit refused to respond, she said, "Please, let's not fight."

Still he said nothing. She rose onto her knees and moved across the mattress. Lifting her hands, she placed her palms against his chest and flashed him a devilish smile. "Why fight, when there are other things I'd rather have us do? Things we do so well."

He took a step back, then another, until her hands could no longer reach him. "Do not try casting another spell. I do not have time to become ensnared in the net of your charms. I must go. If there is a map to my camp, as you claim, I must get back and warn my men."

Katelyn sat back on her heels, watching him pull on his clothes. She sighed, then said, "There is a map, Brit. But I didn't give it to Ross. Even if I'd wanted to draw a map to your camp, I couldn't have. I don't have any idea where it is."

As he buttoned his shirt, he gave her a brief glance. "More lies, *gringa?* You were at my camp for many weeks. You must have some idea where it is located, and when I returned you here, I did not take the precautions of using a blindfold or traveling at night, as I should have. You saw the route we took from the time we left my camp until we arrived at your door."

"But it didn't matter that you didn't blindfold me, or that we traveled during the day. Don't you understand what I'm trying to tell you? I have no sense of direction. My father used to tease me—" Seeing a muscle in his jaw jump, she pressed her lips together in annoyance, then said, "It's the truth, whether you want to believe it or not. I know your camp is in the mountains, but I have no idea which mountains or which direction to take out of town to get there. You have to believe me, Brit."

He didn't reply, but continued getting dressed. Tired of both his accusations and his refusal to listen, she decided to voice her suspicions. "I think Marco gave the map to Ross."

His fingers momentarily stilling in their process of buckling his gun belt, he remained silent. "Brit, listen to me. Marco knows the location of your camp; you defeated him in a knife fight; he's probably very angry, and this is his way of seeking revenge. Don't you see, the man selling information to Ross has to be Marco?"

Teeth clenched, he swung around to face her. She was still kneeling on the bed, naked. He forced himself to ignore her heaving breasts, kiss-swollen lips, and flushed face. "What I see, *gringa*, is nothing more than a convenient lie, one you are telling to cover your own involvement."

"I swear it isn't a lie. Please think about what I said. It makes sense that Marco would be the one who—"

"I will listen to no more of your talk about Marco." Picking up his hat and jamming it on his head, he said, *"Adiós, Katelyn."*

With that, he turned on his heel and left the bedroom. A few seconds later, she heard the front door click shut. Grabbing her robe, she stuck her arms into the sleeves as she ran into the parlor. She pushed the curtain aside and looked out the window. He had already been swallowed by the encroaching darkness.

Dropping her forehead against the cool glass, she wondered if she'd ever see him again.

Nineteen

Grace and Jake walked arm in arm along K Street, returning from their after-supper stroll through town. Stopping in front of the stairs leading to her apartment above the Barnes laundry, Grace said, "Would you like another slice of pie?"

Jake looked down at her. "No, 'fraid not. Food is the furthest thing from my mind."

"Oh. And what is on your mind?"

He removed her hand from the crook of his arm and squeezed her fingers. "Grace, I love you, you know that, don't you?"

"Yes, Jake, I know. And I love you."

Jake's eyes widened slightly. "Do you? I mean, I know you said you thought you were falling in love with me. But are you sure now that you do?"

Grace chuckled. "Oh, yes, Jake. I'm absolutely sure." Grabbing his hand, she pulled him toward the stairs. "Come on. I have something to show you."

His brow furrowing, he balked. "What is it?"

She turned to face him, her dark eyes glowing with promise. "It's in my bedroom."

"Your bedroom—" He eyed her suspiciously, then suddenly smiled. "Are you saying what I think you're saying?"

She nodded, returning his smile. "Now come on. Time's a-wasting."

Jake laughed, then hurried up the stairs behind Grace, his heart pounding wildly.

When they arrived at the doorway to her bedroom, Jake pulled up. "Gracie, are you sure you want to do this? I mean, us not being married and all. We can wait until we say our I do's, if you want."

"Jake Fletcher, are you proposing?"

"Reckon I am." He grasped her hands and folded them inside his larger ones. "Will you do me the honor of becoming my wife?"

"Yes," she whispered, never taking her gaze from his. When he didn't respond, she said, "Now, are you going to take me to bed or not?"

Jake threw back his head and laughed. "Aye, you saucy-mouthed wench, I am." Releasing her hands, he put his arm around her shoulders, then steered them toward the bed with its patchwork counterpane.

"Would you like me to give you a few minutes?"

Though she wanted to refuse his offer, now that the moment was upon her, Grace realized she did need the time to undress in private. Looking up into his hazel eyes, she nodded.

He dropped a brief kiss on her mouth, then left the room.

On the Thursday following Brit's weekend visit, Katelyn sat at her desk in the *Argus* office, working on the newspaper's books. Hearing the door open, she looked up to see her employee enter the office, then smiled.

"Did you have a nice evening with Grace?"

In spite of his efforts to prevent it, Jake felt the rush of blood to his face. *Nice* didn't begin to describe the previous evening. But he couldn't, he wouldn't, tell Katelyn that his relationship with Grace had become intimate. Keeping his gaze averted, he smiled as he recalled their passion. Finally in a soft voice, he said, "Aye. She's the finest woman I've ever known."

Katelyn stared at his profile for a moment, wondering about that secret smile and the dreamy quality of his voice. Before she could say anything, he spoke again.

"I asked Grace to marry me last night."

"Oh, Jake, how wonderful! I knew you two were meant for each other. I'm so glad you finally decided to keep company with Grace."

"I have you to thank for that, Katie."

"Me? What did I do?"

"If you hadn't left town and sent that note over to my lodging house, I might never have worked up enough courage on my own to talk to Grace."

"Grace told me almost exactly the same thing," Katelyn said with a laugh.

"Did she? Well, it's true."

"You're giving me too much credit, Jake. All I did was unknowingly give you a little shove in the right direction. You did the rest."

"I don't see it that way, Katie. And I just want you to know, I'm beholden to you."

Katelyn smiled. "Well, you two are my closest friends, and I'm glad I could help, even if . . ." Seeing his attention had wandered, her brow furrowed. Were his upcoming nuptials the reason for his preoccupation?

When the real reason dawned, she grinned. *Well, well. Not only are Jake and Grace engaged, looks like they've also become lovers.* Her smile slowly faded. *I hope your love thrives and grows stronger, my friends. I'd hate to see someone else go through the agony my love for Brit has brought me. Love should bring joy and hope, not sorrow and despair.*

Heaving a sigh, she turned back to her desk and the pile of bills waiting to be paid. She rubbed her eyes, then pinched the bridge of her nose. It seemed she wasn't any more successful running the *Argus* than she was with her personal life. She'd just finished posting the current receipts in the ledger, and she knew there wasn't enough money to pay everything she owed. As much as she dreaded the prospect, she realized she'd have to start making the rounds of the local business owners again. With Mr. Danbury having done as she'd feared—storming in to see Jake while she was away and withdrawing his business—the paper was falling deeper and deeper into debt. There had to be somebody in town willing to run advertisements in the *Argus*. She'd just have to keep looking until she found them.

Sighing again, she started sorting through the bills to decide which suppliers she would pay, and which she would have to ask for an extension.

A few minutes later, Katelyn was jarred from her work by Jake's voice.

"Oh, Katie. I almost forgot to tell you. The Vulture struck again."

"What?" She swung around to face him. "Where? When?"

"The Vulture robbed some miners down by Sonora on Sunday last."

"Last Sunday? Where did you hear that?"

"I was coming by the sheriff's office, when a rider came in with the report."

Katelyn's heart pounded loudly in her ears. "How far is Sonora from here?"

"Close to a hundred miles, I reckon. Why?"

She stared at him for several seconds, then turned away.

"What is it, Katie? All at once you're looking sorta funny."

Unable to meet Jake's gaze, she said, "I . . . I'll be fine. I guess I ate something that didn't agree with me."

Shoving the ledger and stack of bills aside, she reached for a piece of paper and her pen. "I'd better write up something to put in the *Argus*. Did you hear any other details about the robbery?"

"There were five bandits, all dark-skinned, most likely Mexicans. They came into a mining camp near the claim called French Bar southwest of Sonora, just after dawn on Sunday morning. The men handed over their pokes of gold, but the bandits weren't satisfied and started rummaging through the miners' personal belongings. Supposedly one of the Frenchmen objected to their taking a miniature of his wife and got hisself knocked senseless for voicing his displeasure. When the other two miners tried to help their friend, they got their throats slit for interfering."

Katelyn frowned. "If all three miners were killed, how does anyone know there were five bandits, that they were probably Mexican, or what they tried to steal?"

"Because they slit the throats of two of the Frenchman, there's little doubt the brigands intended to kill all three. But they must've forgot about the one they knocked senseless with their fists. He didn't die from the beating. Leastways, he ain't died yet. He was able to tell the authorities what happened."

"How seriously was he hurt?"

"He was beat up pretty bad, I guess. But so far he's holding his own." Jake shook his head. "Ain't that about the lowest thing you've ever heard tell of? A man gets his brains kicked in, just because he wanted to keep a picture of his wife."

"Yes, it is," she replied, wondering what reason the thieves could possibly have for taking the miniature. The painting certainly would have no value to them unless it was in an expensive frame. And that didn't seem likely. "Can you think of anything else?"

Jake rubbed his chin. "No, reckon that's all I can remember."

"Okay, I'll write this up, so we can get it in this week's edition."

Jake nodded, then took off his jacket to begin his day's work.

Katelyn sat staring at the notes she'd made and a blank sheet of paper for a long time. What should she do? She couldn't report the robbery had been committed by *El Buitre* and his men, because it would be a lie. Whoever had robbed and attacked those Frenchmen was not The Vulture, not when the real bandit by that name had been in her bed at the time.

As she contemplated what to do, a conversation she'd had with Brit came back to her. It was after his knife fight with Marco. Brit told her he and Marco had disagreed about how to treat his robbery victims. Marco wanted to live by his own set of rules: steal everything and leave no witnesses, while Brit refused to hurt anyone.

Was Marco not only selling information to Ross as she suspected, but had he also formed his own gang and committed the latest crime? Had he stolen everything, then attacked the men with the intention of leaving no witnesses? She shuddered at the thought.

She also recalled Brit emphatically denying he'd ever robbed anyone other than the hated Yankees. He claimed his sole target had always been those who had brought so much suffering to his people. Yet she knew for a fact there had been attacks on people of other races and heritages. Both she and her father had reported such crimes in the *Argus* a number of times.

So what did all of that mean, and what should she do about it? All at once the last few months were too much for her. She pushed her chair away from her desk and rose. Gathering her papers together, she started for the door.

"If I'm not back before you leave, will you lock up, Jake?"

"Sure thing." His brows pulled together. "Are you sure you're all right? And what about the article about the robbery?"

"I'm fine. I just need to lie down for awhile. I'll do the

article later. Don't worry, I'll have it ready so you can set the type first thing in the morning."

Jake nodded after her, wondering at her odd behavior. Shrugging, he turned back to his work.

Two nights after returning to his camp, Brit sat with Tomás in his cabin.

"Lutero said you told him to pack, that we are leaving this camp earlier than usual. Is that true?"

"Yes. We will head for our southern camp in the morning."

"Did something happen while you were gone?"

Brit stared into the fireplace. "Yes. There is supposedly a map being circulated which shows the location of this camp."

Tomás frowned. "And you believe the map exists?"

"I have no choice. I must assume there is such a map, otherwise I could be putting every man in this camp in great danger."

After a moment, Tomás said, "Do you know who made the map?"

Brit's jaw tightened. He gave a curt nod. "Yes, I know. She denies it, but I do not believe her."

"You think the *gringa* who was here, the woman you are in love with, is responsible?"

Brit turned a cool glare on his friend. "And you find that so hard to believe?"

Tomás shook his head. "I did not say that. You said you accused her of making the map?" At Brit's nod, he said, "What did she say?"

"She said she has no idea where our camp is located, that she has no sense of direction, that there is no way she could have drawn the map."

"And you think she lied?"

"Why should I not think so? She has lied before, so she could have lied about this as well."

Tomás fell silent, mulling over what his friend said. "You know, *amigo mío,* her explanation does make sense."

Brit snorted. "How can it make sense?"

"Have you forgotten when she tried to escape from our camp? You found her north of here, deeper in the mountains, traveling in circles. Why would she try to escape by going that way, unless she truly did not have a sense of direction?"

Brit considered his words. He'd never known anyone who did not have some natural sense of direction. Was it possible Katelyn lacked even the smallest trace of what he'd always assumed everyone possessed? Did that explain why she'd run the wrong way when she tried to get away from him the night he took her from her home? And what about when he'd found her after she'd escaped from his camp, and she couldn't tell him which direction to take to find the saddle she'd left behind? The corners of his mouth turning down, doubt began to chip away at the accusations he'd made.

Finally, he said, "If she is not the one who betrayed us, then who could it be?"

"There is only one other person who has been here, who is not one of us."

Brit's scowl deepened. "You are suggesting it was Marco?"

"*Sí,* Marco."

"*Madre de Díos,* not you, too?"

"What do you mean me too?"

"Katelyn also told me she believes Marco is responsible."

"I think she may be right." At Brit's skeptical look, he continued, "He was very angry when he left here, after the two of you fought. You know how much he hates losing. I would not put it past him to betray you to get even."

"He would not be that stupid. He has a very hot temper, and yes, he was angry when I ordered him to leave and not come back. But he knows I would come after him, if I thought he had done such a thing."

"If our camp is found and you are killed or captured, there would be no need for him to worry about having to face you."

Brit blew out a weary breath. "Yes, that does makes sense, Tomás. But regardless of what you and Katelyn say, I am still not convinced it was Marco who betrayed us." Running a hand over his face, he added, "I no longer know what to believe."

Several hours later, Brit sat alone by the fireplace, Katelyn's journal resting in his hands. He had refused to read from the book since he first accused her of breaking her promise. After the conversation he'd had with Tomás, his confusion about Katelyn's betrayal stirred the need to read more of her words.

He stared at the book for a long time, running his fingers over the cover. Taking a deep breath, he opened the journal and flipped to where he'd stopped reading, the entry about her putting off answering Ross Carter's proposal.

The next entry had been written in his camp soon after their arrival. As he read her description of him, a smile curved his lips. That she thought him handsome pleased him. Her next words erased the smile. "Ah, *querida,*" he murmured. "You are not plain as mud." His heart ached with the pain he felt in her words.

Thinking back to the first time he'd seen her, he was startled and embarrassed to realize his initial impression of her had been exactly that—plain. That he now considered her one of the most beautiful woman he'd ever known, did little to ease his conscience.

Perhaps she wasn't naturally beautiful. True beauty wasn't just a person's physical appearance. Beauty came from what a person was inside. That thought made him frown. When had he changed so drastically, to think the outward appearance of a person meant so little? He equated the beginning of his reversal in attitude with his meeting Katelyn Ferguson.

Turning his attention back to the journal, he continued reading. Most entries were brief character sketches of his men and their day-to-day activities at the campsite. Other entries were anecdotes of her stay.

I was especially bored today so Armando and Juan took it upon themselves to entertain me. I was surprised to learn Juan likes to sing. After a bit of cajoling on my part, I convinced him to sing, while another of the men played a guitar. Though I did not understand the words of the hauntingly beautiful song, I was very moved by Juan's truly wonderful voice. Armando told me the song was popular at wedding fiestas. Such celebrations, I was astounded to learn, could last as long as five days and are filled with eating, drinking, singing, and dancing. After I badgered him unmercifully Armando showed me some of the dances performed at fiestas. He is very light on his feet, and I especially liked the jarabe and the jota. Though Armando offered to teach me, I declined. I doubt I could ever learn the steps of either dance.

Brit smiled at the picture of Armando dancing for Katelyn, then immediately sobered. He never knew Juan had a good singing voice, or that the young man even liked to sing. Though annoyed Katelyn had learned something else he didn't know about his men, he continued reading.

The more he read, the more the truth became apparent. She had not used the journal to record information about him for use in her newspaper editorials. Conceding that on this, at least, she had not lied, he refused to consider whether the concession should also be extended to the other falsehoods he'd accused her of telling.

When he read the entry she wrote after learning why he'd become *El Buitre,* he clenched his teeth together in silent fury. *Let the law handle it, bah! Both the law officials and the courts would do nothing. They were just more* gringos, *siding with the Yankees, who were trying to send those of us they called greasers from the mine fields.*

Still seething, he continued reading. Katelyn's next entry, the one about their first kiss, immediately cooled his anger. He smiled at her description of that kiss and how it affected her, vividly recalling his own heated reaction to the moment.

The rest of the entry was not so amusing. She told of her intention to escape. Her claim of having no sense of direction brought his eyebrows together in a fierce scowl. He tossed the journal down in disgust.

Pressing the heels of his hands against his eyes to ease the sudden ache in his head, he thought about what she'd written. Was it possible her words were true, that she really had no idea where his camp was located?

He dropped his hands from his face and stared into the fire. Perhaps she had been covering for herself. Perhaps she'd written the entry, knowing he'd eventually read her words and believe her denial of having revealed the whereabouts of his camp.

Thinking about her coming up with such a plan, he frowned. Such a scheme seemed much too elaborate, even for a woman bent on revenge. If she wanted his camp found, why would she deny breaking her promise? If she wanted him caught and punished as she'd claimed, she would have gloated over her success, anxious for him to know she was behind his demise.

Was this another instance where he had wrongly accused her of lying? As difficult as it was to consider, had he thought the worst of her at every turn, when in fact she had done nothing to earn his scorn?

Still not sure what to believe, Brit rose from the chair. He would go for a walk before retiring. Perhaps the cool night air would help him find the answers he sought.

Katelyn was just locking the door to the *Argus* office on Saturday, when someone grabbed her from behind. "What are you doing?" she said, struggling to free her arm. "Let go of—" Finding herself being spun around to face the person clutching her elbow, the demand died on her lips.

"Ross! For heavens sake, let go of me! People are staring," she said in a harsh whisper. "What's gotten into you, anyway?"

His fingers eased their tight grip, but he did not release her. "And I'd like to know what's gotten into you."

"What are you talking about?"

He held up a newspaper with his other hand. "This is what I'm talking about. What the hell's the matter with you?"

"What's the matter with me? You're the one acting like a raving lunatic. Now which paper are you waving in front of my face?"

"This is today's *Argus*. Now do you understand?"

Stiffening her spine, Katelyn sent him a fierce glare. "No, I do not understand. I have no idea what you're trying to say."

Ross took a deep breath, then exhaled slowly. "What I'm trying to say is, you knew the robbery at French Bar was the work of *El Buitre*, yet you refused to name him."

Katelyn shrugged off his hand. "And just how is it I know The Vulture was responsible?"

"Because the man who survived the bloodthirsty bandit's attack said so."

"But how does the man know it was *El Buitre* who robbed and beat him?"

Ross opened his mouth, then snapped it shut. He stared

at Katelyn through narrowed eyes for a moment, then said, "I don't intend to continue arguing with you on this subject, Katelyn. I don't understand you. I thought you wanted the bandit caught, just like the rest of us. But this article certainly doesn't sound like that's what you want. If the man's to be caught and punished, it's our duty to help accomplish that end, which means using The Vulture's name when we receive word a robbery was committed by his gang. Now, next time you will do that, won't you?"

"Don't you tell me what to do, Ross Carter. I'll run the *Argus* any way I see fit. Do you hear me?"

The expression of Ross's face would have been laughable, had Katelyn not been so furious. "Oh, before I forget. I want to give you my answer to your proposal." When she was sure she had his attention, she leaned closer and said, "My answer is no. I'd sooner marry . . . *El Buitre* than the likes of you."

"You can't be serious? You're just upset. When you calm down—"

"I am not upset," she said, her voice raising slightly. "And I am most definitely serious. I do not want to marry you, Ross. Not now, not ever. I can't put it any plainer than that."

He stared at her thoughtfully for a moment. "Is there any chance you'll change your mind."

"No, there's no chance whatsoever. Now, at the risk of sounding rude, would you get out of my way?"

When Katelyn started to move past him, Ross snapped out of his momentary shock. Stepping in front of her, he said, "But what about the *Argus?* Will you consider selling the paper to me?"

"I see I really broke your heart with my refusal, didn't I, Ross?" Before he could answer, she added, "I haven't decided if I want to sell. But I'm sure you'll be pleased to know, if I make that decision, you'll be the first person I contact." Disgusted by the anticipation and greed she saw on his face, she started past him a second time, grateful he didn't try to stop her. Not looking back, she headed down K Street.

Twenty

The following day, Katelyn attended mass at the St. Rose of Lima Church. Though she was not Catholic and didn't understand a word of the Latin-spoken mass, just being in a church of Brit's faith made her feel closer to him. Her hands clasped beneath her bowed head, she prayed for his continued safety.

After leaving the church, she went for a walk. As she strolled through town, she made a decision on something she'd been contemplating for the past few weeks.

When she arrived in front of the *Argus,* she figured she might as well get started on the decision she'd made. She entered the newspaper office, locked the door behind her, removed her bonnet and shawl, then headed for the back room.

Rummaging through the storeroom, she finally found what she was looking for: the wooden crate containing her father's notes. After his funeral, she had packed them away and had Jake carry the crate to the back room. She had never been tempted to look through his papers on *El Buitre* until now. Brit's story of the treatment he and others received in the mine fields had opened her mind to the possibility that her father might have been right. Then the latest robbery attributed—wrongly—to The Vulture, made her realize how the bandit's exploits had been greatly exaggerated, not just in this instance, but probably in others as well.

There was no doubt Brit had taken up a life of crime.

But she needed to know if the reasons he gave were accurate. To do that, she planned to do some investigating of her own, beginning with her father's notes.

She dragged the crate from the storeroom over to her desk, then carefully opened the lid. Searching the contents for the file Cyrus had kept on the bandit, she found several folders marked Research, and pulled them out of the box.

Taking a deep, steadying breath, she sat down, then opened the first of the folders. Inside was a collection of newspaper clippings. Sorting through the articles, Katelyn noted they were from various newspapers around California, the *Sonora Herald, Alta California* and *Stockton Times*. Most of the clippings were about the bandit dubbed *El Buitre,* and the editors' outrage at the man's crimes. A scant minority objected to the unfairness of the treatment all Spanish-speaking received. "Shame! Shame!" one article read. "For the savage way many of our contemporaries have treated the so-called greaser."

A knot forming in her stomach, Katelyn laid the folder aside. The second folder contained a collection of handwritten notes, all penned by Cyrus Ferguson.

The first few were written not long after the name *El Buitre* had been given to the bandit playing havoc with the entire mining area. Cyrus expressed his interest in the man, his plan to dig into the bandit's background if possible, and how he one day hoped to interview the man.

I find this bandit, El Buitre, a most interesting fellow. I can only wonder what tales he could tell, if I were able to speak to him in person. I have this inexplicable feeling he is not what he appears. That beneath the bandit veneer, there is a man like the rest of us, a man who has something in his past to explain his life of crime. To begin my research, I must first learn the history of the mine fields, to find out why so many are against those who speak Spanish.

The next few pages were filled with a chronology of events in the area, beginning with the discovery of gold by James Marshall.

Katelyn quickly scanned the first page. Foreigner Miners' Tax. The words jumped out at her. Brit had mentioned something about the tax, and how it had angered him. Apparently her father had felt the same way, based on the note he wrote in the margin. "What has gotten into the men of our newly formed state legislature, thinking they can exclude all 'foreigners' from the mines? California is a state now, sworn to support the U.S. Constitution, which says all men are created equal."

The knot in her stomach pulled tighter. *Dear God, what have I done by not looking into the reasons for the crimes Brit has committed?*

Other notes made by her father contained eyewitness accounts of the crimes committed by The Vulture, and even descriptions of the man. Some reported him as being tall and muscular with a long moustache, while others claimed he was short, stout, and clean-shaven.

The last note Cyrus wrote before his death read: "All *Californios* have a complaint against the Yankees, and justifiably so. As to the man known as *El Buitre,* I have not been able to determine his specific complaint."

Katelyn closed her eyes and took a deep, shuddering breath. Well, perhaps she was a bit late, but she would dig deeper and find the answers her father—and now she— wanted.

The next morning, Katelyn waited impatiently for Jake's arrival at the *Argus*. Most anxious to talk to him, the wait was nearly unbearable. At last, the front door opened and Jake stepped inside.

"Morning, Katie," he called, coming around the counter. "You're here mighty early."

"Yes, I know. Jake, come sit down for a minute."

His eyebrows lifted. "Sit down? But I have work to do."

"Work can wait a while longer. I need to talk to you."

Jake removed his coat, then sat down in the chair next to her desk. "What is it? Are you feeling poorly? You're looking peaked this morning."

"I'm fine. I just didn't get much sleep last night." She opened the desk drawer and withdrew the folder containing her father's notes. "I want to talk to you about Papa's research on *El Buitre.*"

"What about it?" he replied carefully.

Sensing his unease with this topic, she said, "I should have paid more attention to Papa's obsession with the bandit. I should have looked in Papa's files before now. I should have done a lot of things." She reached over and squeezed one of Jake's hands.

"I want to finish what Papa started, Jake."

"So, where do I fit into your plans?"

"Papa talked to you about his work, didn't he?"

"Aye."

"Well then, I want to know everything you talked about. I want to know anything that might help me."

Jake stared at her for a minute, his brows pulled together. "Are you sure this is what you want to do? Won't it just bring up more sad memories about your father's passing?"

"Yes, I'm sure. And no, the sad memories are past me now. I want to do this, because I owe it to Papa. It was his dream, and now that he's gone, I've decided I want to finish it for him."

After a moment's silence, he said, "Okay, Katie. What do you want to know?"

"Tell me about the Foreigner Miners' Tax."

He made a sound of disgust in his throat. "If that ain't the most harebrained idea the state legislature ever come up with. Just 'cause the Mexicans were better at finding gold than us Yanks—who knew next to nothing—the damned authorities listened to the complaints of the Yankee miners and levied the tax."

"Is that when bandits like The Vulture took to robbing?"

"Not right at first, though there was plenty of trouble when tax collectors were sent to the mine fields. Anyone who refused to pay the tax was ordered out of the mines. Not long after that, we started hearing stories of violence and robberies."

"And was *El Buitre* responsible for all the trouble?"

Jake chuckled. "Not likely. There's no way one man could be in so many places and rob so many people in the short amount of time between some of the robberies. *El Buitre* isn't the only bandit around this part of California, he's just the most famous."

"In reading Papa's notes, he indicated the miners' tax was repealed in '51."

"Aye, it was. The legislature made the decision after all the tension and violence broke out against the tax collectors. Then, of course, there was also the issue of whether the tax was constitutional. When the tax was repealed, it had only been in effect for a little over a year. But by then, it didn't make any difference. Prejudices were already too deep, hatreds too strong."

Katelyn sat back, thinking about what Brit had told her. He had said the same thing, that even after the tax had been lifted, the Yankees still didn't want any greasers in the mines. At last she said, "Why didn't you tell me all of this when I started writing the editorials about *El Buitre?*"

Jake gave her a small smile. "At first I didn't say anything, because you were so grief-stricken over losing your father. Then when your grief turned to vengeance, I knew you would never listen to anything I had to say about the man you held responsible for Cyrus' death."

"I suppose you're right. I wouldn't have listened to you," she replied. "But that's changed. Now I want to hear anything you can tell me. What do you know about the *Californios?*"

Jake scratched his head. "Not a lot, I reckon. It's the name folks who were born in California to Spanish-speaking parents call themselves. Some years back they went by *Españoles* or *Mexicanos,* but since neither of those names reflects where they were born, they now prefer *Californios.* Most of them have lived here for many generations. Their ancestors originally came from Spain to settle on land granted them by the Spanish crown."

"Didn't the Miners' Tax apply only to those who weren't born in the United States?"

"Aye, that was its intent. Except no one would listen to the *Californios'* claims of being U.S. citizens. Because they were born here, the Treaty of Guadalupe-Hidalgo gave them full citizenship. But the tax collectors refused to honor the treaty, and considered all Spanish-speaking miners foreigners."

"That's what Brit said," she murmured.

"Who's Brit?"

Katelyn looked up to meet Jake's confused gaze. "Has Grace said anything to you about what I told her a few weeks ago? About where I was back in July?"

He shook his head. "Grace told me you and she talked about it, but she wouldn't tell me what you said." He looked down at his callused hands. "I thought you and me were close friends, Katie."

"We are, Jake. I didn't mean to hurt your feelings by telling Grace first. But I just couldn't hold it in any longer, especially not after she guessed part of it."

Jake lifted his head to stare at her. "What do you mean? What did she guess?"

"That I was with a man," she replied in a low voice.

"A man?" The muscles of his jaw tightened. "If some no good scoundrel hurt you, Katie, they'll have me to deal with."

"It wasn't like that, Jake. I admit, I did fear for my safety at first, but except for a few cuts and scrapes caused by my own foolishness, I didn't get hurt. And I wasn't in any danger, unless you call getting lost in the mountains with no food dangerous."

"Lost in the mountains? Katie, I think you'd better start from the beginning."

She sat back with a sigh. "First, you have to swear what I'm going to tell you will go no further than Grace."

"I give you my word."

"Okay, here goes. The night I left Sacramento, a man was in my apartment when I returned from the town council meeting. He said he was taking me with him, then ordered me to pack a bag and write the note to you.

"We left town on horseback and rode for the better part of two days. When we arrived at his destination, he introduced himself as Roberto Cordoba, but that I knew him by another name, *El Buitre.*"

"You're pulling my leg?" When she shook her head, he said, "It was really the bandit hisself?" He leaned forward, his eyes wide with disbelief.

"I know it's hard to believe, but it's true. He told me the reason he'd abducted me was so that I could get to know the real *El Buitre,* that he wasn't the vile person I'd described in my editorials."

Jake's eyes widened even more. "He'd read your editorials?"

Katelyn laughed. "Yes, but that's not the only thing about the man you will find unbelievable. He was educated at Oxford. He reads Shakespeare. And he can handle a knife better than the best street brawler."

After a few moments, Jake said, "So, who's this Brit you mentioned?"

"It's a long story."

He sat back in his chair. "I ain't going anywhere."

* * *

An hour later, Katelyn finished her tale, having omitted only the intimate details of her relationship with Brit.

"So, what do you think?" she finally asked when Jake remained silent.

"I wish your father were alive, so he could hear what you just told me."

"Me, too. Papa would have liked Brit."

"I think I would like him, too."

Katelyn smiled. "I'm sure you would." Her smile faded, her heart aching for the man she loved.

"So, what are you going to do with Cyrus' notes?"

"I'm not sure," she replied, her brow furrowed. "I know Brit committed robberies, so there's no way I could help prove him innocent. It's just that I want to do something to show people that he isn't the horrible, bloodthirsty bandit he's been portrayed as being."

"I doubt you'll do any good, Katie. People have their opinions, and I doubt anything you could say will change them."

"You're probably right, but I still have to try. I feel as though I owe it to Brit for the things I said about him."

Jake fell silent, tapping his fingers on the corner of Katelyn's desk. At last, he said, "Are you sure there isn't another reason for your wanting to do this?"

She met his gaze for a brief moment, then stared down at the folder in front of her. "I love him."

A pain wrenched his heart at the hurt he heard in her softly spoken words. Covering her clasped hands with one of his, he gave her an encouraging squeeze. "Oh, Katie. I wish there was something I could say to help, but I'm afraid I don't know what it would be."

She gave him a tremulous smile. "That's okay, Jake. There's nothing anyone can say." Forcing her sadness aside, she said, "Well, I'd better let you get started on your work. I've kept you from it long enough."

Rising from his chair, he started to say something, then

changed his mind. As he walked behind her, he gave her shoulder a gentle pat.

The next morning, Katelyn went to see Grace before going to the newspaper office.

"Grace, can I ask you some questions about when you lived in the mine fields?"

Grace turned from a pile of mending, a needle in her hand. Soon after she started doing laundry for the miners, she learned they would also pay handsomely for her skills with a needle.

"Ask away."

"You lived in one of the mining towns northeast of here, didn't you?"

"Yes. My husband and I arrived in California in the spring of '50, and came up the Sacramento River by steamer. We lived in a one-room cabin on our claim on the middle fork of the American River, up near Auburn."

"Did either you or your husband ever see any of the other miners mistreated while you were there?"

Her eyebrows drawn together, she said, "I'm not sure what you mean."

"Was there any prejudice against any of the miners, maybe a particular nationality?"

"There were men who disliked everyone, no matter where they came from. Men like that were prejudiced against anybody they saw as a threat."

"What about the Spanish-speaking? How were they treated?"

"There were several men mining near our claim from Argentina, though the others called them Spaniards. I never saw anything firsthand, but my husband told me how some of the miners would get drunk and start shouting 'Down with the Spaniards' and 'Drive every foreigner off the river.' That summer, the miners' tax was imposed. The men from

Argentina and most of the other Spanish-speaking men left the area. The few deciding to stay did so at their own risk."

"You left the mines before the tax was repealed?"

"Yes. My husband died of cholera in October, seven months after we got here, then I moved down here to Sacramento and opened the laundry."

When Katelyn fell silent, Grace said, "Why are you asking me these things? Is it because of what you told Jake yesterday?"

Kathelyn met her friend's inquisitive gaze, then smiled. "I should have known Jake wouldn't waste any time telling you what I told him."

Turning back to her mending, Grace said, "I can't believe you actually spent an entire month in a camp of outlaws."

"Sometimes I have a hard time believing it myself."

"Katelyn, are you sure you know what you're doing? I mean, going through Cyrus' files and digging into the past. What will that prove?"

Katelyn drew a deep breath, then exhaled slowly before responding. "I don't know if what I'm doing will prove anything. But I do know it will make me feel better."

"Well, if there's anything either Jake or I can do, just speak up."

"I will, and thanks, Grace."

During the next several days, Katelyn spent every available minute going through her father's files and rereading her own articles about the crimes committed by *El Buitre*. After carefully cataloging each crime attributed to The Vulture, she discovered a very telling pattern. There were two distinct types of crimes: those where robbery was the only motive, the victims—all Yankees—never hurt; and those where victims of assorted nationalities were robbed, then assaulted or killed, their cabins or tents often set afire.

More and more of Brit's claims were proving to be true.

A few days later, word reached Sacramento about a robbery at Mokelumne Hill where *El Buitre* had committed the latest of his heartless murders and robberies. Five Mexicans reportedly had entered a camp of Chinamen, killing two and severely wounding the others, then made off with two thousand dollars in gold.

Refusing to write an article naming Brit as responsible, Katelyn made a decision she'd been toying with for several days. She planned to visit the area where so much of the trouble between the Yankees and the Spanish-speaking had taken place, where the Foreigner Miners' Tax had caused such havoc. She wanted to talk to the people who lived through those times. Based on the newspaper clippings her father had saved, the counties of Calaveras and Tuolumne, once hotbeds of anti-Mexican activity, would be where she'd start.

When she told Jake about her plan late the next afternoon, he said, "Are you certain that's a wise idea, Katie?"

"Yes, I do. I think Papa was right, there is another side to *El Buitre's* story, a story that should be told. And I hope to be the one to tell it."

"I already told you, nobody will listen to anything you have to say. Though it ain't right, nobody cares what provoked the man to a life of crime. They consider him a bandit, a murderer, and every other sort of criminal, and the only thing you'll change will be the way they think about you. They'll turn against you, Katie. They'll call you names. Names you won't like. I'm asking you to reconsider."

She shook her head. "I don't care what the people around here think of me. If they're so narrow-minded they refuse to believe the truth, so be it. I'm taking tomorrow's stage to Jackson."

Jake wiped a hand across his brow. "Okay, I see that I can't change your mind. But at least let me or Grace go with you."

"No, I'm making this trip alone. You and Grace need to

stay here and see to business. Don't worry about me. I can take care of myself."

"What about Ross?"

Katelyn stiffened. "What about him?"

"Don't you think you should tell him you're leaving? He was madder than a wet hen last time."

"I don't need to tell him a damn thing," she said with her chin high, bringing a chuckle from Jake. "I told him I wouldn't marry him, so now he has no excuse to come snooping around the *Argus*. Promise me you won't let him try to take over this time."

"You have it, Katie. Now that I know you ain't marrying that sorry good-for-nothing, I won't let him get beyond the front door."

She smiled, then said, "I guess I'd better get home and pack a bag. I'd ask you to see me off in the morning, but the Forrest Line stage leaves at four."

"Don't be silly, Katie, four in the morning isn't too early for these old bones. I'll come by at three-thirty and walk you to the stage. The Forrest Line runs from the Crescent City Hotel, doesn't it?"

"Yes, but—"

"I'm walking you to the hotel," he interrupted in a firm voice. "And I won't take no for an answer."

Katelyn's smile broadened. "Okay, okay." Giving him a quick hug, she said, "I'll see you in the morning."

Twenty-one

As Katelyn and Jake said their good-byes in front of the hotel, five Forrest Stage Line Concord coaches waited abreast in the street, the teams of horses nervously pawing the ground. Katelyn hugged Jake one last time, then stepped up into the coach heading for Sonora. Even with the ungodly hour of departure, the coach was full. Katelyn sat pinned between a miner who immediately scrunched down on the seat and fell asleep, and a whiskey drummer from San Francisco who had no such intention.

By the time the stage stopped for breakfast at Twelve Mile House a little more than an hour later, Katelyn already had a pounding headache from a combination of the salesman's nonstop ramblings and the cloying scent of his cologne. Breakfast, such as it was, consisted of salt mackerel, salty ham, hard biscuits, and thick coffee, and did little to ease the throbbing in her head.

After crossing a suspension bridge over the Cosumnes River and passing through Ione Valley, the stage rumbled into Jackson right on schedule: 11:00 A.M. sharp. Planning to continue her journey the following day, Katelyn gratefully bid her traveling companions good day, then headed down Main Street.

Though she wanted to begin her investigation right away, she first sought a hot meal and a room for the night. A nap and a sponge bath refreshed her immensely and erased the last of her headache. It was time to start seeking answers to her questions.

Katelyn spent the rest of the day searching for someone who would talk to her about past troubles in the mine fields, both before and after the Foreigner Miners' Tax was imposed.

A few men she spoke with offered their opinions on the tax and the expulsion of foreigners from the mines, but it was only the typical Yankee biased view. Then, when the men discovered she was interested in the other side of the issue, their attitude changed. The looks of disgust on their faces and their curt dismissals told her they were no longer willing to talk to a newspaper reporter who was, in their eyes, nothing but a damned greaser-lover.

She bit her tongue to hold in a scathing retort, then swallowed her disgust and continued her search for information.

Unfortunately, all the Spanish-speaking men she approached were even more skeptical. In spite of her claims of wanting to hear their side, they were not willing to trust a stranger, especially a *gringa*. Though they weren't as rude or belligerent as the Yankees, they refused to speak.

Realizing the mission she'd given herself was going to be more difficult than she'd imagined, she left Jackson on the next day's southbound stage.

Her reception in each mining town she visited— Mokelumne Hill, San Andreas, Angel's Camp—was initially open and warm. After all, a new female was always welcome in towns where the population was more than ninety percent male. But as soon as she started asking questions, the treatment she received changed to formal coolness. The answers she received were only icy stares and closed mouths.

Refusing to give up, she boarded the Forrest Line coach after each unsuccessful stop and continued her southward trek to her final destination: Sonora.

There had to be someone who would say more than, "The

greasers got what they deserved." Yet, as she walked Sonora's narrow, hilly streets, each person she questioned who claimed to know nothing, made Katelyn wonder if trying to find some answers was just a waste of her time. She'd been in the mining area the better part of four days, and had yet to learn anything of value. And to make matters worse, her money was nearly gone. Food and lodging were unbelievably expensive, plus the twenty-dollar stagecoach fare back to Sacramento would take nearly the last of her cash. She had no choice but to head home on the morning stage.

Depressed with her lack of success and depleted coin purse, she sat in a restaurant, idling pushing her food around on her plate.

"The steak is not to your liking, *oui?*"

Jerked from her daydreams, Katelyn started at the sound of the slightly French-accented voice. Looking up from her partially eaten meal, she blinked with surprise at the person standing next to her table. A petite, dark-haired woman of perhaps thirty-five, wearing a dress of magenta silk and matching feather-trimmed bonnet, stared down at her.

"Yes. I mean no, the steak's fine. I guess I'm not very hungry."

"Perhaps, *mademoiselle,* you are not feeling so well." The woman gave her a gentle smile, her pale green eyes filled with concern.

"Who are you?"

"Forgive me. My name is Manette Boudreau, and you are?"

"Katelyn Ferguson," she responded. Setting down her fork, she shoved the plate to the center of the table. "Actually, I'm feeling fine. I've just had several horrible days, riding in those miserable, uncomfortable stagecoaches, then having everyone act like they've suddenly gone deaf when I talk to them."

The woman's smooth brow furrowed. "Where are you

from, and why would anyone act like they're deaf when you speak to them?"

"I'm from Sacramento," Katelyn said, pushing away from the table and standing. "I own the *Sacramento Argus,* and I came to this part of California to do some research. Unfortunately, I haven't been able to find anyone who will answer my questions." Dropping some money onto the table, she turned to leave.

"What kind of research are you doing?"

Katelyn looked over her shoulder at the woman following her from the restaurant, but said nothing until they were outside. "I'm trying to find out about the trouble between the Yankees and those they call foreigners, especially the Spanish-speaking."

"Ah, *chérie.* It is no wonder no one would talk to you. That is not a good subject to discuss. There is still a great deal of bad blood over that very issue." When Katelyn didn't respond, she said, "Why are you interested in such problems?"

"Actually, there are a couple of reasons. I think the entire truth has never been told about how the Yankees treated the other miners in towns like Sonora."

"That is one reason," Manette said when Katelyn didn't offer more. "What is the other?"

"My other reason is . . . personal." Katelyn turned and started walking down Washington Street.

Lifting the hem of her skirt, Manette lengthened her strides to catch up. "Would you mind if I walk with you, Katelyn? It is not often I can enjoy the company of a bright young woman like yourself."

Katelyn cast a sidelong glance to the woman walking beside her. "Why is that?"

"Most people in town, especially the women, don't want to associate with me."

"Why not? You're obviously educated, you dress well, and your manners are perfect."

Manette laughed. "That makes little difference. For you see, I own a parlorhouse."

"A parlorhouse?" Katelyn said with a squeak. "But, that's a—" Feeling the heat of a blush creep up her cheeks, she clamped her mouth closed.

"Oui, a bordello. Does that disturb you?"

"No. It's just that I never met anyone who owned a . . . well, one of those places."

"I see no shame in what I do. After all, I am a business-woman. I supply a service men want and need, and they are willing to pay very well for what I provide." Seeing the thoughtful look on the younger woman's face, she added, "Do you not run your business the same way? You produce a newspaper which people are willing to buy, *oui?"*

Katelyn nodded. "Yes, that's true. I guess I never thought of it that way," she replied. After a few moments of silence, she said, "How long have you lived in Sonora?"

"I arrived in San Francisco from New Orleans in April of '49. I moved here a month later."

"Then you were here when all the trouble started?"

"Oui."

Katelyn stopped short and swung around to face a sur-prised Manette. "Will *you* answer my questions?"

The Frenchwoman stared at her thoughtfully for a mo-ment, then said, "I will answer them as best I can, *chérie."*

"Thanks, Manette. Now, where can we go to talk?"

"I was going to fetch my dog and take him for a walk. Would you like to go with us? We can talk while Bouffon runs after rabbits in the forest."

"Bouffon?"

"Oui, it is French for clown. When you see him, you will know why I gave him such a name."

Sitting on a boulder on a hillside above Sonora, Katelyn and Manette watched Bouffon run helter-skelter through the pine trees scattered across the foothills. The dog was a New-foundland, an enormous ball of black fur who took great joy in being allowed a few moments of freedom from his leash. Katelyn had never seen such a large dog. Bouffon's sweet, gentle nature was in direct contrast to his size. Performing a variety of tricks to gain the attention he loved, he was indeed a clown.

"What is it you want to know?" Manette asked, pulling her cloak more tightly around her shoulders against the cool October wind.

"What was it like when you first came here?"

"Sonora was like paradise. After the oppressing heat, the smell of the docks in a city as large as New Orleans, I was enchanted with this little town. It is so very beautiful here at the edge of the mountains, especially at night when every house shines with the light of lamps and—" She cleared her throat. "Forgive me for getting sentimental, *chérie.* Now what did you ask me? Oh yes, what it was like when I first arrived. Though beautiful, Sonora was also a very wild town. Liquor was sold around the clock. My plans to start a parlorhouse with a gambling room were met with boisterous approval. I opened my business in a building made of canvas and adobe with the two girls I brought with me from New Orleans.

"Besides drinking, gambling, and paying for time with one of my girls, the men found other ways to entertain themselves. One of their favorites was held every Sunday afternoon: a bear and bull fight." At Katelyn's sharply indrawn breath and the look of horror on her face, Manette's mouth curved into a weak smile.

"I see you feel as I do. I have never witnessed a more cruel or sickening sport." Manette shuddered, pulling her cloak more closely around her. "The town grew quickly, the number of men willing to pay for female company increasing so fast I had to bring in more girls. I bought a piece of land on the edge of town and had a house built, this one large enough for both my business and my private living quarters.

"Barely a day went by without some sort of trouble. The Yankees had no tolerance of anyone from south of the Rio Grande, and they were especially hostile to those more experienced in mining. They just couldn't stand other miners, particularly the ones they called greasers, being more successful at finding gold."

"Surely not all Yankees shared that opinion?" Katelyn said. "I can't believe they all hated those who spoke Spanish."

"You are correct. Not all Yankees agreed with the ignorant prejudice that *Mexicanos* and other Spanish-speaking were nothing more than half-civilized devils. The Yankees were such fools. They were so wrapped up in their bigotry they never noticed that many of those they despised were highly educated and impeccably mannered gentleman."

"So, why didn't the ones who weren't prejudiced step in and stop what was happening?"

"They were afraid of the hatred filling their countrymen. They feared they would become the target for so much hate if they tried to stop the persecution. It was easier to ignore what was happening, rather than facing retaliation for interfering."

"There were a lot of Spanish-speaking miners around here, weren't there?" Katelyn said.

"*Oui.* Sonora was first settled by *Mexicanos;* they named the town for their home province in Mexico. When the Yankees in the northern mines first started ordering the *Mexicanos,* along with the Peruvians and Chileans, to leave, the number of Spanish-speaking miners in and around Sonora continued to increase. The Yankees' obsession with ousting all foreigners didn't end with the northern mines, but spread here to the southern mines as well. It was a constant battle for the *Mexicanos* and other foreign miners to stop Yankee claim jumpers."

"And the Foreigner Miners' Tax only made things worse,"

Katelyn whispered. "I can't believe my own countrymen were stupid enough to pass that law."

Manette nodded. "I agree with you. Sonora was in a state of turmoil for days. The foreign miners banded together, calling secret meetings and drawing up petitions to fight the tax, which they flatly refused to pay. But when the tax collectors and their armed posses wouldn't accept what the foreign miners offered to pay and threatened to send them from the mines by force, most *Mexicanos* and many others gave up and left town. One of those who remained was said to have threatened the sheriff and was stabbed to death. By September, Sonora had lost almost three quarters of the population, sending the town into very hard times. Many businesses closed. The *Herald* even stopped publishing, because there was no one to read the paper."

"How did repealing the tax in '51 change Sonora?"

"Some of the miners who'd left came back, hopeful they could live a normal life. They were disappointed to learn Yankee attitudes and prejudice had not changed."

"What about the *Californios?* How were they treated?"

"The Yankees made no distinction between those from Mexico, Chile, or Peru and the *Californios*. All were beaten and driven off their claims or killed, for no reason other than the Yankees wanted what they had. All Spanish-speaking were equally resented. Even the Chinese, who replaced the *Mexicanos* as the lowest of all humans in the eyes of the Yankees, were not whipped or hanged like the ones they called greasers."

"Whipped and hanged," Katelyn said in a low voice. "Did those things actually happen?"

"Oui. A gambling tent owned by *Mexicanos* was raided one night by a group of Yankees. Four *Californios* were accused of stealing five pounds of gold. The men were convicted by a travesty of a court and flogged. As horrible as it sounds, those men were lucky. They could have been branded or ear-cropped. Like other *Mexicanos* found guilty,

they might not have lived through their punishment. Or, like some, they might not have made it to court at all. They could have been hauled to the nearest tree at the whim of their accuser, or by an angry crowd of Yankees bent on their own form of justice."

Staring down the hillside toward town, Manette shuddered. "One night, a *Mexicano* and an Irishman got into a fight over one of my girls in the downstairs parlor of my business. I entered the room just as the Irishman shouted, 'No greaser is going to touch a French whore.' Then he pulled a knife. The *Mexicano* was only defending himself when he retaliated and stabbed his tormentor. When the Irishman died of his wound later that night, a mob came for the *Mexicano*. I tried to tell them it was a fair fight, but they were in a frenzy and would not listen. They dragged the man from my girl's bed and out into the street. At the edge of town, he was lynched."

One hand pressed to her throat, Katelyn said, "Dear God. What would make men turn against one another that way?"

"Greed. Jealousy. Ignorance. It is sad such things continue to stand in the way of everyone's living together peacefully."

Katelyn nodded, but said nothing. For a few minutes she watched Bouffon chase after a squirrel. When the dog tired of the game, he came back to where she and Manette sat. His tongue lolling from one side of his mouth, he dropped onto his rear haunches at the feet of his mistress and laid his great head on her knees.

Ruffling the heavy coat of her pet, Manette said, "Have you asked all of your questions, *chérie?*"

Startled from her thoughts, Katelyn said, "What do you know about the man called *El Buitre?*"

Slipping Bouffon's leash around his neck, the Frenchwoman rose from the boulder. "I have to get back. Walk with me, and I will tell you what I know."

Katelyn stood and moved next to Manette. "Have you ever met him?"

"Non. At least, I do not think I have. No man has ever introduced himself to me as The Vulture. But perhaps he visited my parlorhouse and I did not know he was the bandit."

Katelyn's heart wrenched at the thought of Brit going to Manette's bordello, but she pushed the painful idea to the back of her mind. "Then you don't know what he looks like?"

"Non, not for sure. I have heard stories about him. He is said to be a handsome *Californio* from somewhere south of here."

"What else have you heard?"

"It is rumored he came here to look for gold, but gave up mining after a female member of his family was savagely raped and killed by Yankees. I do not know if that is true, for most of the men who were in the area when the attack supposedly took place are no longer here. But I do not doubt such a vile thing actually happened, something that would send any man into the arms of banditry."

Katelyn nodded. Sticking her hands into the pockets of her coat, she remained silent on the walk back to town.

In front of Manette's parlorhouse, an enormous, two-story, wooden structure with a balcony running the full width of the second floor, Katelyn turned to the older woman. "I really appreciate your talking to me, Manette. You've been a great help."

"My pleasure, *chérie.* Will you join me for supper tonight?"

Katelyn shook her head. "I'm taking the stage back to Sacramento in the morning, and I'll be going to bed very early."

"Well, then godspeed, Katelyn Ferguson."

Shaking the offered hand, Katelyn smiled. "It's been a pleasure making your acquaintance, Manette Boudreau.

Good-bye." Giving Bouffon one last pat, she turned and started toward the main section of town.

Manette watched her walk away and whispered, *"Au revoir."*

Back in her room in the United States Hotel, Katelyn opened her carpetbag and pulled out the folder containing her father's notes. After rereading everything Cyrus had written, she read what she'd written upon her arrival in Sonora.

> *I have visited Mokelumne Hill, called Mok Hill by the locals, but was unable to learn more about the trouble there several years ago between Yankees and the Frenchmen who raised the French flag to celebrate a sizable gold find. One miner known as Fuzzy told me all "furriners" should go back where they came from, a perfect example of the prejudiced attitude of so many Yankee miners. In San Andreas, I tried to glean some information about the Chilean war Papa mentioned in his notes. Again, I was told in no uncertain terms, the greasers—this time the Chileans mining in a nearby area known as Chile Gulch—got what they deserved— a fight ending in their departure from the mines. Though I found men willing to tell me the Yankee side of things, no one would answer my questions regarding the foreigner viewpoint on the issue.*

Thinking about what Manette had told her, statements confirming Cyrus Ferguson's suspicions, Katelyn again chastised herself for not taking more interest in her father's work. She'd still be ignorant of the prejudices the *Californios* and other Spanish-speaking miners suffered at the hands of her fellow Yankees, if it weren't for Manette, or more importantly, if not for Brit.

Brit. She closed her eyes and thought about the man she

loved and the last time she'd seen him. They'd had such a good time, talking and laughing, and making love during the day they spent together. Less than two weeks had passed since that weekend, yet it felt much longer. She missed him. If only— She halted her line of thinking. Making wishes that could never come true would do no good. Such foolishness would only cause more pain.

Opening her eyes, she pulled out a clean sheet of paper and began writing.

What I have learned in Sonora confirms Papa's beliefs. El Buitre was driven to his life of crime by the Yankees' ill use of his people. After the Californios were called names, degraded because of their heritage, and finally forced from the mines, the man who came to be known as El Buitre struck back by the only means left to him. Banditry. While strictly speaking The Vulture is a criminal, his reason for becoming a bandit was actually self-defense. But more than his own life, he was also trying to defend the life of his people, people many Yankees continue to hold with total disregard. It shames me to admit I once shared such disregard. Now that I know the error in my thinking, I don't know what I can do to rectify the situation. The miners I encountered in the towns I have visited are not going to change their biased opinions because of anything I have to say. Jake was right. If I tried to convert everyone's thinking, no one would pay me any heed. In fact, they'd probably run me out of town, like they have so many others. Yet, I know in my own mind and in my heart, I have found the answers I sought. But, until others are willing to listen, I have no choice except to be satisfied with having learned the truth.

Twenty-two

Katelyn sat in the Concord coach on the return trip to Sacramento, grateful none of her traveling companions—two middle-aged businessmen and a young married couple—found it necessary to fill every minute with mindless chatter. Bracing herself to keep the coach's rocking motion from jarring her into the broad-shouldered young man sitting next to her, she rested her head against the back of the leather seat and closed her eyes. She hadn't slept well the night before, her mind constantly dwelling on what she'd learned from Manette.

Thinking of the bordello owner brought a smile to her lips. *Papa would roll over in his grave, if he knew I'd actually spent time with such a woman.* Her smile faded. She didn't consider Manette a bad sort, and now that she thought about it, she doubted Cyrus Ferguson would have either. After all, Cyrus thought *El Buitre* was not all bad, that a good man had been concealed by the facade of a bandit, so he likely would have given the same benefit of the doubt to a woman running a bordello.

Katelyn drew in a deep breath. This trip had been worth it, even though what she learned might very well end up going to the grave with her. Lulled by the coach's constant, gentle bouncing, she slipped into a light sleep.

She dozed off and on, rousing when they pulled into one of the towns on the route, then slumping back against the leather seat when their journey continued.

Only a few minutes after rumbling out of Jackson, the sharp retort of a gun and the loud cursing of Grady, the stage driver, yanked Katelyn from her slumber.

"What's happening?" she whispered to the man sitting next to her.

Trying to calm his wife, the man turned to look at Katelyn long enough to say, "Bandits."

Katelyn's eyes widened, her gaze snapping to the window. She couldn't see anything, yet the stagecoach was definitely bouncing to a halt.

When the last of the dust cleared and the coach stopped its rocking, a voice came clearly from outside. "You, driver and your guard, throw down your guns. Do it, now!"

One gun, followed by a second, flashed past the window and hit the ground with a thud.

"Bueno. Now the strongbox."

There was a scraping sound as the two stage line employees pulled the strongbox from the coach's front boot beneath the driver's seat. With a grunt the men hefted the box, then tossed it to the ground.

The man giving the orders said something in rapid Spanish, then suddenly the stagecoach door was jerked open. A dark shadow appeared in the opening. With the sun at the man's back, only his silhouette was visible from inside the coach. Motioning with the barrel of the pistol gripped in his right hand, he said, "Now, it is your turn, passengers. I want you to step out here, slowly. Then move away from the door with your hands in the air." The man backed away from the door, moving into the sunshine.

From her position by the window, Katelyn studied him while the other passengers prepared to leave the stagecoach. He was of average height, a wide-brimmed hat pulled low over his forehead hid his face, and straight black hair brushed his broad shoulders. He wore a leather vest over a linen shirt, and a bandana loosely encircled his neck. A row of silver buttons ran down the outside of each leg of his fitted trousers. The buttons from his knees down were not fastened, allowing the bottoms of the trousers to flare over his boots. Her gaze traveled back up to his waist. As the others left the stage, she watched the man's grip tighten on the gun he held.

The two businessmen exited first. Then the third man stepped down, turning to help his wife. When Katelyn moved to the door, her skirts bunched in one hand, one of the businessmen took a step toward her. "Miss Ferguson, here, let me—"

"Do not move," the leader of the bandits shouted. "And keep your hands up." Grunting with satisfaction when the man obeyed, the leader chuckled. "So you were going to play the gentleman and help the lady, eh? Do not worry, *señor,* I can be of assistance to *la señorita.*"

Moving closer to the stagecoach, the bandit gave Katelyn a stiff bow, then grabbed her elbow and helped her to the ground. "Which of you men does *Señorita* Ferguson belong to?" he said, looking at the two men traveling without a companion.

Katelyn tried to jerk her arm free, but the man's grip was too tight. "I don't belong to anyone. And I'd appreciate your unhanding me." Glaring up at him, her gaze moved from his shadowed face, over the whisker-roughened jaw, and down his neck. Seeing the line of red puckered skin just above the bandana, she frowned. What was it about the man that— His sudden bark of laughter jerked her from her thoughts. She lifted her gaze to stare at his wide grin.

"Ah, so full of fire. I like that in a woman." Using the barrel of his pistol, he pushed the brim of his hat away from his face. Ignoring the gasp from the woman he held, he turned to his men. "Check the rest of the passengers. I will see what valuables this one carries myself."

When he started to pull Katelyn away from the stage-coach, she balked, struggling to free herself.

"Now, see here," the stage guard said, taking a step forward. "You've got no call to manhandle a woman that way." He took another step. "She ain't—" The retort of a pistol, the acrid scent of gunpowder, and a splotch of blood on the man's chest ended his protest. Eyes wide with shock, the guard crumpled to the ground, then lay still.

Fighting the nausea welling in her throat, Katelyn's head rang with the vibration of the gun fired so close to her ear. She turned to look at the man next to her, smoke still wafting from the barrel of his raised pistol. No, she hadn't been wrong. The leader of the bandits was Marco Chavez.

"Why did you have to kill him?" she said in a fierce whisper. "He was only looking out for my welfare, and he wasn't even armed."

Marco merely shrugged. Turning, he pulled her farther from the stagecoach.

"Oh, that's right," she said when he stopped. "I forgot how you always kill everyone you rob. That's why you and your men aren't wearing masks, isn't it? You plan to kill the rest of us, too."

Holstering his gun, Marco swung her around so they stood face-to-face. "What are you talking about? Why do you think that is my plan?" His eyes narrowed, he cocked his head to one side, better revealing the scar running across his neck. When she remained silent, he gave her a shake. "Talk, *gringa!*"

"Because Brit said your rule was steal everything, then kill all witnesses."

Marco's back stiffened. "Brit?" Staring down at the flushed face of the woman glaring at him, his gaze moved over her blond hair and light eyes. A smile slowly replaced his scowl. "Well, Brit does not know me as well as he thinks. Why would I kill such a lovely *gringa* . . ." He ran his fingers down her cheek, then lowered his hand to squeeze one breast. "When there are so many enjoyable uses for her alive?"

Katelyn held herself still, determined not to show her

fear. She knew what a ruthless man Marco could be, and she had to stop antagonizing him. When he lowered his head toward hers, she pressed her lips together, bracing herself for his kiss. Just as his mouth was about to touch hers, the shout of one of his men stopped him.

"Jefe, we have all the valuables and the gold from the strongbox. We should finish here and leave, *pronto."*

Staring down at Katelyn, Marco said, "I have thought about you many times since the first time I saw you, *gringa.* I wanted to find you, but I had no idea where to look. And now, we meet again. My luck has always been very good, eh?" He flashed her a wide smile.

"You weren't so lucky the night you fought Brit," Katelyn said before she could halt the words.

Lifting his hand to the puckered skin on his neck, a fierce gleam leaped into Marco's eyes. After a moment, he said, "I do not agree. What happened that night has led me to you, something I had hoped for. Finding you is the luckiest thing that could have happened to me, and has given me the opportunity to complete my final revenge against *El Buitre."*

"What are you talking about?"

"You, *Señorita* Ferguson. You will be my final revenge." Seeing the confused look on her face, he said, "I can think of no better revenge than having his woman after he is captured."

"What makes you think I'm his woman?"

"I know Roberto Cordoba. He would not have a woman at his camp unless she was warming his bed."

"But I'm a newspaper reporter. I could have been at his camp to interview him for a story."

He threw back his head and laughed, a demonic sound sending chills up Katelyn's back. "That is very amusing, *gringa.* But I do not believe you. My plan is perfect. Brit will be rotting in his grave, while I am enjoying his *gringa* woman."

She said nothing, unable to force words past the enormous lump in her throat. She didn't doubt for one minute that Marco meant what he said. Unable to bear looking into his face, twisted with demented rage, she turned away.

When he jerked her handbag from her wrist, she started, but did not protest.

"You are not wearing any jewels," Marco said. "So, let me see what you have in here." He rifled through the small purse, confiscating her small cache of coins and stuffing them into his pocket. He tossed the other contents onto the ground, and was about to do the same with a small ivory card, until he turned it over.

"The *Sacramento Argus*," he read aloud. "K.A. Ferguson, owner and editor." Rubbing the card across the stubble on his cheek, he smiled. "Well, well. So that much of what you told me is true. If my plan had gone as I originally intended, we would have met earlier, *Señorita* Ferguson. It seems we were destined to meet."

"What do you mean?"

"It is nothing." Throwing her empty handbag onto the ground, he grabbed her elbow again and hauled her back to the stagecoach. The rest of his men had mounted their horses, their guns pointed at the other passengers and the stage driver.

Before Katelyn could move, Marco bent and brushed a quick kiss across her lips. Touching his fingers to his hat brim, he whispered, *"Adiós, Señorita* Ferguson. Until we meet again."

Resisting the urge to scrub her mouth with the back of her hand, Katelyn watched him leap into his saddle in one lithe motion. Marco flashed her one last smile, said something to his men in Spanish, then wheeled his horse around and kicked it into a gallop. One by one, his men did the same.

When the bandits disappeared from view, Katelyn and the others gave a collective sigh of relief.

"Damn Vulture," Grady grumbled, hurrying over to the fallen guard.

Katelyn looked up sharply. "What?"

"When is the law gonna catch that no good, son of a bit—er . . . biscuit?" he said. "There ain't a person in California who's safe, not until The Vulture is caught and stopped once and for all."

"You think the man who robbed us was The Vulture?"

"Well, of course, he was, Miss Ferguson," one of the businessmen said, moving to help Grady with the body of the guard. "He spoke Spanish didn't he, and he sure looked like a greaser."

Her lips pressed together in distaste at the epithet she had come to hate, Katelyn watched the two men carry the dead guard to the back of the stagecoach, then lift the body into the rear boot. Though it pained her to blame Brit for a crime she knew he didn't commit, she had no choice. She couldn't tell these people she knew the identity of the man who robbed them, any more than she could tell them the man wasn't *El Buitre.* Finally she said, "I guess you're right. He must have been The Vulture."

"Damn right," the second businessman said, stooping to pick up his wallet. "Stole every cent I saved to open a hardware store in Sacramento. I don't even have the money to get back to Missouri."

"At least he didn't kill us," Katelyn added, grateful Marco had spared their lives, though what he had in mind for her would be infinitely worse.

As the stagecoach reached the edge of Sacramento, Grady shouted for someone to fetch the sheriff. By the time the stage pulled up in front of the Crescent City Hotel, the sheriff, Lester Pierce, had been notified of the holdup and was on his way.

One by one Sheriff Pierce questioned Grady and each

passenger, painstakingly writing down each person's statement. Katelyn purposely allowed herself to be the last one
interviewed.

"Okay, Miss Ferguson, it's your turn. Tell me what happened," he said.

For a moment Katelyn studied Sheriff Pierce. His face
was heavily freckled, as were his hands and forearms, making him look younger than his forty-plus years. She could
see a lock of russet hair curled over his forehead beneath
the brim of his hat. He stared down at her with impassive
green eyes, his thin lips turned down slightly at the corners.
There was nothing in the man's expression to give her a
clue about what he was thinking.

When Katelyn didn't respond, the sheriff said, "Take your
time. I know this must have been a terrible ordeal for you."

She looked down at her clenched hands, wishing she
could say, "Yes, but not for the reason you think." Instead
she nodded, then lifted her head and began reciting the
events of the holdup, leaving out her recognition of the bandit leader and what he'd said to her.

When she finished, Sheriff Pierce was quiet for a moment, then said, "The other passengers and Grady think the
robbery was committed by that murderous bastard, the Vulture. You agree with that, Miss Ferguson?"

"I . . ." Running her tongue across her lips, she took a
deep breath, then exhaled slowly. "I can't be sure, Sheriff."

"He and the others spoke Spanish, didn't they? And they
looked Mexican?"

"Yes," Katelyn replied.

"Well, then, I reckon it had to be The Vulture and his
men, wouldn't you say?"

Realizing the sheriff wasn't going to let her get out of
answering the question, she squeezed her eyes closed for a
second, then nodded.

* * *

Bone-tired from the fourteen-hour stage ride and the ordeal of the robbery, Katelyn headed for her apartment and bed. Surprised to find a light coming from the *Argus* office, she turned toward the front of the building.

She opened the door, then stepped inside. "Jake, what are you doing here? It must be close to eight."

Straightening from his work, he smiled. "Katelyn! Well, if you ain't a sight for sore eyes. I was just giving the press a good cleaning. Grace went to her ladies' meeting, so I needed something to do." Wiping his hands on a rag, he crossed the office to stand in front of her. "If you'd let me know you were coming home today, I would—" His smile faded. "Is something wrong, Katie?"

"My stage was held up by bandits this side of Jackson."

"Held up! Dear God, are you all right? They didn't hurt you, did they?"

"No, I'm fine, Jake. I'm just tired. I was planning on going straight to bed, until I saw the light."

"You go ahead, Katie girl. You've had quite a day. Why don't you join Grace and me for breakfast?"

She gave him a weak smile. "I'd like that." Turning to leave, she said, " 'Night. I'll see you in the morning."

Over a steak and eggs breakfast in Grace's kitchen, Katelyn told Grace and Jake about the stage holdup, how the sheriff had interrogated her, and how she had agreed with the other passengers on the identity of the band of thieves.

"Was it really him?" Grace said, pouring each of them another cup of coffee.

Katelyn shook her head. "I couldn't tell the sheriff I knew it wasn't *El Buitre*'s gang that robbed the stage. If I had, he would have demanded to know how I came to have such knowledge, then asked other questions I couldn't answer."

"From what you've told me," Grace replied, "holding up

the stage you were on isn't the first robbery wrongly credited to The Vulture."

"That's true. I don't know how many crimes he's been charged with that he didn't commit, probably a lot. Even I contributed to the number, painting him with a guilty brush like everyone else, without taking the time to check out the stories."

Grace reached across the table and grasped the younger woman's wrist. "Don't go blaming yourself, Katelyn. What's done is done. This time, you had a good reason for naming his band responsible. So don't be too hard on yourself."

Swallowing the sudden spurt of tears, Katelyn smiled. "I know. But it still hurts, knowing I accused the man I love of a crime I know he didn't commit. What I learned in Sonora proves Papa was right. Brit is a good man. But he was backed into a corner, because of the way he and his people were treated by the Yankees. The only way he could retaliate was to become a bandit. Yet there's nothing I can do about it." She heaved a weary sigh. "Jake, what you told me before I left is true. I doubt I can ever reveal what I learned. After hearing the names I was called in the mining camps, there's no way anyone would keep an open mind and listen to what I have to say."

Jake rose from his chair and moved behind Katelyn. Laying one rough hand on her shoulder, he gave her a squeeze. "I wish I could say something to ease your pain, Katie. But I'm afraid I don't know what it would be."

Placing her hand atop his, she curled her fingers around his much larger ones. "I know, Jake. There's nothing anyone can say."

After a few moments of silence, Jake cleared his throat, then said, "Katie, there's something else I have to tell you."

As he moved to the kitchen window, she frowned, wondering at the anguish she heard in his voice. "What is it?"

Staring out into the sunny October morning, he said,

"Yesterday, the state legislature announced a plan to stop *El Buitre*."

Katelyn sucked in a sharp breath, her heart pounding loudly in her ears. "What plan?" she whispered.

"They decided to offer a reward for The Vulture's capture. Five thousand dollars. Dead or alive. And just in case the reward isn't enough encouragement, they also commissioned a detachment of mounted State Rangers to find and bring him in."

"Why now?" She pounded her fist on the table. "Why would they do this now, after all the time they sat on their hands, doing nothing?"

"They finally got off their duffs in response to citizen pressure, I reckon." When Katelyn didn't respond, he added, "The rangers left last night to look for the bandit's hideout."

Katelyn sat back in her chair, stunned. For so many months she had devoted herself to just such an occurrence, working tirelessly to get the legislature to take action. Yet, now that they had, the knowledge, and worse, the consequences, formed a hard knot in her stomach.

"No one knows what he looks like," she said in a low voice. "Such a large reward is bound to prompt men into ambushing any man who even vaguely looks Mexican and is unfortunate enough to cross their path."

"Yes, that's true," Grace replied. "The lure of five thousand dollars will be too strong to resist for a lot of folks, putting all Spanish-speaking men at risk. But I don't see what can be done to prevent it."

Katelyn nodded, staring at her clasped hands. Perhaps she should protest to the state legislature. She quickly discounted such a notion. Besides drawing unwanted attention, the only thing protesting would accomplish would be getting herself labeled a hypocrite.

She glanced over at Jake, then back to Grace. "I'm so afraid for him." The sympathetic looks on their faces did nothing to ease her pain.

If Brit were found, there was no hope for his survival, not after the state of California had given its blessing to his being shot down like a rabid dog. Though she wanted to believe there were honest men who would do everything they could to bring a wanted man in alive, as Grace had pointed out, the large reward would be a powerful motivator. Katelyn also knew that hatred for *El Buitre* and the thirst for revenge ran deep in the town's citizenry. Hadn't she contributed to those feelings with her editorials? The realization pulled the painful knot in her stomach even tighter.

Thanks to her, there were any number of men who would gladly be the one to run the bandit to ground. And even if by some miracle, Brit was brought in alive, he would eventually be hanged for his crimes, either at the court's order or hauled from jail by an angry crowd bent on holding a lynching.

The idea of the man she loved dying sent a shudder rippling through her, pushing the pain in her stomach up to grip her heart with a paralyzing ice-cold fist. The result was a fear like she had never known.

If only there were some way to give Brit a second chance, a chance to erase his past life of crime and start over as a law-abiding citizen. She drew in a deep, shaky breath, then exhaled on a sigh.

The situation was hopeless; there was nothing she could do.

Twenty-three

Brit and Tomás sat near the dying fire, deep in a canyon containing their winter camp in the Coast Range Mountains. The hour was late; most of the other men had already sought their bedrolls. Even Brit's hounds, Paco and Pepe, had left his side to find a place to spend the night.

"You are very quiet tonight, *amigo mío*," Tomás said. "Something troubles you?"

Brit merely grunted in reply, poking at the fire with a stick.

"You know, if we are to arrive at the *Rancho del Sol Poniente* in time for the baptism on All Saints' Day, we must leave no later than next Friday." When Brit didn't respond, he said, "Have you changed your mind about attending the baptism of your sister's child?"

"No, I will be there." Brit tossed the stick into the fire, sending a shower of sparks into the air. "There is something I must do before we head south. I am leaving at the break of dawn and will be gone several days." Meeting the concerned gaze of his friend, he said, "Do not worry, Tomás, I will return no later than Thursday evening, so we can still leave for my parents' *rancho* on Friday. But in case I am delayed, take half the men and head south. I will catch up with you."

"This something you must do, it is Katelyn Ferguson?"

A muscle jerked in Brit's jaw. "What concern is it of yours?"

Ignoring the cutting words, in a low voice, Tomás said, "You are my friend, and I do not like seeing the hurt filling your heart reflected in your eyes. I am afraid if you continue to see her, you will only make the pain worse."

Brit pressed his lips together, shifting his gaze away from Tomás. He knew his friend spoke the truth. Seeing Katelyn again probably would worsen the pain in his heart. But it didn't matter; he had to see her one last time.

Ross closed the door of the parlorhouse behind him, incredibly relaxed from the stimulating hour he'd spent in Colette's room. He strolled down Front Street, his thoughts lingering on how well the French whore had learned to please him. Perhaps it was time to set her up as his mistress, then he could— The sudden presence of someone at his elbow jerked him from his musings.

"Who are you, and what do you want?" he asked in a fierce growl, sorry he hadn't thought to carry his pistol.

A soft laugh floated to him in answer. "Do not be afraid, señor. I mean you no harm. I just want to talk."

Ross halted, then swung around to face the other man. "Talk? I don't have time for more talk. Especially when all your previous talking has done no good."

Marco lifted his chin. "What are you saying, señor? I told you where the camp of El Buitre was located, and I hear the rangers your government hired found it only yesterday."

"Yeah, they found it all right. But there wasn't anyone there, in case you didn't hear that part. The camp's been abandoned for weeks, the trail so cold, even the ranger's best tracker couldn't follow it."

"Ah, so that is why you are so upset. I am sorry for that, Señor Carter. I did not think El Buitre would leave his summer camp so soon, but it does not matter. He has another—"

"I don't want to hear it. The rangers are in charge of the

search now, and with the reward the legislature offered, I'm confident the bastard will be found very soon. So I don't need to pay more of my gold for more of your worthless information. Our business association has ended."

Marco curled his hands into fists. He longed to tell Ross Carter he now knew the identity of the woman he'd seen in Brit's camp, longed to see the expression on the *gringo's* face when he learned she was none other than the woman Carter had once planned to marry. But Marco held his tongue. That information was his alone to savor. He wished he had time to pay the *gringa* a visit, but his men were waiting for him at the edge of town. There would be time enough for his final revenge after Brit was captured.

He slowly uncurled his fingers, forcing himself to relax. "It is just as well, *señor.* Now that a reward has been offered for *El Buitre,* I do not feel safe coming here." Taking a step backward, he said, *"Adiós,"* then disappeared in the shadows of the night.

Ross grunted in reply. After a few seconds, he turned and resumed the walk to his favorite saloon.

A week after learning about the reward for Brit, and two days after his camp had been found, Katelyn lay in her bed, unable to fall asleep. Worry was her constant companion, banishing her appetite and plaguing her with insomnia. Rolling over, she squirmed to find a more comfortable position. A noise outside the front door of her apartment stilled her movements.

Her first thought was that Brit had come to see her again, but she quickly amended her thinking. With a reward on his head and a detachment of rangers possibly bearing down on him, he wouldn't risk coming to Sacramento.

Being as quiet as possible, she slipped from her bed. She carefully moved one hand across the top of her dresser, hoping to find something she could use to defend herself.

Wrapping her fingers around the wooden handle of the only thing she could find, she tiptoed toward the bedroom door.

Just as she stepped into the parlor, the knob of the front door rattled, sending her heart into double time. There wasn't time to dash across the room and take up a position by the door, so she crouched behind the nearest chair. Holding her breath, she waited for the person forcing the lock to enter the room.

The door swung inward. Someone crossed the threshold, then carefully closed the door. The intruder stood perfectly still for a few seconds, then finally moved farther into the room. Based on the sound of booted footsteps and the size of the shadow the person cast, Katelyn knew a man was sneaking across her parlor. When he drew even with Katelyn's hiding place, she sucked in a deep breath, raised her impromptu weapon, and leaped out from behind the chair. The downward arc of her arms ended with a thump to the man's shoulder, followed by his grunt.

Before she could get in a second blow, the man grabbed her arms and pinned her against his chest.

"Katelyn, what are you trying to—" He sneezed. "Do? And what did you hit me with?" Whatever she'd used to club him was pinned between their bodies, one end just under his nose. He sneezed again.

"Brit! Thank God." She sagged in his arms. "I didn't think it was you, so I grabbed the only thing I could find to defend myself."

He released her and moved across the room to light an oil lamp. Turning back to her, he studied her *weapon,* then howled with laughter. "What were you planning to do with that?" He nodded toward the feather duster clutched in her hands. "Tickle your intruder to death?"

Her back stiffened. "When I heard the doorknob rattle, there wasn't time to search for a real weapon. Besides, the duster has a stout handle, and might have done some real damage, if I'd gotten in a better whack." When he didn't reply, but only laughed again, her voice turned cold, "What are you doing here? Don't you know a reward's been issued for you?"

His amusement fled. "So I have heard."

"And do you know your hideout was found last week?"

"Yes, I know that as well, something I wanted to discuss with you."

"Surely you don't still think I drew that map?"

He shrugged, then crossed his arms over his chest.

"Brit, I told you I couldn't have described where your camp was located if my life depended on it. You have to believe me."

He stared at her for a long moment. As much as he wanted to call her a liar, he did believe her story. He merely shrugged again, then said, "If you say so."

"Do you also know a detachment of rangers has been commissioned to find you? They could have followed you here."

"I know about the rangers, but no one followed me." He moved closer, his dark gaze searching her face. "What is it, *cardillo mio?* Why are you being so obstinate? I thought you would be glad to see me."

"You shouldn't have risked coming here, Brit. The legislature means business; they want you captured." She swallowed hard. "Or killed."

"You sound like that would bother you, *querida.* Or can it be, you do not want me to be caught in your home, or more precisely, in your bed?"

Her face burning with embarrassment, she lifted her chin defiantly, but refused to respond.

He raised one hand and ran his fingers down her flushed cheek. "Or perhaps there is another reason. Are you responsible for the government changing their mind on stopping *El Buitre?*"

She blinked up at him. "Why do you keep accusing me? I had nothing to do with it." Seeing his skeptical look, she

shook off his hand and drew herself up to her full height.
"Well, I didn't. The legislature made the decision while I
was in Sonora, and I didn't hear about—"

"Sonora? You went to Sonora?"

At her nod, he said, "What in God's name made you do
such a stupid thing?"

Katelyn wanted to tell him the truth. The words were on
the tip of her tongue, but she bit them back. Telling him
she'd gone to Sonora because she thought she owed it to
him would serve no purpose, any more than telling him she
could do nothing about what she'd learned while in the
southern mining towns. Finally, she said, "I went there on
newspaper business. And as I started to say, I didn't hear
about the reward or the rangers until the day after I got
back."

He didn't reply, just continued to stare at her with a penetrating gaze. She opened her mouth to tell him about Marco,
but the heat in his eyes derailed her train of thought. He
took the feather duster from her and tossed it onto the settee, then lifted her arms and wrapped them around his neck.

Pulling her fully against him, he kissed her long and hard,
then lifted his head. "Ah, *querida,*" he murmured against
her lips. "You taste so good. You feel so good." He ran his
hands down her back, over her buttocks. The thin gown
separating him from her naked flesh inflamed his desire
even more. "I did not come here to argue."

"Why did you come here?" she said in a breathless whisper. His husky laugh sent a shiver of excitement up her
spine. A stab of heat settled between her thighs.

"I needed to see you again," he replied, then in Spanish
he added, "You have become a part of me, a part of my
heart, my soul, and I had to see you."

Before she could reply, he lowered his head and captured
her mouth in another kiss. Lifting her into his arms, he
carried her into the bedroom, then eased her down on the
bed.

As Brit quickly stripped off his clothes, Katelyn never took her gaze off him. She watched him remove his shirt, then his trousers, the well-defined muscles of his arms and shoulders flexing with the effort. When he stood next to the bed, naked, she shivered in anticipation. She longed to run her fingers through the silky black hair covering his chest, to feel the smooth, hard muscles of his stomach, to wrap her hand around his thick arousal.

He leaned over the bed, and with one swift movement pulled her nightdress up over her head, then tossed it on top of his pile of clothes. Stretching out next to her, he wrapped his hands around her waist, then shifted her position until she lay atop him.

The startled look on her face made him chuckle. "What is it, *querida*? You do not like the position of a *vaquero*?"

"*Vaquero*?"

"*Sí*, the one who rides atop the powerful stallion."

She blinked with surprise, then smiled slowly. "So, you're comparing yourself to a powerful stallion, huh?" She wiggled her hips. "That's awfully arrogant, don't you think?"

"I only spoke the truth," he replied with a wink. "You did not answer *my* question, *querida*. Do you like this position?"

"Yes, I like it," she said, wiggling her hips again. His arousal jerking against her belly, his hips lifting off the bed widened her smile. "I like being a *vaquero* very much."

"I thought you would," he replied, returning her smile. "Now bring that lovely mouth down to mine, or I might change my mind and toss you onto your back."

She giggled, then lowered her head until her mouth was only a fraction above his. Her tongue peeked out to touch the corner of his mouth. The groan rumbling in his chest made her bolder. Using the tip of her tongue, she outlined his lips in a slow, measured movement.

He remained still for as long as he could stand the torment of her actions. When his control started to slip, he grasped the back of her head to halt her ministrations. "I can take no more of your teasing. I want you. Now."

Seeing the heat of his desire reflected in her eyes, he lowered his hands to her waist. "Bring your knees up to straddle me," he murmured. She complied, allowing him to lift her while she shifted her legs. When her knees were pressed to either side of his hips, he said, *"Bueno.* Now, join us, *querida.* Make us one."

She reached between them, wrapping her fingers around his manhood. He throbbed in her hand, bucking against her palm. Never taking her gaze from the almost pained look on his face, she guided him to her, then carefully lowered her hips.

Brit released her waist, letting her complete their joining at her own pace. She eased down slowly, stoking his already sizzling desire even hotter. With one quick, final movement, she took all of him inside her warmth.

He groaned, his hips lifting upward in reaction to her silken heat and the contraction of her muscles around him. Nothing had ever felt better.

Hands splayed on his chest to brace herself, Katelyn started a gentle motion—a slow rhythm of lifting, then lowering her hips. Soon the slowness of her movements was not enough. She increased the tempo, alternately pressing against his groin when he lifted his hips from the bed, then rising until he was nearly withdrawn when he dropped back onto the mattress.

Brit reached up to run his thumbs across the tightened tips of her breasts. She moaned, arching her back to allow him better access. When he gave each hardened nub a gentle pinch, she sucked in a sharp breath. And when he pulled her forward to lave each nipple with his tongue, her gasp changed into another moan.

Rotating her hips, she continued to grind against him, rocking forward, then back, in an increasingly frantic rhythm. The warmth between her thighs grew hotter, spreading outward through her body as if her blood was on fire. Her breathing quickened. Her hands moved from his breastbone, running down over his ribs, trailing across his belly, then up his sides to return to his chest.

Cupping her face with his hands, he pulled her down until her mouth was just above his, her hair falling around them like an exotic curtain of gold. "Kiss me, *querida,*" he murmured. "For I cannot stand another minute without tasting your sweet lips."

Her heart near to bursting with love, Katelyn did as he bid. The kiss was long and deep, her tongue dueling with his in the same pattern as their bodies.

When he broke the kiss, his voice was a low rasp. "I hope you are near your finish. I do not want to leave you, but I fear I cannot last much longer."

He prayed he had enough self-control to hold back until she was near her release. Grasping her shoulders, he pushed her back into a sitting position, then slipped one hand between their bodies. At the first touch of his fingers on her swollen flesh, she jerked in reaction. A soft gasp escaped her lips.

Continuing to thrust upward, he matched the pace of his hips with his fingers. Katelyn's breathing changed to harsh little pants. Her hands clenched the sheet on either side of her knees. Her hips rocked in a steadily increasing rhythm.

Abruptly, her movements halted, her breath hanging suspended in her throat. With a soft cry, she started pushing against him again, harder and faster. Hearing his shout of joy, then feeling the throb of his manhood deep inside, she closed her eyes to savor the moment. She had only a second to relish his pleasure; her own desire demanded to be appeased. Head thrown back, she let her climax overtake her, a series of powerful spasms racking her body. When the spasms passed, she shuddered, then with a sob fell forward onto his chest, her face pressed to the hollow at the base of his neck.

Brit found the strength to bring his arms up around her, lightly running his hands over her back. After a few moments, he said, "Are you all right?"

She nodded, her hair tickling his chin.

Brushing the soft strands away from his face, he tightened his embrace. How could he leave this woman, the woman who had stolen his heart? He sighed. No matter how difficult, he had no other choice.

Later, as they lay next to each other, Katelyn said, "I'm so glad you weren't at your camp when the rangers found it."

"I moved the camp after you told me about the map."

"Then you believed me when I said, if I'd drawn the map, I wouldn't have bothered telling you about it?"

"I am responsible for my men. I could not take chances with their lives, so I had them pack up camp and head out of the mountains."

Realizing he hadn't answered her question, she fell silent. After a few moments, his voice jarred her from her thoughts.

"I should leave," he said, starting to roll to the edge of the bed.

"No, not yet. Please," she replied, grabbing his arm. "Please stay for just a little longer."

Seeing the pleading in her eyes, the softness of her mouth, Brit silently cursed his inability to resist her. He slipped one arm beneath her shoulders, then pulled her close. "All right, *querida,* I will stay for a few minutes more."

Her smile tore at his insides, but he refused to let her see his inner hurt. To ease the ache, he captured her mouth in a blazing kiss. He slowly ran his hands over her body, testing the silkiness of her skin, burning the texture and shape of her curves into his brain.

Lying on their sides, facing each other, Brit made gentle, yet urgent love to Katelyn once more. If he must spend the rest of his life without her, he wanted—no, he needed—one more memory to tuck away for safekeeping.

After her second shattering climax, Katelyn fell into a

light sleep. The bed shifting with Brit's weight roused her. In silence, she watched him get out of bed and pull on his clothes.

When he turned back to the bed, she had scooted into a sitting position, the sheet tucked under her arms. The smile she gave him wrenched his heart. "I must leave now."

"Where are you going?"

"You do not need to know."

"I won't tell the rangers," she snapped. "If that's what you're worried about."

He smiled. "Ah, still so much my prickly golden thistle."

"Please don't make fun, Brit. I only asked because I . . . I'll worry about you."

"You should not worry about me, *querida*. And it would be better if you did not know where I am going."

She stared at him for a moment. In a soft voice, she said, "Are you coming back?"

He didn't answer immediately. Finally he said, "I do not think so." Seeing the stricken look on her face, his anger at the helplessness of the situation surfaced. "Do not look at me with those sad eyes," he said more sharply than he intended.

Her chin quivering with her efforts to control the threatening tears, she whispered, "I can't help it. I love you, Brit. That's why—"

"Stop it!" he ordered fiercely. "Do not speak of love."

"But why? I—"

"Do you not see?" he said, cutting her off again. "It does not matter that you love me, or that I love you. For you know as well as I, there can be no future for us. I am a wanted man, and thanks to reporters like you, I now have a very large price on my head. I cannot, I will not allow you to be placed in danger because of what I am."

After allowing himself one last, brief kiss on her soft mouth, he turned to leave.

She clamped her lips together, determined not to lose her composure. But one sob escaped.

His shoulders stiffened at the pitiful sound, but he never broke stride as he left her bedroom, her apartment, her life.

Closing her eyes, Katelyn let her head drop back against the headboard. She had never known such paralyzing pain. Brit had finally spoken the words she longed to hear: he loved her. Yet in the same breath, he had also broken her heart.

Twenty-four

After Brit left, Katelyn remained slumped against the headboard, strangely dry-eyed, for a long time. Then the flood of tears came in one torrential wave after another, until she finally fell into an exhausted sleep just before dawn.

She awoke with swollen eyes and a pounding head. She forced herself to get up and make herself a cup of tea. Afterwards, she went back to bed. Though it was Wednesday and Jake would be expecting her at the newspaper office to start laying out the week's edition, she was unwilling to face him, or anyone else.

As she lay in her bed, staring at the wall, she realized she hadn't told Brit about the stage holdup or Marco's threats. Surely Brit would want to know what Marco had planned. Then again, perhaps Brit's not knowing was just as well. The only thing telling him would have accomplished was increasing his anger. He'd already expressed his ire over her going to Sonora in the first place. And besides, he had enough on his mind; she didn't need to add to his burden. Perhaps Marco was only bluffing. Maybe his threats had only been an attempt to scare her.

She shivered, pulling the covers up tighter under her chin. Closing her eyes, she drifted to sleep, praying she never learned whether Marco had made empty threats.

It was just past one o'clock, and Jake was locking the *Argus* door when Katelyn finally arrived.

"Katie, you had me worried." Noting her puffy eyes, he

opened his mouth, then snapped it shut. The look on her face told him she didn't want to answer any questions.

Opening the door, then stepping aside to let her pass, he said, "I was just going to get a bite to eat. Would you like me to bring you anything?"

"No thanks, Jake. I'm not hungry." When he didn't leave, but stood just inside the doorway, running his hands around his hat brim, she said, "I'm fine." Seeing the uncertainty on his face, she added, "Really, I'm fine. Now, go have your dinner."

After a moment, he nodded, donned his hat, then turned to leave. "I'll be back shortly."

She gave him a halfhearted wave, then sighed. It had taken all of her strength to get up, bathe, and dress. She longed to return to her apartment and crawl back into bed. Determined not to give in to her melancholy, she headed for her desk and the pile of work awaiting her.

The next few days passed in a blur for Katelyn. She rose before dawn and went immediately to the newspaper office, where she worked until past dark. Only when her eyes were too tired to keep open any longer, her hand so numb with writer's cramp she couldn't hold a pen, did she return to her apartment for a cold supper and another night of fitful sleep.

Though she knew both Jake and Grace were worried about her, she told them nothing. The pain of her broken heart was still too raw. Perhaps eventually she could tell them why she went through the days by rote, barely speaking, barely eating. Some day she would share her pain. But for the time being, she suffered alone.

Brit stepped through the *sala* door into the courtyard located in the center of his parents' home. He drew a deep breath of the refreshing air. The day was especially warm for early November, the sky cloudless, the wind barely ruffling the olive trees shipped from Spain at his mother's request and planted in the courtyard.

"Are you also looking for some peace and quiet, *mi hermano?*"

Brit started, turning to stare into the shadowed interior of a large vine-covered arbor. When he saw the oldest of his sisters, Natalia, and her new daughter, he smiled. *"Sí.* It is much quieter out here."

"Tomás and Rosita are arguing again?"

He nodded. "My head hurts from their constant bickering. I do not know why he puts up with her."

"It is simple. He loves her."

Brit grunted. "What of our sister? Does she love him?"

"Sí, Rosita loves Tomás very much."

"She has a strange way of showing how she feels. Why does she continually pick fights with him? Why does she not marry him and settle down?"

Natalia laughed. "You should know the answer to your question. Rosita has always been her own person, more independent than the rest of us put together. She is not like me. She is in no hurry to become a wife and a mother. Rosita wants to enjoy her freedom as a grown woman, to experience life."

"Tomás may have something to say about that."

"It is as I said, he loves her. If he truly wants her to be his wife, he will wait."

Brit fell silent, mulling over the rough road his friend had before him. Natalia was right, Rosita was definitely an independent young woman, much to their mother's dismay. But as Natalia had pointed out, if Tomás and Rosita really loved each other, their future would eventually have them as man and wife. Not like his own future with Katelyn—nonexistent.

A crushing pain settling around his heart, he turned to leave.

"No, do not go back inside." She patted the cushion next to her. "Come, sit beside me. We have not had a chance for a private talk since you returned two weeks ago."

Brit waited until the pain eased in his chest. When he could breathe easily again, he moved across the courtyard, then stooped to enter the arbor. Sitting down beside his sister, his gaze moved over her oval face, large dark eyes, and the single thick braid draped over one shoulder. Natalia looked wonderful, literally glowing with the joy of motherhood. He shifted his gaze to the month-old Ana snuggled in his sister's arms. After a moment, he said, "Was there something you wanted to talk about?"

"How have you been? You have not visited our family home in a very long time. Mamá has been nearly sick with worry, and both Rosita and I share her—"

His back stiffened. "There was no need. As you can see, I am fine."

Natalia's dark eyes flashed, her full mouth pulling into a frown. "Do not be insolent with me, Roberto Brit Livingston y Cordoba. Just because you are my older brother, you do not have the right to talk to me in such a way."

Meeting his sister's angry glare, he lifted one shoulder in a shrug, then dropped his gaze back to the baby. "Sorry," he murmured. "I have a lot on my mind."

"I have noticed how preoccupied you have been since you arrived. Talking about whatever is on your mind will help. Perhaps there is something I can do to make you feel better."

Relaxing his stiff posture, Brit smiled and shook his head. "You always were the one who wanted to make things right. You could never stand it when Antonio and I got into a fight. You would insist we make up immediately." His smile faded. "I am afraid there is nothing you, or anyone else, can do this time. But I thank you for the offer."

She stared at her brother's pinched features for several seconds, then rose from the settee. "Here, hold Ana for a minute," she said, handing the sleeping baby to him. "I need to speak to Vicente." She bit her lip to stifle a laugh at the sheer panic on Brit's face. "Do not worry, big brother, she will not bite."

Holding his breath, Brit gingerly took his niece and cradled her against his chest. When the baby didn't stir, he exhaled slowly.

"I will be right back." Natalia took a step back, then another, moving slowly toward the door to the *sala*.

When she returned a few minutes later, she quietly stepped into the courtyard, stopping to peek around the edge of the arbor. What greeted her gaze brought an immediate smile. Brit was gently rocking a wide-awake Ana, singing to her softly in Spanish.

"You have taken a liking to your godchild," she said, approaching her brother and daughter. "Just as she has taken a liking to you."

He glanced up at her and smiled. "We were just getting acquainted." He ran a fingertip across one downy cheek. Ana gurgled, wrapping one tiny fist around his finger. His smile broadened. "You have a beautiful child, Natalia."

Returning his smile, she said, "You will make a wonderful father."

Brit's smile disappeared. Silently, he handed Ana back to her mother.

Natalia took a seat, grabbing his arm when he started to rise. "No. Please stay." When he sat back down, she said, "Who is this woman that troubles you?"

Blinking with surprise at his sister's perception, he slouched against the settee's back in stunned silence. Finally, he lifted his shoulders in a weary sigh. "You do not know her."

"She has hurt you? Is that why you have been so quiet since your return?"

"No, she has not—" He jumped to his feet. "It is hard to explain," he said, running a hand through his hair.

"But you love her, yes?"

"Yes," he replied in a soft voice, "I love her. But—"

"And she loves you?"

"Yes. But—"

"What else matters? As long as you—"

"You do not understand, Natalia," he said sharply. "It does not matter how we feel. She and I both know we can never be together."

"That is ridiculous. If you love each other, surely, you can—"

"Enough," he said in a near shout, bringing a squeak from Ana. Seeing the hurt in his sister's eyes, he crouched down next to her. "I am sorry, Natalia," he said more softly. "But I do not want to talk about this. Have I made myself clear?"

She opened her mouth to make a retort, but the hard set of his jaw changed her mind. Clamping her lips together, she lowered her head and nodded.

"I want you to promise me you will tell no one about this conversation." When she didn't reply, he placed his fingers under her chin and forced her to look at him. "I will have your promise, Natalia."

Her anger softening at the hurt she saw lurking in the depth of his eyes, at the pain she heard in his voice, she whispered, "Sí, I will promise, but only if you will promise me something as well."

Dropping his hand from her chin, he drew his eyebrows together. "What would you have me promise?"

"You should talk to someone, Brit. It is not good to keep so much pain locked inside."

"Do not start again, Natalia. I told you, I cannot—"

"I understand," she said, reaching out to grasp his hand. "Truly, I do. But one day you will be ready to talk. Vicente and I will be returning to our *rancho* soon, so I will not be here to offer my help. When that day comes, I want you to promise me you will talk to Papá. He is a good listener and a very wise man."

Brit pulled his hand out from under hers, straightened, then stepped back. When he didn't respond, she said, "Promise me, *mi hermano*."

He closed his eyes. The muscles worked in his jaw. Finally he said, *"Sí, te prometo."*

A few days after his talk with Natalia, Brit decided he had to find something to keep him busy. It was time to start turning his land into a real *rancho*. Though he wasn't sure he could ever live in the house he planned to build, he and a few of his men began the back-breaking process of hauling stone from the nearby mountains.

Once enough stone had been brought to the site he had selected, Brit spent the next week working on the ranch house. Whenever Tomás or one of the others asked about returning to the north, he gave a noncommittal answer, or avoided answering their questions altogether.

Though he loved his family, he stayed away from his parents' *rancho* as much as possible. He preferred staying on his own property, in spite of the lack of a roof over his head.

Only on Sundays did he return to the *Rancho del Sol Poniente*. His mother became despondent after Natalia, Vicente, and Ana left to return to their own home, and she appealed to Brit to help ease her sadness. Margarita wanted the rest of her family to be together on Sunday, and he could not disappoint her by turning down her request.

But even that one day each week was hard on him. The adoring looks and loving touches his parents openly shared became very painful to endure. He had always dreamed of a marriage like his parents, that one day he would take a wife who would make his life complete. Yet now that he'd found the woman to make those dreams come true, he could no longer bear being around his parents. Watching their happiness was like a knife in his heart, a constant reminder of what he would never have.

He spent a lot of time reflecting on his life. Though he would not change what he had done, the choices he had made, the price he must pay became apparent. His punishment for becoming a bandit was a life sentence of loving a woman he could never have.

In an effort to forget such painful thoughts, he worked himself from the first rays of dawn until well past dark. He hoped the long hours of physical labor would leave him too exhausted to do anything other than fall into an instantaneous sleep once he sought his bedroll.

At first his theory worked relatively well. Then, as his body got used to the rigorous schedule, sleep came less and less easily. Finally he gave up and spent his evenings reading Shakespeare's sonnets or Katelyn's journal by firelight.

Though he knew he should probably toss both books into the fire, he couldn't make himself do so. In truth, destroying either book would accomplish little. For, just as he knew many sonnets by heart, he had committed many of Katelyn's entries to memory as well.

Once he started reading her journal again, it became increasingly difficult to keep her from his thoughts. Preferring to work alone, he directed the other men to begin building corrals and the first of several barns, then devoted his time to the ranch house. Unfortunately the solitude he wanted also allowed his mind the freedom to wander. And invariably, his mind dredged up memories of Katelyn. It was another painful realization to discover his life now resembled a line from one of the sonnets he knew so well. *When to the sessions of sweet silent thought I summon up remembrance of things past.*

Fear became Katelyn's constant companion over the first few weeks following Brit's visit. Word continued to filter back to Sacramento regarding the rangers' pursuit of *El Buitre*. They were being led a merry chase up and down the valley, a chase Katelyn knew would inevitably end with the outcome the legislature envisioned.

Dragging herself out of bed each morning became more and more of a chore. She was more tired when she awoke than when she went to bed. Lately, she arose not only exhausted, but nauseous. Even at meal time, her favorite foods no longer tasted good. Often just the smell turned her stomach.

At first, she thought her easily upset system was her body's reaction to having been pushed too hard with little sleep and even less food. But after a week of the same symptoms, she began to suspect her malady had a different cause.

For a few days she refused to acknowledge her suspicions, hoping if she didn't think about it, the situation would go away. But one morning, six weeks after she'd last seen Brit, she finally accepted the truth. During his last visit, she had conceived his child.

Later that morning, Katelyn arrived at the *Argus*, pale but humming.

Jake's eyebrows rose. "Well, Katie, you're certainly chipper this morning."

"Yes, I'm feeling better today." Hanging her coat and bonnet on a peg, she said, "Would you mind going next door and asking Grace if she can have dinner with us? I need to talk to both of you."

"Be glad to. Can you tell me what this is about?"

Katelyn gave him a secretive smile. "I'd rather wait and tell you both, if you don't mind."

"Okay, Katie. I'll be back directly."

"You're what?" Grace and Jake said in unison at Katelyn's announcement over dinner.

She chuckled at the startled looks on her friends' faces. "I said, I'm with child."

"And just how did that happen?" Jake said in a fierce whisper.

Patting his hand, Katelyn replied, "Now, Jake, don't tell me you don't know how babies are conceived? I would have thought a man your age must have had plenty of experience in the process."

His cheeks burning, he said, "I know the how of it, Katie! And my experience is none of your concern. We're talking about you, and how you got herself into this predicament."

"Jake, settle down," Grace said. "There's no need to badger Katelyn." Turning to the younger woman, she said, "I take it Brit's the father?"

Katelyn nodded. "He came to see me about six weeks ago, and we . . . well, you know." Feeling a blush creep up her neck and face, she dropped her gaze to where her hands gripped her coffee cup. "When he left that night, he said he wouldn't be back."

"Is there some way you can contact him?"

Katelyn shook her head. "I asked him where he was going, but he wouldn't tell me. Even if he had, I would never send word to him about the baby."

"That's nonsense, Katie." Jake said. "As the babe's father he should be told, so he can come back and make things right."

She lifted her gaze to meet Jake's glare. "I want him to come back because of *me*, not because of our baby." She watched the anger in his eyes cool, his fierce expression soften. Unable to bear the sympathy she saw on his face, she swallowed hard, then looked away.

Grace broke the long silence when she said, "So what are you going to do?"

Katelyn sighed. "I don't know. I only accepted the fact that I'm with child this morning, so I haven't had time to think about what's going to happen next." She took a sip of coffee, then continued. "I will have to decide what I'm going to do about my future. I'll have to leave Sacramento, but I'll make—"

"Leave?" Jake said. "Grace and me aren't real family to you, but we feel like we are. Why can't you stay here with us?"

"You know why, Jake," Katelyn replied. "Folks won't accept my having a child without the benefit of a husband. I'll just have to go somewhere else. Maybe I'll go to San Francisco. I can say I'm a widow, that my husband died in one of the mines before our child was born. I'm sure that's happened before."

After a moment, Grace said, "When do you think you'll leave town?"

"I'm not sure," she replied, staring at her now-empty cup. "I have some time before I have to make a decision." There was no way she could leave Sacramento until she knew Brit's fate. Once he was— Not able to finish the thought, she suppressed a shudder.

Lifting her head, Katelyn looked at Grace, then at Jake. "There's one thing I'm sure of. I want this baby more than anything. I can't describe the incredible joy I feel because I carry Brit's child, or—" She paused to swallow the sudden lump in her throat. "Or the incredible sadness because there is no way to prevent my child from growing up without knowing his father."

Twenty-five

By the second week in December, Brit's *rancho* was beginning to take shape. His men had finished constructing the main corrals and a large horse barn, and he had completed laying the stone for the house. With winter approaching, he hoped to have the rest of it finished in a few more weeks.

"Have you selected a name for your *rancho?*" Tomás asked one day, during the break for their noon meal.

Brit stared at the stone walls and wood framing of his partially built house. "No, not yet."

After a few minutes of silence, Brit said, "I have decided it is time for *El Buitre* to retire."

Tomás looked over at his friend through narrowed eyes. "You no longer want to seek vengeance for the way our people were treated, for Mirabella's death?"

"What I have accomplished is enough. Nothing can replace a life or erase the suffering our people have endured, but it is time to put all of that behind us."

Tomás thought about that for a moment, then said, "What about the rest of the men at the winter camp? Should I send word to them?"

"No, I will go there myself. Some of the men may not like my decision, so I should be there to face them." Setting his plate aside, he got to his feet. "Would you like to go with me, or do you not want to leave my sister?"

Tomás rose to stand beside him. "I will go with you."

"*Bueno.* We will leave day after tomorrow. In the morning, I will ride over to tell my parents of our plans. Do you want to ride with me, so you can kiss Rosita good-bye?"

"No, you can do it for me," he replied. "Tell her I said *adiós,* and I will see her when we return."

Brit chuckled. "You are hoping to prove the truth of a line from *Isle of Beauty.* The one that says 'absence makes the heart grow fonder'?"

"If I am not around her so much, perhaps she will not take me for granted."

This time Brit laughed. "As you wish, *amigo mío.*"

Brit, Tomás, and several other men made the two-day journey to the winter camp of *El Buitre,* arriving on the evening of December fourteenth. Paco and Pepe yipped with excitement, their tails wagging wildly at the return of their master. As Brit swung down off his horse, Armando hurried over to him.

"*Jefe,* it is good to see you. With the rangers so close, we were worried something had happened to you."

Brit's hand stilled on one of the hounds. His gaze snapped from the dogs to Armando's face. "Close? What do you mean?"

"The rangers have been searching these mountains. They passed very close to our camp several times."

"We saw no signs of their presence when we came into the canyon," Tomás said.

"You came at the right time. They headed north, but if they find any of the trails we have used, they could circle back."

"Yes, that is very possible, Armando," Brit replied. "We came to tell you to break camp. We have no further use of this canyon."

"We are moving to a new campsite?"

"No. *El Buitre* rides no more. We are going home. To stay."

Armando crossed himself, his lips moving in silent prayer. "That is welcome news, *jefe*."

"Will any of the men find fault with my decision?"

Armando pulled on one side of his mustache. "There may be one or two, but do not worry. When they see how the rest of us are eager to return to our families, they will forget their objections."

"I want the men to start breaking camp immediately. Tell them to pack everything. Before we leave in the morning, I want this canyon stripped of all evidence of our presence."

"Sí, I will get them started at once."

Brit and Tomás walked across the canyon floor to the campfire. The rest of the men offered their greetings before hurrying off to do Armando's bidding.

"Should someone go to Stockton to tell Jorge?" Tomás asked, after filling his plate with food and sitting down next to Brit.

"Yes, he must be told it is no longer necessary to gather newspapers for me. I will see if one of the men is willing to delay his return home a little longer."

"I will go," Tomás said.

Brit turned to look at his friend, a fork of food halfway to his mouth. "You? Why are you volunteering?"

"Why not? I do not mind riding to Stockton," he replied. Seeing his friend's eyebrows lift in question, he lowered his voice and added, "If I return home after being gone only four days, Rosita will not have had a chance to miss me."

Brit swallowed a chuckle, then continued eating. After a moment, he said, "As you wish. It is possible you will have to wait to see Jorge. He may be out of town on a stage run. He could be gone for several days."

"That does not matter. I will wait for him."

The following morning, Tomás left the camp and turned

north. Brit set out with the rest of the men, their supplies, and his dogs, heading south.

Early in the evening of December sixteenth, Jake had just left the *Argus* office for the day, when the sheriff stopped him.

"Jake, could I talk to you for a minute?"

"Sure thing, Les. Why don't you come inside—"

"No." Glancing inside the newspaper office, he said, "I need to speak to you in private. Come on, let's move down the street a ways."

Jake nodded, then followed Sheriff Pierce. When they stopped a block from the *Argus,* Jake said, "What's this about?"

"I got word a couple of hours ago that *El Buitre* has been killed."

"Killed? By the rangers the legislature hired?"

"Yeah. Caught up with the bastard and some of his men in the Coast Range earlier today. When the gang tried to run, the rangers shot and killed the whole lot of 'em.

"So, why are you telling me this?"

The sheriff removed his hat, ran a hand through his hair, then settled the hat back on his head. "The body of The Vulture is being brought here, arriving sometime tomorrow, I reckon. Before I authorize payment of the reward, I want to be absolutely sure the rangers got the right man."

Jake felt a chill dance up his spine. "And?"

"And I was hoping you'd ask Miss Ferguson, if she'd come to my office to identify the body."

"You can't be serious? You'd actually ask a woman to do that"

"I wouldn't ask her, Jake, if there was any other way. But there's no one else to do it. Grady, the stage driver, is out of town on a run, won't be back for two or three days. And I can't find hide nor hair of the other passengers. Either they were just passing through Sacramento, or they've already left town."

Jake cursed softly, running a hand across his face. "I don't know, Les. Are you sure there's no one else?"

"I'm sure. Of all the folks riding on that stage when it was robbed, only Miss Ferguson is in town."

Drawing a deep breath, Jake blew it out slowly. "All right. I can't promise she'll do it. And mind you, I won't try to change her mind if she refuses. I'll talk to her, but not tonight. I'll do it first thing in the morning."

"Fine. Let me know her decision." Nodding his head in farewell, Sheriff Pierce moved down the street.

Jake stood stock-still for a long moment, his thoughts dwelling on what he had agreed to do. *Dear God, how will Katie react when I tell her the man she loves has been killed?* Rather than heading for his place as he'd planned, he turned and hurried to Grace's laundry.

As soon as Jake stepped through the door, Grace knew something was very wrong. His face was blanched of color, his brow furrowed with deep lines. "Jake, what is it?"

"Oh, Gracie," he murmured, pulling her into his arms and holding her close.

Grace could feel the tension in his body, the rapid beat of his heart. "Jake, you're frightening me," she said against his neck. "Please tell me what's wrong."

Relaxing his embrace, he held her at arm's length. "The sheriff just told me the rangers killed *El Buitre* this morning."

"Oh, sweet Jesus," she cried, her fingers digging into his arms. "Does Katelyn know?"

"No. Les wants her to identify the body."

Her eyes went wide. "You have to be joking."

He shook his head.

"How can he ask a woman to do such a ghastly thing?"

"He claims he wouldn't, except she's the only one in town who's seen the bandit's face."

"But that wasn't—"

"Aye, I know. Except the sheriff doesn't know that."

"So, maybe the man killed wasn't Brit!"

"Maybe. But maybe it was. Even though I don't want Katie to be the one to make the identification, she's the only one who will know for sure."

Grace nodded, her heart aching for her close friend. "When are you going to tell her?"

"In the morning. I haven't the heart to burden her with the news tonight."

"Will you stay with me tonight, Jake? I don't want to be alone with my thoughts of what's ahead for Katelyn."

"You know I will, Gracie. I'll be here."

The following morning, Jake had just removed his jacket and was rolling up his shirtsleeves, when Katelyn burst through the *Argus* door.

"Jake, I just heard some boys talking on the street," she said in a breathless voice, rounding the counter and approaching him. "They said *El Buitre*'s been killed. Have you—" Seeing the look on his face, she sucked in a surprised breath. "You knew." Closing her eyes, she swayed drunkenly.

Taking her arm, Jake helped her over to her desk. Dazed, she sank down onto her chair.

"You knew he'd been killed," she whispered. "You knew, and you didn't tell me? How could you do such a thing?" Her eyes filling with tears, she stared up at him with disbelief.

Crouching down in front of her, Jake grasped her hands between his. "That's not the way of it, Katie. The sheriff told me last night, and I admit I should have told you right then. But I couldn't do it. You need your rest, with the babe and all, so I didn't want to upset you any sooner than I had to. Please believe me, Katie."

After a long silence, she drew in a shaky breath and nodded. "What did Sheriff Pierce tell you?" Her voice quivered with the pain she fought to keep in check.

"Les said he got word yesterday afternoon that the rangers had tracked down and killed The Vulture and the rest of his gang in the mountains southeast of here."

Katelyn sniffed loudly. "What else did he say?"

"He told me the body of *El Buitre* is being brought into town today and . . ." Jake squeezed her hands tighter. "Oh, Katie, I wish there was a better way of saying this, but I don't know how. Les wanted me to ask you to identify the body."

What color was left in her face drained away, leaving her a chalky white. She blinked at him, her eyes glassy. She opened her mouth, but no sound came out.

"Katie?" He chafed her hands between his. "Are you all right?" When she finally nodded, he exhaled a relieved breath.

Releasing her hands, he got to his feet. "I'll go tell the sheriff you can't do it."

"No." Her voice was a mere squeak. Clearing her throat, she said more loudly, "No. I'll do it."

"But you shouldn't upset yourself any more than you already are. In your condition, the shock of what he wants you to do could be dangerous for the babe."

"I'm fine, Jake." She got to her feet, forcing her knees not to buckle. "When will—" The front door banged open, and a disheveled Grace rushed into the office.

"Jake, you shouldn't have let me oversleep. I wanted to be—" Grace slid to a halt, her gaze fastened on Katelyn's pale face. "Oh, Katelyn, I wanted to be here when Jake told you. He promised me he'd wake me."

Moving to the younger woman, she wrapped an arm around Katelyn's shoulders. "Are you okay? Can I get you anything?"

"I'm all right, Grace." Looking over at Jake, she said, "When will the body arrive?"

"Body?" Grace said, dropping her arm to her side. "You're not really going to do what the sheriff wants?"

"Yes." When Grace opened her mouth to respond, Katelyn held up one hand. "You can't change my mind, so don't try." Glancing over at Jake, she said, "Either of you. I have to know if Brit was killed, and there's only one way to do that."

Grace and Jake exchanged an anxious look. "We'll go with you, if you want," Grace said.

"No, that's not necessary. And besides, that would look strange, don't you think?"

When they nodded, she said, "Now, back to my original question. When is the body supposed to arrive?"

"The sheriff didn't know for sure," Jake replied. "He just said sometime today. Should I go over to his office and find out if he knows any of the particulars?"

"Yes, please. I . . . I think I'll go lie down for a while. Let me know when you find out where the body is being taken, and what time I'm expected."

Jake nodded, slipping one arm around Grace. Together they watched Katelyn move woodenly across the office, then out the front door.

"My heart aches for her," Grace whispered. "She's been through so much, and now she's faced with the possibility of identifying the body of the man she loves, the father of her child. Why does one person have to be given so much sorrow?"

"I don't know, Gracie," Jake responded. "I just don't know."

Katelyn lay curled on her bed, staring at the wall. She had no idea how much time had passed since she'd heard the report of *El Buitre*'s death and returned to her apartment.

For her, time was frozen in place, and wouldn't move again until she knew the truth.

She must have fallen asleep, because she was jolted awake by someone pounding on her door.

"Katie, are you in there?"

She sat up, then struggled to her feet. "I'm here, Jake," she called into the parlor. "Just give me a minute."

Checking the clock, she was surprised to find she had slept the morning away. She opened the door, then stepped aside to let Jake enter.

"Is it time?"

"Les said to come by his office at two. They'll . . . um . . . have the body ready for you by then."

"Two. That's over an hour away."

"Aye, I know. I thought maybe you'd want to get something to eat first."

Katelyn swallowed. "No, I don't think so. But maybe I could drink a cup of tea."

"Okay. I was just going over to Grace's for dinner. Would you like to go with me?"

"Yes, I'd like that. Just let me get my shawl."

At ten minutes before two o'clock, Katelyn left Jake in Grace's kitchen and headed for the sheriff's office. The tea she'd drunk had done little to ease the enormous knot in her stomach. As she drew closer to the place where she was expected to perform the grisly chore of viewing and identifying a dead man, the knot tightened even more.

A crowd had gathered outside the sheriff's office, their voices raised in a rumbling din. When Les Pierce caught sight of her, he shouted for everyone to step aside. The men grumbled, until they turned and saw Katelyn. Pulling their hats from their heads, they immediately quieted and shuffled backward to make room for her to pass. The path they created revealed a makeshift bier of sawhorses holding a wooden coffin.

She hesitated only briefly. Steeling herself for what lay ahead, she walked toward Sheriff Pierce's position at the foot of the coffin. The rest of the men instantly crowded close, forming a half-circle behind her.

"Now, Miss Ferguson, I want you to take your time," Les Pierce said, cupping her elbow with one hand.

She nodded, unable to get any words through her tight throat. Slowly, she shifted her gaze to the coffin. Squeezing her eyes shut for a second, she prayed for strength, then took a step closer.

The man's boots had been removed, his trousers were covered with dust and dried blood, as was his shirt. She could see at least two gunshot wounds in his chest, places now black with coagulated blood. She fought down the nausea, then forced her gaze upward.

Seeing the man's face, so peaceful in death, her vision started to dim. It was as if she viewed the scene through a tunnel. The pounding of her heart grew loud in her ears. All other sounds faded, as if they came from a great distance.

"Miss Ferguson, are you all right?"

"Come on, lady, what's taking so long?" someone groused.

"Yeah, hurry it up," another said.

She swayed on her feet.

"Hey, Sheriff, I think she's gonna faint."

Sheriff Pierce tightened his grip on her arm, saving her from falling. "Miss Ferguson?" he said, giving her a quick shake.

Katelyn's head snapped back. Pulling her gaze from the dead man, she looked up into the heavily freckled face of the sheriff.

"I know this isn't the kind of thing ladies are asked to

do," he said. "But I need your answer. Now, do you recognize this man?"

"Is it *El Buitre's* body, or ain't it?" one of the men yelled.

"We're waiting, Miss Ferguson," the sheriff said. "Is this The Vulture?"

Her throat clogged with emotion, she blinked back tears, then managed to say, "Yes, it is."

"You're sure?"

Pulling a handkerchief from her handbag, she nodded.

Releasing her arm, the sheriff smiled. "Thank you, Miss Ferguson. I appreciate your taking the time to do this. I know it must have been hard on you."

She tried to smile, but failed. She wanted to tell him he couldn't possibly know how hard it had been, but she remained silent.

"Would you like me to have someone escort you home?"

She shook her head. After glancing one more time at the coffin, she pressed the handkerchief to her mouth, turned, and walked away. The shouts and laughter of the men celebrating the demise of the bandit, *El Buitre,* echoed in her head.

Katelyn had barely stepped inside the *Argus* door, when Jake was at her side.

"Katie, how did it go? Was it him?"

She opened her mouth, but no words came out. Silently, she crumpled to the floor.

"Grace, come quick!"

By the time Grace reached him from the back of the office where they'd waited for Katelyn's return, Jake was sitting on the floor, the younger woman's head resting against his chest.

Kneeling beside them, Grace loosened the collar of Katelyn's dress, then felt her forehead for fever. "She just fainted. She'll come around in a minute."

Even before the words were out of Grace's mouth, Katelyn stirred. She lifted a hand to her face, then slowly opened her eyes. Blinking with surprise to see Jake and Grace peering down at her, she said, "What happened?"

"You fainted. If I hadn't caught you before you hit the floor, you could have put a nasty lump on your head."

Sitting up, Katelyn frowned. "Fainted? I've never fainted in my life."

"Well, you just did," Grace said with a smile. "It isn't any wonder. You've been under a terrible strain, and you didn't eat anything before you left."

Seeing the confusion in Katelyn's eyes, Jake said, "Don't you remember where you were a few minutes ago?"

Her brow furrowed, then cleared. "I remember. I was at the sheriff's office."

"And?"

"He wanted me to identify the body of *El Buitre.*"

"For god's sake, Katie, get on with it."

Katelyn blew her nose, then said, "I told the sheriff it was *El Buitre.*"

"Oh, Katelyn, I'm so sorry," Grace whispered.

"That's what I told the sheriff." Katelyn lips opened in a huge smile. "But it wasn't Brit! The body brought to town was the man who robbed my stage—Marco Chavez. Since the rangers thought they killed The Vulture, I decided to let them go on thinking it." She quickly sobered. "You two have to swear you won't tell anyone what I did."

"Of course, we won't," Jake replied and Grace quickly agreed.

Struggling to get to her feet, Katelyn allowed Jake to help her up. "Come on, Jake. We have a paper to get out."

"Paper? But it's only Wednesday."

"I know. I was the one who told Sheriff Pierce the man laid out in that coffin was *El Buitre,* so I think I should be the one to report it in a special edition of the *Argus.* Don't you agree?"

"Aye, Katie," Jake said with a chuckle. "I agree."

Twenty-six

Yesterday the bandit El Buitre *made his final visit to our fair town. He arrived, not in his usual manner of sitting astride his horse, but wrapped in canvas and slung across his saddle. This reporter was asked to personally view the body to make sure there was no mistake in the identity of the dead man. Taking my civic duty seriously, I obliged, and hereby dutifully report the vile bandit is now in the hands of a greater power. We pray he will be forever condemned to the great abyss of purgatory. Now that* El Buitre *no longer poses a threat to our safety, we can rejoice in life once again, able to go through our days without fear of having our purses stolen or our lives snuffed out. Do not let the death of this most sought-after bandit be in vain. Seize the opportunity his passing brings forth: a chance to begin life anew. Please join us in thanking the Rangers, who refused to give up until they found The Vulture and ended his reign of terror once and for all. This is indeed a grand day for not only the citizens of Sacramento, but for the entire state of California.*

Katelyn read again the words she had written, now printed on the front page of the *Argus'* special edition, then sighed. Having penned an editorial claiming the man she loved was dead left her with a strange mixture of emotions: guilt for having lied to first the sheriff and now the readers of her newspaper, elation for having been the one to give Brit the chance to put his past behind him if he chose to take it, and hope for his survival.

But even if Brit were alive, would she ever see him again? Thinking of the child she carried, she knew she couldn't wait too long for the answer to that question. In a few more weeks, her secret would become obvious. And rather than risk the ridicule of the townsfolk, she had to formulate plans for her future.

Since she had no other family, there was no reason to move back to Chicago. Just thinking of the wind and cold she had endured each winter in Illinois sent gooseflesh over her arms. She would definitely stay in California. As she'd suggested to Grace and Jake, San Francisco would be her destination.

Her thoughts were interrupted by the office door swinging open and banging against the wall. Turning toward the sound, Katelyn's halfhearted smile of welcome changed to an annoyed frown.

Ross Carter closed the door, moved around the counter, and swaggered toward her. "Aren't you going to say hello, Katelyn?"

"Hello, Ross," she answered automatically, wondering what brought him to the *Argus*. He hadn't been around since the day she told him she wouldn't marry him. "What do you want?"

His eyes narrowing slightly at her curt tone, he forced himself to smile. "Just wanted to congratulate you on the special edition. You beat us all to the punch with the news of The Vulture's death."

He moved to stand next to her chair, peering at the sheet of newsprint on the desk in front of her. "Yes sir, that Washington Press of yours sure does a fine job," he said, running his fingers over the masthead.

Katelyn's frown deepened. "Is that all you—" Her brow

abruptly cleared. "Tell me something, Ross. Are you still interested in buying the *Argus?*"

Startled, he jerked his hand from the newspaper, his gaze snapping to her face. "What are you saying?"

"Just answer my question, Ross. Do you still want to buy the paper?"

"Yes, I want the *Argus*. But I'd like to know what made you change your mind."

Shoving her chair away from the desk, she rose and moved across the office. She had to come up with something convincing.

Swinging back to face him, she said, "As you're aware, I only took over the paper to avenge my father's death. Though I knew little about running the business, I felt I owed it to him. But now that the man I held responsible for Papa's death is also dead, my thirst for vengeance has been quenched. Therefore, my heart is no longer in the paper, and frankly, I'm tired of the continual struggle to keep the *Argus* going." She swallowed her self-disgust before she added, "Ross, you would be doing me a huge favor by taking the *Argus* off my hands."

He contemplated her explanation for a few moments, then said, "So, *El Buitre*'s death is the reason you're suddenly willing to sell out. Hmmm, how ironic. I helped change your mind, and didn't even know it."

"What are you talking about?"

Hands clasped behind him, he rocked back on his heels. "As it happens, I had something to do with that blasted bandit meeting the end he so richly deserved."

"You?"

"If not for the information I was able to learn about The Vulture and pass on to the authorities, they might never have found him."

Katelyn snorted, then coughed to cover the sound. Knowing she'd have to stroke his ego in order to get some answers, she gave him a sweet smile. "You're right. Your help was invaluable. Now that *El Buitre* is gone, can you tell me who gave you the information?"

"Gave me? Hah, I had to pay, and pay dearly I might add, for what the man knew about the bandit."

"Who was he?"

Ross lifted his shoulders in a careless shrug. "I haven't the faintest idea." At Katelyn's skeptical look, he said, "Names weren't important. Even if I'd asked, he wouldn't have told me. Anyone who insisted we meet in a deserted alley at midnight, isn't going to reveal his name."

"Midnight? So you don't know what he looks like either?"

He shook his head, then frowned. "He was just another damned greaser, as far as I was concerned. Except, this one had a grudge against The Vulture."

"Grudge?"

"Yes. He said it was something personal. Probably had to do with the scar on his neck," he responded, moving to stand by the printing press.

"I thought you said you don't know what he looked like."

"I don't. He was always rubbing the side of his neck. I figured it was a nervous habit, until Col—uh . . . an acquaintance of mine told me about the puckered scar."

Katelyn whirled around. *Oh, my God. I was right. It was Marco!* She clamped a hand over her mouth to stifle a gasp. If Ross noticed her shocked reaction to what she'd just learned, he would certainly ask questions she had no intention of answering.

Just as she'd suspected, Marco had sold information about Brit, while he and his own gang committed far worse crimes—crimes blamed on The Vulture. Such duplicity filled her with impotent rage. If only Brit had believed her. *I'm glad Marco's dead. If the rangers hadn't killed him, I gladly do it myself.* Recalling the feel of his mouth on hers, she repressed a shudder.

"Katelyn! Are you listening to me?"

"What?" Snapping out of her momentary lapse, she faced Ross. "I'm sorry, what did you say?"

"I asked you when you wanted to complete our deal for the *Argus*."

Katelyn made some fast decisions. She would give Brit a month; she couldn't wait any longer. If she didn't hear from him by then, she would have to accept some painful facts: he had been killed, or he still believed she had betrayed him, or he had lied when he declared his love and wanted nothing more to do with her.

Ignoring the anguish such thoughts spawned, she said, "You can take the paper over in two weeks. But since I'm not sure what I'm going to do, I'd like to stay in my apartment for a couple of weeks after that, if you're agreeable."

"Fine. Fine. I'll be moving everything out of here anyway, and I've no plans to do anything with the building for the time being." He ran a hand almost lovingly over the press. "Two weeks," he said in a soft voice. "That would make me your new owner on January first." He grinned. "A perfect way to start a new year."

Tomás pulled his horse to a skidding stop in front of Brit's new barn, then leaped to the ground. "Lorenzo, where are you?" he shouted.

Lorenzo Sanchez came running from the barn, then slid to a halt. "What is it, Tomás?" Lorenzo asked, grabbing the reins tossed to him by his older brother.

"Where is Brit?" he said, reaching up to remove his saddlebags from behind the saddle.

"He is working in his house. Is there something wrong?"

"No," Tomás replied, smiling at his brother for the first time. "If Brit is here, then nothing is wrong."

Frowning at Tomás's strange comment, Lorenzo shrugged, then turned to lead the horse inside the barn.

Tomás draped his saddlebags over his shoulder, strode

purposefully across the yard, then jumped onto the newly constructed veranda which ran the full width of the house.

Stepping through the doorway, Tomás called, "Brit? *¿Dónde estás?*"

"Tomás, is that you?" Brit's voice came to him from deep in the house.

"Sí."

"It is about time you returned. Come down the main hall to the last room on the right."

As Tomás started down the hall, he said, "I would have been here sooner, but I had to wait three days for Jorge to return." He found Brit working in the largest of the home's bedrooms. Openings had been left on the southern wall for a window and a set of doors opening onto a smaller veranda on the rear of the house.

Looking around the room, Tomás whistled. "I am impressed, *amigo mío.* You have accomplished much since your return. This will be the bedroom of *el patrón,* your room, *sí?*"

Brit moved to look out the window opening. "It is supposed to be the bedroom of the *patrón.*"

Tomás's eyebrows rose at Brit's strange reply, but he made no comment. "I am glad to see you are well. I was concerned when I heard the news."

Turning away from the window, Brit said, "When you heard what news?"

"Then you do not know? You have not read the newspapers from the past week?"

"I do not have time to read. Now tell me what news concerned you."

Tomás flipped open one of his saddlebags, pulled out a roll of newspapers, and handed them to Brit. "The newspapers say *El Buitre* has been killed. Jorge had no way of knowing you needed his help, so he had already collected these papers on his run through Sacramento. He was extremely upset by the reports, which said you had been killed

by the rangers. His concern grew when he found me waiting
for him. He was afraid I was at his home to confirm his
fears. Unfortunately, I could not be absolutely certain you
were alive—though I assured Jorge you were—until I arrived here today."

Brit only half-heard Tomás's explanation. Stunned, he
stared at the headline of the first paper. *El Buitre* Shot Dead.
He scanned the article, picking out bits and pieces of information. He had supposedly been cornered by the rangers
in the Coast Range Mountains on December sixteenth, then
shot to death when he and his men tried to run. The Vulture's body was taken to Sacramento, where positive identification was made by newspaper owner Katelyn Ferguson!

"What the hell," he grumbled, tossing the paper aside.
He quickly scanned the articles about *El Buitre* in several
other papers. Though each reporter had embellished his article with his own choice of adjectives to describe the bandit
and his deeds, each reported the same set of facts regarding
the identification of the deceased. The body brought to Sacramento was identified as that of The Vulture by a woman
who had seen the bandit before, a Miss Katelyn Ferguson,
whose stagecoach had been held up by the notorious villain
on the return trip from Sonora several months earlier.

"Damn her," he whispered, crumpling the paper in one
fist.

"Who?" Tomás said, craning his neck to see what had
upset his friend.

"She did not tell me her stage was held up."

"Ah, you are talking about Katelyn. I wondered when I
read about her, if you knew about the stage robbery."

"Yes, Katelyn," Brit replied in a tight voice. "I knew she
went to Sonora. I told her it was a stupid thing to do. She
never mentioned her stagecoach was held up on the return
trip."

"I understand why," Tomás said under his breath. Louder,

he said, "We did not rob the stage she was on. Who could have done it, and why were you blamed?"

"Every crime in nearly all of California was blamed on *El Buitre*. That robbery was no different."

"That still does not explain why she would say the man killed by the rangers was *El Buitre*."

Unable to come up with a plausible explanation for her behavior, Brit did not reply. Tossing the other newspapers onto the floor, he stared at the one he held in his hands—the *Sacramento Argus*.

In a low, but firm voice, he read Katelyn's editorial aloud. When he finished, he paused for a moment, then whispered, "Why, *querida?*"

Tomás cleared his throat, then said, "Perhaps, *amigo mío*, she is giving you a chance to start over without a price on your head."

His brows pulling together, Brit said, "What makes you think she would do such a thing?"

"The one sentence she wrote, the one about the chance to begin life anew. Is it not possible she also meant those words for you, that you should be allowed a new beginning?"

Brit shifted his gaze from the newspaper still clutched in his hands to the window and the stream beyond. Was that truly Katelyn's motive? Or could there have been another reason?

While he worked on the house, Brit continued to mull over Tomás's words for the remainder of the afternoon and into the evening. When darkness forced him to quit, he headed for the barn. Now that one structure on his ranch was finished, he no longer had to sleep outside, but spent his nights on a bed of straw in an empty horse stall.

Lying on his makeshift bed, his hounds sprawled next to him, he idly stroked Paco's head. Though Brit was bone-tired, his mind refused to quiet. He recalled every minute he'd spent with Katelyn, going over each of their conversations. Unable to shake her from his thoughts, he finally gave up trying to sleep. After lighting a lantern and hanging it on a nail above his head, he reached for her journal. He reread all of the entries she wrote after they met, then all the newspaper articles recounting the death of *El Buitre*. By the time he finished, the questions plaguing him remained unanswered.

There was one thing he knew for sure. His love for Katelyn. He loved her more with each passing day. So why was he reluctant to accept what she had done at face value? Perhaps her proclaiming the dead man to be *El Buitre* was an elaborate ruse to lure him to Sacramento. By making him think it was safe to visit her, he would ride into town and fall neatly into the trap she had set. He would be arrested, then no doubt sentenced to hang, and she would be proclaimed a heroine.

He found it hard to believe the woman who professed to love him would do such a thing. Still, she had blamed him for her father's death and admitted she wanted vengeance. And although she claimed she loved him, could her desire for revenge overrule her personal feelings?

He rubbed his eyes, then pinched the bridge of his nose. It was well after midnight, and still he had solved nothing. In fact, he was more confused than ever.

Paco raised his head, turning large sad eyes on Brit. *"Sí,* I know, it is late. You and Pepe are anxious to go to sleep and not be disturbed, eh?"

As if on cue, Pepe stretched, then yawned.

"Too bad the two of you cannot talk. I could use another opinion." He scratched each hound behind the ears, then rose to turn out the lantern.

Once again stretched out on his bed, Brit's thoughts drifted to his last private conversation with Natalia. Perhaps it was time to make good the promise his sister had managed to wrest from him.

Just before he fell asleep, he made a decision. In the morning, he would ride over to the *Rancho del Sol Poniente* and speak with his father.

Twenty-seven

Brit walked down the main hallway of his parents' home, his boot heels clicking on the tile floor. Reaching his father's office, he stopped, took a deep breath, then knocked on the thick oak door.

When he heard his father's muffled call to enter, he opened the door and stepped into the room, his footsteps hushed by thick carpet.

"Buenos días, Papá."

Ricardo Livingston looked up from the sheaf of papers on his desk, then smiled. The network of fine lines surrounding his dark green eyes deepened with the smile on his tanned face. At fifty-five, his dark brown hair had only a few strands of gray, his tall, muscular body sported not a bit of fat. Pushing his chair back, he rose and came around his desk.

"Brit. It is good to see you," he said, shaking his son's hand. "What brings you here at such an early hour? Your *mamá* has not yet left our bed. She will be disappointed if you do not stay long enough to spend some time with her."

"I will make sure I speak to *Mamá,* before I leave."

"Good. Now what can I do for you?"

Brit moved restlessly around his father's office, unsure of where to begin. Finally, he said, "I came to talk to you."

When his son fell silent, Ricardo took a seat behind his desk, then said, "What is it you want to talk about?"

Running a hand through his hair, Brit took a deep breath, then swung around to face his father. "I met a woman."

The pain he detected in his son's declaration took Ricardo by surprise. "And that troubles you?"

Brit strode back to the desk and sat down in a leather chair across from his father. "Let me start at the beginning." At his father's nod, he began speaking in a low, even voice.

"When I returned to the mine fields after Mirabella was buried, I started reading what the newspapers wrote about me. The editorials in one newspaper, the *Sacramento Argus,* were especially vocal about the crimes of *El Buitre,* and how the bandit should be dealt with. I decided I had to see the person who wrote such hostile and vengeful words, so I went to Sacramento. I learned it was the owner of the *Argus* who wrote the editorials."

"This woman you mentioned?"

Brit nodded. "Once I saw her, I could not rout her from my thoughts. I wanted her to know the truth about *El Buitre,* not the foolishness she spouted in her newspaper, so I went to her apartment that night and—" He stopped to clear his throat. "I told her I wanted her to get to know the real Vulture. Then I took her to my camp in the Sierra Nevada."

Ricardo's eyes went wide. "You abducted a woman from her home? My god, Son, did you not consider the consequences of such actions? You could have been arrested for kidnapping!"

"I am not proud of what I did. But she made me so angry, and I was so confused by my attraction to her. I was not thinking straight."

"All right, so what happened?"

Brit told his father about the time Katelyn spent at his camp, returning her to Sacramento, and his subsequent visits to her apartment. He was completely honest, holding nothing back. Though his father's expression changed at several points while Brit's story unfolded, he did not interrupt.

After his son finished, Ricardo remained silent, elbows

braced on the arms of his chair, fingers steepled under his chin. At last he said, "That is an incredible story, Brit. But the question remains, what are you going to do now?"

"That is why I came to talk to you. I need some advice on what I should do."

"No one can tell you what to do. You will have to decide the path you must take on your own. However, I do want to ask you something, which may help you make your decision. In spite of everything that has happened between the two of you, do you truly love Katelyn?"

"*Sí, Papá.* I love her with all my heart."

"And do you want her to be your wife?"

"*Sí.* More than anything."

"Then if you want something badly enough, you must work to get it." Seeing the doubt flash in his son's eyes, he said, "All things are possible, Brit. Do not ever doubt that. You have but to look at your mother and me, to see the truth of my statement. I loved your mother from the first moment I saw her, and I was determined to let nothing stop me from spending the rest of my life with her by my side. There was no obstacle I could not conquer: not the differences in our cultures, our religion, or even the strong objections of her parents." He flashed Brit a wide smile. "At least you do not have the problem of overprotective parents to contend with in your circumstance."

Brit managed a weak smile in return. "That is true, but I am not so confident Katelyn and I will ever be together."

"If she loves you, it is very possible. You said she told you of her love. Do you believe her?"

"I think she loved me once. But I am afraid I may have killed that love. I have hurt her so many times, the things I said to her, the names I called her. And the last time I went to Sacramento, I told her there was no chance we could ever be together, not with a price on my head."

"But that has changed. There is no longer a reward for

El Buitre. Everyone thinks he was killed. Something Katelyn had a large part in, from what you have just told me."

"Yes, though I cannot figure out why she did it."

"Perhaps Tomás is right. Perhaps you have been given something most people never get: the chance for a new beginning."

Brit stared at his father for several moments, then said, "I wish I knew for sure."

"If you want her as your wife, you must go to her. You must convince her of the depth of your love, and that she must forgive your harsh words. If you love her as much as you say, you should be willing to do those things. If not . . ." He shrugged his wide shoulders. "Then it was not meant to be."

Brit drew in a deep breath, then blew it out. Rising from the chair, he said, "Thank you, *Papá.* You have given me much to think about. I will let you know when I have made my decision."

On January second, Katelyn watched Ross Carter's men haul her father's printing press from the *Argus* office with a sense of relief. Running the newspaper after agreeing to sell to Ross had been harder than she'd anticipated. When he came by the office every day to check on the soon-to-be-his Washington Press, she had seriously considered moving the date of the sale ahead. Signing the sale papers earlier would have been worth it, not only to stop his annoying visits, but also to relieve herself of the burden the paper had become. For purely spiteful reasons, she refused to let his behavior sway her, and let the original date stand.

After Ross and his men left, Katelyn released a weary sigh and glanced around the nearly empty office. *Now what do I do?* Though she didn't regret selling the *Argus,* she realized she now had to find ways to occupy her time, ways besides longing for what could never be.

She spent the next several days keeping busy by sorting through the few things left in the newspaper office, packing what she wanted to keep, and making a pile of what she wanted to discard. Then she started on her apartment, filling trunks and boxes with personal belongings and household items in readiness for her move.

The evenings were the worst to get through. Too tired to continue packing after darkness fell, she was left with hours to fill, hours of trying to keep Brit from her thoughts. In an effort to occupy her mind, she started sewing baby clothes, and once in a while she visited Grace and Jake.

Since her friends had married in a Christmas Eve ceremony, Katelyn didn't spend as much time with them as she had in the past. Seeing their obvious happiness, knowing they lived as man and wife, were constant reminders of her own circumstances. Every time she saw the tender looks they exchanged, their gentle touches, she longed for Brit all the more. He was never far from her thoughts.

She tried to keep abreast of the news, constantly watching for reports of new robberies in the area and worrying for his safety. Each day without a new crime reported kept alive her hope that he had not been killed, and brought the comfort of knowing he had not returned to the life of a bandit. But each day also brought grief. Although she tried to ignore the passage of time, the deadline she had given herself was fast approaching.

Late one afternoon, two days before she was to leave Sacramento, she glanced around her parlor, then let out a weary sigh. How she would miss the tiny apartment. All she had left to pack were her clothes. Everything else was boxed, ready to ship to San Francisco by steamer in the morning, a day ahead of her own departure. Before she started on the last of her packing, she decided to rest for a few minutes. Though her morning sickness had passed, she still tired easily.

She had just taken a seat in her rocking chair and closed

her eyes, when there was a knock on the door. Her heart speeding its rhythm, she rose and moved across the room. Taking a deep breath, she reached out and opened the door. Her heart sank.

"Oh, Grace. Jake. Hello."

Grace's brow furrowed at Katelyn's lackluster greeting. "We aren't disturbing you, are we?" Grace said.

"No, I was just packing. Would you like to come in?" She moved back to allow them to step into the room.

"We can only stay a minute," Grace said, taking a seat on the settee. Looking at all the trunks and boxes filling the small parlor, she said, "My, you've been busy."

"Yes, I have." Motioning for Jake to have a seat next to his wife, Katelyn said, "What brings you by this afternoon?"

"Katie, we just wanted to tell you our plans," Jake said.

"Plans?"

"Yes, I sold the laundry today," Grace replied. "So we'll be leaving town, too. But probably not for a couple of weeks."

"Leaving? Where are you going?"

"We haven't decided yet," Jake replied. "We're planning to travel around California a bit, until we find a place to our liking. I think it's time I did something besides working as a printer's devil. I've always fancied owning some land, where I could raise cattle."

"And I'm looking forward to doing laundry and mending for just the two of us," Grace added with a chuckle.

"That's wonderful," Katelyn said. "I know you'll be happy wherever you end up."

Grace nodded, then said, "Have you decided what you're going to do in San Francisco?"

"I'll try to get a job with one of the newspapers there. Before Papa died, I never had any designs on working in his office for more than a few hours a week. But I've discovered I really do like writing. I just hope the newspaper editors in San Francisco won't object to hiring a woman."

"They'd be fools if they didn't take you on," Jake said. "You're a fine reporter, and don't let some narrow-minded jackass of an editor tell you any different."

Katelyn laughed for the first time in many days. "I hope there are others who will agree with you."

"You'll let us know where you're living?"

"Of course, I will, Grace."

Rising from the settee, Jake said, "We'd best be on our way, Gracie."

Accepting her husband's hand, she got to her feet. "Are you sleeping all right, Katelyn? You look tired."

Shrugging, she said, "I've had a lot to do." She nodded to the pile of boxes. "Packing and everything."

"Promise me you'll go to bed early tonight?"

She smiled at Grace. "Okay, I promise."

As they moved to the door, Jake said, "I'll bring a wagon by first thing in the morning to take these boxes down to the freight office." Before he followed Grace outside, he turned to Katelyn. Kissing the top of her head, he said, " 'Bye, Katie."

"Good-bye," she whispered, closing the door softly behind them.

Brit walked down K Street, anticipation quickening his pace. Approaching the office of the *Argus,* his pulse rate picked up. Stopping to glance through the front window, his blood froze. The office was empty.

Fear gnawing at his middle, he hurried to the alley and turned toward the apartment at the rear. Nearly bumping into a couple as they came around the corner of the building, he mumbled an apology but kept walking.

At the front door of Katelyn's apartment, he stopped to steady his nerves. Closing his eyes, he filled his lungs with a deep breath, then exhaled slowly. He raised a hand—surprised to see he was actually shaking—and knocked on the door.

It seemed like hours rather than seconds before the door swung open. Katelyn stood in the doorway, a smile curving her mouth.

"Jake, did you forget some—" Her fingers tightened on the door to keep herself from falling. This definitely wasn't who she expected when the knock came only seconds after Jake and Grace left. One hand pressed to her chest, she stared up at the man standing on her porch.

Brit found his throat clogged with emotion. He could only gaze at the woman he had ridden four days to see. Katelyn looked tired and pale, but otherwise the lovely face framed by pale blond hair was a balm to his aching heart.

"Are you going to invite me inside?" he finally managed to say in a raspy whisper.

"Brit." His name came out in a soft gasp. Snapping out of her shock, she moved back. "Yes, of course. Please come in."

He took a step into the parlor. His brows pulling together in a deep frown, his gaze swung from the boxes to her face. "You are moving?"

"Yes. I'm leaving Sacramento the day after tomorrow."

"Why?"

"I . . . I sold the *Argus,* and I decided to move some place where the memories aren't so painful."

After a long, strained moment, he said, "I do not want you to leave, *querida.*"

"But I can't stay in Sacramento." Refusing to explain, she changed the subject. "Why are you here?"

"I wanted to see you, to talk to you."

"Talk to me? What about?"

Finding this extremely difficult, he finally blurted, "I want to know if you really return my love?"

Katelyn blinked up at him, her eyes wide. "Yes, I do."

"Are you sure, what about—"

She stepped close enough to press her fingers to his lips. "I love you, Brit." In fascination, she watched his shoulders relax, the tightness leave his face.

He curled his fingers around hers, then pressed a kiss on her palm before releasing her hand. "What about the way I treated you, the things I said to you? Can you forgive me?"

"Brit, there's nothing—" Seeing the hard set to his jaw, she reached up and rubbed the pad of her thumb across the cleft in his chin. "Of course, I forgive you."

After a moment, he nodded. "I want you with me, *querida*. I have thought of you constantly, my heart aching for you. As soon as I heard *El Buitre* had been laid to rest, I have thought of nothing except coming for you."

"That was almost a month ago. Why did it take you so long to get here?"

"I wanted to come sooner, but— Do you remember when I told you I would not allow Mirabella to set our wedding date?"

At Katelyn's nod, he said, "And do you remember the reason I would not let her do so?" She nodded again. "Ever since my last visit, I have been working on my *rancho*. I finished the house the day before I left for Sacramento."

"What does all that have to do with me?"

Cupping her chin with one hand, he smoothed the furrows on her brow with the other. "I want you to be my wife, Katelyn. Will you marry me?"

If not for his hand under her chin, she would surely have fallen. Grasping his forearm to maintain her balance, she whispered, "Yes."

Letting out a whoop of laughter, he grabbed her waist and swung her around in a circle.

When he set her back on the floor and her own laughter faded, Katelyn looked up into his face. "Brit, there's something I must ask you." She cleared her throat, unsure how to word what she had to say. "Are you sure you can forgive me for giving myself to another man, for not being a virgin for you?"

"There is nothing to forgive, *querida*."

"But . . . but you were so angry when I told you about Mason."

"*Sí*, I was very angry. But not with you. My anger was directed toward the man who took your maidenhead with the false promise of marriage. He was the target for my anger, not you."

Feeling the sting of tears, she quickly blinked them away. "Oh, Brit, I love you so much."

"And I love you," he whispered, before lowering his head to press his mouth to hers. At first his lips just brushed hers, teasing for more. Then with a soft growl, he pulled her into his arms and kissed her hard.

When he finally pulled away, his chest heaved with his labored breathing, desire sang in every fiber of his body.

"Do you still have a bed, *querida?* Or have you packed it as well?"

Chuckling, Katelyn flashed him a smile. "I needed a place to sleep for two more nights, so I have done nothing with my bed."

"*Bueno*. Though I would have made love to you on the floor, I am glad we will have the comfort of a bed. Do you not agree?"

"Yes," she replied, wrapping her arms around his neck and rubbing her breasts against his chest. "Will you shout for me, Brit?"

Though startled by her request, his body reacted instantly, his aroused flesh swelling even more to press painfully against his trousers. "You like it when I shout my pleasure?"

"*Sí, muchísimo*," she replied, running the tip of her tongue over his lips.

Sweeping her up into his arms, he started toward the bedroom. "Then, let us find ways to make me shout, eh?"

* * *

Much later, Katelyn cuddled close to Brit, head on his chest, one leg draped over his thighs. She sighed with pleasure. She couldn't believe she was going to marry the man she loved. Nothing had ever felt this wonderful.

Brit kissed the top of Katelyn's head, the fingers of one hand lightly rubbing her back. "Why did you do it, *querida?*"

Raising her head enough to look into his face, she said, "Do what?"

"Why did you tell everyone the man the rangers brought in was *El Buitre?*"

She braced herself on one elbow, the other hand resting on his chest. "Brit, the man the rangers killed was Marco Chavez."

Seeing his eyes widen with surprise, she said, "After I went to identify the body, I learned my suspicions were correct. Marco did betray you; he was selling information to Ross Carter. I didn't tell you this before, but when I returned from Sonora, my stage was held up. I recognized the man leading the bandits from the night he was at your camp. It was Marco. I'm—" Recalling the robbery, a shiver racked her shoulders. She couldn't tell Brit about Marco's threat, someday maybe, but not yet. "I'm glad he's dead."

"He finally got what he wanted," he replied in a soft voice. "He wanted to be a famous *bandido*. Now, thanks to you, he will actually be *El Buitre* for eternity."

When Katelyn didn't reply, Brit said, "You did not answer my original question. Why did you say Marco was *El Buitre?*"

"I had several reasons." Katelyn dropped her gaze to his chest. "We all make mistakes. Goodness knows I've made my share—like blaming you for Papa's death. Anyway, when I went to see the man the rangers killed and found Marco, not you, lying in the coffin, I realized I had a choice to make. I decided you should be given a second chance, a chance to start over. I said Marco was The Vulture so you could begin a new life, if you wanted to. That's one of my reasons, the other one is . . ." She paused to gather her thoughts. "The other reason is I wanted to give our child a chance to perhaps one day meet his father."

Brit's body went rigid, then slowly relaxed. Sitting up, he grasped Katelyn's shoulders and held her at arm's length. "Our child? Are you telling me you are carrying my child?"

She nodded.

"Why did you not let me know?"

"It happened the last time we were together. When I realized I had conceived, I had no idea where you were, or how to contact you. That's why I was planning to leave Sacramento. I couldn't stay here, unmarried and carrying a child."

"Ah, *querida.* I am sorry for the pain you must have felt. If I had known, I would have come for you sooner. I swear."

She offered him a weak smile. "You're happy about the baby?"

"Very happy. You have given me a chance to start a new life, and I promise, you will never be sorry. We will spend our new life together as Mr. and Mrs. Brit Livingston. We will live in our new house, where we will raise this child . . ." He gently laid his palm against her stomach. "And hopefully many more, on the *Rancho de Principios Nuevos.*"

Katelyn's brow crinkled in concentration. "The ranch of new beginnings?"

Brit smiled. *"Sí.* You not only gave me a second chance, a chance for a new beginning, but you also gave me the inspiration for the name of our ranch. Do you like it?"

"Yes," she whispered, lying back down on the bed and tugging on his arm. "The name is perfect, absolutely perfect. Now come down here."

One dark eyebrow lifted. "What, I did not shout loudly enough the first time?"

"No," she said with a giggle. "Not nearly loud enough."

Epilogue

Katelyn sat on the bedroom veranda, rocking a sleeping child. Her gaze moved over the land now lush with spring grass, the stream cutting across the property, the mountains to the west. She smiled. How everything had changed since she moved onto the ranch as Mrs. Brit Livingston.

Because of her husband's hard work and a group of dedicated workers, the *Rancho de Principios Nuevos* was doing very well. Solazo was proving to be an even better brood mare than Brit had predicted. According to him, the three colts she had produced in the five years they had lived on the ranch would all be prize-winning horses.

Katelyn smiled again. There must be something in the ranch's water supply, since she had also given Brit three children in the same time span. If Brit was proud of his horses, he was doubly so of his two sons and the daughter Katelyn held in her arms. To have a husband who loved his children so much was a gift for which she never failed to give thanks.

In spite of her full schedule—taking care of the children and overseeing the running of the house—she managed to find the time to write an occasional article for the local newspaper. Someday, when she had more time, she wanted to write a book about the infamous *El Buitre,* a book which would tell the truth about the bandit.

Unable to imagine life being any better, she drew a deep breath of fresh spring air, then exhaled slowly. How she loved the ranch, her children, and most of all her husband. Smiling, she dropped her head against the back of the rocker and closed her eyes.

Brit found his wife dozing on the veranda, a sleeping Marcela wrapped in her arms. He smiled, his heart swelling with love. He loved his sons, Jonatán and Esteban, but it was his two-year-old daughter who had completely bewitched him. Looking at her perfect little face, with her mother's nose and stubborn chin, his high cheekbones, and surrounded by a tangle of curly hair as black as his own, his smile widened. *My sweet Marcela, such an innocent in your sleep. So unlike the little imp who flashes those blue eyes at me when she begs for another sweet. You must be a bruja just like your mamá, for she, too, threw a spell over me I could not break.*

His gaze moved to the woman who would forever hold his heart. Recalling their rough beginning, he offered another prayer of thanks for allowing this blond woman, his golden thistle, to become his wife. He swallowed the sudden lump in his throat. Life could not be sweeter.

Watching the gentle rise and fall of Katelyn's breasts as she slept, seeing the soft skin of her neck just begging for his touch, Brit felt himself harden. Time had certainly not lessened his desire for his wife. Reaching for the silk bandana wrapped around his throat, he grinned.

He teased the end of the bandana across his wife's cheek, then bent to nuzzle her neck. "Wake up, *querida.*"

Katelyn's eyelids fluttered, then lifted. She met his gaze and smiled. Seeing the piece of red silk dangling from one hand, she said, "What are you doing with the bandana?"

"I was thinking we should put it to use."

Her brow furrowed. "What are you talking about?"

"Do you not remember the time I visited you in Sacramento when you told me about a bandana?"

She shook her head.

"It was when I awoke and thought I had dreamed about the night we spent together. You described for me what we had done before we went to sleep, how you used my bandana to make love to me." Seeing a flare of blue fire in her eyes, he chuckled. "Ah, I see I have jogged your memory."

He bent to press his lips to hers, his tongue teasing her mouth open. After a long, leisurely kiss, he lifted his head. "It just occurred to me that we have never tried to duplicate your fantasy. I think we should explore the idea in great detail. What do you think, *querida?*"

"What about Marcela?"

"The children's *dueña* will take care of our daughter. Here, let me take her." He bent to lift the sleeping child from her mother's arms.

Pulling the bandana from his hand, Katelyn rose from the chair, then glided past him into their bedroom. "Do not be long."

In a few minutes, he returned to find Katelyn sprawled on their bed, naked. She held one end of his bandana in her right hand, the other was tied to the headboard. An enormous flood of desire rushed through his veins and settled in his groin. "I instructed the *dueña* to keep Marcela, Jonatán, and Esteban occupied for the rest of the morning."

Katelyn's eyebrows lifted. "It's not yet nine o'clock. That gives us three hours. Don't you have work to do?"

He pulled his shirt over his head, then reached for the buttons on his trousers. *"Sí,* we have three hours," he replied in a raspy voice. "And no, the only thing I have to do is make love to my wife."

She watched him remove the rest of his clothes in silent appreciation, desire building between her thighs. When he moved toward the bed with his usual, easy grace, she said, "I heard one of our men say Solazo is with foal again. Is that true?"

Stretching out next to his wife, Brit said, *"Sí,* it is true."

"Well then, I suggest we get started. I certainly can't let a brood mare get ahead of me in producing babies on this ranch." She flashed him a flirtatious look. "Do you think you're up to it?"

Momentarily startled, a slow smile appeared on his face. He grasped her wrist, then moved her hand lower. Wrapping her fingers around his aroused flesh, he whispered, "I think I am definitely *up* to it. What do you think, *cardillo mio?*"

Please turn the page for an
exciting sneak preview of
Arlene Holliday's next sizzling
historical romance
Dancer's Angel
coming soon from Zebra Books

One

"Company in the parlor, girls." The husky voice of Ruby, the stout, bewigged madame who sported a fake beauty mark next to her painted mouth, drifted up the stairway to where Angelina Coleman stood on the second-floor landing.

Angelina sucked in a deep breath, hoping to ease her trepidation. This was the moment she'd been waiting for, the moment she'd tried to prepare for over the past week . . . the moment she dreaded. Could she really do this? Would she be able to go ahead with what she'd told James Murray, owner of the brothel he called the Murray House? Thank goodness neither he nor Ruby knew the truth. If they found out their newest girl wasn't as experienced as she'd allowed them to believe . . . She shuddered. The idea of being auctioned off like a prize bull made her skin crawl.

Pushing those unsettling thoughts aside, Angelina rubbed her damp palms along the skirt of the dress she'd selected for the evening ahead.

Fashioned of rose-colored silk, the dress had a fitted waist, short sleeves, and a narrow skirt. Her only concession to the nature of the business where she would appear in the dress, was a neckline dipping much lower than she would have preferred. Glancing down at how the gown revealed the upper swell of her breasts, she realized worrying about her exposed flesh was a waste of time. Her reputation had undoubtedly suffered one crippling blow as it was—and about to endure a more damaging whack—so the cut of her dress didn't matter.

Releasing her held breath in a long sigh, Angelina wondered again at the unfortunate string of events leading up to her working in the Murray House.

She didn't regret her father's decision to leave Georgia. To help his ailing wife, Douglas Coleman had sold their home in January of '85, and a month later moved his family west. Sarah's physician suggested the warm, dry climate of southwest Texas might be beneficial to her failing health. Arriving at the ranch Douglas had purchased sight unseen to find the buildings in sad need of repair and the land long neglected, had been a real disappointment. But Angelina had never shied away from hard work. Raised in a household with a mother ill with consumption and a sister lame from a childhood fall, she'd never known a time when she hadn't worked. When she should have been out having fun with young people her own age, she was home cooking, sewing, or waxing furniture. She'd missed many social events while growing up in Savannah, but she wasn't bitter. She'd gladly worked to help her family, and had done so again on the run-down ranch, laboring next to her father, while her sister Chloe looked after their mother.

Then, six weeks after their arrival, a freak accident took Douglas Coleman's life, leaving Angelina solely in charge of her family. She might have been able to handle the added duties thrust upon her, if the vice president of the El Paso Bank hadn't paid the Coleman ranch a visit just a day after her father had been laid to rest. If not for Elliot Wentworth, the mortgage papers bearing her father's signature and Wentworth's suggestion on how the debt could be paid, Angelina would not be standing on the second floor of a Utah Street brothel about to—

"Are you all right?" Jenna whispered, pulling her from her musings.

Angelina shifted her gaze to the woman with hair the

color of toffee, one of the two close friends she'd made since coming to the Murray House. Jenna's full bust swelled above the deep décolletage of her dress, the rest of her well-rounded figure filling out the dark lavender silk equally well. Seeing compassion reflected in her friend's hazel eyes, Angelina swallowed the sudden lump in her throat. "I don't rightly know. I thought I was, but now . . ." Unable to voice her fears, she turned to watch the rest of the brothel's stable of painted ladies move to the head of the stairway.

The first in line, Penny, a tall, leggy redhead who used Garnet as her *nom d'amour,* started down the stairs, moving in a slow, deliberate rhythm, each step accompanied by the exaggerated swinging of her hips. Though Garnet disappeared from view, Angelina could picture what was happening downstairs in her mind's eye, having witnessed the arrival of the house prostitutes many times, from her former place at the piano on the other side of the parlor.

Each *femme de joie* would descend the stairs, strutting and wiggling, every move carefully choreographed to make the men in the parlor crazy to pay for their time. At the foot of the staircase, each woman paused until Ruby announced her, then moved to mingle with the gentlemen clientele.

After Garnet was announced, Inez moved into position. A *chola*—mixed Spanish and Indian blood—with a tawny complexion and jet black hair and eyes, Inez was known to her customers as Lucinda. Next was Sadie, working under the name Coral, a plump blonde with leaf green eyes, deep dimples, and a full mouth.

Angelina knew a moment of panic. She thought she had prepared herself for what lay ahead. But now that her turn was fast approaching— A shiver racked her shoulders.

"You don't have to do this, Angelina."

Her gaze moved from the stairway back to Jenna's face. The heavy application of face powder, rouge, and lip paint on the young woman she had come to care about, always took Angelina by surprise. The makeup made Jenna look older than her eighteen years, hiding the sprinkling of freckles across her nose and cheeks, camouflaging the youthful glow of her skin. Though four years younger than herself, Angelina was amazed at Jenna's maturity, at how much she knew about life.

Staring at her friend, Angelina managed a wistful smile. "I wish I could agree, but I can't. I have to do this. Mamma and Chloe need me. You know if I continue working as the piano player, it would be years before I could pay off my contract. I had to find a faster way to pay Mr. Murray. I had to find a way to get out of here, so I can move back to the ranch." She drew a deep, shuddering breath. "You know that's why I made the decision I did, Jenna. There was no other choice."

Jenna stared at her for a long moment, then said, "I really wish you would reconsider. Though I've told you everything I can, I'm still not sure you're ready."

Angelina squeezed her eyes closed. What would happen later that evening couldn't be worse than the awful pawing, leering, and crude suggestions she'd endured during the past few months as the brothel piano player. Could it? Forcing herself not to dwell on the answer, she opened her eyes, then said, "Waiting will only postpone the inevitable."

"I suppose." Jenna started toward the stairs, then turned back. "Don't forget about the La Clydes."

Angelina felt the heat of a blush creep up her cheeks. She shouldn't be embarrassed after Jenna's lengthy instructions regarding the use of the white petrolatum, something she was told was an absolute necessity in a brothel. Yet she still found such subjects much too private to discuss as nonchalantly as one would discuss the weather. Realizing Jenna was waiting for a response, she finally said, "No, I won't. You'd best get downstairs. Ruby will be fit to be tied, if she has to come up here after y'all." Before Jenna could turn around, Angelina impulsively gave the woman a hug. "Thanks for your help."

Returning the hug, Jenna dropped her arms, then took a step back. "As soon as I start down that stairway, I become Topaz. Remember?"

"Yes, I remember." *And I'll be Angel.* Angelina shivered at the name the men in the brothel had given her. She definitely didn't feel like an angel, not with what she was about to do. But as she'd just told Jenna, she had no choice. She had taken on the responsibility of paying off Papa's debt on the ranch, staunchly refusing to let her mother and sister lose their home. She would do what had to be done.

Squaring her shoulders and lifting her chin, she moved to the head of the stairs. She heard Ruby shout, "Gentlemen, for your pleasure, please greet the lovely Topaz," then the hoots and hollers of the men in the parlor. After whispering a quick prayer for the strength to get through the evening, Angelina summoned the cold veneer she wore while downstairs, then lowered one high-heeled foot onto the first step.

Kit Dancer shifted in his chair near the bottom of the staircase, his body taut with anticipation. Not long after his return to El Paso four months earlier, he'd started hearing the stories being circulated about the woman who would soon be making her entrance into the parlor of the Murray House.

At first Kit hadn't paid much attention to talk of the piano player called the Ice Angel. He already had a woman on his mind—another employee of a house of ill repute, a prostitute he called Red. As soon as he returned to El Paso, he'd headed for the brothel where he'd last enjoyed Red's company. Turns out he made the long trip from Galveston for nothing. Red had been moved to another city on the circuit of French-owned *maisons de joie* soon after he'd left town. Her moving on was probably just as well. He'd never intended to spend more than a couple of nights in her bed anyway.

The voice of the madame shouting for quiet jerked Kit back to the present. As each of the painted and perfumed doves wiggled her way between the tables, greeting the customers with a smile or a wink, he watched impassively. Once again he wondered why he remained in El Paso. He had no ties to the town, no reason to stay. Hell, he even knew Red would probably never return. Still he stayed, picking up odd jobs here and there to supplement the money he'd salted away. For the first time in his thirty years, his life was at loose ends. He'd given up bounty hunting after the fiasco of his last job, and he sure as hell had no desire to pin a badge on his chest again. So, there he was in El Paso, sitting in the parlor of a brothel—one much more lavishly appointed than he was used to—with no idea what he wanted to do about his future.

A hush fell over the crowded parlor. Whispers of "Here comes Angel" drew Kit's gaze back to the stairs. He straightened in his chair, his pulse increasing at the prospect of seeing the woman who'd caused such a stir: the former piano player whose rare smiles and cold-as-ice appearance had prompted the men in town to call her the Ice Angel. Talk about the woman hadn't piqued his interest, until he heard she had reverted to her former profession, trading her piano stool for a bed in the brothel. Now that she was his kind of woman—no commitments, no words of love, just a plain and simple business deal for uncomplicated, mutually enjoyable sex—he'd decided he should see this Ice Angel for himself.

Forcing himself to relax, he eased back in his chair, watching the woman descend the stairs, his eyes shadowed by the brim of his hat. Though slimmer than the others, the rumors of Angel's beauty hadn't been exaggerated. Flawless skin the color of rich cream, large, heavily lashed eyes outlined with kohl, a full, pouty mouth painted a dark red, and deep brown hair parted in the center and pulled into a simple, yet elegant knot at her nape, combined to make her the epitome of every man's dream. Yet most notable to Kit was the lack of emotion on her lovely features. No happiness. No anger. Nothing.

She reached the floor of the parlor, then paused, hands clasped in front of her, eyes downcast. Ruby waited several seconds, letting the anticipation build before she said in a booming voice, "Gentlemen, may I present the final Murray House lovely. Angel."

When Angel remained at the foot of the staircase, Kit's brow furrowed at her stiff posture, the tightness of her clenched hands. Then a brief word from the madame brought her head up with a snap. As Angel started past his table, she turned to look in his direction. For a moment, he looked directly into eyes the color of a fine, aged whiskey. What he saw came as a shock. What appeared to be resignation, coupled with a deep-as-the-bone sadness, filled her eyes. His fascination increased. Staring deeper into her gaze, he detected something else. A fire burned deep within this beauty, a fire held at bay by some unknown force, a fire he instinctively knew would burn hotter than any he had ever experienced. Just thinking about being the one to ignite that blaze sent a sizzling stab of desire to his groin.

This woman displaying an unemotional, controlled coolness, whose eyes spoke not only of incredible sadness but of extraordinary fire as well, intrigued him far more than any woman he'd ever known. For a reason he didn't understand, a reason that went beyond physical desire, he had the overwhelming need to find out what went on behind those sad, golden brown eyes.

Kit exhaled slowly, willing his heart rate to slow to normal. He pushed his chair away from the table, then got to his feet. Approaching the crowd of men vying for Angel's attention, he elbowed his way to the front, ignoring the curses and howls of protest. Finally, the vision in rose silk stood before him, her posture stiff, her gaze moving warily over her admirers.

"Evenin', Angel. Can I buy you a drink?"

Angelina started at the soft, masculine voice. She shifted her gaze from the horde of disgruntled men stubbornly holding their ground, to the man standing beside her. Noting how the well-defined muscles of his chest, arms, and legs filled out his black attire, she held her breath while lifting her gaze. Unable to make out his features beneath the shadow of his hat brim, she felt a momentary stab of disappointment.

She exhaled, then said, "I don't imbibe." Realizing her words had sounded rude, when the man dressed entirely in black had done nothing to deserve such behavior, she added, "Just because I don't partake of spirits doesn't mean y'all can't enjoy a glass of your favorite libation. I'd be happy to keep you company, Mistuh . . . ?"

Her soft, southern drawl washed over him, sending his pulse into another fast cadence. Clearing his throat, he replied, "Dancer. Kittridge Dancer. But please call me Kit."

After a moment, she said, "All right, Kit."

Glancing over his shoulder, he said, "Okay, fellas, the lady's with me. Better luck next time."

The men gave a collective sigh of defeat, then moved off to find another form of entertainment.

Kit grasped Angel's elbow, then escorted her to the shadowed end of the small bar across the room. He asked for a whiskey, then turned to his companion. "That's definitely not a Texas drawl. Where are you from?"

He watched a small flicker of pain flash across her features, before she said, "I'm originally from Savannah."

"Savannah. That's a long ways from west Texas. You been working the circuit of brothels?"

Her back stiffened. Forcing herself to swallow the retort on the tip of her tongue, she said, "No, I have not."

"So what brought you to El Paso?"

"It's a long story," she said in a low voice.

"I got plenty of time," Kit replied, surprised he hadn't given up his notion of finding out what went on beneath the icy facade and hustled her upstairs to ease the intense ache in his groin. Though he was strongly attracted to Angel physically, for the first time in a very long while, he looked forward to sharing a conversation with a woman. There would be time enough later for sharing pleasures of the flesh.

Angelina stared up at the man's shadowed face, wishing she could see more than the deeply tanned skin of his square jaw. He seemed sincere, yet she knew the men who frequented the Murray House did so for only one reason: to relieve their physical urges. So what was she supposed to do now? How could she pay off her contract, if all this man wanted to do was talk? Still, talk would be infinitely preferable to— She repressed a shudder. But could she tell this man how she'd ended up working in an El Paso brothel?

The touch of his hand on her forearm jarred Angelina from her thoughts. As his long, blunt-tipped fingers trailed up her arm, she shivered. An unfamiliar warmth swept through her body, settling low in her belly. Swallowing hard, she said, "I'm afraid my life might be boring to y'all."

"You wouldn't bore me, Angel. Nothin' about you could ever—"

A loud crash behind them cut off Kit's words. Turning toward the sound, he saw one of the tables had been overturned. The men responsible were squared off, knees bent, feet spread, clenched fists raised. Several more of the customers jumped to their feet, eager to join the fray.

"Damn," Kit muttered under his breath. He managed to pull Angel to the side of the room, before all hell broke loose in the parlor. More tables were overturned, chairs went flying, followed by a body catapulted by a vicious blow from an angry fist.

Ruby shouted for the fighting to stop, but if the men heard, they paid her no heed. Her painted mouth pinched with annoyance, she skirted the room, then shoved through the front door. Lifting the police whistle—identical to the one each brothel madame had been issued—she drew a deep breath, then blew with all her might.

A shrill sound rent the air. Still the combatants did not slow their punches. When Ruby came back inside, she motioned for each of her girls to move the kerosene lamps. Fire was a constant threat in a town as hot and dry as El Paso, and making sure anything that could start a blaze was kept out of harm's way was always a priority.

Angel reached for the lamp nearest her and quickly turned down the wick. A thin trail of smoke swirled up the glass chimney, then drifted into the room in a tiny black cloud.

"You'd better get upstairs, Angel," Kit said, leaning close to her ear, "before you get hurt. Ruby's whistle will bring the police in no time."

Shifting her wide-eyed gaze from the lantern she held, she nodded. He stared down into her golden brown eyes, expecting to find fear or disappointment reflected in their depths. Instead, he saw what looked like relief. Surely she wasn't relieved her evening had ended without— The arrival of the El Paso police halted his musings.

As he was ushered out of the Murray House with the rest of the patrons, Kit was already looking forward to the following night. Now that he'd seen the Ice Angel for himself, he was intrigued. He also knew she had been given an incorrect nickname. Though an Angel she might be, he knew without question she was definitely not made of ice. Angel needed a man to ease the sadness in her eyes, to break through the icy facade she insisted on presenting. Most of all she needed someone to set her inner fire ablaze.

Kit figured he was just the man for the job.

Dear Reader:

When I started writing historical romance, I had some definite ideas about what I wanted to give readers. My first goal was to create entertaining books which would bring to life the excitement and the adventure of my favorite period in America's past—the Old West. Next I wanted to sprinkle in a little humor, add a little passion—okay, a lot of passion—and finally throw in a dog, a horse, or a goat (yes, there's a goat in *Dancer's Angel*) to satisfy my animal lover nature. But most importantly, I wanted my books to provide readers with an escape, whether it be from a difficult boss, irate customers, yelling kids, or just the demands of everyday life.

I hope I've succeeded in meeting my goals in *Summer Wind*. I also hope you'll watch for *Dancer's Angel* in the fall of '96.

My next project is a short story for the Zebra 1996 Christmas anthology. Then I'll be working on a book set in southwest Texas in the 1840's about a sultry healing-woman and a hot-blooded Texan.

I love to hear from readers and always respond. Please write to:

P. O. Box 384 Paw Paw, MI 49079-0384

Arlene Holliday

JANE KIDDER'S EXCITING
WELLESLEY BROTHERS SERIES

MAIL ORDER TEMPTRESS (3863, $4.25)
Kirsten Lundgren traveled all the way to Minnesota to be a mail order bride, but when Eric Wellesley wrapped her in his virile embrace, her hopes for security soon turned to dreams of passion!

PASSION'S SONG (4174, $4.25)
When beautiful opera singer Elizabeth Ashford agreed to care for widower Adam Wellesley's four children, she never dreamed she'd fall in love with the little devils— and with their handsome father as well!

PASSION'S CAPTIVE (4341, $4.50)
To prevent her from hanging, Union captain Stuart Wellesley offered to marry feisty Confederate spy Claire Boudreau. Little did he realize he was in for a different kind of war after the wedding!

PASSION'S BARGAIN (4539, $4.50)
When she was sold into an unwanted marriage by her father, Megan Taylor took matters into her own hands and blackmailed Geoffrey Wellesley into becoming her husband instead. But Meg soon found that marriage to the handsome, wealthy timber baron was far more than she had bargained for!

DISCOVER DEANA JAMES!

CAPTIVE ANGEL   (2524, $4.50/$5.50)
Abandoned, penniless, and suddenly responsible for the biggest
tobacco plantation in Colleton County, distraught Caroline Gil-
lard had no time to dissolve into tears. By day the willowy redhead labored to exhaustion beside her slaves . . . but each night
left her restless with longing for her wayward husband. She'd
make the sea captain regret his betrayal until he begged her to
take him back!

...QUE OF SAPPHIRE   (2885, $4.50/$5.50)
    Talbot-Harrow left England with a heavy heart. She was
    America to join a father she despised and a sister she
    ... She was certainly in no mood to put up with the in-
    ...ctions of the arrogant Yankee privateer who boarded her
    ...sacked her things, then "apologized" with an indecent,
    ... kiss! She vowed that someday he'd pay dearly for the lib-
erties he had taken and the desires he had awakened.

SPEAK ONLY LOVE   (3439, $4.95/$5.95)
Long ago, the shock of her mother's death had robbed Vivian
Marleigh of the power of speech. Now she was being forced to
marry a bitter man with brandy on his breath. But she could not
say what was in her heart. It was up to the viscount to spark the
fires that would melt her icy reserve.

WILD TEXAS HEART   (3205, $4.95/$5.95)
Fan Breckenridge was terrified when the stranger found her near-
naked and shivering beneath the Texas stars. Unable to remember
who she was or what had happened, all she had in the world was
the deed to a patch of land that might yield oil . . . and the fierce
loving of this wildcatter who called himself Irons.

*Available wherever paperbacks are sold, or order direct from the
Publisher. Send cover price plus 50¢ per copy for mailing and
handling to Penguin USA, P.O. Box 999, c/o Dept. 17109,
Bergenfiled, NJ 07621. Residents of New York and Tennessee
must include sales tax. DO NOT SEND CASH.*

JANELLE TAYLOR

ZEBRA'S BEST-SELLING AUTHOR

DON'T MISS ANY OF HER
EXCEPTIONAL, EXHILARATING, EXCITING

ECSTASY SERIES

SAVAGE ECSTASY	(3496-2, $4.95
DEFIANT ECSTASY	(3497-0, $4.95/$
FORBIDDEN ECSTASY	(3498-9, $4.95/$5.95)
BRAZEN ECSTASY	(3499-7, $4.99/$5.99)
TENDER ECSTASY	(3500-4, $4.99/$5.99)
STOLEN ECSTASY	(3501-2, $4.99/$5.99)

Available wherever paperbacks are sold, or order direct from the Publisher. Send cover price plus 50¢ per copy for mailing and handling to Penguin USA, P.O. Box 999, c/o Dept. 17109, Bergenfield, NJ 07621. Residents of New York and Tennessee must include sales tax. DO NOT SEND CASH.